PURSUIT

PUR

A NOVEL

RANDOM HOUSE

SUIT

THOMAS PERRY

NEW YORK

Library of Congress Cataloging-in-Publication Data
Perry, Thomas.
Pursuit / Thomas Perry.
p.   cm.
ISBN 0-679-45306-7
1. Ex–police officers—Fiction.   2. Serial murders—Fiction.
3. Mass murders—Fiction.   4. Murderers—Fiction.   I. Title.
PS3566.E718 P87 2002
813'.54—dc21   2001040365

Printed in the United States of America on acid-free paper
Random House website address: www.atrandom.com
2 4 6 8 9 7 5 3
First Edition

Book design by Victoria Wong

To Robert Lescher

ACKNOWLEDGMENTS

I'm grateful to my editor, Kate Medina, for her encouragement
and helpful suggestions on this and earlier books.

PURSUIT

1

Daniel Millikan looked down at the thirteenth corpse. This one was at the back of the restaurant kitchen, dressed in a white uniform with a ridiculous paper hat on his head that was supposed to keep his hair out of the food, and a long apron that had been filthy even before the blood had gushed down to soak it red. Millikan corrected himself. This was the first corpse, and the one a few feet from it was second. The others, logically, came later.

He bent to let the light catch the tile floor just right so he could tell if there had been any wet footprints in the kitchen, but there had not. There were none in the dining room either: the killer had been here, done his work, and locked the door behind him before the rain had begun. Time in the restaurant had been stopped at—he would guess —around nine-thirty. The light, misty spring rain had not reached Louisville and begun to gleam on the street pavements until late at night, after Daniel Millikan had finished his speech at the conference and retired to his hotel downtown. He had still been awake and noticed it when the rivulets began to run down the window of his room. He had been frustrated because he needed to catch the plane back to California at seven tomorrow morning, but he had been too agitated and restless to sleep.

He never felt tense while lecturing his own students at the college in Los Angeles, but the audience tonight had been people he thought of as grown-ups. They were serious men and women of his own generation who had heard of him and—at least some of them—read his books. They had come to take a look at the expert . . . or, more accurately, at the alleged expert. They had listened to his lecture on the interpretation of homicide evidence with a polite attentiveness that he could only call professional. In the faces of the grown-ups there was always a reserve, something they held back or maybe even disguised, possibly because they had worked homicides and, unlike Millikan, expected to do it again.

He had considered pouring one of the little bottles of scotch from the bar cabinet into a glass, diluting it with tap water, and swallowing enough to help him sleep. He was glad that the two cops had arrived in the lobby and rung his room before he had done it, instead of after. Lieutenant Cowan's voice on the telephone had been courteous but confident: after delivering that particular lecture, Millikan could hardly say he would not dress and go with the police to look at a homicide scene. Right now, he was glad that his brain was functioning quickly and efficiently, but he knew that when he got back to the hotel, he was going to want that drink.

Millikan studied the angle of the body, judged the steps from the back door: ten to twelve. It was easy to see where the boning knife had come from. The row of black-handled kitchen knives in the gleaming stainless steel rack had only one gap. The killer had slipped in the back door and silently cut the dishwasher's throat with the knife he had found. That was a disquieting sign. This killer had been right about too many things: that there would be a weapon where he could reach it; that it would be at least as good and as sharp as anything he could buy and carry; that it would not be of any use to the police, because tracing it led only to the rack on the wall; that he would be quiet enough to take twelve paces unheard and formidable enough to fall on a healthy, strong man in a brightly lighted room and kill him without so much as knocking over a pan or letting him cry out. Millikan judged the distance from the back door to the body again—a good thirty feet. Maybe this killer was invisible.

Millikan looked in the other direction, toward the swinging door to the dining room. After the dishwasher was dead, the killer had dropped the knife into the soapy water in the sink. Then one of the waiters had come in from the dining room. The killer had not tried to reach into the sink to retrieve the knife or pulled out his gun. He had simply broken the waiter's neck, let his body fall into the blood that was already draining onto the tile floor beside the first man, and gone on.

He had walked the next ten feet to that door, stepped into the dining room, and started shooting. The shooting should have been comforting to Millikan, because that was what lots of lifelong losers had chosen as their final act. In those cases it was half murder and half suicide, because they were trying to induce the police to come and put them out of their misery. If the cops didn't appear right away, they usually shot themselves. But this time, the shooting was full of signs that something else had been going on.

The killer had not simply arrived at the restaurant, burst in, and pulled out a gun. He had come first to the front of the building, put a chain and padlock on the front door, and covered the window with a CLOSED sign before he had gone around to the back. That was disturbing. It had been meant to keep new customers from coming in, of course, but it also ensured that once the shooting started, the only way out would be to step over the shooter. This killer had known too much about the way people would behave: they wouldn't even try. The ones near the front door would grasp the handle and get the bad news. The ones farther from it would go low—try to hide behind tables and chairs and each other—and a few would just be paralyzed, too amazed to do anything but let their jaws drop open. This killer had known what to expect.

The shooter had selected. Probably the first round was the one he put through the forehead of the man at the third table. The position of the body indicated the man hadn't dodged or ducked, just looked up and died. The others had come after. They were sprawled, hit anywhere—backs, faces, whatever was visible—when they ran or crouched. Millikan had one more thing to look for. He walked along the far wall, then stood at the front door, examined the backs of seats and the vinyl upholstery of the booths. He lingered for a moment over the spot where the bodies of the two children lay.

Lieutenant Cowan was at his elbow. Cowan was aware that Millikan had made the full tour now, and that he had seen it all. "What do you think?" he asked. Cowan seemed to be in his early thirties, but he had that red-faced, apoplectic look that two of Millikan's uncles had developed when he was a child. They had looked as though it would take only one more aggravating circumstance to make them explode. Millikan pursed his lips, then looked down again. "I don't envy you. I think you've got the genuine article here."

"What do you mean—the genuine article? A random shooter? We figured out that much. All we had to do was count."

Millikan shook his head. "Not a nutcase. A pro."

Cowan seemed to be struggling to keep his reaction from being impolite. Millikan was doing the department a favor, and he was an important man, a name. "Why would a professional killer come in and do all these people in a restaurant—little kids, like this? Did somebody pay him for the first dozen people he saw?"

"He wants you to think he's a guy who wears camouflage fatigues around the house. He wants you to think that tonight he got a big headache and heard Jesus tell him he wanted new angels. But that isn't who he is. He came for one of these people. Just one. My guess would be this guy over here with his brain blown out of the back of his skull. He shot him first."

Cowan's face compressed in a wince, his eyes squinting at the floor. "I'm not sure what to do with that."

"What I'd suggest is that you look as hard as you can for the shooter from now until dawn. You won't find him, but you might learn something you'd like to know about him. Then find out who would have paid to have one of these people killed, and get that person into a very small room. Offer him a deal that he can't pass up."

"A deal—on thirteen people?" Cowan was shocked.

Millikan shrugged. "It's the way you get a hired killer." His eyes turned away from Cowan and returned to the front wall of the restaurant. He bent over and walked the length of it.

"What are you looking for now?"

"Holes." Millikan gestured at the door. "None there, either, except the ones that went through somebody. None anywhere. He comes in the back, silently takes out the dishwasher—"

"He was the cook," said Cowan. "Or one of them. The others went home when the last meal of the night was delivered."

"All right, the cook. He does him with a knife he finds. It doesn't affect him at all. He puts the knife in the sink to let the prints soak off. The waiter comes in and surprises him, but not enough to do any good. He gives the waiter's neck a twist and drops him on the way into the dining room. He pulls out the gun he brought. His hand is absolutely steady—no fear, not even any nerves. He pops eleven people, with no misses, and at least one fatal round for everybody." Millikan paused and looked into Cowan's eyes. "No misses. Ever see multiple handgun fatalities with no misses before? Once the first round goes off, people are running, dodging. Then he steps back out, and he's gone." Millikan looked around him again, then sighed. "Maybe the deal isn't such a good idea, but it's worth a try. I don't think this is a guy I'd rat out for a shorter sentence. I'd take my chances on an appeal."

Cowan's jaw was tightening and opening, chewing on nothing. "Because he's a good shot?"

"No," said Millikan. "I'm a good shot, you're a good shot. It's because he's got no more feeling about any of this than a pike snapping up a few minnows. As soon as he thought of it, these folks were dead." Millikan began to button his raincoat. "When your forensics people are done, I'd appreciate it if somebody would send me a copy. I'm curious about him. And tell your D.A.'s office I'll be happy to fly back and serve as an expert witness if you get him."

"What could you say in court?"

"Same as I told you. He's trying to look like somebody who went berserk, but he's not. He's a pro. If you get him once, this is a guy you really don't want to let out again. Not ever."

"You don't seem to think we'll get him."

Millikan avoided his eyes. "I hope you do."

Cowan seemed to soften a bit, hoping for some trick, some secret. "We're doing everything we can right now—going house to house. They called in another shift. They're stopping people on the streets for a mile around to see if they saw or heard anything. I don't want bodies dropping all over the place."

"That won't happen," said Millikan. "There's not enough work in a city the size of Louisville to keep him occupied. He's had a lot of practice, so if he lived here, you would have noticed. I think he came to town for this." He looked at his watch. "Can you spare the man who picked me up to take me back to the hotel? I've got to check out and get to the airport."

"Sure," said Cowan. "He's waiting out there." Cowan hesitated. "I appreciate your coming to take a look. You spent practically the whole night here."

"Don't worry about it," said Millikan. "I'm sorry I couldn't tell you anything more optimistic."

The two men shook hands at the door, and Millikan muttered, "Good luck." He stepped out onto the sidewalk. The rain had begun again, so he hurried toward the open door of the patrol car.

Millikan's plane for Chicago left at seven A.M., but with the delay in Chicago he didn't reach Los Angeles until seven in the evening. He spent the next two days preparing the final examination he was going to give in a week. He was in his small, cramped office in the basement of an old brick building at the university when the call came.

The voice was a woman's. She asked for Professor Millikan, then said significantly, "We're calling from Louisville."

"This is Daniel Millikan," he said.

"Is this a convenient time for you to speak with Mr. Robert Cushner?"

Millikan could tell that Robert Cushner was a name he was supposed to know. The woman's voice had conveyed that there was no question that Millikan would be willing to talk to him, only when. But she had said the only word that was necessary: Louisville.

"Now is fine," he said.

There was a click and the background noise disappeared. A man's voice said, "Professor Millikan?"

"Yes?"

"I understand you were called in to examine the scene of my son's murder."

Millikan felt a wave of heat rise up his back and stiffen his spine. "Your son?" He recovered. "I'm very sorry, Mr. Cushner. I happened to be at a conference at the University of Louisville. The police knew I was there, because a few of them had attended some of the seminars. One of them called and asked if I would examine a crime scene. The names of the victims weren't known at the time, so I didn't recognize your name. Please accept my condolences. It's very sad that he was in the wrong—"

"He wasn't," interrupted Cushner. "He wasn't some unlucky by-stander or inconvenient witness or something. He was the target. Now, I understand you took one look at the mess in there and knew that."

"Oh," said Millikan. His son was the young man alone at the third table, the man with the hole through his forehead. "It was only a theory."

"It's the theory the police have accepted, but they didn't see it for themselves. You did. Lieutenant Cowan says so. His bosses had everybody looking for an angry maniac for hours until he could convince them you were right. You picked out my son as the intended victim."

Millikan began to feel a growing sense of discomfort. "I think Lieutenant Cowan has made me sound more perceptive than I am, and more involved. I was a visiting forensics teacher who was called in to give an opinion. I did that and left. By now the police have moved way past my guesses, and done some real investigation. Any questions you have about your son's murder should be directed to them."

"I want to hire you to find the killer."

Millikan gulped in a breath, then blew it out slowly to give himself time to get the answer right. In Mr. Cushner's voice he had heard sadness and despair and anger. "I'm afraid I can't do that. I'm very sorry."

"I know you're a professor. You can take a leave, and they won't fire you. If you'll take off a year to try, I'll pay you five years' salary. If you find him, I'll double that."

"I'm sorry," said Millikan. "I haven't been a police officer for fifteen years, and being one meant I didn't do that kind of work on my own. Now I'm a teacher. Your best hope is the police department. They'll do everything that can be done."

"I'm not telling them to drop the case," said Cushner. "But I know how things work in big organizations. It's everybody's job, so it's nobody's. I need a man who is the equal of this . . . this monster. I want him searching every day, every night, thinking about him and hunting him. My son was a decent, strong man who left a wife and two children . . ."

Millikan stopped listening to the words. He had learned a long time ago that there was nothing to be gained by letting these stories into his mind, because once he did, they never left. There were already too many of them, and they were all true and always the same: a mind, a will, hopes, all blown off like smoke, and the survivors ruined forever. He was aware of the sound, but blocked the meaning and waited. It was like waiting for a train to pass.

He closed his eyes tightly, but when he did, he saw the son, the lone man at the third table, the one who had died first. As he surveyed the rest of the room in his memory, looking at each of the others, he felt the temptation growing but he clenched his teeth, just in case it became too strong. He knew what had given him the thought. It was "a man who is the equal of this monster." The voice went on, and Millikan could not block out the pain in it. But he knew better than to let that sound convince him.

He considered the voice critically, reasonably. This was clearly a rich, powerful man. He had just offered roughly a million for his son's killer. Not everybody could do that. The parents of the other dozen people couldn't, so unless Millikan spoke, all the families would have to make do with what came for free. His memory wandered among the bodies again, most of them young and attractive people a couple of hours before he had seen them, all lying in pools of their own blood. He thought of the two children lying dead on the floor, both girls about ten years old, both taken with shots in the back. He knew a secret, and it was something that Cushner had already come to suspect: the Louisville police had already done everything they were able to do. Suddenly he heard himself saying, "There is a man . . ."

"What?"

Millikan was shocked at what he had done. He had to say the rest of it now. "There is a man. He's not a nice man. If you are willing to give him what he charges, he might help you."

"Who is he?" asked Cushner with eager impatience. "Where can I find him?"

Millikan hesitated. "Let me look him up." Millikan didn't have to look him up. His number was one of five printed in the last page of his address book, without names or addresses beside them, but this one he knew by heart. There had been times in his life when he had sat and stared at the number, repeated it to himself over and over, feeling the temptation to dial it. He would toy with the idea, imagining how the call would go: he would say his name, and Prescott would remember him, then take over his problem.

He had always resisted. As he remembered that, the enormity of what he was doing settled on him. He had decided to do it because the man was rich, and it would cost money. But the money was just numbers, not worth worrying about. What was important was the guilt. He was about to involve the old man in it, but only to share: he would not be able to shift it off his own conscience.

"Professor Millikan?"

The old man was waiting. Millikan closed his eyes again. "His name is Prescott. He's . . . a kind of specialist, who takes a certain kind of case. What he does isn't exactly illegal, or at least nobody's proven that it is. But it's—"

"Did you find his number?" The voice was strong and sure.

Millikan admitted, "Well, yes . . ."

"Then give it to me."

Two days later, Cushner took the same early-morning flight that Millikan had taken. A few hours after he reached Los Angeles, he was in the restaurant at his hotel, waiting. It was a dim, old-fashioned room where waiters spoke in quiet voices and then disappeared. At precisely eight o'clock, as arranged, a tall, slim, athletic-looking man with light hair and gray eyes stepped up to the maître d' and spoke quietly with him, then allowed himself to be ushered to the table. Cushner could see that he wore simple, conservative clothes—a navy blue summer-weight blazer and gray slacks. Not a dandy, at least. When the man came closer, Cushner was reassured to see that he was not a young man. He was at least forty-five and his face had the look common to men who had proven their worth through some kind of work that didn't involve merely pleasing people.

"Mr. Prescott?" said Cushner, and began to get up, but Prescott only nodded and said, "Sit down." Prescott sat down across from him, and said quietly, "I've taken the time to read some of the press reports in the Louisville papers. Are they mostly accurate?"

Robert Cushner answered, "Yes, as far as I know." He stared across the table at Prescott, and suddenly understood. Millikan had not been taking all that time to search for a telephone number. He had been trying to give himself time to refuse, probably trying to get himself to lie and say he'd lost it. This Prescott was exactly the kind of man a vengeful father yearned for—a hard, violent, cold man—but Millikan had almost kept the phone number to himself.

Millikan need not have bothered to feel guilty for the sake of Robert Cushner, but apparently he did not know that. Maybe Millikan did not have children, and he certainly had not had a predator set his filthy eyes on one, or he would have understood. He was supposed to be a famous criminologist, so he should have known not to hesitate. He should have known about the purity of fire, the hot hatred that burned up all compunction that a normal good man would feel, a man who had been left undisturbed and intact. Revenge is not sweet, a luxury. It's a necessary restoration of balance in the universe.

When Cushner looked at Prescott's face, he had to raise his eyes a little because Prescott was tall. His height conveyed the impression that he was thin, but he wasn't, exactly. He looked like a runner or a swimmer, with shoulders and arms that were hard, with long muscles. The face was unchanging, the features relaxed but never in motion, as though there were no such thing as surprise. His was the face of a man in a room by himself. The eyes were different—bright and alert, but without sympathy: they did not veil the fact that they were looking at you but not feeling what you felt.

Cushner said to Prescott, "My son's name was Robert too. He was a very special person, not just to me, but to everybody who knew him. He left a wife and two children. The little one probably won't even remember what he looked like. Right now, he cries every night. The older one thinks her father was killed because she talked her mother into taking them to a movie, and that made her father have to eat alone in a restaurant."

"Excuse me, Mr. Cushner." Prescott's eyes were cold and piercing, but his voice was quiet and calm. "You want to tell me why you would pay me money to find his killer. That isn't what I want to hear. I'm not just coming to this problem for the first time, the way you are. I don't need to be convinced that you have a reason. I'm not interested in what you feel, or how you got to feeling it. I'm not interested in you at all. The one who matters is the one who killed him. That's all I can help you with."

Cushner looked at him for a long moment. "You're right." He started over. "What can I expect—written reports, or calls, or what?"

Prescott said, "If what you want is reports, the Louisville police will give you reports for nothing."

Cushner was uncomfortable. He shifted in his seat, then admitted, "No. I guess that's not what I want. I want you to find him and make sure he never does it again. But I'm talking about you and me, how we do business."

"I get three hundred thousand to start," said Prescott. "When I come back with proof that it's over, you pay me three hundred more. Then I go away."

"But how are you going to do it? How can you expect to find him if the police can't?"

"I don't expect to find him," said Prescott. "I'll wait for him in a place where he's going to be."

"How can you do that?"

"I get to know him."

2

James Varney saw the end of the big hotel pool coming toward him for the last time, the lines between tiles resolving their blurriness into clean, straight edges. His right hand touched the wall with its last stroke. A mile. He reached up with both hands and pulled himself to the deck, then walked to the men's shower and stood rinsing the chlorine off his skin. He savored the feeling in his muscles, mildly tired but stretched and comfortable: it was a good way to finish.

He had risen at five, come to the hotel exercise room while the other guests were still asleep, and done a good approximation of his usual weight training. Then he had spent time on a treadmill and a stationary bike before he had gone into the pool. He could see the clock on the wall at the other end of the locker room. It was nearly nine, and he was ready to buy the morning newspapers and eat breakfast. He stepped into the locker room, took some towels from the counter, dried himself, and began to dress.

After Varney did a job at night, he liked to get into a car and drive until morning, or until he heard the first announcement on the car radio. That usually put him far enough away so that he could drop out of sight for a time, watch television, read the papers, and wait.

On his way to Louisville this time, he had stopped in Columbus, Ohio, and registered at this big, comfortable hotel. Columbus was only 214 miles from Louisville on Interstate 71, so he had selected it as a convenient stop on his way home. But now he had lingered in Columbus for five days. Whatever agitation of the authorities that might have added any risk to highway travel was well over by now. He supposed it was time to continue his journey home.

When Varney traveled, he studied the junior-level executives and salesmen in their late twenties or early thirties he saw in airports and hotels, and made sure he looked and dressed the way they did. But he was not what they were. He was a special person.

James Varney had experimented at living a life of adventure since he was eleven years old, but he had not been able to get the last of the obstacles out of his way until he was nearly eighteen. After that, things had been more to his liking, and he had been able to get what he needed.

The experiments had started with Aunt Antonia. She had taught him simply by being in his way. In those days, the family had lived in a big old house in Oakland, California, all dark brown wood, with a big cold kitchen and a great, broad, creaky staircase that always collected dust beneath the railing and next to the wall. The staircase led from the foyer, just opposite the front entrance, up to a row of dark, musty rooms on the second floor. The tiny one at the head of the steps was his, the big master suite at one end of the hall belonged to his parents, and another just like it was set aside for Aunt Antonia. The other three bedrooms were furnished with beds and mismatched furniture, but nobody ever went into them except when Aunt Toni nagged his mother into stripping the beds and washing the sheets and blankets, then pointlessly making the unused beds again. Days like that had made the boy sad.

Aunt Antonia was of no more relevance to the life of the family than the cocker spaniel that was always at her heels, and she was no more pleasant. Each time another member of the household came in the front door, she would be there to complain and criticize, her shrill voice accompanied by the dog's cranky yapping. They both continued bravely and unremittingly as long as the enemy was in sight. Sometimes when an attack was interrupted, they even waited in siege outside a bathroom door for the next sortie, when they would stage a flank attack and keep up harassment barrages until the next time a door was closed to them.

Each time the intruders departed again, she and the dog both collapsed on the long couch in the study, letting nervous agitation disappear in contemplation of the new wrongs the enemy had committed during this engagement. This new list of crimes would provide fresh rallying cries to inspire them when they repelled the next invasion.

An older person might have taken a more complex view, and decided that Aunt Antonia had some pleasure in her life—even that she enjoyed her warlike outbursts—and that as a living organism, she had a right to them. But Jimmy was a child, and such thoughts did not occur to him.

When he set his mind to killing her, his concerns were simple and practical. It had to be done in a way that would lead no conceivable investigator to him. That was pure instinct. And it had to be done in a way that ensured she and the dog would go together. He knew it was likely that once she was dead, the dog would be put to sleep too, but he felt that he must not rely on this. If there were some kind of mysterious adult sense of propriety or even sentimentality that he had not noticed because he did not feel it, they might keep the dog alive. He could hardly expect to kill the dog later.

He set about stalking his aunt and her dog, being careful not to let them catch him at it. He would get up early every morning through the summer by the simple expedient of leaving the east window of his room uncovered so the rising sun would wake him. Then he crept to her door, watched, listened, and waited. By the end of a week he knew all of her habits, and he began to plan.

He would follow her from place to place at a distance, recording in his mind when she did things and how she did them. He devised all sorts of causes for her death. She could go too close to her open window on the downhill side of the house, where the driveway was dug in deeper so the car could go into the garage under the first floor. The fall from her room would be at least forty feet to the concrete pavement. She could plug in her coffeepot when the kitchen stove was on and the pilot light out, and blow herself up. She could fall on a kitchen knife. She could be mistaken for an intruder and shot by his father in the night. Her own dog could be infected with rabies and bite her, so they would both die a lingering, simultaneous death. Each of these ideas had faults. He had to settle for electrocution.

He waited until all of the conditions were right on a hot August evening. When he heard her bathwater run for a long time and then stop, he listened for the music on her radio. When he heard it, he walked in, tossed her dog into the tub beside her, and pushed the radio in with them.

In the end, there was no real investigation, because the adults who rushed in as soon as they could get up the stairs thought they knew everything instantly. The dog had barked out of playful overexcitement and jumped into the tub to be with its mistress, knocking the radio into the water. The commotion had first brought the boy in—a second tragedy, to have one so young confronted with the sight of his electrocuted, naked aunt and the ugly, dead little dog—and then everyone else.

The boy's parents had behaved as though they were convinced, not that they had pieced together the sequence of events using inferences and imagination, but that they had seen it, somehow, having seen all of the evidence immediately afterward. The policemen who arrived a few minutes later and did such things as unplug the radio and make everyone leave the bathroom found no fault with the parents' story. They went away convinced that they had investigated. Later, the coroner's report had made the tale unassailable: she and the dog had definitely died of electrocution, hadn't they?

The boy was aware, at the instant when he dropped the radio into the water, that he was taking an irrevocable step. He knew he was casting off his innocence, but he did not think of it as a descent into evil. It struck him as a first, necessary step into adventure. He had stopped cowering in shadows, depending for comfort on not being noticed. He had, instead, seen circumstances as a chance to mold the future to his will. As it happened, the effort at improving the future had failed because he'd had incomplete information. Aunt Antonia was the wife of his father's dead brother, and thus no real relation to the family.

A week after the funeral, his parents packed all of their belongings and his. They sat him down and explained that the house had belonged to Aunt Antonia. Because his father had been in what he called "a bad patch," she had allowed them to live with her for a time. The boy had wondered at this, because at the age of eleven, he could not remember having lived anywhere else. But now, her will had been read. The house and the money they had all lived on were going to her sister, a woman none of them had ever met, who lived in Omaha. The house was going to be sold, and even if it weren't, his parents did not have enough money to pay the heating bills for a place that size.

The boy had noticed that when his parents packed, they took with them a number of things that he had never seen anyone use but his aunt. He saw a woman's watch, rings and necklaces, a silver tea set, a couple of antique clocks from her bedroom, a set of hairbrushes and a mirror with mother-of-pearl inlays. He knew from the many suddenly empty surfaces in the house that there was more that he had not seen them pack.

As he grew, the event diminished in his memory: his effort had turned out to have been of little consequence or advantage. He had acted well and decisively, but the forces of the universe were not easily moved. He was still not given the kind of attention that he felt his parents should give him. They were still just as distracted and, if anything, busier than before. Gradually, he came to see that they were simply that way: people of little account. After that they bustled about in the usual way, frantic and occasionally noisy, but he knew it was of no importance to him.

When their scheming and hustling seemed to gain them some money, they would squabble over it, because they had each spent it in their minds already. His mother would have a new dress, usually, and his father would be in a bad mood because he had bet his share on something that had not behaved as he had predicted: a horse, a team, some cards.

At some point the next year, a change took place, but it was minor too. His father disappeared. The noises in the periphery had been louder lately, but had not changed in character. After one of the small temporary victories, his father had gone out as usual, but he simply hadn't come back. The boy at first assumed that he had gone off somewhere to get over his usual remorse in solitude. A few days later he noticed that his father was still not around, but the boy assumed that he'd come and gone without his noticing. The next time the boy thought of it, he asked his mother where his father was, and she gave

him an unusually sour look. She said, "I don't know, and I don't care."
He waited for a moment, suspecting that she did care. Because he did
not ask, she added, "I guess life is too much for him. Things were fine
for him when I was at his beck and call anytime. But after you came
along, I was too busy to take care of two babies." There followed a day
or two of dire mutterings, at times against his father, and at times
against him.

The man he was used to was gone, but he was replaced by others.
Some would stay for a month, but others would simply be a knock on
the door or a phone call. Late at night there would be whispers, creak-
ing stairs, or the thump of a shoe dropping on a floor above his head.
It didn't matter which it was, because the ones who came were empty,
just more people of no account to keep his mother occupied at the
edge of his vision.

The good part was that the constant squabbling about money
had ended. Whatever negotiations she had with the men who stayed
or passed through were carried on out of earshot, and seemed to be
resolved mostly in her favor. The things she liked—new dresses,
makeup, hair and nail work—were in plentiful supply. But he still was
alone most of the time. He got up and went to school, came home, ate
what was left over from the dinners she had shared with her male
guests, washed the dishes, and went out again. If he was home in time
to be gone again by the time she woke up, he had nothing to fear from
her displeasure.

For years, he made no further forays into the world of adventure he
had glimpsed in the death of Aunt Toni. He prepared. He got up in the
morning and did his sets with weights, chinned himself, did crunches
and push-ups, showered, and went to school. Then he came home,
did his homework, ate what he could find around the house, and went
out to run a few miles. When he came back he did a second workout,
showered, and went out again to walk the night streets.

He detested the weak, so he worked and sweated to be strong and
hard and fast. Failure was humiliating and brought unwelcome attention, so he avoided trouble by doing his homework and getting good
grades.

In the second month of his senior year of high school, it seemed to
occur to his mother, all at once, that he existed. It was as though while

he was young and small he was able to be invisible, but by that October, he had grown too big to ignore. He had to endure detailed recitations of her daily life. He had to endure less specific lists of sacrifices she had made for his sake. He had always had to hear her say that having him around was such a terrible burden that she could not stand it any longer. But now he had to experience a strange new set of indictments: the complaints against his father that had been silently refined in her mind during six years of resentment were now delivered to the boy as though the transgressions were his.

Varney waited. He concentrated on his routines, for he was of a curiously disciplined temperament. He worked harder and longer, and maintained his silence. This was a method he had perfected in order to stay invisible when he was small, and he found it worked nearly as well now that he had been rediscovered. He lasted until June. On the afternoon of his graduation he came home with a diploma and began to pack for his life of adventure just as his mother was waking up.

She came out of her bedroom and stared at him, then went back in to get her robe. When she came out this time, she had tied it so tight at the waist that her eyes were bulging. She said in a voice like cracking glass, "What do you think you're doing?"

He shrugged. "I just graduated. Time to go."

She shrieked at him, "You bastard!" Then she began to pace. "I raised you all by myself! I gave you everything you ever had! Everything you ever did was because I did it for you! Now you're just going to leave?"

He looked at her, puzzled. She had always said that he was a burden and she wanted him to leave. "What else?"

"What else? You ask me what else? You can get a job and do the same for me. You can—"

He was already shaking his head. "No." He wasn't angry. He wasn't interested in any more trouble. He went on packing. He had not anticipated this. From the moment when he had been old enough to decipher her words, she had said she couldn't wait until this day. But the fact that her reaction was the opposite wasn't enough of a surprise to disturb him. It simply explained a few of her most recent tirades. She had noticed he was grown into a man. She had not been trying to hasten his departure. She had simply identified him as an adult male—someone who could be induced to get money for her.

He had almost finished packing, since he owned very little that he wasn't wearing. She saw the diploma and it seemed to outrage her, as though the piece of paper was what had caused him to offend her. She snatched it off the couch, tore it in four pieces, and tried to hurl it at his face, but the pieces merely fluttered to the floor at her feet.

She looked around her, and then her eyes settled on the suitcase. She snatched the handle. "These are mine!" she shouted. "I paid for everything! You want to go, you're not taking anything of mine with you."

He looked at her for only a second, then picked up the pieces of his diploma and walked to the door.

She screamed, "You'll be back! You're going to need me!"

He thought for a moment. "If cannibalism comes back in style, I might come back to cut up your fat ass and sell it. Otherwise . . ." He shrugged, stepped out, and closed the door. His life of adventure began.

That had been ten years ago, and Varney did not often think about those days anymore. He finished his breakfast in the hotel dining room, reread the editorial in the Columbus Dispatch, folded the paper, and returned to his room. For the next half hour, he packed and made leisurely preparations to leave, glancing now and then at the television set and feeling pleased. In the editorial, they had referred once more to the "senseless massacre of thirteen people in a Louisville restaurant." Senseless meant that they still had not seen the sense of it: the job was a clean one. Senseless was good.

3

Prescott stood at the front door of the restaurant, then stepped to the side and stared in the window past the FOR LEASE sign. He raised his eyes a few degrees, and he could see the folding steel grate extended across the storefront two doors away. This was probably where the killer had been standing when he had noticed the lock.

The new padlock the owners had put on the grate stuck out a little. Prescott walked toward the store, looking at the pattern of cars on the street, listening for engines and counting, gauging speeds. There had probably been more cars parked at the curb on this side that night, because the restaurant had still been in business, but it wasn't a street that had much foot traffic. He reached the padlock, then gave himself a few seconds to open it in his mind. The killer had probably carried a shim pick in his pocket. No, Prescott decided, it had been a small, all-purpose set, because the killer had been improvising.

Prescott walked back to the door, stopped for a couple of seconds to simulate putting the chain and padlock on the door and hanging the CLOSED sign on the knob, then went around the small building toward the rear. There was a little parking area in the alley where trucks could unload supplies, and spaces for five cars—the boss, the two cooks, the two waiters. He stopped and looked in one direction, then the other. There was nothing for the length of the alley that would have concerned the shooter: no big light fixtures, no other businesses that were open at night. Instead, there were dumpsters, piles of empty boxes, long dark stretches, and places where he could climb a fence or step between buildings and be on the next street in seconds. Prescott began to feel a faint echo of the killer's sensation. This looked good to him— safe, almost—but the time was going by, and the opportunity was too good to pass up. He went to the back door and used the key to open it, then put the key away and propped the door open six inches with the doorstop.

Prescott stepped back into the dark alley again to clear his mind. The police had finished here a few days ago, and had returned the building to the possession of its owner. Prescott had presented himself as a potential tenant and gotten the keys for the night. Now he had to forget those details, and see this place as the killer had.

Within a few seconds, he had succeeded. He looked at the light falling from the open door onto the rough, pitted pavement at his feet. In his mind, the door was open because someone in the kitchen had opened it. The cook had done it to disperse the heat and steam and food smells. The last meals of the evening had been served. Soon the dishwasher would arrive to help with the cleanup in the kitchen while he waited for the last customers to leave the dining room. This way he wouldn't have to bang on the door to get in.

Prescott stepped close to the door, looked inside, and listened. The killer's ears would have been what told him where the cook was. He took the pistol he carried in his jacket and moved it to his belt at the small of his back, so he could reach it but it would not get in his way. He leaned into the doorway and waited until the sounds the cook was making moved away, then farther away, toward the sink at the end of the room.

He saw the knives where they used to hang on the rack. He scanned for the one: most were big, flat, and unwieldy. The serrated edge of the bread knife had a small attraction, but the blade was thin and flexible. The boning knife was the one. He took three deep breaths, and drifted in. He did not tiptoe slowly in but floated quickly to the rack, his hand already feeling the handle so it came into his grip smoothly, without pause. There was still a space of about twenty feet to cross, and he moved even more swiftly. Then his left arm came up to hook around under the man's head and jerk it back, and his right brought the blade across the throat in a single cut. He stepped back quickly to avoid the blood and the falling body, preparing to strike again not because it would be needed but because that was the correct way to complete the motion. He remained poised to thrust for two seconds, then dropped the knife into the hot, soapy water in the sink and took two steps toward the door.

The polished wooden surface abruptly swung inward at him, and a waiter nearly collided with him. There was no time for decisions. The killer's body did what it had practiced so many times: the legs pushed off to dodge aside and pivot, ending behind the waiter. The hands shot up, one beside the waiter's jaw and the other to the opposite side of the head, and they pushed hard to turn the head against the body's momentum and break the neck. The killer let the body drop on its back beside the other one.

Prescott moved to the swinging door. He stopped at the hinged side and reached to the small of his back for the pistol, pulled the slide to cycle it and put a round in the chamber. He felt the need to proceed quickly, but he used one second to visualize the dining room he had seen through the front window: where the nine customers had been seated, where the waiter and the boss had stood, and the places where they might have moved. He stepped through the door smoothly, his gun already aimed at the table where Robert Cushner sat. Bang!— through the forehead. Bring the gun to the right ten degrees, the arm still extended. The boss and the waiter both at the front of the room, the boss at the little podium where there used to be a reservation book and a telephone, and the waiter leaning against the wall near him. Two shots for them, one in the waiter's chest because he was young and already on his feet, and one through the boss's neck because he was near the phone—probably a head shot that was a bit low, but maybe a slip of the mind and not the hand, because the killer was aware he might try to use the phone. Then there were the two who dashed to the door—the young guys. They had been sitting in the booth by the window, and getting out the door had looked easy to them. By then the killing had seemed intended to be a clean sweep. He pictured them tugging on the door handle, and sensed a small, amused chuckle. Why was that? They looked funny: pulling on the door, pulling harder, their eyes widening with the bad news. BAM BAM BAM. Their bodies collapsing.

He moved his arm to the left, and found the parents with the two little girls. The husband popped up, probably with a vague intention of protecting the others, but making his chest an easier shot. Then the wife, clinging to him as he went down, a shot through the head. The two ten-year-old girls taking a step to run, two shots placed identically between the shoulder blades.

That left the young couple under the front window. The man had pushed over a table and lay on top of the woman to shield her from the bullets. Prescott saw the table in his mind, felt the impulse to fire through it ten inches from the floor, so the man would die on top of her, then to fire through it again to kill her. But he did not allow himself to be that sloppy. He took four steps around the fallen table, stopped at their feet, and fired through the man's head, then his back, down into the woman's chest. Both dead.

Incredibly quiet. Listen for noises from the street: cars stopping? People rattling the door? Nothing. He looked around him. There was nothing more to do but pick up the spent brass casings. First the two that had ejected to his right while he was shooting the couple. Then the bunch to the right of the kitchen door: three for the men at the locked door, two for the waiter and the boss, one for Robert Cushner. Eight. Then four for the parents and two children. Twelve.

He looked around again. Good. Brilliant. Only one shot into the target's head, so Cushner looks no more like the target than any one of several others. The young couple share two holes, and that looks like random craziness. Shooting two little girls in the back makes it conclusive. All the brass casings are up. The cops use those to figure the order of shots, and now they won't have them, or the distinctive marks a firing pin and extractor make on them that can reveal the model of the gun. There was a moment of elation, and Prescott savored it, tested it, and felt the delayed beating of the heart, the slug of fresh, oxygen-laden blood to the brain. Pride: I'm so fucking smart. A look at the bodies—a still life, juicy, cut fruit with a few dead fish laid beside it on the wooden floor, their eyes already clouding over. A work of art.

He turned and stepped to the kitchen door, switched off the light in the dining room, then backed through to the kitchen. He stopped to look down toward the spot where he had sliced the cook, to be sure he saw where the blood had run. Five quarts in a grown man, and a good bit of it pumped out on the floor while the heart was still beating: step carefully. But it's okay: the tile floor in the kitchen has a little slope to it so water will go down to the drain when they wash it. The knife— take it? No, what the hell. Leave it in the sink.

First a new clip in the gun, then the back door. Stop, listen, then out quick and shut the door so the light won't shine out into the alley and the door will lock. Walk at this pace—not in a big hurry, but not loiter- ing in a dark alley, either. Don't cut between buildings. This isn't an emergency, so there's no need to take the chance. Come out at the end on the side street. Now to the car and go. I'm gone now. There is no more connection to that restaurant than there is to any other place I see driving down this road. It's done.

The elation is taking over. The pay. Yeah, that's good too, but it's al- most beside the point. Reliving the sense that everyone else in the room is slow, as though they're moving with weights tied to them. He had always been ahead of them, a superior being. He was still ahead, only this time he was ahead of the cops: they would never figure out what he had just done. Prescott pulled the car to the side of the road and turned the engine off. It was power. This killer had to be stronger and faster and braver, but mostly he had to be smarter, because that made the difference. If he was smarter, they were all in his power. If they were smarter, then he was in theirs. He could not allow them this giddy pleasure; he could not allow them to make him that afraid.

Millikan was grading final examinations when the telephone rang. The voice was the one he had been dreading for days. "Danny Mil- likan," it said. "It's me."

Millikan sighed. "I'm not in this. I gave him your number, and that's all. I'm not involved."

"I wanted to thank you for the referral. It pays pretty well."

"No, you didn't," Millikan said irritably. "You don't do this for the money any more than the other killer does. You need the kick to keep your heart beating."

"Actually, what I wanted to thank you for was giving the old man the stuff from the cops—the crime-scene photographs, and the reports. You knew he would give them to me. What good would they be to him?"

"You're welcome," said Millikan. "Now—"

Prescott interrupted. "You were there, weren't you—at the restaurant? That's why you gave him my number."

"Yes."

"You think it was Cushner first, then the rest?"

"That's what I think."

"I didn't see any misses—none in the walls or the furniture."

"There weren't any."

"Did he scoop up the shell casings too? I don't see any pictures with brass, and no circles on the floor."

"Right. No brass, no prints, no footprints in the blood, no identifiable fibers or hairs."

"You have to wish somebody noticed him before he got this good at it, don't you?"

"Yeah," said Millikan. "I told the cops to find his client and make a deal for his name."

"How promising is that?"

"The suspects are three big companies that wanted to take over Cushner's business. The directors are retired senators, the chairmen of other companies, college presidents. There's nobody to squeeze." He was silent for a moment. "He's yours now."

"Don't worry," said Prescott. "If your luck holds, you may never hear from me again. I don't need to check in with cops very often."

"I'm not a cop anymore," said Millikan. "I teach."

"You teach people to be cops."

"What is it? What do you want?"

"I spent the night at the restaurant. I can feel him. There's something there at each step."

"It's different," admitted Millikan. "I could feel that much."

"He's told us a lot. The padlock shows me he's learned to open locks: probably took a locksmith course somewhere. He was in a hurry, but he spotted the lock and went right to it. That was because he knew he could open it, how long it would take. And he didn't know the back door was open, either, but he knew that there would be a door, and that he would be able to open it. Then there's the cook."

Millikan couldn't help himself. "That was the thing that struck me, too. He's got a gun, he knows the front door is locked because he just locked it. Nobody can leave if he fires. Why sneak thirty feet across a lighted kitchen, find a knife, and risk a fight with a good-sized guy?"

"To show us he can. He can cross that distance in about three seconds without making a sound, grab the right knife and strike—once, with certainty—and step back before the first drop of blood hits the floor."

"What are we talking about—martial arts?"

"I think so. I'm not sure what kind, yet. Other people can sneak up on a guy like that and cut his throat. But this one took a quick look and knew he could do it a hundred times out of a hundred, or he wouldn't have tried. He didn't need to. It was just the best way to do it. He has to do things that way."

"The shots?"

"Right. More lessons, more practice. He must spend enormous amounts of time on firing ranges—probably combat ranges, with moving targets and pop-ups. He's been perfecting himself."

Millikan sighed and rubbed his eyes.

The silence caught Prescott's attention. "What?"

"You want me to get somebody in law enforcement to give you some lists, don't you? Black belts, regulars at shooting ranges, and all that."

"No," said Prescott. "You know what this guy is like."

"I do," said Millikan. "He's the loner of all loners. Maybe a charmer, but even if he is, no real friends. Smart enough to avoid the notice of the authorities, or even of people who would put his name on a list for authorities."

"He's convinced himself he's the best," said Prescott. "That's his vulnerability."

"Very likely," said Millikan. "I'm not sure it's a vulnerability."

"Of course it is. He's not the best," said Prescott. "I'm the best."

"What do you want?"

"I want you to tell him."

4

Varney watched in fascination. A week ago, he had never heard of this Millikan jerk. Here he was on CNN, and they were calling him a leading expert on homicide. Varney gave a mirthless little laugh. A leading expert on homicide wasn't some professor. It was somebody like Varney.

It was Millikan's turn to talk. "We're accustomed to having authorities, from the president on down, say killings like these are 'senseless,' or I believe the usual term is 'random and senseless.' They're neither: the killer knows exactly what they were for."

The interviewer saw a way to make his discussion appear coherent, and appear to be in control. "All right, then. Take the Louisville restaurant murders we just saw in our opening clip. What were they for?"

"Let's ignore the superficial reason: some small offense that might have gone unnoticed, jealousy, money. What I'm talking about is the underlying reason. The killer doesn't think he's unilaterally attacking. He thinks what he's doing is retaliating for things that were done to him, or making a pre-emptive strike to avoid something he fears in the future."

"Specifically in the Louisville case, how would you know that?"

"The way I came to know it is thirty years spent interviewing dozens of killers and hundreds of eyewitnesses. But I did examine the crime scene in Louisville the night of the murders, and I've been following the case since then. I believe the case will be solved in a few weeks. We'll be able to interview the perpetrator and find out exactly what—"

The moderator had been itching to interrupt, but one of the panelists was quicker. It was Cameron, and Millikan wasn't surprised. "What we'll find out is that it was a disgruntled employee, or a customer who got thrown out of the place that night. It would have been nothing, except he was able to get his hands on a gun."

"As my friend Mr. Cameron knows, I'm not a fan of guns," said Millikan. "But that's changing the subject. We were talking about why, not how. What we'll find is that this was a child who was abused or neglected at home. When he went to school, he was picked on or taunted, and nobody protected him. He's been spending the rest of his life protecting himself from threats that have already come and gone—making himself less emotionally vulnerable to his parents, less physically vulnerable to the people who picked on him in school. Obtaining a gun is only one of the things he did to make himself more formidable. He's not a good argument for gun control, because he's not somebody who would have been harmless without a gun and simply killed because it was convenient. He's a great argument for doing something about the way our society raises many of its children."

"It's easy to say that," snapped Cameron. "But it comes down to 'What can we do?' We can't disqualify a few million people from having sex and producing children. We can disqualify civilians from owning firearms."

The moderator was getting panicky now. He could see the clock telling him he had six minutes to bump this squabble out of the endless circular argument about gun control and turn it into a news story. He said, "Professor Millikan, I want to get back to something you said earlier: that the case would be solved in a few weeks. What makes you believe that? Have the police made a break in the case?"

"No," said Millikan. "It's not the police. What's happened is that the case struck a chord in unexpected quarters. A donor has put up the money to hire Roy Prescott."

The interviewer was intrigued. "Roy Prescott?"

"He's a private homicide specialist. Mr. Cameron and I are both acquainted with his work, and I understand he has good leads already. I would say it's a matter of time. A few weeks, at most a few months."

The interviewer unexpectedly turned to Cameron. "Mr. Cameron, I noticed that when Professor Millikan said earlier that it was nearly over, you didn't disagree. Did you know this too?"

"No." Cameron's eyes were on Millikan. He seemed to be getting over a shock. "I didn't."

The interviewer sensed that he was on the edge of something.

"Can you tell me more about Roy Prescott?"

"I have no comment." It was a statement that the moderator had never before heard on his show. Panelists didn't say that. They interrupted and shouted to get more time to make comments. He could see that Cameron's expression was peculiar. He was staring at Millikan, intrigued, barely blinking.

"Then, Professor Millikan, can you do better?" It was a mild barb for Cameron, to get him going again, but he was like a member of the audience now. "What makes you confident that this specialist will catch the killer?"

"The best analogy I can think of offhand is a bear hunt," said Millikan. "A bear isn't merely big and fast and strong, with long teeth and claws. He also knows what he's going to do in a crisis, and when the time comes, he does it very efficiently. But the reason bears are an endangered species and we're not, is that the hunter also knows what the bear is going to do. His larger brain is the only advantage that matters."

The moderator tried to ignore the frantic waving of the producer, who was spinning her finger in the "wrap-up" sign. He glanced at Cameron, hoping to get a reaction in the last seconds, but Cameron seemed stunned. Reluctantly, the moderator conceded that it was too late to go on. "My thanks to Michael Cameron, former district attorney of Los Angeles and now congressman, and to Professor Daniel Millikan, author of *Manifestations of Guilt,* the standard text on homicide. Tomorrow night my guests will be Lilian Horvath, animal-rights advocate, and Dr. Garth Fillmore of the Boston University medical school, on the use of animals in research."

The camera zoomed in for his close-up, and he said, "Be there." The producer sighed and shook her head at him to show that he had cut it too close, but he shrugged happily. He had made it again, even gotten the promo in.

Varney felt the intense heat of anger on his shoulders and the sides of his neck all the way up to his scalp, so strong that he began to have the peculiar tunnel vision he sometimes noticed during a fight. But this time, there was a shortness of breath, a sensation that his lungs were partially filled with sand so there was little room for air. It was not the clean, good anger that he felt when he was fighting back. It was outrage, a bitter sense of unfairness. They were saying things about him that he couldn't answer. They said he was stupid, that they knew everything he was going to do before he did it.

He tried to reassure himself. That pompous, stupid son of a bitch on television couldn't do anything to him. His theories were designed just to make all the fat-ass spongeheads excited enough to sit through the next commercial.

He tried for a moment to get past his anger. It wasn't really that Millikan guy he was thinking about. He was just the big mouth that went on television. He was so stupid, he had told Varney something he couldn't have known any other way. He went to his computer and turned it on. He called up the phone directories and began to search.

A few minutes later, Millikan came out of the elevator into the underground parking garage. He looked at the big purple number 3 painted on the wall, then looked at the letter painted on the nearest pillar: D. His rental car was in G, somewhere on the other side. He came around the back of the elevator and saw that his car was the only one left in the visitors' row. Cameron was standing beside it.

He took a deep breath and blew it out as he walked toward the car. When he was close enough so it wouldn't be wasted, he put on a false smile. "Pretty good, Mike. Maybe they'll give us our own show."

Cameron didn't accept the proffered pleasantry. "I waited because I want to know about Prescott."

Millikan stopped walking and stood still. "I said it because he asked me to."

"Asked you to?" Cameron frowned and stared at Millikan as though he were trying to climb a hill he had never suspected was there.

Millikan nodded. "That's why I'm here. They've been asking me to come on for a year. I called them and said if they were going to do a show on the topic, I'd be willing to go on. I'm going to be on four other shows in the next week, just so I can mention Prescott."

"Why are you doing anything Prescott asks? You arrested the bastard."

Millikan shook his head. "Once, fifteen years ago, he allowed me to comfort myself with the fantasy that I was hauling him in to face questioning and a possible murder charge. He knew that very little evidence would be found, and he knew that it all supported him. He had removed everything that didn't." He paused. "Otherwise, I suppose he would have killed me too."

"If you know that, then why do him a favor?"

"It's not a favor. It's an act of calculation. I was in that restaurant in Louisville right after it happened. I think that the one who did it is one of the special cases. He's somebody we can't afford to have walking down a street where our families walk. I don't like Prescott. It costs me something to know I put Prescott into play. Well, tough for me. What I feel is nothing compared to the damage this killer has already done. He's not going to stop unless somebody stops him. We both know Prescott is the best bet for doing that."

"But you were a police officer."

"I was," said Millikan. "And you were a D.A. We both followed all of the rules."

"What does that mean?"

"It means that maybe the reason we retired and went on to other things was so we could sell out for a good cause. You're one of the best lawyers in the country. You know that even the half-assed gun control we already have is unconstitutional, but you argue for more as though it weren't."

Cameron glared at him, but then his shoulders slumped in a sad, tired way. He looked older. "What the hell am I supposed to do? Wait for the Second Amendment to be repealed while thirty thousand people a year get killed? You know goddamned well it'll never happen."

Millikan shook his head. "I voted for you. If I lived in your district, I'd vote for you again."

Cameron nodded sadly. "I'll see you, Danny." He walked off toward the other end of the floor, where a driver was waiting for him in a Lincoln Town Car.

Millikan got into his rental car and picked up the road map from the passenger seat. This was the second time in thirty-six hours that someone had called him Danny—just like the old days.

Varney stopped walking at the phone booth, then took a last look around. There was nobody near enough to hear him, and there would not be anytime soon. The gas station had been closed for hours. He put in the first two quarters, dialed the number, and listened to hear how much more he needed to deposit to reach Los Angeles, then pushed those coins in too. He wanted to hear the voice. He knew he would probably only hear a recording, but it might be a recording of Prescott's voice. The voice would help him judge things—the man's size and weight and age, the regional accent. The phone rang once, twice. The click was wrong. A man answered, not a recording. "Yes?"

Varney felt annoyed. He had just wanted to hear the man's voice.

"Yes?" the man repeated. "Hello?" Varney knew that the man wouldn't talk unless he signified his presence. He needed to let the man know he was listening. He breathed loudly so he could hear the sound in the earpiece, and instantly felt foolish. It was what perverts did to scare women.

Prescott laughed, a deep, open-mouthed guffaw. "A breather?" he said. "You're a breather? It's you, isn't it? What's on your mind? Oh, I know. You're calling because you heard they had hired me and you want to make a deal. I'm afraid I can't do that on this one. I understand your feelings. You know you went too far this time, and you want to be forgiven and get out of it. I'm afraid I can't let you do that."

Varney's head was throbbing, and the tunnel vision was coming back. He could almost see this man—tall and thin, with long hands, and he had an accent like a big fucking cowboy. He whispered, "You stupid fucker. I called to tell you you're dead."

"Not very convincing," said Prescott. The whispered voice sounded young, so Prescott made his tone patronizing. "But I understand. You want me to be scared, just like you are. I'm afraid it's not possible. That's just one of the differences between a boy and a man."

"You forget, I know who you are."

Prescott's voice came back with a slight frustration. "Now, there's an example of one of the other differences. You think you did a pretty good job back there in Louisville, don't you? You stole a padlock and chain for the restaurant door. Don't you know that, even at night, stores have surveillance cameras aimed at their front doors? I got you on tape, Slick. That's more than you know about me. I can pick you out anytime, but you won't see me coming."

Prescott paused and listened to the silence. He hoped that the man on the other end was feeling a moment of pure terror: of course there were surveillance cameras. Every time some poor jerk broke into a liquor store they had him on tape. How could he have forgotten? Prescott waited patiently for the outburst.

The voice was sick with anger. "You're full of shit."

"Too bad you slipped up that way on your first try."

Varney said, "There were no mistakes, and it wasn't my first."

"Oh? What else have you done? How many?"

"I don't keep track," said Varney. "Enough."

"You're not old enough to lose count," said Prescott. "I know you're scared to say what they were. I'm just asking a number."

Varney said, "Columbus, Ohio, a year ago in November. Phoenix in January. Houston in April. Pittsburgh in May. Danville, Illinois, in May. Biloxi in July. L.A. in July."

"What are those?"

"Look them up. You'll see."

The line went dead. Prescott hung up the telephone and sat in his office, looking down at the surface of his desk. He should have been up and pacing and feeling jubilant. He had succeeded. Having Millikan go on TV had worked. He'd had no right to expect the man would see Millikan so soon. But what had happened did not feel pleasant enough to be a victory.

When Prescott had been a boy, there had been a house down the street where he stopped on the way to school. He waited until a younger boy and his sister appeared, then walked with them. The younger boy was one of those whose only hope was to grow into an adult as quickly as he could: he was no good at being a child. He was skinny and unprepossessing and wore glasses. The worst thing about him was that he was smart, and he had so little sense of what other people were really thinking that he didn't hide it, or make a joke out of it, as Prescott did.

So Prescott walked with them, made sure they got into their class-rooms unmolested. He told other people he protected them because his mother made him. It wasn't quite a lie, because if his mother had known, she would have. She would have stopped what she was doing in the kitchen and trained those big brown eyes on him for a second and said, "Too bad there's nobody around with the guts to stand up for those two until they get a little older." Then she would have gone back to what she was doing, pretending it had nothing to do with her. After a day or two, she would have asked, casually, "How are those Beeman kids getting on?"

The Beemans had an older brother, much older, maybe twenty-five. He lived three streets over, in a house that had two trucks parked in the driveway at night because he had an exterminator business. He was always gone too early in the morning to take the kids to school, and came home too late to pick them up. But one day after school, Prescott saw that one of the trucks was parked in the driveway at the house where the young boy and girl lived, and the older brother was there, sitting on the porch in his work clothes, drinking a Coke out of a can. He said, "Prescott. You're a good man." Prescott was twelve. "You want a summer job?"

Prescott said he did, without knowing what it was or what sort of pay to expect. He went home and asked his mother if that was okay, and she said it was just fine, as parents did in those days. Two weeks later, school ended and Prescott went to work. He had to get up at five and be outside Carl Beeman's house to help him load his chemicals, traps, and tools. They worked until dark.

Prescott gained fifteen pounds that summer and grew two inches. By the end of August, he was lean, tall, and tanned, and as strong as some men. He had also listened to Carl Beeman talk. Beeman was not like his little brother. Carl was thought of as on the slow side of aver-age, but he was given credit for his compact, functional body that had been toughened by the endless physical labor that only small busi-nessmen are willing to endure. Prescott discovered that Carl had also developed his mind during those years, in the eccentric way peculiar to people of a contemplative temperament who spend a lot of time alone.

Carl Beeman made most of his money on rodents. He knew every-

thing about mice and rats: how they had made their way into a building, what they had been eating, how long they had been there, how
many there were. He would climb into an attic, go down into a basement, walk slowly around the outside of the house, a skilled hunter
scouting the habitat before he made his plan.

As the summer went on, Beeman began to talk to Prescott while he
worked, teaching him in low tones just above a whisper, and Prescott
learned. The owner of the house was a bystander: the business was between Beeman and the mice. The adversaries understood and recognized each other, engaged in a primal battle for dominion over this
space. The human beings whose names were on a paper filed in the
county courthouse were as irrelevant to Beeman as they were to the
mice. Although these people, in a way, fed and housed both sides of
the struggle, they took no part in it and seldom saw the places where
major battles were fought. Beeman was a good enough businessman
to be sure the customers saw the casualties—rodents he carried out in
plastic bags that didn't need to be transparent but were.

Slowly, Prescott discovered that Beeman respected and sympa-
thized with the mice. They were perfectly normal animals doing what
animals did. They struggled for food, a warm, dry place, and safety.
They had a good strategy: they shared a house with another, larger
species that used it almost exclusively during daylight, so they used it
mainly at night. The attributes of the larger species rendered it harmless to mice except for one quirk of evolution: the big, slow daylight
creatures had Carl Beeman's phone number.

Each campaign was carried out over a period of a week, with Beeman using a variety of tactics, checking daily to see how each had
worked. Had he blocked all the entrances? Had the corn treated with
strychnine been nibbled? Carried off? What were the mice doing on
their side—chewing their way out? Prescott sighed. It was thirty-five
years later now, and he had become Carl Beeman. He had been right
about this adversary, and he had picked the right way to get the adversary to call. It had taken Prescott only a couple of days to select the
right poison and deliver it. The killer might spend the next couple of
days walking around ignoring it, but it would gradually work its way
in and begin to hurt.

The killer would call again. He had to, because the need was hard-wired into his brain. He didn't just have to practice until he was smarter and stronger and more powerful. This was his destiny, the little play that he had been inadvertently raised to act out. He had been struggling to defeat the enemy that was older and bigger and had somehow always thwarted him and kept him down but had, at the same time, been oddly invisible, missing, impossible to even identify. Prescott stared at his hands. To volunteer for that role in this particular drama, a man would have to be crazy. He pushed the REWIND button on the tape recorder, picked up a pen, and waited to copy the words onto a notepad.

5

rescott spent his days getting ready. Everything he would
need had to be laid out, examined, taken apart, then packed
in exactly the right order. When that had been done and re-
done, he passed the time in the big central library in downtown Los
Angeles scanning old issues of newspapers on microfilm. He carried
with him the list of cities that the killer had mentioned—Columbus,
Phoenix, Houston, Pittsburgh, Danville, Biloxi, and Los Angeles—
and the months when he had supposedly visited each one.

Each night, Prescott set up his bed on the couch in his office. He
had selected the suite for nights like this. It was in a high-rent high-rise
office building on Wilshire Boulevard. The other tenants included a
few financial managers for the very rich, and several attorneys who had
clients with high visibility and rapidly fluctuating reputations, so the
security men downstairs were the cold-eyed suspicious sort rather
than the kind who could be sent out to bring you lunch or get your car
detailed. After hours, the elevators required a key to work. His office
was on the ninth floor behind an unmarked polished oak door that
had been reinforced on the inside with quarter-inch steel panels. The
building's upper windows were one-way glass, and Prescott's wall on

the hallway side was lined with tall filing cabinets that looked very businesslike but were filled with unopened reams of blank paper. If a bullet went through the wall and pierced the back of a filing cabinet, there was no chance it would come out the front.

He slept within a few feet of the telephone on his desk because he knew the killer's call would come at night, almost certainly between two and five. The killer would know as well as he did that this was the time to take an enemy off guard. It was when sleep was deepest, and when police raided armed suspects. This killer would feel the need to stake a claim on the night.

On the fourth night at three A.M. the telephone rang. Prescott gave himself one ring to clear his mind, one to take a drink from the glass of water beside the telephone so his voice would not sound dry and scratchy from sleep. Then he picked up the receiver. "Yes?"

There was the breathing on the other end again. The anonymity the killer had relinquished by being goaded into speech the first time was something he seemed to believe he could get back, even though part of his mind must have known that Prescott recorded his calls.

Prescott said, "Oh, it's you, breather. What's up?"

What answered him was a whisper. "Just making sure you're where I wanted you to be."

"Yep," said Prescott. "You can stop looking over your shoulder for now, and get some sleep. I'm not in that much of a hurry. I'll get to you when I've gotten my schedule cleared. I've got a chore that's a bit more important than you are right now."

The whisper was angry. Prescott's overconfidence was ugly, like a swelling that needed to be lanced. "Didn't you check the jobs?"

"What jobs?"

"Phoenix, Houston, Pittsburgh . . ."

"Oh, your list of cities," said Prescott. "I was going to make an attempt, but when I had a minute, I couldn't see much in it. Los Angeles and Houston each have over a thousand homicides a year. You taking credit for all of them, Slick?"

"No."

"I did try Danville, because that seemed like it might be a manageable number, but I don't seem to find any mention of anybody dying in any interesting way in the month of May."

"Abel Tucker."

"Who's that?"

"He's the one I got there. In L.A. it was Donald Pearson. In Houston it was Sidney Obermeyer. That ought to be enough."

"Well," Prescott said doubtfully, "I'll check and see if I can dig up your press clippings. But what are they supposed to tell me—that you're bad?"

"It doesn't matter. It's better if I show you what I do."

Prescott sensed that something about the voice had changed. He decided to concede something. "I've seen what you do."

"Do you have a family?"

"Nope," he said. "I tried it once, when I was young and optimistic, but it doesn't fit with this kind of life."

"Who do you love?"

Prescott chuckled, hoping that the alarm he was beginning to feel was not audible in his voice. "Nobody."

"There must be somebody you care about, somebody that will get your attention."

Prescott had been listening attentively to the voice. He had begun to identify the change he had heard. The voice had started out querulous and sullen, but as the words had begun to be about killing—not the people he had killed, but about plans to kill someone new—it had gained strength. It had deepened, gotten quicker and more lively. The change was shocking, frightening. This was not the sort of killer who could be convinced to go off and do something else just because it was safer or more lucrative. Killing wasn't hard. It didn't scare him or worry him or repel him. As soon as he had started thinking about it, talking about it, he was confident and eager. Prescott had to deflate that mood, make him think differently. "Well, as I said, Slick, you'll have to wait your turn. I've already got somebody else who needs my attention right now. After I've got him, I'll get to you. Just in case you lose your nerve again, where should it be?"

"Where?" The voice was genuinely confused.

"Sure," said Prescott. "You think you can handle it, we'll meet someplace."

There was a silence on the other end that was part amazement and part outrage: How could this man think he was that stupid? The fact that Prescott had even tried this was proof that he was utterly sincere in his contempt. Varney gave a quiet, voiceless chuckle that came out as empty air. "I think you need a demonstration first."

"Killing some unsuspecting little old lady is not going to convince me of anything, so don't bother." Prescott's own voice sounded a little hollow to him. He knew this man really was thinking of murdering somebody else, just to rattle him. He had to stop it.

"I don't mind. It's no trouble. It'll be easier to talk to you after."

Prescott forced his face into a false smile, in the hope that it would change his voice subtly to hide the concern he felt. "Do I strike you as somebody who cares about strangers?"

"Yes. You do. It'll be a cop. Maybe two. Just so you know I don't have to do easy ones."

Prescott said, "No! Come and get me, not them."

"Them first. Then you."

Prescott heard the click as the killer hung up. He pushed the button to get a dial tone, and quickly punched in a number.

Millikan approached the telephone on the table beside his favorite reading chair in the living room with foreboding. These days nobody called Millikan after ten at night, and a deviation from the expected was not welcome to him. The telephone began its second ring, and he snatched it up to silence it so it wouldn't ring again in the bedroom and wake his wife. "Hello."

"Millikan."

Millikan controlled his irritation, then let it out slowly. "I thought you weren't going to call me again. I'm doing what you asked."

"It worked. You can stop now. He's called me twice. But there's something I can't keep to myself."

"What is it?"

"He's going to kill a cop."

Millikan was silent for a moment, trying to overcome his shock and concentrate. "Why?"

"To show me he can do it—no, that he will do it. He wants me to sweat. He's going to show me that he can do just about anybody, any-time he wants. Then he'll come for me."

"Jesus," muttered Millikan. "Did he say when, or where, or any-thing?"

"No. He's neurotic—defensive and hostile—but not delusional. Whatever is wrong with him makes him aggressive, but it doesn't seem to make him reckless."

"Why are you telling me?"

"Because if I call the police and tell them who I am and what I heard, they won't do what they need to do. If you tell them, maybe they will."

After Varney had pushed down the hook on the pay telephone to sever the connection with Prescott, he had stood with the phone to his ear for a minute or two, surveying the area around him to be sure there was no one nearby who might have overheard. Now he hung up the telephone and began to walk. That son of a bitch thought he was stupid. He could hardly contain his rage. He was not going to be as easy as Prescott seemed to think. Varney was not stupid, and he was beginning to work on exactly how he was going to prove it.

He was walking along Hertel Avenue in Buffalo in his sport coat, carrying a grocery bag from the store where he had stopped to make the phone call. He watched a police car drift up the street past him, knowing the car wouldn't stop. He knew the profile they were trained to look for, and he had made himself look different from it. He looked like a young man whose wife had sent him out after midnight because they were out of formula for the baby. Varney was not stupid. He had even been to college before he'd left California.

It was only a two-year college, but he could have gone to a four-year place. He just didn't have the money. As it was, he'd had to be inventive just to eat and sleep under a roof. He had left home at the beginning of summer, when high school ended. He had seen a HELP WANTED sign in the window of a hamburger place, and worked there for a while. He had gotten an idiot pleasure out of laying the burgers on the tray and popping them into the oven, then timing the french fries and getting the shakes lined up just in time to get the burgers out and bagged and on the hot table in time to sell them.

Then in August, the manager had taken him aside at the end of the shift and asked him if he wanted to train to be an assistant manager. Varney had looked at the manager—Darryl Sams, his name was—and it was as though he had suddenly awakened from a dream. That had been all it took, looking at Darryl. He was chubby, with narrow shoulders and pants that went up to his solar plexus. He wore a tie in the colors of the franchise that was too short. His small, close-set black eyes were dumb and worried about nothing visible, the way a dog's were. Darryl meant well, but Darryl was Exhibit A. He was what Varney would become if he stayed and worked hard for ten years. He could get a new paper hat that said MANAGER and get to come home from work smelling that same smell of rancid cooking fat every night.

Varney had been filled with terror that turned into anger. He'd had to get out, to burn up this temptation: this looked like an opportunity, but it was a trap, an offer of slavery made when he was just a step from starving. Varney was making so little money that when he dumped the burgers that had been too long on the hot table, he always secretly diverted one for his dinner. Darryl was trying to look like a benefactor, but he was the enemy. Varney turned a wry, malicious stare at the small, dumb, eager eyes. "Are you shitting me?" he asked. "You think I want to end up flipping burgers when I'm thirty-one?" Darryl was thirty-one. It had only been a week since the girls at the cash registers had put a candle on a hot cherry tart and sung "Happy Birthday" to him. His smile flattened, his dumb eyes seemed to cloud over, and his chubby face slowly turned pink with hurt and humiliation.

Varney said, "I was going to quit this week anyway." He thought quickly. "I've got to leave for college. This is my last day."

Darryl was so dumb that Varney had managed to distract him from his wound. The smile returned. "Well, good luck, Jim. I know you'll do great."

Varney was already taking his apron off. "Damn right," he said. He headed for the rear door without looking back. Darryl called out, maybe in an extreme attack of stupidity, or maybe because a tiny dose of venom had remained in his system from Varney's insult. "If you ever need the job back, just come and ask me."

Varney kept walking for a few steps and then stopped and began to turn around. But then he heard the steel door swing shut and lock. He considered going back in the front door, vaulting over the counter, and beating Darryl senseless, but he controlled himself. He resisted because he was smart, not the kind of fool that Prescott obviously thought he was.

He spent the next few days feeling lost. He had begun the summer sleeping at the house of his one high school friend, until the friend's parents had made it clear that this could not be a permanent arrangement. After that he had spent a period going to parties. He had walked the neighborhoods surrounding the college listening for loud music. When he found a party, he would join the crowd on the lawn or drift in the front door, left open for ventilation. He would pretend to be a college student from out of town who was passing through. He would meet people and talk them into letting him sleep on their floors. If he couldn't charm anyone, he would help clean up the litter and mess from the party and then appear to fall asleep in the yard. But after a few weeks the parties had become too exhausting. He rented a cheap studio apartment.

After he quit the burger job he hitchhiked to the community college, showed them his taped-together diploma, and registered. The tuition was free, so he was able to give reasonable attention to his studies for almost a month. Then he needed to turn his attention to supporting himself.

Stealing from college students was unbelievably easy, and he found that he had a talent for it. He would watch students in his classes, and at the various lunch counters and coffee places around the campus. When he found a girl who had money and salable belongings, he would follow her to learn where she lived. One night he would watch her apartment until she went out, then slip inside and take what he could find. Slowly, by increments, he became an expert.

He began by prying doors with a crowbar he carried in his backpack, or breaking a window. But as he broke into more and more apartments, he became adept at coaxing door plungers and window latches out of their receptacles without doing much damage or taking too long. He became quieter, more familiar with the shapes and proportions of apartments. He learned where obstacles would be placed, where prizes would be hidden, and the way an open space sounded in the dark.

During this period he paid more and more attention to his physical training. He was now a black belt in Tae Kwon Do. He made a deal with the master of the dojo. He taught two classes of white and yellow belts in exchange for his own lessons. That gave him more practice and more training. He made a trip every other day to the college gym, where he lifted weights and used the machines, ran on the track, and showered in the locker room.

It was at the gym that he learned about the gun club. He was getting dressed one night when he noticed a small xeroxed announcement tacked to the bulletin board. It said SHOOTING CLUB, then, underneath, THE CLUB IS NOT SANCTIONED BY THE COLLEGE, clearly a condition for posting it on campus. It said the club was made up of college students who were interested in shooting and had discovered they could get price breaks on all sorts of things if they banded together. They had reserved a part of a local firing range for Monday and Wednesday nights at eleven, when older, preferred customers had gone home. Along the bottom of the announcement were tear-off tags with a phone number. He took one and put it in his jacket pocket.

He showed up at the firing range the following Monday to look things over. The club consisted of a dozen young men who seemed to belong to several factions. There were a few farm boys who were bemused by the distaste and dread other students felt for a simple household contraption no more mysterious than a pencil sharpener. There were a couple of fanatical marksmen who had become enraptured by firearms at an early age and spent much of their free time trying to compress a pattern of shots into a one-inch space. A couple of tinkerers seemed most interested in replacing things on their weapons with custom pieces that, to the naked eye, were identical to the original parts but were claimed to be vastly superior. There were two ROTC officer candidates who seemed to be under the impression that some day they would be called upon to fight a war with pistols. Varney had never held a firearm in his life, but that made him more welcome. He was seized upon with missionary zeal, as each of the factions interpreted his ignorance as an opportunity to create a convert. He could not afford a weapon, but each of the members of the club was eager to let him try one of theirs, to instruct him in its use and features and quirks.

After three meetings, Varney realized that he would have to get money to pay for the ammunition he was using. He stepped up his burglaries and moved his hunting ground to neighborhoods far from his college. Now he would go to a neighborhood at dusk and spend an hour or two walking and looking. Then he would select the best house to rob.

That was how he started his own gun collection. He always began by looking for money and jewelry, and now that he was in houses where middle-aged men lived instead of tiny apartments where students lived, he began to find guns. He was good enough with a pocketknife and screwdriver to open some doors and many windows, so he often had time to hit three or four houses in a single night. He had trained himself in years of exercise and martial arts so he could easily use a tree or a drainpipe to climb to a vulnerable upper window.

Using his stolen guns, he sharpened his shooting skills with the same determination he applied to everything else he chose to do. He slyly courted the attention of the club members. He let the accuracy purists believe he was a natural ally in their debates about bullet shape, muzzle velocity, and barrels. He listened with sincere attention to the tinkerers and let them teach him to dismantle, clean, lubricate, adjust, and modify his weapons. He also assented to the ROTC cadets' belief that all target shooting was preparation for the future moment when the bullet must burrow its way through living flesh.

He joined them in separate outings to a combat range, firing rapidly at flat comic-book villains with bristly jowls and sneering lips who mechanically popped up or lurched forward at him. Combat shooting became his strongest event; he outdid his two companions on his first day. He had been training his reflexes to be quicker, his coordination more finely tuned, and his muscles stronger in eight years of martial arts. By breaking into houses while people slept, he had been training his eyes and ears to an acuity that had gone beyond response and become intuition.

Varney had been slowly, doggedly making himself into the vision of perfection he had invented when he was a child. He was an adventurer. He still had to show up at classes at the community college, but the work remained easy. He had enrolled with the intention of going on to a university at the end of two years, so he took a standard liberal arts curriculum. But the college served a clientele of students who had finished high school without being able to read comfortably or to make much sense of algebra, so keeping up with them did not distract Varney much from pursuing his other activities.

After a year, he was burglarizing difficult houses, bigger buildings with broad, open lawns, high fences, and alarm systems. He got more cash and better jewelry. He also found some merchandise he had never seen in smaller houses. They were certificates—stocks and bonds with elaborate scrollwork and filigree borders like his diploma. He took them because they looked valuable and weren't heavy, but after a few months, he had too many of them in his apartment to ignore. One day when he went to Wally's Pawnshop, one of the places where he sometimes sold his loot, he brought a few and asked Wally about them.

Wally shrugged and shook his head. "That's not a business I can get into." He lifted his hands to keep them far from the stock certificates, in an exaggerated gesture.

Varney asked, "Then where do I go?"

Wally winced as though something in his belly had begun to hurt him. "I'd forget it."

The boy persisted. "You said it's not business you do. But if it's a business, somebody must do it. Who?"

Wally's resistance did not weaken. He said quietly, "A little guy can't do anything with securities. The only ones who can are big—people you don't want to know." He could see he was making no impression. "People you don't want to know you."

Varney let the subject drop, but he did not forget it. He was not a petty businessman like Wally, he was an adventurer. A week later, he tried asking another of his buyers. This was Dave, proprietor of Genuine Gems. Dave was not as cautious as Wally. He muttered, "I could get you in touch with some people."

The fences were all nominally independent, but nearly all of them did some business with a group they called the wholesalers. When they bought merchandise of suspicious provenance from people like Varney, they would keep it out of sight. About once a month they would be visited by a pair of men who would look the stuff over and make an offer. The wholesalers would also offer the local shopkeeper a variety of merchandise picked up the same way in other cities. By a combination of barter, haggling, and cash payment, a deal would be struck. They would take the local valuables, leave the valuables from elsewhere, and move on to the next city.

Dave agreed to offer these men the securities at the standard price—2 percent of face value. He explained to Varney the realities of the business: a good diamond ring of a carat or less from across the country would go quickly, with little risk. Anybody could sell it. A thousand shares of Microsoft had to be handled in special ways, and only certain people could move them. As he put it, "You have to be huge." Selling stolen securities involved big, dangerous maneuvers, like forming a corporation, having the corporation obtain a business loan and letting the bank hold the securities as collateral, then converting the loan to clean, untraceable cash and the corporation to thin air. Another way was to actually pretend to be the man whose name appeared on the securities, use them to obtain credit, and buy pieces of merchandise—jewelry, cars, even houses—then resell the merchandise and leave the buyer, the credit underwriter, and the original merchant to fight it out. All of these methods involved big numbers, complicated transactions, and the ability to keep institutions from asking any of the right questions.

The wholesalers were not big enough to accomplish schemes of that sort. When they sold Varney's certificates, they were only acting as middlemen for much larger interests in New York. It was this transaction that brought Varney to the attention of the people Wally had told him he didn't want to know. The money was, for Varney, a fortune nearly forty thousand dollars. To them the money was a tip. But there were certain things about the young man that interested them. The securities had come from twenty-two different robberies, done over a period of a year. This meant he had the qualities of patience and caution, which they admired, and secretiveness, which they worshiped. They advised the wholesalers to keep an eye on him and watch his development. It was well known that people who did not take their advice were the very definition of stupid and did not deserve to live.

The wholesalers already knew quite a bit about Varney. Several of their fences had purchased items from him, and each confirmed what the others said. He was quiet, steady, and reliable. He was a relief to them, after the legion of mentally impaired, volatile maniacs who came in with something they'd taken in a smash-and-grab or a purse snatching that they expected would keep them in crystal meth for a month.

But the wholesalers were waiting. They knew every aspect of the stolen-merchandise business in a way that no young sneak thief could know it, and they knew that the odds would catch up with Varney. When the inevitable happened, that would be the test. Either he would cease to be a factor in the local trade, or he would kill somebody.

One night, he went into a rich neighborhood in San Francisco that he had never hit before. He walked for a time, trying to select a house. The night was unusually warm, and he could hear the faint hum of air conditioners coming from some of the houses, which told him the windows were all closed and latched. There were lights on in the windows of others. Now and then, if he lingered near a house too long, a dog would bark, and he had to move on. Finally, he found one that seemed not to present too many obstacles. He stood outside the gate for a few minutes, listening and studying the building. Then he saw something that made him decide.

He was over the fence and up the broad lawn like a shadow. He climbed a trellis, careful to place his hands and feet where they would not tangle with the climbing roses. He reached the second floor, where there was an open window. He was sure that a place like this would have an alarm system, but whatever circuit included an open window had to be turned off. He slit the screen with a knife and slipped inside a bedroom. There was no one in the bed.

He moved to the doorway and cautiously looked up the hall. There were bedrooms, all with their doors closed, and no sign of light under them. At the other end of the hall was a faint glow. He froze and waited. There was no sound. The light was not like an incandescent lamp, so he decided to look more closely. He slowly moved up the hallway. The glow was a computer screen. There was a screen saver, with colorful tropical fish moving from left to right and disappearing. He took two deep breaths. It was all right. The room was an office, and the computer was probably left on all the time. There was nobody awake. He was halfway down the hall toward the office, so he decided to start his search for valuable items there. He heard a creak behind him that might be a person in one of the bedrooms. He retreated to the nearest door, but found the room absolutely empty, with nothing to hide behind. He knew he had time for only one more guess. He stepped to the office, slipped just inside the doorway, and waited.

He had chosen wrong: the room was not empty. He heard the hollow rattle-scrape sound behind him, and knew it: a handgun being grasped and lifted from the wooden bed of a drawer. He gave it a half second, so the man's arm would be in motion, rising toward the level of his chest. Then Varney abruptly squatted, slapped the floor with the palm of his hand, and dived across the open doorway.

The gun went off and punched a hole in the wall where Varney's chest had been. Varney caught a glimpse of the man while he was in motion. The man was about forty years old, crouching beside the desk wearing sweatpants and a T-shirt, and his black hair was tousled. He must have been working at the computer and fallen asleep on the couch. The man popped up, startled by Varney's low dive, and pointed the gun downward. The man overcompensated in aiming his second round, this time firing into the carpet at his own feet.

Varney rolled, brought his knees up to his chest in a crouch, then quickly did something that was not what anyone else would do, and few could do: he sprang up, took a running step up the wall, pushed off, and hurled his body into the man with the gun. The man was knocked down, his head hit a chair, and the gun bounced on the carpet. Varney picked it up, fired it into the man's forehead, checked the magazine to be sure it had a few more rounds, then went down the hall to the room where he had heard the creak.

He opened the door and found it empty, then opened all of the others. He returned to the office and considered his situation. Maybe the reason the man had kept a gun in this room was that there really were valuable things here. Varney could see the gun had come from a small, open door on the right side of the desk, with a key sticking out of the lock. He pushed the door open a bit farther with his foot, and saw that it was a small safe, with three shallow drawers, like trays. The gun must have been locked in there in the front of the safe.

Varney wanted to run, but he kept the fear under control. The house was big, a stone structure set back on about two acres of land, but there seemed to be nobody here except the man. The only open window was down the hall where he had come in. If the three shots had not been heard by the neighbors in their big houses, then the danger was over.

He put the gun into the back of his belt and began to empty the contents of the drawers while he listened for sirens and car engines.

There were banded stacks of cash, a couple of fancy watches, two gold rings, and a sheaf of documents that looked to Varney like stock certificates. When he had what he could carry, he went down the hall, out the window, and down the trellis.

Two days after he sold the securities, he received a visit at his apartment from two of the traveling men who worked for the wholesaler. They had learned that the name on the securities—Robert Haverly—was a name the San Francisco newspapers had printed as the victim of a burglary and murder. Varney had shown the aptitude the wholesalers had been told to watch for.

All these years he had been stubbornly preparing himself for a life that was different, more intense and exciting than the drab busy-ness that occupied other people. Now he had shown that he was ready to find out precisely what that life was.

6

Varney made his reservations so that his flight to the West Coast left the next afternoon. He would land at night. There was no reason to wait even one extra day and give Prescott time to dream up some kind of trap. Varney could use the flying time to sleep and plan.

This, he had decided, must be a virtuoso performance. Its purpose was not practical but psychological. He had listened to Prescott's laconic, skeptical tone, and it had given him a strong urge to wake Prescott up. Prescott had been overconfident, absolutely certain that he could assume Varney was no threat, although he knew nothing about him. It was time to teach Prescott something about Varney, to let him know that this time he had made a fatal miscalculation.

Varney rented a car at the airport, then drove north past the center of the city into the San Fernando Valley. He had to assume that Prescott would have called the L.A. police as soon as he had hung up, and that by now they were all on edge and preparing to be attacked. He was still in their jurisdiction but far from Prescott's office, and he was willing to bet that the police here had taken the warning less seriously. All cops patrolling this late at night were tense, suspicious, on guard.

They already seemed to have adrenaline trickling into their veins at a steady pace before anything happened, because they were never at ease. He had decided that the place to do his hunting was in the suburbs, where the people were richer and the cops weren't treated like an occupying army. They would be calmer, and easier to approach.

He had decided that a good place to find what he wanted was a hospital, so he went to Valley Presbyterian because it was the biggest one he knew of in the area. He parked his car a few blocks away on a quiet residential street and walked back. He walked the circuit of the hospital to study the entrances, exits, and parking lots carefully. Then he extended his walk around once more to stop near the emergency room. He found a concrete bench in a little niche that people seemed to use as a smoking area, sat down, and watched.

He had sat for only a half hour in the dark before he saw what he had been waiting for. The police car came up the driveway toward the emergency-room entrance quickly, but without flashing lights. There were two cops in the front seat, the smaller one behind the wheel. The car coasted smoothly up to the curb in front of the emergency-room entrance and stopped. Both front doors swung open, and the cops got out.

The one on the far side of the car was a big man who immediately opened the back door on his side, leaned in, and pulled out a thin passenger who seemed to think there was still a roof over his head. Even after he had taken two unsteady steps away from the car he was still bent over, as though he didn't want to bump his head. The cop said something to his partner and ushered his charge toward the double doors. The person was not handcuffed, but seemed not to be entirely free, either. He straightened and became recognizable as a teenaged boy in a T-shirt that had been stretched out of shape, and he had a trickle of blood running from his hairline down the side of his temple to his neck. He had to be a victim, Varney decided: a loser.

The shorter cop had come around the front of the car to help but had found nothing to do, and now returned and approached the open door on the driver's side. Varney could see that this one was a woman. Her dark hair was tied back in a tight bun, and the body armor under her shirt made her look rectangular. The heavy, blunt-toed black shoes she wore seemed calculated to make her walk like a man. She got into the car quickly, restarted the engine, and drove it around the building to a reserved space by the wall at the edge of the driveway.

Varney was up and moving into the darkness along the wall as soon as she started the car. He reached the spot he wanted while the car was still moving, then crouched and froze. He was twenty feet from the driver's door, behind a large electrical-circuit box in the shrubbery by the wall. He listened for her footsteps as she hurried along the driveway by the dark wall to join her partner in the emergency room. She came along quickly, almost trotting, and he knew from the sound that he had chosen the right place to hunt. She was busy, her brain was fully occupied, and she was not feeling any sense that she could be threatened. She hurried past his hiding place, but he didn't move until she was two paces beyond him and her peripheral vision would not help her

He sprang. His right hand delivered a blow to the side of her head to stun her, then moved smoothly to her wrist so she could not reach the big, blocky grip of the pistol in its holster. His left forearm was around her throat. He crushed the trachea and let his weight drag her down, then quickly broke her neck. He pulled her pistol out and stuck it into his belt at the back, then lifted her body and propped it in the driver's seat of the car with the feet out on the ground and the steering wheel holding her up as though she were sitting there listening to the police radio. He searched the leather cases on her belt for useful tools. He found a set of handcuffs and a short, broad-bladed knife for cutting seat belts to remove accident victims from cars.

He went back to his hiding place and waited. It was a pleasant surprise to him that the male police officer was coming out of the hospital alone. Either the victim they had brought was being admitted or the cop was wondering what had become of his partner and had left him for a moment. The cop called, "Marianne!" but he didn't seem alarmed when she didn't answer him or move. Instead, he quickened his pace toward her, and gave Varney a chance to take him.

The cop did not hear Varney, but he seemed to have a sudden suspicion that made him spin to look around him. Varney was already in the air, and the knife was in his right hand. Varney knew better than to try to cut through the Kevlar vest, so he slashed at the throat above it. The cop looked surprised, then lowered his head and saw that his blood was spurting into his hands. Varney went low and kicked to sweep his legs out from under him, then plucked out his sidearm and tossed it out of reach. He stood beside the body and waited until the cop had lost consciousness.

When Varney was sure the cop was dead, he considered slipping off into the darkness to his rental car. But things were going so well that he decided to take a risk. He took the man's wrists, dragged him to the side of the police car, opened the rear door, and backed in, then hauled the body in after him. He climbed out the other side and stepped to the front. He pushed the female to the passenger side, strapped her upright with the seat belt, took her place behind the wheel, and started the car. He knew he probably had little time to do what he wanted, but he judged it would be worth the effort.

Two hours later, the telephone in Millikan's living room rang. It was very late, but he had not been to bed. He picked up the receiver on the first ring. "Yes?" he said.

Prescott's voice came on. "He did it."

"How? When?"

"Not long ago. He just called me."

"Do you believe him? There's nothing stopping him from lying."

Prescott's voice was tired, but insistent. "I recorded it. Listen."

Millikan could hear a hissing sound, then, "Prescott. In the morning they're going to find the bodies of Marianne Fulco, badge number 4852, and Jonathan Alkins, badge number 3943. You should get a kick out of them."

Millikan heard Prescott's voice come on again. "Thanks for trying to warn them, Danny."

Millikan said quietly, "I'd better let them know."

Millikan got out of his car and walked slowly and cautiously toward the row of police cars and emergency vehicles parked along the side of the road. There were more than usual for a murder scene, but he had expected that. When a police officer was murdered, there was always anger and sadness at the death of a colleague, but there was also a public-safety concern.

People who did this were something special. They were attacking someone they knew would be heavily armed and well trained and who could get reinforcements almost instantly by pressing a radio button and asking for them. But most alarming, they were killing a person they almost certainly had never seen before. What they hated had to be the uniform. And that made several thousand other people potential victims.

Millikan moved toward one of the cars near the center of the line and a cop came around it, walking briskly toward him with his hand up, palm outward, as though to stop him. But now they were both illuminated by a set of headlights. "Millikan," he said, and lowered his arm.

"Hi, Pete," said Millikan, and stepped closer. "Did they tell you I was coming?"

"Yeah, but I didn't recognize you at first." He shook Millikan's hand. "I thought you might be the first of the reporters." They began to walk toward the park together. Carrera was much taller than Millikan, and he had always made the most of his height, carrying himself with his spine straight. Now he glanced down at Millikan, just moving his eyes and not his head. "It's good to see you, Danny."

"I'm sorry it has to be like this," said Millikan. "How's Denise?" He brought back a memory of children. "And the kids?"

"Not bad. We split up a few years ago, but I still see the kids. I'll tell Denise you asked about her. And how's your family?"

Millikan could tell that Carrera was as embarrassed as he was. They had seen each other every day for years, but after all this time, neither could remember the names of the other's children. "We're fine," said Millikan.

Carrera said, "They say you knew this was going to happen: predicted it."

"Not me," said Millikan. "Roy Prescott. He got a threat from this guy. I decided I should be the one to call it in."

Carrera nodded slightly, but the name Prescott seemed to puzzle him. "Makes sense. I'll show you what we've got."

As they approached, two other cops turned their heads and made moves as though to challenge them.

"It's all right," Carrera said softly. "It's Lieutenant Carrera."

Millikan said quietly, so only Carrera could hear, "Why is everybody so jumpy? Trying to keep something back from the reporters to sort out false confessions?"

"You'll see."

Millikan came down the hillside to the picnic area of the park. The police car was stopped among the wooden picnic tables. There were several people from the forensics team stepping gingerly around the car, shining lights on every inch of ground, and others taking pictures or brushing surfaces for fingerprints. Millikan came closer.

When Millikan started around the car, the nearest forensics officer, a woman named Dale Chernoff, spun her head toward him with an expression that was almost angry.

"Hello, Dale," he murmured.

She nodded and gave him a small, sad smile as she returned to her work. He stepped past her, saw the picnic table, looked down at the ground beside it, and winced. It was all clear to him now. The two bodies had been posed.

The killer had placed the two of them on the ground beside the table. He had yanked the male officer's pants down to his ankles. He had done the same to the female officer, but had removed her shoe from her left foot so he could get the trouser leg all the way off on that side and fit the male officer between her legs.

The cops were working in full force on the crime-scene preliminaries because they really wanted this killer. But they were working fast too, out of an almost instinctive compulsion to protect the bodies from the gaze of outsiders. The police wanted them in body bags before the reporters came.

"Dale, can I go in beside them yet?"

"Yeah," she answered. "We're done there."

Carrera stepped closer, at his shoulder. Millikan glanced into the car and said, "They were killed somewhere else. The bodies were driven here and dumped. Where did it happen?"

"Outside Valley Pres. They had just dropped off a kid that had been hurt in a fight at a party."

"Any prints?"

Carrera shook his head. "The best hope was Marianne's shoe. That's the female—Officer Marianne Fulco. She had them all spit-shined like a marine. And this character pulled off one of them to get her pants off. If there was going to be a print, the heel of that shoe was probably where it would have been. He was wearing gloves."

"He brought gloves?"

Carrera shook his head. "They had just brought in this kid who was bleeding. They put on disposable rubber gloves, and the box was still on the car seat."

"He's good at using what he finds." Millikan knelt beside the bodies. "Whose blood is that?"

"The male. Officer Jonathan Alkins. He had his throat slashed. Looks like the guy used Officer Fulco's knife. It's on the floor in the back seat."

"I think I see this," said Millikan. "He must have waited in the dark until the two of them were separated somehow. One of them must have been in the car or near it, probably listening for calls. That would be Fulco."

Carrera raised an eyebrow, but he didn't ask how Millikan knew.

Millikan said, "If he used her knife on Alkins, he had to get her first." Millikan lowered his head nearly to the grass to look at the woman's face. The eyes were open, the mouth gaping.

"See her neck?" asked Carrera.

"I'll bet it's broken," said Millikan. "He did that in Louisville, too: a quick twist to the head from behind." Millikan looked down toward the feet at the crumpled pants, and his eyes passed along her belt. "He took their sidearms?"

"Right. He tossed Alkins's in the bushes by the hospital, but he kept hers, and a couple of ammo clips."

"I wonder why he didn't take both?"

"I wonder why he did any of this," said Carrera. "He didn't do this to get guns. You say he's from out of town, so it can't be retaliation. And leaving the two of them like this . . . it's just sick, mean stuff."

Millikan looked back at the bodies one last time. "He was trying to show that he could kill just about anybody, just for the hell of it, anytime he wants."

"Who is he trying to scare—you?"

Millikan shook his head. "Not me. I was convinced by what I saw in Louisville. But Roy Prescott has been hired to look for him, and he was trying to rattle him."

Carrera's head spun to the side to stare at Millikan. "Roy Prescott? What a waste. Prescott. Shit."

Millikan stepped away and began to examine the car. The interior was blotched with fingerprint powder, and the bloodstains were still clearly visible. They confirmed the details of the story he had already constructed, but he could tell that he was not going to learn any more until Dale Chernoff's report had been completed. He studied the ground and walked up the gentle slope to examine the angle of the indentations left by the car tires when it had pulled off the road. Then he walked up the shoulder of the road a hundred yards, trotted to the other side, and tried to determine what had made the killer choose this spot. Did he know L.A. well, or had he seen one of the signs at the entrance to the park and assumed that any park was adequate for his purpose? Millikan decided it could have been the signs. The raised roadbed let the killer see that there were no lights, no cars in the park.

Millikan stood still and watched the line of officers with flashlights walking along, staring at the ground and searching for the killer's footprints. They wanted him so badly, and they knew nothing about him. They would probably never know enough. The thought reminded him of why he was here. He had to go somewhere to call Prescott and tell him what he had just seen. After that, he was through.

Prescott sat in the dimly lighted lobby of the office building and waited. It was situated directly across Wilshire Boulevard from his own building. It did not enter his mind that the killer might not show up. He had killed the two cops, and Prescott was next. The only question to be settled was whether this was the right time. This one had a lot of braggadocio, but he was not about to do anything crude. He was not like any of the others Prescott had known. It was important to plenty of them that they be smarter than anybody else, and being smarter required that they act carefully in situations like this, when their professional competence was in question. But this one was simply better at it.

Prescott knew the general tenor of what this one was thinking. But he could not yet know the details, and the details were what got a man killed. Prescott had managed to insinuate himself into this one's brain, and get him to focus. That was a necessary step, but it had brought on the rest of the job more quickly than Prescott would have liked. It was like setting a fire at the entrance to a cave: there was no question that what was in there would be out shortly, but whatever it was, it would be moving fast and looking for the guy holding a match. This one had fooled him. Instead of coming for Prescott, he had stopped to kill two innocent people. Now Prescott could only wait and hope that he would be faster, or stronger, or maybe just luckier.

He watched the lighted lobby of his building, where the two security guards sat behind the big counter. There was a console above them with twelve little television screens that showed nothing much this time of night but empty hallways and the locked main entrances of the building. Prescott had to admire the two men. Since he had been here, they had both looked at the screens pretty regularly, in spite of the near certainty that there would be nothing more on the screens than there had been every time before: right angles and bare surfaces.

A lot of buildings around here had security guards with fancy uniforms and no sidearms. To Prescott, that defied logic. Anything that could be handled by an unarmed man wearing a uniform was not something that Prescott had much concern about. When he had been looking for an office to rent, he had paid special attention to the security guards. As soon as he had verified that at the building across the street they all carried sidearms, he had been able to proceed to their mental equipment. Rent a cop companies had a bad record as judges of character. They ran a quick check to see if the job candidate had any felony convictions under the name he happened to be using on his application, then hoped for the best. Most of the best-known serial killers of the past thirty years had, at one time or another, been security guards.

Before he had signed the lease, Prescott had taken the time to stop in at different times over a week to chat with whatever men were on duty, to be sure there were no symptoms of craziness or ineptitude. His excuse had been that he wanted to introduce himself and be sure they all recognized his face. There was some truth to it: the instant of some emergency wasn't the moment when Prescott wanted a scared man with a gun to have to choose between him and an intruder.

He stared across the street at the lighted lobby again, then looked up and down the sidewalks and at the cars going by. He was hoping to spot this shooter on his first scouting visit, before the game had even started. He wanted to see him when he was still sitting in a car outside and counting floors and windows, or walking in a leisurely way down the sidewalk, gazing up at the sides of the building to search for ventilator grilles that a fat fifty-year-old architect would not have considered accessible but might serve as an entrance to a man in his late twenties who killed people for a living.

The thought reminded Prescott again of his summers working as an exterminator. He had learned to look at buildings the way a rat would look at them—with a mind that was without preconceptions concerning the purpose or suitability of openings, free of awareness of what they were designed for—merely gauging their sizes and shapes against the capabilities of his body to climb or squeeze or flatten itself. This killer would be like that. He was accustomed to using whatever he found. But before he committed himself this time, he would take a long, hard look, and Prescott would know him.

Prescott could only guess what he might look like, because Prescott had lied about the surveillance videotape in the store in Louisville. When the killer had stopped in front of the steel grate to open the padlock and chain, the camera had caught nothing useful. Prescott had counted on making the killer hate and fear him enough to keep him from remembering clearly some things he had seen and done, so that he would not to be able to disprove Prescott's assertion.

The killer had stepped to the center of the grate to steal the padlock, but the center was directly in front of the door. The camera mounted inside the building had been aimed at the door, so that if an intruder opened the door and entered, it would catch him full on. But the store had been closed, and the big CLOSED sign had been hanging over the glass upper half, blocking the view. All Prescott had seen was a blurred, shadowy shape drift from the right side of the alcove to the sign, then pause for a couple of seconds to unlock the padlock, take it with its chain off the grate, open the grate, and grab the CLOSED sign as he slid off to the right again.

Prescott caught movement in the corner of his eye. In the lobby of the building, one of the security guards was up and walking. He went to the elevator. The other guard, a younger man, kept fiddling with something at the console in front of him, staring closely, but he said something that made the older one stop, look back, then change his course. The older man called something to the younger man, waved his arm, and then moved quickly to the staircase. The younger man stood up and hurried toward the rear of the building, out of Prescott's sight.

Across the street, Prescott was already through the glass doors and hurrying out onto the sidewalk. His eyes first moved up and down the street—what had he missed?—then up at the windows of his own building. There was nothing obvious enough to see from here. He waited for a car to pass, then trotted to the center line before the next one arrived, and waited for three cars to race by in the other direction before he dashed the rest of the way across. He had his key in his hand when he reached the big glass door in the center. He turned the key, punched his entry code into the panel beside the door, heard the buzz, and jerked the door open to slip inside. He listened for footsteps from beyond the elevators, but he heard none. The younger guard must have been heading for the other set of stairs at the rear of the building.

Either an alarm had been tripped somewhere in the building or they had seen something in one of the television screens on their console. He stepped around the desk to see: the screens were all black. Prescott looked at the three rows of alarm indicators: all were glowing a steady green.

He wondered for a moment whether his punching the keypad and coming in had reset the system and made a break indication go away, but he dismissed the idea. They must have seen something on one of the television screens before they had all gone out, or they would not have known where to go. He was pretty sure he knew what they had seen.

Prescott stepped to the elevator, but stopped himself without pushing the button. If he rode up that way, then when he reached the ninth floor, the indicator light above the ninth-floor doors would go on, the bell would sound, and somebody—either a scared guard or a killer—would be standing in front of them when they opened. At least if Prescott went up the stairs, he would not be the one making the most noise. He slipped into the rear staircase and started upward.

He climbed the stairs as quietly as he could, rushing up a flight and then crouching at the inner rail at the top of the flight to look and listen. The younger security guard must have left the stairwell already, because there was no noise coming from above. Prescott was particularly worried about him. The older guard was one he had seen a number of times, one of the men he had talked to before he had leased an office here. His name was Chet or something like that. No, Cal. The younger guard was one Prescott had never spoken to, and he might very well take a look at Prescott and assume he was the problem. Prescott stopped at each floor, cautiously opened the door to the hallway a crack, and listened. On the fifth and sixth floors, he heard nothing. On the seventh, he put his hand on the grip of his pistol. He wanted it where he could reach it, but he didn't want to have one of the guards see him in profile holding a gun, and pop him.

While he was climbing, he revised a few theories. The killer must have wanted, as he had expected, to get into Prescott's office. But everything else was wrong. Prescott had expected him to case the building tonight, not make an attempt on it. Somehow or other, this killer had skipped a couple of steps. He was already past the alarm system and inside the building. He had somehow disabled the electronic surveillance system. The only mistake he seemed to have made was to assume he could do that without having the guards notice it and come after him.

It was disconcerting to be wrong about so much, but Prescott was still certain that the killer would be on the ninth floor trying to get into his office.

Prescott moved to the stairwell door on the eighth floor, opened it a crack, and listened. He heard nothing, so he slowly, carefully pushed it open another six inches. There was still no sound. He slipped out and eased the door shut behind him. The best way to do this was to let the complete emptiness and silence of the building magnify and sharpen his senses. He needed to know precisely where the three men in the building were. He moved close to the elevator door, put his ear to it, and listened. There was no hum. He moved to the front stairwell, the one he had seen the older guard, Cal, enter. He put his ear to the door and listened, then opened it a crack and saw the shoes.

The body was lying face-down on the landing above him, and the feet protruded over the highest step. Prescott climbed higher, and knelt to reach for the carotid artery to feel for a pulse, but withdrew his hand without touching it. The head had been wrenched to the side and the neck broken. The gun was still in its holster.

Prescott stepped over the body and out of the stairwell onto the ninth floor. He moved to the first turn of the hall, then kept going past the corner into the center, staring at the hallway along the barrel of his gun. There was nobody in sight. He waited, listening for footsteps, then carefully made his way toward his office. Each of the possibilities suggested itself to him: the killer had planned to wait inside the office until Prescott showed up in the morning, but the security guards had made it impractical; the killer wanted to booby-trap the office, so when Prescott opened the door he would be either perforated or fricasseed. Prescott hoped that was what it would be, because that took time, and the killer would be fully engaged for a few more minutes.

What worried Prescott most was the younger guard. Could this guy have killed them both already? No, the older guard had been killed silently. At that point the younger guard had still been alive: there was no reason for silence if there was nobody alive to hear. The second one, he would simply have shot. Prescott moved into the corridor where his office was. As he silently approached, he kept his eyes on the doorknob, watching to see it turn. He had never let the photographs of the bodies in the Louisville restaurant fade from his mind: all rapid, clean shots done without moving anything but the gun arm. If Prescott saw this character, he probably wasn't going to get more than one shot unless the first one cut flesh.

He stepped to the door, moved to the side, set his left hand on the knob, and held the pistol in his right. He formed a clear, sharp image of the office in his mind, tracing the way every shape would look from here. Whatever did not perfectly conform to that picture had to be shot, a round placed in the middle of it instantly.

Prescott heard the elevator bell ring and he spun, then froze. He heard the elevator doors open. If the killer was in Prescott's office, he must have heard it too. Prescott couldn't let the young security guard stumble into the middle of this. Prescott held his gun in front of him and began to back away from his office. He heard the elevator doors slide shut. He backed to the turn in the hallway and looked. The indicator lights lit up as the elevator descended.

Prescott dashed to the stairwell and slipped inside. He bent over the body again, checking for the keys. The elevator would not work unless it was operated with a key. The older guard's keys were still clipped to his belt. Prescott shoved his gun into his jacket pocket, grabbed both railings, and began to vault down the steps four and five at a time.

On the fifth floor, he paused and opened the door to look at the elevator. Above it, he could see the number two, just lighting up. He kept going, trying desperately to reach the lobby in time. When he arrived at the ground floor, he was winded, but he flung open the door, his gun ready. The elevator was open, the lobby deserted.

He ran to the telephone at the security console and dialed 911. As soon as he heard the click of the connection, he said, "My name is Roy Prescott, and I'm at 98503 Wilshire Boulevard. An armed killer has just murdered a man and left the building. He's extremely dangerous, and he's dressed as a security guard." Prescott paused and then added, "Might as well send the bomb squad too. He's the sort of person who may have left a little something."

7

Prescott sat in his office and piled objects into cardboard boxes that had once held reams of paper, and put others into big trash bags. He didn't mind being evicted. The trip wire had been easy to find if you knew what you were looking for, and the gun it had been connected to had not even gone off when Prescott had disconnected it. There had been no reason after all to call the bomb squad.

The building manager had arrived to see the guys in padded suits coming out of his building a couple of hours later, and he'd seen the bomb-sniffing dogs and the trucks. He'd heard all the crap about pipe bombs and booby traps, and had wondered just how much inconvenience and aggravation the rent on one office was worth. That had been before he had even heard about the murder. No, Prescott recalled: murders. The other guard who had been killed for his uniform and gun was part of it, too.

He had given Prescott twenty-four hours, but Prescott had let him off easy. As soon as the evidence guys had sprinkled half the building with black fingerprint dust and stiff-armed all the other tenants to keep them from coming into their offices, he had come in and gotten to work packing. The office was not much use to him now. This was not the kind of killer who would keep trying the same thing in the same place until he got it right. He had already proven that he was a man who could, and would, do anything. The next try would be something entirely different.

Prescott had just about finished his packing. The furniture-rental people would be coming in a few hours to pick up the desk and chairs, the table and filing cabinets. He checked his watch, then looked at the telephone and answering machine. It was possible that he had figured this guy wrong. He had assumed that as soon as this killer knew that Prescott had not gotten his head blown off, he would make his way to another pay phone and call. The ring was like the answer to a question. He picked up the receiver and said casually, "Yeah?"

"How do you feel, Roy?"

"Sorry to disappoint you, Slick."

"You scared yet?"

"Me?" said Prescott. "Not possible. Every day brings its own little benefits."

"Like what?"

"Well, you know, I guess I spoke prematurely about having you on videotape. It seems I was misinformed and you didn't get picked up too well. But last night you showed up right in the lobby of my building. I got to watch you for a couple of hours while you were pretending to be a guard. I got to know your face, the way you move. And there was that perverted business with the two cops. I'm starting to feel like I know you."

"You don't know shit."

"When I get around to coming for you, I'll pick you out right away."

"I'll look forward to that."

"Where?"

"Where what?"

"If you're looking forward to it, you must want it to happen. Of course, life is tricky. A lot of the time you get all eager about something, and then when you finally get it, it's not anywhere near as pleasant as you thought. But that's your problem. Tell me where you want to meet, and I'll be there."

"You must be crazy. You think I'm going to tell you where I am?

You'd have a thousand cops surround the place and set fire to it. You could sit home on your ass and watch it on TV."

Prescott's voice was slightly different, and Varney detected the change. It was quieter, curious, penetrating. "You haven't done any research on me yet?"

"Yeah. I found your telephone number and address in the phone book."

Prescott's voice resumed its usual jovial, mocking tone. "Address. That reminds me. After your antics last night, my landlord bought out my lease. I'm evicted."

"Oh," moaned Varney. "So sorry."

"It's okay," said Prescott. "He had to pay me double what I paid for the year's lease, so you took care of my last two years' rent. Since I already wrote it off as a business expense, it's about half pure profit. The only reason I mention it is that I'm moving to a new address. Got a pencil?"

"You want to give me your new address?"

"Sure. It's 87875 Sunset. The phone number will be the same, but it might take a couple of days to get it transferred."

"Why are you giving me this?"

"Why not?" said Prescott. His voice was quiet and penetrating again. It gave Varney a cold, eerie feeling that made him want to shake it off. It sounded as though Prescott were inserting the words directly into his brain, without any physical mediation from the telephones, or even his ear. "You aren't going to do anything to me."

"Wait and see."

Prescott's voice was amused. "Now that I've seen you, I understand why you're afraid to tell me anything. You've been scared all your life. Before I knew who you were, I saw you sitting in the lobby and I felt sorry. I thought, A young guy who's spent all that time working out in the gym, building up his biceps and shoulders, must have had a miserable time as a kid. Probably got kicked around a lot by normal kids. You overdid the lats a bit, and the abs too, by the way. It's nice to have a thin waist, but you look a little like a girl."

Prescott heard the click, and knew the killer had hung up. He put the receiver back in the cradle, unplugged the telephone and answering machine, and put them in the box. He supposed he had gone a bit

too far this time, but the murder of the two cops and those two poor
security guards had made him impatient.

He had believed from the beginning that he would need to call this
one's manhood into question, but it had to be done with some sub-
tlety, not by flat-out saying he looked like a girl. That had been just
plain stupid. Prescott had been patiently, relentlessly fitting himself
into a role. Prescott needed to be a perfect fit, and he needed never to
appear to be trying to be perfect. He simply had to embody all of the
qualities that this man had been searching for, as though it were a miracle: he had to be all the people this man had ever hated.

Varney walked from the pay telephone into the men's room. He felt
reassured in shopping malls, because no matter where in the country
he was, they were exactly the same. This one was in Redondo Beach,
but it could just as easily have been in Buffalo. The entrances and exits
were the same, and even the stores. They were heavy with unobtrusive security, but that did as much to keep Varney from having to
watch for problems as it did for anybody else. He went into one of the
stalls and sat on the toilet to calm down. These calls always left him
feeling agitated and unsatisfied, as though he had been trying to
scratch an itch but couldn't reach the spot.

He could not ignore what Prescott had said: "You haven't done any
research on me yet?" The sound of it had been chilling. To Varney it
had been like a hostile teacher, one who had contempt for him, saying,
"You haven't done the assignment?" There had been an eagerness in
the sound, amusement. The unspoken part was, "Then you're going
to fail." Why hadn't he done some research? He had not been taking
Prescott seriously enough. Varney had decided almost immediately
that he could defeat Prescott's defenses. Varney had seen the keypads
and locks and security guards, and known that the way to get in was to
be one of them. He had said that he had seen something on the camera in the ninth-floor hallway, so that the old guard would go up.
Then he had unplugged the cable that went to the recorders and mon-
itors. Simple. Prescott should have walked to his office next morning,
pushed open the door, and gotten a hole in his chest. He should be
dead. Instead, he was telling Varney that he didn't know enough.

Prescott reminded him of Coleman Simms, and that made talking to him worse. Varney calculated. It had been nearly eight years ago, when Coleman Simms would have been about the age Prescott seemed to be now. They both had that kind of accent that was partly West and partly South, and they used some of the same words. Coleman had called everybody "boy" or "Slick" too, with that air of superiority that made him sound like a combination of an old-time gunslinger and a marine sergeant. It was as though he had such a backlog of experience behind his voice that most of it wasn't even available anymore: he had beaten better men than you without bothering to put out his cigarette, and the ones that had been a challenge, that had made him rock-hard and leathery, were all dead, because he had killed them.

Varney remembered their first meeting. The two messengers from the wholesalers had taken an entire day to drive him out to a ranch in the high desert east of Los Angeles, pulled off the road, and walked with him to a house about three hundred yards in, where there was a man standing alone, waiting. That had been Coleman Simms. Coleman had been about six feet three, thin in the way that basketball players were—with shoulder and muscle, but elongated, like a reflection in a funhouse mirror. He had big, red hands with long fingers and knotty knuckles, and pale, empty blue eyes that always squinted because he had an unfiltered cigarette hanging from his lip. Once in a while he would take it out and make a whispery "Teh" sound to spit a small flake of tobacco off the tip of his tongue. He wore jeans that always looked unfaded and brand-new, as though that were his version of dress-up, hard leather shoes, and a business shirt in a plain color with no stripes or patterns.

That first day, he had said to the two messengers, "Thank you." He waited long enough to see them walk all the way back to their car parked just off the main highway, get inside, and drive away before he turned his attention to Varney. "Before we get to know each other, I want to be fair. You're young, and probably smart as a spare tire, so I'll spell it out. Right now, you have a choice. You can walk out to that road, stick your thumb out, and get a ride back to L.A. in a few minutes. No questions asked. What I want to talk to you about is a job. If you get it done, there will be a lot of money. If you like it, there will be plenty of others—all you want. But it's the kind of job that, once we talk about it, you're going to be on a very short list of people who know. If you turn it down, and the others think you talked about it, you have a problem. Am I being clear to you?"

Varney nodded. "I'll never tell anybody. You can talk."

Coleman Simms took the cigarette out of his mouth, flicked it into the dirt, and stepped on it. The blue eyes looked into Varney's with frank curiosity. "You ever kill anybody besides that guy you robbed in his house?"

Varney looked away from him toward the road, then around him at the low, dry weeds of the pasture, then quickly back at the blue eyes.

"Don't worry, Slick," said Simms. "I'm not a cop trying to get you to confess. I'm not wearing a wire. You don't have to tell me who it was, or where. Nod your head or shake it."

Varney nodded.

"Good enough," said Coleman Simms. "I'll tell you how this works. There is a guy. You won't have to meet him or know his name. He won't know mine or yours. He is going to give a fence like the ones you do business with a pile of money. Our two friends who drove you out here will pick it up and bring it here, minus their cut. A couple of days later, I'll take you to a place where a different man lives. You'll kill him. I'll bring you back here. You will get twenty-five thousand in cash."

"How much do you get?"

"Twenty-five," said Simms. "If you live through this one, you'll get thirty next time, and I'll get twenty. You start doing them alone, you'll get forty." He stuck another cigarette on his lip, lit it from a Zippo with a big flame, and the squint returned. "If there's somebody big— somebody with some real risk to him—the pay goes up."

"What about this one?" Varney asked. "Who is he?"

"He's just some unsuspecting citizen who's pissed off the man who's paying."

"If it's so easy, why don't you do it and keep the whole fifty?"

That was the first time he saw Coleman Simms smile. "Oh, I've done a few that way. Quite a few. That's what paid for this ranch, and for what I got put away. I'm getting to the point where I can afford some luxuries."

"What does that have to do with me?"

"Well, this guy lives in a big house. You've been making a living as a second-story man, so I think it'll be easier for somebody like you to get inside. I also think splitting some jobs will be a better way of managing the business. If somebody hires me to kill his worst enemy, probably other people know they were enemies, so his name is going to come up. The police will squeeze him and squeeze him. If he's weak, he might give up and tell them some names. I've always tried to put a middleman or two between the customer and me, but now I can afford something better—protection from the middleman. If anybody along the line ever gives me up, he's still got to worry about you."

"What makes you think I'd kill anybody for that?"

This time when Coleman Simms smiled, his eyes crinkled and his teeth showed. "It's just a little feeling I have. Once we get good enough at deer hunting, we find it hard to put up with much from the deer." He spat out an invisible flake of tobacco. "Besides. It don't much matter whether you do it or not after I'm dead. What does me good is that while I'm alive, they'll think you will."

For four years Varney had worked with Coleman Simms—no, he admitted to himself now, surrounded by the quiet bare tiles of the men's room—for Coleman Simms. Coleman had always been the boss. He had always treated Varney like an apprentice. When Varney made a mistake, he was "dumb as a pile of cow shit." When he questioned Coleman's decisions, he was an "uppity little shitweasel."

In the end, it was Coleman who had made the mistake that mattered. The day came when Varney knew everything that Coleman knew, and Coleman had been too arrogant to see it coming. All that had been necessary from then on was for Varney to learn where the jobs were coming from. Maybe Coleman had seen it coming. After Varney had shot Coleman in the back of the head, he had needed to drag the body into the field to bury it. He had put his hands under the armpits to lift it a little, and found that under his shirt, Coleman had taken to wearing a bulletproof vest.

Varney heard two men come through the door into the men's room. He stood up and flushed the toilet, then went to the sink to wash his hands. He would go to the public library to see if he could use one of the computers. He would look up what he could find about Roy Prescott.

8

An hour later, Prescott moved his boxes into his new office
and left them in a corner unopened. The place was much
like the last one, only on Sunset the lawyers down the hall
were more likely to be entertainment lawyers than corporate or criminal, and most of the other offices were occupied by talent agencies or
small film-development companies that lived off the excess money
and vanity of some actor or director.

The telephone jack was about all he was interested in for the moment, and he was in a hurry, so he plugged in his phone and answering machine and left. He took the elevator down to the street level, so
he could get back in his car and drive to his rented storage space near
the airport on his way down to the marina.

A number of years ago, Prescott's wife had announced to him that
he was not temperamentally suited for marriage—something he had
begun to suspect on his own—and asked him to move out of their
house. Prescott had learned a couple of years later that a man in his
business should not live in a house at all. After the divorce, he had
bought a small house wedged in on a short, unremarkable street in
Van Nuys. It was shaded by old magnolia trees that dropped thick,

brown, leathery leaves on the pavement and lawns year-round, but added white, rubbery flower petals in the spring and summer, and grenadelike woody cones in the fall. His name had not been known to people he had not met face-to-face. Since his hunting had been conducted in cities far from Van Nuys, all that was required for safety was that he never give up on a hunt until it was finished, leaving some killer free to follow him home.

The house had appreciated in value through the eighties, as every piece of land in California did even if it was situated on a toxic-waste dump astride the San Andreas Fault. He had done what all the world seemed to consider inevitable—sold it and bought a better one. The second house was two miles away in Encino, south of Ventura Boulevard. He selected it for its appropriateness to his high income, paid five times as much for it as for the last one, and then remodeled it with an awareness that things sometimes happened to people like him if they momentarily forgot who they were.

It was a two-story Spanish-style stucco rectangle in the middle of three acres of land, with a high wrought-iron fence around it. He installed an electric gate, had a row of decorative spearheads welded to the top, and planted climbing roses along the fence that rapidly grew into a dense, thorny barrier. He dug up trees and ornamental gardens and had the yard graded with the regularity of a putting green. He had motion-sensitive security floods along the eaves that went on when anything as large as a cat crossed too near the house. They bathed the empty, featureless lawn in blinding light that converted it into a kill zone like the margins around prisons. The windows were equipped with steel shutters, and beneath each of them was a hollow window seat containing a flashlight, a cell phone on a charger, and a loaded Smith & Wesson nine-millimeter pistol.

He lived there for about three years before a job took him into the woods north of Minneapolis. He had been hired as a subcontractor by a private detective. The detective's name was Paul Mellgrim, and he was a highly visible man who had made his name protecting celebrities and handling the investigations that surrounded their many lawsuits. Mellgrim was searching for the daughter of a studio executive who had been a student at the University of Minnesota. He had traced her movements, and found that she had been easy to follow until ten o'clock one evening when she'd left a coffee shop near the campus, said good-bye to a few friends outside the door, and walked off the face of the earth. Mellgrim had called Prescott and said, "I'm telling you, I got a real strange feeling about this. Ugly."

It was ugly. The day after the call, the girl's red Porsche turned up in Duluth painted green and with different plates, all ready for resale. Prescott arrived just as the state police and a group of local volunteers were starting on a sweep through the forest in St. Croix State Park. The place surprised him. It was only ninety minutes north of Minneapolis, but it was a kind of wilderness that he had not been expecting. The forest ran right to the highway. If a car entered on the only road in, it drove five miles through uninterrupted woods before it even reached the first ranger station, where visitors were supposed to stop voluntarily and buy a pass. Three times on the way in, Prescott had needed to slow down to let deer bound frantically across the road.

The reason for the sweep was that a biologist who had been busy following the trail of a tagged bear had come across the remains of a young girl in the forest. The body had been mutilated so badly that it was a good thing the biologist had been the finder: he had been able to assure everybody authoritatively that she had not been mauled by a bear. The preliminary examination that had been carried out in the city had confirmed his claim for any remaining doubters, but it had raised another: the girl wasn't the one Mellgrim had been looking for. Prescott had parked his car and joined the search. It had taken hours of fighting blackflies and sweating through low brush, often losing sight of the line of searchers and staying with them by the sounds they made. But they found the bodies of four more girls, all killed with about the same ferocity and dumped in the woods.

Prescott recognized the pattern without waiting for the state police to get around to discerning it. One body belonged to a girl missing much longer than the others—nearly two years—but the third had died only two months after the second, and the fourth only two weeks after the third. The fourth was the one Prescott had come to Minnesota to look for, the daughter of Mellgrim's client. The one that had set the sweep in motion, the one the biologist had found, was the most recent. She had been killed only a week after the fourth.

The pattern that sexual psychopaths often followed was asserting itself with unusual intensity this time: two years, two months, two weeks, one week. The first crime was some kind of power experiment, usually an abduction for the purpose of rape. The killing had probably not been planned. More likely, it had been the result of an impulse, or panic. That had ended the incident, but an unexpected problem had arisen after the girl was dead. The killer, consumed by the stew of emotions he felt—fear, shame, remorse, self-hatred—had looked back on it, and remembered. And when he'd remembered, he'd discovered that he liked it. He'd run through it in his memory, and reliving it had made him sexually excited. After a long interval, he'd become so obsessed with repeating it in his mind that he'd wanted to repeat it in the world with a new girl.

He'd tried to duplicate his first experience, and when he had, he'd made some more discoveries: he'd found that his fear had been groundless, because this time the crime was planned, and it was much easier. He'd found that once he had done this to the first girl, the shame and remorse had become meaningless: they were fake. He'd quickly begun to realize that he had never really felt those things. They were just ideas imposed on him by a repressive society, and he had imagined feeling them because he was supposed to. But now his mind had been expanded. He knew far too much to fool himself again. That took care of the self-hatred; he had transcended all rules.

After that, he'd become more and more attached to what had become his new purpose in life. Before long, he had turned himself into something that even he had probably never imagined existed at the start—a predatory creature that wandered in the night searching for victims, needing to feed on their fear and pain. Prescott judged that the man who had left the girls in the woods was reaching some final stage, doing practically nothing now but killing.

Prescott selected his decoy carefully. It was not hard to find a tall, thin blonde of about the right age in Minneapolis. This one was good at impersonating a University of Minnesota co-ed, because it had not been many years since she had been one, and she still returned to some of the hangouts from those days often enough to fit in. Her name was Stella Kaspersen, and she was working as a private detective out of an office on the other side of the river. He spent four hours with her one afternoon, partly letting her convince him that she knew exactly what he wanted her to do, and was capable of doing it.

It was Prescott's theory that the man knew there were three or four policewomen out acting as decoys each night, but that he was very good at spotting the traps: there were always observation vans somewhere within view, and at least two chase cars around a corner. Prescott believed that the police operations offered a special opportunity. The sight of the policewomen would make the killer agitated, more eager to strike than he had been in the past. Those police operations would also keep him away from whole parts of the city. Any other place might suddenly become very dangerous for a woman alone at night.

Prescott and Stella Kaspersen began to work the streets in areas the police were not covering. Four nights later, they were at their third stop, and Stella was walking alone down the empty sidewalk away from the quiet bar where one of the girls had sometimes been seen. A man in a four-wheel-drive utility vehicle pulled over and asked her if she wanted a ride. She replied haughtily that she didn't, then walked faster, as though her reply had been a way of hiding fear. But as she and Prescott had rehearsed, she was hurrying from a lighted, open street toward a dark parking lot at the end of an alley. Prescott watched the man from the dark space between two buildings nearby. He saw that Stella's fear and revulsion were not disappointing to the man. They were making him more interested.

When Stella was in the alley, the man watched her for a moment, then pulled his vehicle over and turned out the lights. Prescott ducked back into the dark space where he had been hiding, and studied the man's face. The man was aware that the police would be using decoys to find him, and that Stella might be one of them. He was using this time to study the area around him to detect the presence of cops. He looked closely at the line of cars parked along the curb for pickup teams, looked at the windows of buildings for spotters. Prescott could tell that he was frustrated and upset: he was not positive that the area was clear, but he was very aware that time was passing. If he let Stella make it to her car, she was going to be out of his reach. After thirty or forty seconds, the man made his decision: he would chance it. He turned on his lights, pulled out, and sped up the alley after Stella.

Prescott broke from his hiding place. He had been expecting the man to go after Stella on foot, but since he had not, Prescott would need his car. He dashed between the next two buildings out to the street where he had left it, got in, and drove up the alley. He pulled in behind the man's vehicle and blocked his exit. When he got out of his car, the man was already pushing Stella away so he could face Prescott.

The man was big and muscular, and Prescott could see in the man's eyes that he was not reacting well: he looked almost glad to see Prescott. In a single, quick motion, he reached into the cab of his truck, came back with a two-foot crowbar, and swung it hard and fast at Prescott's head. Prescott stepped back only long enough to let the claw of the bar get past his face, then lunged forward while the man's arm was across his body trying to stop the bar's momentum to begin the backhand swing. The heel of Prescott's right hand pounded into the middle of the man's face to drive the bones of his nose up into his brain.

Then Prescott called the police and waited patiently. They arrested him, as usual, but Stella had already begun her narrative of his heroism, and her version got better with repetition. She seemed to have judged that a little exaggeration was warranted by the edgy, slit-eyed look both of the cops gave Prescott, and she had determined not to tolerate having equivocal judgments issued by the authorities. Prescott and Stella were allowed to leave the station at the same time the next morning.

Prescott flew home to Los Angeles and received a big check from Mellgrim's client. But when he arrived he discovered that Stella's wild tale of his uncanny brilliance and his deadly combat skills had made it, undiluted and not tempered by skepticism or even common sense, into the wire-service reports, and then onto national television news.

Prescott had still lived happily enough in his house in Encino until one night a month later. He awoke to the flashing of the light on the silent alarm and the low buzz it made in his room when the perimeter of the house had been breached. He began to move silently down the back stairs, his gun in his hand, gliding through the darkness. He slipped out the back door onto the lawn, and quietly made his way around the house to the window where the intruder had entered. As he approached, he noticed that a dim illumination from inside the house was throwing a square of light on the lawn.

The silence was shattered by a piercing electronic shriek, and the square of light seemed to brighten. Prescott stepped forward and looked in the window just as the fire alarm reached 120 decibels. The flames rose from the center of the living room floor and blossomed outward at the ceiling, with thick black smoke pouring ahead of the brightness toward the dining room and the staircase. The color of the flames—bright yellow with blue fringes—told him it was gasoline. The front door swung open and he got a glimpse of a man wearing a blue windbreaker and jeans slipping outside.

Prescott sprinted around the corner of the house in time to see the man running hard toward the front gate. Prescott strained to gain on him, the balls of his feet digging hard into the grass and his strides lengthening. The man pushed on the gate, then realized it would not open, and reached up to pull himself to the top.

Prescott stopped twenty feet from him and aimed the gun. "Don't leave just yet."

When the man dropped to the driveway and turned to face him, the explanation settled on Prescott all at once. In the brightness of the fire, Prescott could see that the man's face and hands were deeply scratched and skinned from going over the fence through the hedge of climbing roses. Trickles of blood ran down his cheeks to his chin, making streaks in the black carbon that had come from the mistake of lighting a big pool of gasoline in an enclosed space. His eyebrows and the hair above his forehead had been singed off by the first flash of ignition, but the eyes glowed with excitement, and the mouth was set in a delighted grin. On the heart of the windbreaker were the words MINNESOTA TWINS.

There followed a fraction of a second that Prescott used by cursing himself for letting this happen. He had been too willing to accept it when the police had insisted that the man who had gone after Stella Kaspersen was a solitary, introverted type who could not have had an accomplice. Prescott had not been sure. The murdered girls had merely been dumped in the woods after they were dead. The way they had first been overpowered and killed somewhere else argued for the idea that there was a somewhere else, and the police had not turned up a suitable spot that was owned or controlled by the man with the crowbar. The police had assured him it didn't mean anything, because that part of Minnesota was full of sparsely populated places where a man could do virtually anything and not be heard or seen. Prescott had assumed they must know more about their territory than he did. Now, a month later, here the nonexistent accomplice was, burning Prescott's house down around his ears.

When the fraction of a second had elapsed, the man's right hand was slipping into the windbreaker's pocket. Prescott had seen from the white-toothed grin in the middle of the black-singed face that this was going to happen, so while the man maneuvered the hidden pistol so he could fire it though the windbreaker's pocket, Prescott took the time to place a shot through the bend of the *M* in *Minnesota*.

While he was bent over the body to check for any unwelcome signs of life, he happened to glance toward his house and see the center beam burn through to dump much of the tile roof into his living room and create a suitable flue for the forty-foot flames to billow upward into the night sky.

As he watched his beautiful, carefully planned house burn down, Prescott admitted to himself that he had become too notorious to live this way. It also occurred to him that in a large city, almost any good hotel had a bed as comfortable as he'd had, a chef who could cook better than he could, and a bathroom that was cleaned more often than he was willing to clean it. He rented a storage space for the possessions he felt he needed to own but didn't want to carry from one hotel to another in a suitcase.

Without the burden of the big house, or the temptation to buy things to put in it, he spent a smaller portion of his income. He put his money into stocks and bonds that were in the physical custody of major brokerage firms, and they automatically fed his checking account every month. If anybody wanted him, they could dial his business telephone number or send a letter to his post office box.

Within a month after the fire, Prescott had effectively disappeared as a physical presence that could be limited at any given moment to a single set of coordinates on the earth.

9

Varney chose the North Hollywood branch library because it was miles from the big central one downtown. It was small enough so that he could see the entrances and most of the employees at a glance. Even if Prescott's suggestion that he do some research was a trap—if Prescott had some insider's way of getting the library's computer-system controller to call the cops as soon as someone started running searches on his name—Varney was fairly confident that he would notice odd behavior in the librarians or patrons in time to get out.

The library was a low brick building at the edge of a huge, tree-shaded park that stretched for blocks in three directions. Near the building, right on the corner where Magnolia Boulevard met Tujunga, there was a life-sized too-bright golden statue of Amelia Earhart holding, oddly, the disconnected propeller of her airplane. On wooden benches near her and at various spots in the park, derelicts and homeless people congregated or slept where the shade would protect them from the ferocious sunshine for a time. It would be easy to slip into one of those groups and sit with that tired, bent-over posture, then make his way slowly to his rented car parked a hundred yards from the freeway entrance on Tujunga.

If that way was blocked, there was a big high school a few blocks down Magnolia. Varney was sure he could move through a big campus like that without being an obvious outsider. He had learned a long time ago that it was easy to take advantage of people's reluctance to stop a stranger and ask rude questions. It took them a long time to convince themselves that somebody should, then that nobody else would, and then to check around them to be sure they would be safe if the answer turned out to be unpleasant. By then he could be around the next corner and out the door on the other side of the building. He considered for a moment. Yes, the high school would be best. After all the news about shootings in schools, no cop would see a high school as a place a man like Varney would try to hide: it was too foolish.

Varney parked and went into the library. There was a sign beside the computers explaining the rules for use. He had to go to the reference desk to give his name, and that would only get him a half hour of computer time. He sighed, then walked off between two shelves of books to pretend to browse while he studied the reference desk and thought about unseen risks. He could perceive none. There was nobody else using the computers at the moment: the kids were in school, and everyone else seemed to be looking at books. He walked up to the desk, showed a bored librarian his stolen California driver's license, and wrote the owner's name on a sheet of paper. Two minutes later, Varney was on the Internet, reading an article about Prescott.

He sat in the old, cool building, half aware of the chattering on the other end of the room near the circulation desk. He knew it would suddenly go quiet if he had a problem. He read the article again. He had chosen the *Los Angeles Times* because it was Prescott's hometown paper, and because it was still one of the big, fat papers that seemed to report on everything. Most of the papers in the country had shriveled over the years to tabloid size, and carried more short wire-service clips and syndicated columns than local news.

The title was "Five-Year Search Comes to an End." It was about Prescott going after some guy named Spinoza who had been selling cocaine out of a house somewhere in L.A. County: Hawaiian Gardens? How the hell could they call a town that? The cops had raided the house, but the guy had already gotten out. He'd shot three little boys on the street nearby, because he knew three kids with holes in them would distract the cops. He had escaped and used his connections with his suppliers to hide in Mexico.

The reporter scored a lot of points against the L.A. police. Instead of getting the cooperation of the Mexican authorities, they had kept looking in Spinoza's old L.A. haunts. Then the crush of an additional thousand murders a year moved the three little boys' case into a kind of limbo: it was solved, just not closed. It was at that point that the neighborhood began collecting money and calling it the Three Boys Fund. By the fourth anniversary of the deaths, and with the help of large donations from a few rich businessmen, the neighborhood had collected enough money to hire their own hunter. They had asked around and kept hearing of Roy Prescott.

Varney looked up from the screen, his eyes moving across the circulation desk, a nearby window, and the doors while he thought. Prescott had already been well known five years ago. A bunch of poor, ignorant people in an apartment complex had heard of him from more than one source, and what they'd heard had convinced them to pay him to go after Spinoza.

He skipped down to the police spokesman's statement: "We don't approve of citizens seeking protection for their neighborhoods by giving money to men who may or may not be honest, or competent, and who, in any case, care nothing about the best interests of the community. In this instance, the issue was not even the safety of the neighborhood. It was revenge, pure and simple. As for Mr. Prescott, the district attorney's office is studying his actions for possible prosecution, as, I believe, are officials in Matamoros, Mexico, and Brownsville, Texas."

Varney scrolled back up the column. Prescott had refused to answer any questions, but the story was clear. He had gone into Mexico alone, worked his way from person to person until he had found, not Spinoza, but Spinoza's new route for moving in and out of the United States. He had waited for Spinoza near Brownsville, Texas, then caught him in Matamoros, Mexico. The details were missing, but the essentials were there: Spinoza was dead and Prescott was not.

Varney scrolled downward through the article, then returned to the opening display. Under the caption "Also in Today's L.A. Times" was the title "Long Hunt Ends in Matamoros." He clicked on the words

and, in a moment, saw something forming on the screen that he had
not dared to hope for: a photograph. His eyes jumped to it eagerly,
then squinted in frustration. It was not very clear. The article said it
had been taken by an American tourist in a car in Matamoros just after
the shooting of Spinoza. There was a covered body lying in the street.
Three uniformed men, all dark and about the same height, were leading a lone man toward a car. He was light-haired, a head taller than
they were, and lean. He was walking away, but he had turned his head
slightly to the side to look down at one of the policemen, so Varney
could almost see a vague profile of the face, but not quite. Looking
more closely at it only made the picture dissolve into the diagonal
rows of tiny dots that composed it.

Varney's half hour was up. He went back to the reference desk to
sign out, then signed in on the next computer. He found other articles. There was one in the *Denver Post*. Prescott had followed some
guy into the mountains in the spring and hunted him all summer
through the resort towns. There was one in the New Orleans *Times-
Picayune* that said he'd gotten himself arrested so he could look for a
man in a parish jail. There was one in Minneapolis where he had
beaten some serial killer to death with—his bare hands? No, there was
something about a crowbar.

The police reactions could all have been written by the L.A. police
spokesman. They hated him. Some implied that he had butted into a
high-profile case just in time to get paid some outrageous fee when
the police would have solved it anyway. All of them said something
disparaging about his "methods." He used excessive force, disre-
garded public safety, ignored the rights of suspects, paid bribes, or
made threats to informants. It was all pretty much what the average
police force did, but they didn't care for having him do it too.

Varney looked up and studied the library again, waiting for a sign
that he was still safe. He watched a group of children—two boys and
two girls—get dragged into the entrance by a woman who was too
openly irritated to be anything but their mother. That made him relax
again. If the police were outside, they might not do anything overt,
but the one thing they wouldn't do was let a bunch of extra kids in the
front door.

He signed off the Internet, stood up, and walked outside. He strolled across Magnolia Boulevard to the bigger section of the park as he re-examined Prescott's remark. When Prescott had asked him if he had done any research, he had meant that if Varney thought Prescott was going to be able to have a squad of cops doing his bidding, then Varney didn't know anything about Prescott. Now, why would he want Varney to know that? Was it because he wanted Varney to think that killing Prescott would be easier than he had imagined? Maybe all he had wanted was to have Varney stumble across the picture of him that was impossible to make out, and feel helpless. And whatever the police thought about Prescott, they would do just about anything to get the man who had left the two dead cops in the park.

He got into his car and drove along Magnolia past the high school, but did not get onto the freeway for many blocks, until he was sure that he had not been followed. At Woodman he found another entrance ramp, drove west on the Ventura Freeway, then turned south on the San Diego Freeway. He was thinking of the way to get Prescott. Reading about him had not helped Varney find any vulnerabilities.

In those articles, Varney had read accounts of Prescott shooting about three people, killing some guy in a hand-to-hand fight, chasing another into a mountain forest where he'd had a suspicious fatal fall. Prescott had found people in seven or eight different ways in places that had little in common. Varney saw nothing in the stories that would tell him what Prescott was likely to do this time. He remembered that there was a man named Donald Ramirez interviewed in the Hawaiian Gardens case. Ramirez was a very common name, but Varney was pretty sure there would not be a lot of Donalds in the phone book. Maybe he would give this guy a call. If Varney pretended to be considering hiring Prescott, a satisfied customer might tell him things that had not been in the newspapers five years ago.

Varney got off the freeway at Marina del Rey and drove to his motel. It was a long, low building across the Pacific Coast Highway from the harbor, where thousands of yachts were nosed up to the docks nearly touching each other, and the masts of sailboats looked from a distance like the forest they once had been. Varney took comfort in the motel's design. It was built in the shape of an enormous horseshoe. The outer sides of the building showed only a row of room doors leading directly to the large parking lot, with one small window for each room.

The inner side of each room had a sliding glass door that led out to an inner court dominated by a heated swimming pool.

The motel was easy for him to find, because it had a high row of shrubs with big white flowers at the edge of the parking lot, and they were all in bloom. He approached the entrance to the parking lot, but he hesitated and let his car go past. There was something he did not like. Varney kept going for another block, then turned into a lot near the boat harbor and parked. He sat still for a moment, then got out.

What he had seen was a brand-new dark blue Cadillac parked at the edge of the motel lot, backed into a space. It was much farther from the building than the other cars. When he was working, Varney spent much of his time in motels, and he knew that motel guests seldom parked farther from the building than they needed to. They had to carry their own luggage in and out, and they liked to keep their cars close, in the belief that proximity discouraged car thieves. Often he saw cars stranded far out in a lot as this one was, but they were always the cars of guests who had arrived late the night before when the lot was full, and slept late in the morning while the rest of the guests checked out. This car had not been in the lot when Varney had gone out this morning.

Varney would have ignored the car, but he thought he had seen a man sitting behind the steering wheel. His speed and the flowering shrubs along the sidewalk had blurred and partially obscured his view. It wouldn't hurt to walk the block to the motel and be sure. He turned away from the harbor onto the next street, then walked toward the side of the motel next to the parking lot.

He came around the building where he could see the man in the car without being seen. The man was tall, with a long left forearm resting on the top of the car door. His head had that same look that Coleman's had once had, the sandy hair cut close at the sides with a bit more at the top combed straight back, high cheekbones, and a slight squint of the eyes in the sunlight. He compared the man with the profile he had seen in the hazy newspaper picture from the old case in Mexico. Prescott had let Varney see that dim, unfocused picture of him walking away as a taunt, just another attempt to unnerve him. But it had confirmed Varney's sense of Prescott's size and body type.

This was Prescott. It had to be. He was parked so the car was aimed at the door of Varney's room. If he chose, he could wait until Varney had driven in and gone into his room, then pull the car across the lot entrance to block the way out. If Varney saw him and ran, he could tromp on the gas and run him down.

Varney turned and walked along the side of the building farthest from the parking lot. There was only one way this could have happened. Prescott had somehow gotten the license number of the rental car last night, used it to get the number of Varney's credit card, and found the motel name through a credit check. Varney gritted his teeth and closed his eyes. He had been stupid to park in the underground garage at Prescott's building. He had planned that when he was at the controls in the lobby, he would erase all the surveillance tapes. He must have missed one for a camera recording the license numbers at the garage entrance. At the time, he had figured Prescott was just a self-promoting blowhard, like the professor on television. Varney had planned to fly here, terrorize him with the deaths of the cops, then come for him and disappear, all in a day. He had been careless.

Varney hesitated. If Prescott had that kind of lead, what was he doing here? He could have given Varney to the police. Varney remembered the newspaper articles. They had been printed over a period of ten or twelve years in different states. There must have been dozens of times when Prescott had collected enough information to turn somebody over to the police. But it didn't appear that he had ever done that. He always wanted to make the kill himself.

Varney turned the corner of the building, considering what he would lose if he just kept walking: his suitcase contained some clothes and personal items that Prescott might be able to use in some way. There would be hair from his brush, fingerprints on the latches. He had left his plane ticket in the suitcase. He had thrown away the stub of the ticket he had used to get here, but the return ticket was still in the suitcase. He had hidden it in a slit he had made in the lining. A thief probably wouldn't find it, but he could not leave the suitcase for a man like Prescott.

He wanted to kill him. Prescott was sitting in that car in a shady spot, probably listening to the radio and patiently, contentedly staring at the door of Varney's room. Varney tried to formulate a strategy. He had no gun. But he could come through the bushes behind Prescott's

car, be at the open window in a second, try to disable Prescott's left
arm and maybe get a hand to his temple, eyes, or throat. But it was
midday, and the car was in the open, far from any others. Prescott
might see him coming. Prescott wasn't just some guy sitting in a car,
either. He was here in the first place because he was expecting Varney,
and he undoubtedly had a gun he could put his right hand on in a second.

Varney was not going to try it. He would have to be satisfied with
simply getting out clean. He entered the motel through the back of
the lobby on the other side of the building, then walked along the side
of the pool in the interior courtyard. He stopped to feel the water,
then moved on until he came to his room. He knew the sliding glass
door was locked, because he had locked it himself. But the lock was a
simple mechanism. The latch was a hook that went over a little bar in
the frame. By the time he got to it, he already had his thin plastic
phone calling card out of his wallet. He stepped close to lean against
the edge of the door, inserted the card between the frame and the window, and pulled the card up. The latch came with it, and he was inside.

Varney closed the drapes, went to the closet, lifted his suitcase, and
checked to be sure it was still locked. Then he snatched a damp towel
from the bathroom floor, wiped off all the knobs and surfaces he
might have touched, slipped out the sliding door to the courtyard, and
walked along the pool to the lobby. He stopped at the desk to accept
and sign the bill that had been charged to his card, and to turn in his
key. He had taken a risk, then compounded it by taking the extra time
to clean his room and leave the right way, but he judged that it would
give him peace of mind later. The man at the desk had to go into a
back room to get the paperwork. Varney could see filing cabinets and
the corner of a desk through the door. He saw the man quickly leafing
through a card file as he spoke to someone in the back room. Then he
found the registration card and the credit card slip and returned. Varney heard another door open and close.

As Varney signed and pushed his key across the counter, he became
aware of a rattling noise outside, but dismissed it. There was nothing
Prescott would do that made a sound like that. The rattle grew louder,
now and then punctuated by a *bump-bump*. It was just a maid pushing
her cart along the side of the building. His heart sped up. The maid!

That's what the clerk had been doing in the back room—sending the maid to make up his room for the next customer. Prescott would see her go in. He took his slip and picked up his suitcase. As soon as Prescott saw where the maid was going, he would come straight to this desk to learn when Varney had left. Varney had to do something, and as each second passed, choices went with it. He turned and moved to the rear door, went out on the courtyard side, and walked back along the pool to the room he had just vacated. As he reached the sliding glass door, he saw the maid grab the two plastic rods to whisk open the curtains to get more light to work.

Varney smiled at her, quickly opened the sliding door, and slipped in past her.

"Sir?" she said, a little frightened. "Forget something?"

"I'm not sure," he said. "I just want to take a quick look." He stayed in the shadows near the closet and stared out past the cart she had used to prop open the door. He could see the parking lot, but his mind stumbled. The dark blue Cadillac was still there. How could Prescott not have seen the maid? But then he saw that the head behind the wheel was gone. Prescott was out of the car.

Varney moved to the side of the door. Prescott wasn't coming to the room on foot. The maid was pretending not to watch Varney, but he could see that her head was held in a stiff-necked angle to keep him in her peripheral vision. He took out his wallet and handed her a twenty-dollar bill.

"Thank you, sir," she said.

"You're welcome," he muttered. "Might as well go out this way."

She didn't answer, but as she watched him sidestep past her cart and out the door she seemed relieved.

Varney looked up and down the building in both directions, then began to walk quickly toward Prescott's car. The suitcase was small, but he hated the weight and imbalance it forced on him, and the visibility of it. If he could ditch it somewhere, he would be just a man walking down the street. With it, people were going to see him, remember him, wonder if he was on foot with a suitcase because he was skipping out on a hotel bill, or if he was a thief. He couldn't leave it, because Prescott might find it and use what was in it to hunt him. As soon as he was away from here, he would try to find a place to open it and at least remove the plane ticket.

He crossed the parking lot, glancing now and then in the direction of the motel lobby. Prescott must still be at the counter, trying to pry some information out of the clerk. At least that would help delay him. Varney passed to the side of the car and looked inside on the unlikely chance that Prescott had left a gun. It was no surprise that he had not. Varney stepped through the bushes and out to the street, then took his last look at the motel. He saw nothing in the direction of the office, but he could see the open door of his room, and he could tell someone was now inside with the maid.

He turned and ran across the street, dodging cars and trucks until he was on the seaward side near the harbor fence, where he had hoped there would be a few other pedestrians to complicate Prescott's view. But the only people around were far away, beyond the fence, on other parts of the vast network of docks and boat slips. He looked back at the lot, and he could see the tall, thin figure emerge from the room. Varney would have to do something better before Prescott reached his car and pulled out of the lot. He tossed his suitcase over the chain-link fence. He took three steps toward it, ran up, digging his toes in, and rolled over to the other side. Then he snatched up his suitcase and stepped off the nearest dock with it.

He ducked under the water, then came up, smelling the film of leaked gasoline that he could see reflecting liquid rainbows on the surface. He moved under the dock, only his head above the surface. He waited patiently, letting the water seep into his suitcase and soak the clothes, so the suitcase would sink.

It was night before Varney let himself drift out of his hiding place under the dock, then pulled his heavy suitcase to a ramp where boats were launched from trailers. He was shivering with the cold. He found his key and opened the lock on his suitcase with shaking fingers, then let most of the water pour out. He stood and walked with care, keeping in the shadows, letting the water drain from his clothes and his shoes. He had only a block to go to find his rental car, but he moved in the opposite direction, because that was where Prescott would be waiting for him. He left the marina and walked along the beach for a half hour, just above the water line, where the sand was wet and firm. The breeze was cold, but after fifteen minutes he began to feel it less intensely. When he stopped dripping and began to feel, not dry, but a granular stickiness on his skin from the salt water, he went out to the pavement again and turned at the first street that would take him off the Pacific Coast Highway. He went to a closed gas station and used a pay phone to call a cab.

He told the driver that he wanted to go to the airport, but when the cab let him off at LAX, he walked to a cheap-looking motel on Century Boulevard, checked in, and opened his suitcase. He took each item out and hung it on the railing over the bathtub. He looked closely inside the lining of the suitcase, then looked again. The suitcase had been locked. The ticket to Buffalo was still hidden in the lining exactly where he had left it. But how could he be sure that Prescott had not seen it?

10

Varney understood what had happened as though he had seen it. Prescott had gone into the room looking for Varney. He had found it empty, then spent a moment teasing himself with the idea of doing this job the sensible way. He had undoubtedly been tempted to sit there with his gun in his lap, watch Varney walk in the door, and then drop the hammer on him: maybe one through the head, or maybe be safe and conservative and put two or three into his chest while he was standing there, caught in the doorway.

But if Prescott had done it the sensible way, the police would have come in, looked things over, and known that they had Varney and Prescott too. He had to sit around outside, observing the letter of the law until Varney showed up in the open air of the parking lot. Then Prescott could have arranged an execution that at least appeared legal.

Well, fuck him. He was the one who wanted to be famous, so he'd had to give up the advantages that notoriety cost. Varney sat on the edge of the tub and the shivers returned. The salt residue on his clothes and skin seemed to draw water out of the air and renew the bone-chill he felt from his hours in the water. He could not get himself to forget the image he had constructed. There is Varney strolling back from the library unarmed, wearing a T-shirt and jeans. Inside the room, sitting in the only chair, which he has moved to the side of the door, is Prescott. He hears Varney's key in the lock, flips the safety off his pistol, raises it to chest height. Varney steps inside, catches something in his peripheral vision, spins toward it, and crouches. His quick compression of his body brings him low and ready to spring, but all it really accomplishes is that he takes the intended chest shot full in the face.

Varney could not delude himself into believing that any action of his had prevented his death from happening. All that had saved him was that Prescott could not have explained things afterward. Varney's hands were numb and tingling. He stripped off his clothes and ran the shower, then stepped into it, letting the hot water slowly restore his body heat.

As he closed the curtain, he caught sight of himself in the mirror over the sink. His hair was stiff and dirty from the surface slime in the boat harbor, his face pinched and white. Even the muscular torso he had worked so untiringly to build looked white and slack, like the flesh of a fish's belly. This trip had been a disaster. He had talked to Prescott on a whim, and gotten so outraged at everything about him that he had decided to take a quick trip out here to put him away. That had been two days ago. Only two days.

He had not needed to do this. Prescott had made it clear that he wasn't even planning to come after Varney yet. Varney had thought that this made now a good time. He had gotten the cops within a few hours after his plane had landed. Then he had gone after Prescott. He had done everything right. Getting into that office building as a security guard had seemed clever, but what had it accomplished? It had forced him to kill two security guards without any hope of ever getting a dime for it.

Now he was worse off than he'd been at the start. Prescott had heard his voice and seen his face. Prescott had found out one of his identities. Prescott probably hadn't seen the plane ticket hidden in his suitcase, but if he hadn't, it wasn't because Varney had outsmarted him. The ticket would have told him the airport Varney had left to fly to Los Angeles. Varney had given all of that to Prescott. All he could do now was get out of town. But first, he had to leave a message.

After he had showered and dried his clothes, he took a nap. When he awoke it was four A.M. He walked to the airport and rented a car using the credit card that Prescott had compromised already. There was no question that Prescott and the cops would find out about it later. That would give Prescott the impression that Varney had not figured out that Prescott knew about it. Later this morning, Varney would give Prescott something else to wonder about.

Varney drove past the motel in Marina del Rey. He parked a half mile away, on a street that ran inland from the ocean, took the tire iron from the trunk of the car, and walked back. The parking lot was about as full as it had been when Varney had gone out eagerly to get Prescott. His mood was terribly different now.

Varney knew he would not have long to wait. It was nearly six. The maid who had cleaned his room in the afternoon was the one he had seen arriving yesterday a bit before seven in the morning, and the desk clerks seemed to change shifts at about the same time.

He came around the side of the motel to the entrance to the courtyard where the pool was. When he had checked into the motel, he had studied it with his usual attention to detail. Whenever the maids cleaned a room, they always threw open the curtains on the big glass doors to the courtyard to give themselves some light. Sometimes they opened a window to air out the room while they worked. When they finished, they closed and locked the window, but they left the curtains open.

He walked along the row of glass doors, searching. The fifth set had its curtains open. He could see the smooth surface of the bedspread pulled tight across the mattress, the pillow still plumped and covered. Varney had already found that the quickest, easiest way to open the sliding doors was to use a telephone calling card, so he used the one he had again, stepped inside, and slid the door shut.

Varney waited and watched through his small front window until he saw the door to the office open and the night clerk walk across the parking lot to a car along the fence, toss a lunch box and a thermos onto the back seat, get in, and drive off. Varney stepped out of the room, made his way to the office, and entered.

The day clerk was just putting his jacket on a hanger in the back room. Varney heard him put something on the rack in the small refrigerator, then heard him close the door, the insulating rubber gasket making a little smack as it sealed. The clerk came out to see Varney leaning forward with his left forearm on the counter. Varney could detect surprise, but no fear. Prescott must not have told him anything about the man he had been there to look for.

The clerk stepped closer. "Good morning, sir," he said, smiling. "Are you coming back to stay with us again?"

Varney smiled back, and nodded. The man looked down and bent slightly at the waist to reach the blank registration cards on the shelf under the counter. Varney's right arm brought the tire iron up from beside his leg, over the counter, and down on the man's skull in a single, smooth stroke. He followed the blow by vaulting over the counter. He landed with both feet on the man's back, but there seemed to be no huff of air, not even a tightening of muscles. Varney straddled him and swung the tire iron twice more. The man's skull was now partly visible through clumps of hair, like shards of a broken bowl of red pudding.

Varney left him, went to the back room, and looked around. There were filing cabinets and a card file to keep track of the current guests. There was a table where people probably sat to take their breaks, and a door on the other side. He could see a couple of cardboard cartons, and the top of one was open. He looked inside, and saw that it had a blanket inside wrapped in plastic. He unwrapped it and tossed it over the clerk's body to cover it so he wouldn't get blood on his shoes. He noticed that his face felt strange, and realized that he had smiled at the clerk, and forgotten to stop smiling. He let the muscles go slack.

A couple of minutes later, he heard the maid's cart rolling along the sidewalk beside the building. He waited until the sound stopped, then cautiously moved to the front window.

He could see the maid had opened one of the room doors and propped it open with her cart. He stepped along the row of doors to the room and listened for a moment, staring into the cart. When he heard her move into the bathroom and begin running water, he pushed the cart the rest of the way in, and quietly closed the door. Then he took a pillow case from the cart and stepped in behind her. She was bent over, cleaning the tub. He wrapped the ends of the pillow case around his fists, waited patiently until she began to rise to her feet, then quickly looped it over her head and around her neck.

She was a small woman, but she bucked and kicked furiously, even after he tightened the pillow case enough to cut off her air and lift her off the ground. He kept tightening it patiently until he was sure she was dead. He lifted her body and dropped it into the bin in her cart that was for dirty linens. Then he tossed over her the pile of sheets she had torn off the bed.

He took a last look around him, closed the door, and walked back to his car. He drove a couple of miles before he stopped at a pay telephone and dialed Prescott's number. He waited until the answering machine beeped. Then he said, "I'm leaving. I left you a couple of good-bye presents at the motel in Marina del Rey. They're to remind you never to come after me again."

As the plane took off, Prescott reached into the pocket of his jacket for some chewing gum and found the crumpled piece of paper. He took it out and glanced at it. The hurried way he had scribbled the name and address of the hotel in Marina del Rey re-created the sick feeling of soured opportunities. This had been a big one, because the killer had believed he'd taken all the right precautions. The killer had been smart enough to disconnect the surveillance cameras in Prescott's building and erase the tapes. But he had not known that the parking garage did not belong to Prescott's landlord. The parking company operated its own surveillance system. Prescott had looked at the tape and seen the license number of the rented car. He had used it to get the credit card number, then gotten a list of other places the card had been used. He had gone to the hotel, and missed the killer. The only advantage he had now was that he knew the city where the plane ticket had been bought.

Prescott closed his eyes and leaned back in his seat. He had been awake for the past two nights, and the long plane ride to New York City would give him a chance to get back his strength and alertness. He would need them soon: New York was just the first stop on the way to Buffalo.

He had always thought of Buffalo as a luckless town. The people were crazy for sports, and the teams always came from behind, made a superhuman effort, and reached second place. The big buildings downtown were graceful and even ornate, built sometime just before or after the place had reached its peak, around 1900. They were built by people who had been optimists—a reflection of an aesthetic that was a little bit out of date even then.

The forces of history had choked off the supply of money and left the office buildings half empty and the factories completely empty. Every time he had been there, he had found another civic advertising blitz announcing another local renaissance that he couldn't quite locate. The last time he had been through, they had remodeled the airport. But it had the feel of public works in third-world countries that had been built out of civic ambition, and that he could imagine someday soon abandoned to the jungle.

If this killer lived in Buffalo, then the luck of the place must have gotten worse lately. Prescott knew the man had not been born there. His speech had no trace of the accent. Prescott supposed it wasn't a bad place for a killer to live. Real estate was cheap. It was on the Canadian border, and not far from Ohio and Pennsylvania.

He took the telephone from the back of the seat in front of him and dialed the answering machine in his new office. He heard it rewind. There were two messages. He sat up straight, put his hand over his left ear to cut the noise, and listened, but this time it was not the voice of the killer.

"This is Daniel Millikan, and it's four o'clock. I'll be home in an hour, and I'll be in all evening. If you don't get me then, call me in the morning at the office." Prescott listened to Millikan reciting the telephone numbers while he let the surprise wear off. He had not expected this. He hung up and dialed.

"Hello?"

"I got your message," said Prescott. "What's up?"

"The L.A. *Times* had an article about what happened at your office. You're out of your mind."

"Yeah, but I know it. Most of the others don't."

"Why do you do this?"

"Answer unpromising phone messages?"

"No," said Millikan. "You know what I'm talking about."

"I know how to do seven or eight things," said Prescott. "All the other ones cost money."

"I want to call this whole thing off. It was a bad idea. I shouldn't have told Cushner how to get to you."

"It's okay," Prescott said. "You don't have to do anything else. Your part is over."

"He's killed two people just to scare you, and two more to get to you. Putting yourself out as the next victim isn't a good idea this time. You know what he is."

"Yeah, I know what he is. He's not going to get hungry—he's done enough of these so he may not need money for years. He isn't going to make a mistake out of desperation. The only ways are to wait for him to get hit by a truck, or get him to come after me." Prescott paused. "And he could be active for a long time. He's young. Late twenties."

"How do you know that? Voices can be deceptive."

"When he came to my office I saw him in the flesh. Thanks for your concern, but I've got to go now, Danny. I'm on my way to New York." Prescott disconnected and returned the telephone to the back of the seat, then lay back and closed his eyes. His mind ranged nervously in one direction, then another, keeping him from sleep.

He found himself remembering his first lesson about killers. He had seen someone while she was alive, and then seen her again after she wasn't. Prescott had been twenty-four years old. He had just gotten out of the service, and had known little more than that he was glad it was over. When he could find no job that paid well or seemed likely to lead anywhere, he had answered an ad in the paper placed by the Emil Vargas Detective Agency. Vargas was lazy, and he was cunning. In his later years, he would hire two or three young men like Prescott, who were strong and tireless and naive, and allow them to put in the two thousand hours of work required for a detective's license in California. He would pay them minimum wage, and accept every case that was offered, without quibbling about the difficulty or danger. When one of the apprentices quit or put in his two thousand hours, another would take his place.

When Pauline Davis had called, Vargas had answered the telephone, written down the name and address, and handed the paper to Prescott because he happened to be in Vargas's line of sight, and giving it to anyone else would have required him to turn his head.

Prescott met Pauline Davis at a small apartment building on Victory Boulevard. She was in her thirties but looked like an ugly teenager, almost skeletally thin, with bad skin and bad teeth that made Prescott suspect she was an addict. Her clothes were the short shorts and loose, translucent blouses that had not been in style during his lifetime except among street hookers. She said she owned the apartment building and needed a skip trace done. A man named Steven Waltek had rented an apartment. Through bluff and evasion, he had managed to avoid paying her for six months, then disappeared. He owed her six thousand dollars, and she wanted papers served on him. Prescott could still hear her voice, see her talking—always a little too fast, with nervous, birdlike movements. When she turned her head to look for the rental agreement, it was like a twitch.

Prescott had listened politely, written everything down, then gone directly to the county clerk's office to see who really owned the apartment building. To his surprise, the tax rolls said Pauline Davis did.

He began to search for Waltek. He visited the landscaping company Waltek had listed on his rental application as his employer. The owner told Prescott that Waltek worked as a trimmer, climbing the big, old trees with a set of spikes on his work shoes and a leather strap, then using a light chain saw to lop off unwanted limbs. He said Waltek had collected his last check a month ago and expressed some vague intention to move inland.

It took Prescott a week of telephone calls to pick up a trace of Waltek. Prescott always made the calls as Vargas had taught him, claiming to be a former employer who owed Waltek some money, or a friend of a friend who had been told to give him a letter. He found a tree service in Riverside where Waltek had applied for a job. There had been no openings, but they had kept his application because he was experienced at a kind of work that not everyone could—or would—do. When Prescott arrived in Riverside, he found that Waltek's address was not in Riverside. It was on a rural road somewhere in the San Bernardino Mountains. He drove for over an hour up narrow, winding roads, through tiny towns that seemed to exist for the benefit of people who came in other seasons—skiers in the winter, or campers in the summer—but never in the spring. The tall pine trees were shrouded in mist nearly to their tops, and on some of the low, shadowy rock slopes there were still half-melted streaks of dirty snow.

His car was an old Chevy he always had to feed with oil after a couple of hours of driving. As it climbed the steep inclines, it began to grind out a high, whining noise that made him hope that when it broke down he would still be able to disengage the transmission, push it around, and coast back down to the last of the little towns.

Waltek's house was not even on the main road. It was up a side road so small that it turned into a mud track a quarter mile into the woods, and Prescott had to pull off into a level space in the forest and walk the rest of the way up. As he walked, the cold and damp and solitude began to affect his enthusiasm. He was arriving, unexpected, to dun some guy for six thousand bucks—some guy who worked in a job that probably didn't pay a lot, and that required him to inhabit the border between courage and recklessness. It also occurred to Prescott that, while a lot of people way out here had guns where they could reach them, Prescott didn't own one. As Prescott walked higher up the slowly vanishing path, he began to listen for any sound to reach him in the silence. He heard nothing, and that made him more uneasy. He came around a curve and saw the house It was in a flat, rocky clearing, sheltered by tall trees on all sides. It was small, with siding composed of half logs nailed to boards so that it looked like a cabin. There was no car, and he could see no way for a car to get here, so he guessed that Waltek must park in a spot near where Prescott had left his car and walk the rest of the way. He knocked, but there was no answer. He supposed Waltek must have found a job, and maybe that meant he could pay. He decided that all he could do was wait.

He sat on the low front steps for a time, then gave in to his curiosity and looked in the side window. The inside of the house consisted of one room at ground level and a loft. The part that he could see was cluttered. There were dishes overflowing from the sink onto the counter, clothes lying on the floor . . . he stopped. What he had thought was a pile of clothes now seemed to be something else.

Prescott moved to another window to look more closely. Then he kicked in the back door and entered. Lying on the floor was the body of Pauline Davis. He could see she had been beaten and probably, in the end, strangled. What had she been doing out here with Waltek? Then he saw the footlocker lying open near the door. There was nothing inside it, and when he bent to look, he saw stains that had to be blood. She had probably been killed in Los Angeles and brought here, so Waltek could bury her where he could keep people away from her grave.

Prescott backed out the door and headed down the path. He made it nearly to the car before he heard the footsteps. He could see Waltek now, just as he had seen Waltek when he'd emerged from the woods—as tall as Prescott, but very wide, with broad shoulders that made his neck seem short, and heavily muscled forearms developed by years of climbing and cutting. The eyes were the part that bothered Prescott all these years later. They were bright and intense, as the eyes of intelligent people often are, but they had a strange opaque quality, as though they were looking inward, the mind always contemplating its own concerns and needs.

Prescott smiled, held out his hand, and said, "Mr. Waltek? My name is Roy Prescott. Our agency—the Vargas Agency—has been retained by a woman named Pauline Davis. She claims that you owe her some money, and she would like to collect it." It was a gamble, an attempt to convince Waltek, not of the fantastically unlikely story that he had other business here, or was a person who had just happened by, only that he had not looked in the window and seen the body of Pauline Davis. Waltek said, "I do owe her some money. I don't have all of it right now, but I can give you some. Come up to the house with me."

Prescott said, "Okay." He felt something like amazement mixing in with his alarm: this man he had never seen before had decided to kill him, and it would happen in a moment. Prescott judged that Waltek was stronger, and he had no plan for saving himself, but there was no time to wait for things to get better. Prescott walked with Waltek for a few steps, until Waltek's eyes drifted away from him for an instant. Prescott pushed off with both legs to give force to his jab, and struck with all his strength. The blow went wide and smacked into the side of Waltek's head below the temple, making the head turn away with its force. Prescott was afraid to take the time to wind up again, so he instantly brought his right elbow back into Waltek's face. Waltek staggered into it, and his knees wobbled. Then Prescott was on him, delivering punches as hard and quickly as he could until Waltek was down. Waltek rolled to the side and reached for something inside his coat, but Prescott pinned the arm there, picked up a rock with his free hand, and brought it down on Waltek's head.

Waltek was unconscious. Prescott dragged him to the foot of a nearby tree, brought his arms around the trunk, took out the pair of cheap handcuffs that were the only implement of the trade that Vargas would allow his employees, and snapped them shut on Waltek's wrists. He went to get his car, but found that Waltek had left a pickup on the road below his, so he could not get out. He had walked about a mile back to a store where there was a telephone.

Now and then Prescott thought about Pauline Davis. Waltek had killed her for practical reasons. He had wanted the six thousand dollars to add to the down payment for his house in the mountains. There had been something about her that made people know instantly that nobody cared about her. Prescott had seen it, and so, he knew, had Waltek. It made her weak, somebody he could kill.

Prescott detected a distracting something in the back of his mind, then remembered what it was. When he had dialed his office number, the machine had said two messages. Millikan had been the first, but he had not heard the second. He lifted the phone off the back of the seat in front of him, took out his credit card again, and dialed. He pressed the code to hear his messages.

"I'm leaving. I left you a couple of good-bye presents at the motel in Marina del Rey." Prescott sat up, the sound of the voice making him wince. "They're to remind you never to come after me again."

That was it, Prescott thought. That was the price of failing.

11

Prescott traveled with a suitcase that had nothing inside it that he couldn't replace within ten minutes in a department store. He bought dress shirts of 60 percent cotton and 40 percent polyester that said permanent press and meant it, some blue jeans, and some worsted trousers with a razor crease. The sport coats were always summer-weight and dark colored. They were the belongings of a man so ordinary as to seem barely differentiated from others, a fictional person that Prescott had invented to keep from being too easily noticed and remembered. He picked up his suitcase at the baggage claim at Kennedy Airport, then took a cab into Manhattan to begin his preparations.

He checked into a hotel on Park Avenue and began making his calls to art galleries. In the next twenty-four hours, he spoke with thirty-six men and women whose voices told him they were genuinely convinced that they were experts. On each call, he patiently explained what he wanted and listened carefully to the response. At the end of his thirty-six calls, he had heard one name twelve times and no other name more than three times. He made three calls to curators of contemporary collections at museums to see whether they had a different sense of things, but it became clear to him that the voices were essentially the same. The name Prescott heard so many times was Cara Lee Satterfield. He dialed her number, listened to her quick, businesslike hello. He introduced himself, told her that he wondered if she would be willing to speak with him about a commission for a special kind of piece—a picture of a man he would describe.

She said in an unhappy monotone, "Did you get my name from the police?"

Prescott said, "No, from an art gallery. Do the police know you?"

"Come to my studio and we'll talk."

"Now?"

"Four o'clock. I'm working now."

Prescott took a cab to the address she gave him, stepped out onto the street, and looked up. It was a brick building that had at some point had some business purpose, but the upper windows were too big for a business, and the frames were too new and expensive to have been from that era. He went into the man-sized door set into the larger garage door, and found himself facing a freight elevator. He stepped into it and pressed the UP button. The elevator rose two stories and stopped at a steel door with a big face on it that looked like a photograph. Prescott looked more closely. The face was an extremely realistic painted portrait of a grandfatherly man with a beard and glasses, crinkle lines at the corners of his wise old eyes, and an expression of mild puzzlement. He seemed to Prescott to be saying, "What do you want here—it wouldn't be something that isn't so good for you, would it?"

The thin woman who opened the door looked about forty. She wore jeans, a sweatshirt, and a pair of sneakers. Her hair had been chestnut brown, but it had been allowed to gray, so there were bright silver streaks in the tightly tied ponytail. Her face had no makeup and it had a bare look as though it had just been scrubbed. She gave a perfunctory half smile as she looked at him sharply. "Mr. Prescott?"

"Yes, ma'am."

"Come in."

He entered and looked at the loft. The high windows and skylight above threw a bright, even light everywhere, bouncing off the white walls to leave no shadows. There was a huge space to his right occupied by several easels, a big workbench cluttered with tubes of paint, brushes soaking in coffee cans, and assorted palette knives and rags.

There was a second bench with a vise, a miter box, a table saw, a few tools.

She led him past that area, through what looked like a living room set on display in a department store. The furniture was modern, simple in its lines, and upholstered in a coarse black fabric. There he could see that a set of stairs led above to a wide balcony with another steel door that was open. Through it, he could see part of a carpeted hallway that seemed to have at least four doorways leading off it, and at the end, a big room with a vaulted ceiling, bookcases and furniture, and a huge window with green things growing on a balcony beyond.

He gravitated to the walls, where finished portraits hung. From a distance, they were different enough from one another to be the work of several painters, but as he drew nearer, subtle similarities appeared. It was not a similarity of feature, but of eye: the artist's interest in the curve of a young girl's cheekbone, the mottled texture of an old woman's skin, somehow the same interest expressed with the same intensity. This was a calm, unhurried treatment, with no flattering smoothing over of features, but the effect was more than flattering. The precise rendering was a fascinated elucidation of the creature who was being recorded and preserved. Cara Lee Satterfield stood a dozen feet behind him, waiting patiently while he looked. He reluctantly relinquished his gaze at a picture of a young woman with shiny blond hair. He was not sure how he could tell, but the woman was proud of the hair, thinking about it at the moment of the portrait. "You're the best I've seen alive," he said without a smile.

"Thank you," she said.

"It's not exactly a compliment, it's more on the order of a congratulation," he said. "A waste of breath too, because you know it."

She looked at him, puzzled, but did not deny it. "I don't think that's a compliment either."

"Nope," he said. "It's not. People have what they have. When what they have is something special, you can always tell they've had to work very hard for it. If it's this special, they've gone more distance than anybody can go just by working."

"That sounded positive rather than negative, so I'll thank you," she said. "Tell me about your commission."

"It's what I said on the telephone," Prescott answered. "I want a picture of a man I describe to you."

"Who is he?"

"My business is finding people who have done bad things," he said.

"I didn't ask about business," she said testily. "I asked about him."

"He's a young guy, late twenties, probably. He gets paid to kill people. I've seen him, watched him for a couple of hours before I knew who he was. Now his image is in my mind, and I want you to put it into a picture."

"If you found your way here, someone must have told you about me. You must know that I'm always pretty busy," she said. "What made you think I would do it?"

Prescott said, "I asked people who was the best, not who needed the commission." He added carefully, "I checked with galleries to find out what they get for your work. Of course I would expect to pay much more for—"

"I don't want to talk about money just yet." She stared at Prescott's eyes. "You can see him, still?"

"Yes."

"Have you talked to him?"

"Yes," he said. "A few times. I've been doing pretty well at getting to know him."

She kept her gaze on him, unblinking, but she was no longer focused on his eyes. "All right. We'll start it and settle the price later, when I decide what it is."

"When?"

She seemed to think the question was beneath answering. She sat down on a couch, pulled her feet under her, picked up a sketch pad and pencil from the end table, and began to work as she spoke. "Let's start with general outline, simplest stuff. You talk, I'll listen."

Prescott sat in the armchair facing her. "His hair is straight, dark brown. His forehead is high and narrow, but shaped, so you can tell there's a very slight ridge where the eyebrows are that disappears as you move in above the nose. His chin has no cleft, but it comes out a little in a slight horizontal oval, the way some chins with clefts do. The nose is thin and narrow, but the nostrils have a slight flare to them." She was sketching furiously as he spoke, and he could tell that his curiosity was going to make this experience miserable. He added, "His ears are small, kind of rounded, and close to his head."

"Eyes big or small?"

"Average, and not particularly close-set, either."

"Tell me about his mouth."

"It's narrow, with the lower lip a little bit thicker than the upper—not red or overly full, or strange."

"How about this part of his face, right here?" She put one hand across her face just above her mouth to touch both cheekbones at once lightly, with thumb and forefinger.

"Only slightly wider than the rest of the face, tapering gradually to the chin."

She worked in silence for a few minutes while Prescott began to feel the curiosity tormenting him again. Then she stood up, spun the pad around, and stuck the pencil in his hand. "Here. Fix the lines where they're wrong."

He looked at the picture in surprise. "Me? I'll ruin it."

"So ruin it. This is just a preliminary step to get the shapes and sizes of things right. Study your memory and make marks. Too wide, too narrow? Eyes too big, whatever." She tossed a gum eraser onto the pad in his lap. "Take your time."

He was disconcerted. The drawing already looked enough like the man to be almost recognizable. He closed his eyes and brought back the image, watched the man sitting behind the console in the lighted lobby, his face unconcerned, at ease while he waited to kill his companion. Prescott began to make lines, faint and tentative at first, then more sure and bold when he saw that the lines made the resemblance clearer.

While he worked, he was aware of her. She was moving around in the kitchen area, moving things, opening cupboards and closing them. After a while he smelled coffee, and she appeared with a big tray that had two cups and a thermos pot, and several kinds of tea cakes. She set it on a table nearby.

She looked over his shoulder. "Good. Very, very good. Leave it now and have some coffee." She pointed at the table. "You don't strike me as the tea-cake type, but they won't hurt you." She poured him a cup of coffee and went to the couch to take up the pad. She used the gum eraser and pencil and worked on the drawing.

He said, "This isn't what I expected."

"Yes, it is," she said. "You could have gone to a police composite artist if you had wanted something simple. You went to a lot of trouble to find a real portrait painter."

"I mean the way you go about it."

"This isn't the way it's done, but this isn't a normal portrait," she said. She looked up and noticed he was surveying the huge loft. "You like my studio?"

"Artists all seem to be nesters. I've seen a few studios that are better than anything the owner ever made to sell." He frowned. "That's not you."

She chuckled. "It's a sick indulgence—something you do when you need to work but can't do anything right. Maybe if I add a skylight, the shadows over here will be gone. Maybe if I move the wall over here in a little bit, I'll have a small corner that glows just right. Then everything will work." She spun the sketch again. Now the lines that he had made had been refined, and had become the new boundaries of the face.

He stared at it. "That's closer."

She cocked her head and narrowed her eyes at the picture, then propped up the pad so it faced him. "Let's have some of those cakes while you get used to him. I want more lines as soon as you see something that's wrong, remember something you forgot." She sat at the table with him. "How did you get to chasing a killer around? Is it personal?"

He shook his head. "Nothing as honest and dignified as that. It's something I fell into a while back."

"How?" she asked.

"Process of elimination," he said. He picked up the pad and began working on it again. "I started out wanting to be a great man, but then I noticed that every time there was a great man, somebody would lay the crosshairs on his forehead. Then I figured I'd be a saintly man. But it meant I would have to deny myself all the things my mama wouldn't have approved of, and end up getting burned at a stake or something. Then I thought I'd settle for being a good man. But no matter how hard I applied myself to it, I couldn't detect that I was getting any better than anybody else. In those days you had to go into the service, so I did. After a couple of years I got out and had nothing to do. I got a job at a detective agency, then started my own. I solved a couple of cases, and got a reputation. At that point, either I could keep making very good money doing that, or I could go start all over again at something I wasn't even good at. So I kept on." He handed the drawing back to Cara Lee Satterfield. "How about you? How did you get to be a famous portrait artist?"

She went to work with eraser and pencil again. "It's a lot like your story." She looked at him with half-lidded eyes, then down again at the pad. "Except that mine is true. I came up from Virginia twenty years ago. I needed to draw, and I needed money. I live in a century when representational art is something that's only in style among people who wear cheese hats to football games and watch pro wrestling on TV. So I did odd jobs—quickie sketches at amusement parks, greeting cards, witness sketches for the police."

He looked around him at the loft, then back at her. "Something else happened to both of you."

"Both?"

"You and this building."

She grinned as she worked. "I bought this place because I couldn't afford SoHo, which was where artists were living then. This was a hellhole, a place where transients and addicts hung out. There had been four or five fires. I got it cheap. I made it secure so nobody could get in, fixed it up a little, and went to work. Over the years, the rent in SoHo got too expensive for artists, and most of them moved in around me anyway. In the meantime, I discovered that no matter how rich and sophisticated you are, you don't want your portrait to be abstract. You want realism, with ten years lopped off." She showed him the portrait.

"That's close," he said. "Really close. I don't know what I could do to it."

"Then let's talk ethnic stereotypes."

"Stereotypes?"

She said, "Nice people don't. But all we're talking about here is looks. You look the way the genes your grandparents brought from the old country tell you to look. The question is, Which old country?"

He shrugged. "His skin is pale. I thought about that when I saw him. His hair is dark brown, almost black. His eyes . . . I wasn't close enough to tell the color, exactly. They looked light, not dark. Blue or gray. The old country is somewhere in Europe on both sides. But it could be anywhere from Ireland to Russia. You see him, you think 'white guy,' but you don't think about a country."

"If he were out in the sun, would he get freckles?"

"Maybe. He doesn't have any right now."

She did some more sketching. "Tell me about how he seems. You talked to him, watched him. What's his personality?"

"I don't really know."

"Guess."

"I think he's got the skills he needs for getting along. If he's supposed to smile, he smiles. If he's supposed to look like he's sad, he can do that. He doesn't feel any of it."

Prescott looked into her eyes. "You understand? He knows what people are supposed to feel and what their faces look like while they're feeling it. He's spent a lot of time practicing—probably in front of a mirror when he was young, and since then by watching people's reactions—but it's all the same. It's like a man doing birdcalls: if he practices enough, he can hit the same notes, maybe not exactly, but close enough to fool a lot of birds. But he's not a bird. He doesn't know what the bird feels when it sings, or what it means. He just knows that when he does it, birds will come close enough so he can kill them."

She looked up from the pad. "He doesn't feel anything?"

"That's not exactly right. He feels hunger, cold, heat, pain, a little fear—too little of that—and there's a big reservoir of resentment or jealousy or something. I haven't quite isolated that to the point where I can put a name to it. He thinks that other people have things that he deserves. He's smarter, stronger, more disciplined. He works harder than they do—has been working harder than they do since he was a child—to improve himself. That's the only sign of fear I've seen so far. Something made him afraid when he was young, I think, and that was how he got started on making himself dangerous . . . 'potent' is probably the word."

"Is he?" she asked. "He has power?"

Prescott looked at her in surprise, as though he had been in a reverie and heard a discordant note. He nodded. "Yeah. Of a sort. We live in a beautiful, warm, cozy society. We don't always know it, but we do." Prescott paused. "He doesn't."

"How is that?"

"We have wars, crime, and so on—but only a few of us, and only some of the time. It isn't a daily experience. For most of human history, it wasn't that way. People had to walk around with a different attitude: heavily armed, watchful, ready to react instantly and violently. What he's done is turn himself into a man from another time and place: training himself physically and mentally, learning the practices of old warrior societies, developing attitudes and skills of men in cultures that had some practical use for that kind of thing, that rewarded it with high status. He's succeeded. He's a killer, just as they were."

"What about the fear? You said he didn't have much."

"Not enough," said Prescott. "There are theories about that, but they're just theories."

"Tell me," she said. "I need to hear everything that comes to mind when you look at him."

"Once in a while the psychiatrists do tests on a certain kind of people—ones who jump out of airplanes a lot, or go for speed records, or whatever. Supposedly a lot of them have a deficiency in a chemical called monoamine oxidase. It's a chemical that regulates other chemicals, and it's released when you're scared. When monoamine oxidase is released, it gives you more dopamine and norepinephrine, so you feel a rush. I think that could be what's going on with him. He needs that rush, like an addict. But both intentionally and unintentionally, he's been making himself resistant to fear. He needs more and more objective danger to trigger it." He sighed. "But all of that stuff is invisible. It doesn't have much to do with a picture."

She handed the drawing to him, a refutation of what he was saying. There was the young, clean-cut man he had seen in the crisp security-guard uniform.

It seemed to Prescott that the last time he had seen the drawing it had been extremely good. The term for it was a "likeness." But now something else had happened. The face was alive. In the skull that had simply been an accurate outline, then a three-dimensional shape, there were thoughts. He tried to analyze this impression, and realized it had to be the eyes. They were watchful in exactly the right way. The mouth was almost smiling, but the eyes were doing something different that made the smile just an extremely convincing lie. In the eyes was cunning opportunism; inside the pleasant young face a different person was waiting, with cold patience, for his chance.

"It's him," he said. "It's the one." He tried to say it more accurately: "It's that man, and it's nobody else." That was what she had done. An hour ago, it had been a picture of the man. In subtle degrees, she had made it more like him, but absolutely not like other men who resembled him. She had eliminated them.

"Good," she said, without surprise. She stood up and took the drawing away from him, then walked toward the other end of the room, where her workbenches and easels stood and everything was paint-spattered.

"Where are you going?" he asked.

"It's time to paint," she said in a distracted voice, without removing her eyes from the drawing. "I'm a painter."

"You already have him," said Prescott, getting to his feet.

She kept walking. "Go sit down. Have more coffee, take a nap or something. This will take some time."

"But why are you doing it?"

"I told you. I'm a painter. I'm not sort of a painter. I don't quit just because some ignorant character comes in and tells me it's good enough for him. It has to be good enough for me."

Prescott sat and drank coffee. He paced the loft, looked out the windows at the night streets below, now surprisingly empty for New York. After a time, he lay on the couch and dozed, then woke. Each time he looked toward the other end of the loft, he could see her still standing, working intently, paying no attention to anything but the sketch and the canvas. It was daylight before she looked in his direction, then beckoned.

He walked to the easel and looked. The killer looked back at him. It was no longer just a representation. Somehow, contained in the painted version, there were all of the things that Prescott believed about this man and had told Cara Lee Satterfield. The painting was more like him than any blown-up color photograph could be. "When can I have it?"

"You don't want this," she said. "You want eight-by-ten photographs of it. I'll take them now."

The photographs took time. Big floodlights on stands had to be moved around, then white reflective screens arranged and rearranged until she was satisfied. She set up a camera on a tripod, took shot after shot, moved the lights and screens, then took more. At last, he heard the camera's automatic rewinder humming. She popped the camera's back open, took out the film, then looked at her workbench, tore the printed address off an old envelope full of slides, and handed him the address and the film. "That's the place to get them developed." She looked around, seeming to notice the daylight for the first time. "What time is it?"

"Nearly noon."

"Good. They're open."

"You're going to want to go to sleep, so maybe we'd better settle your fee before I go." He reached into his jacket and pulled out a checkbook.

She held up her hand. "No," she said. "That's not going to be enough."

"I keep this account's balance pretty high," he said.

She shook her head. "That's just money. This is magic. It's a collaboration, an experience. I figured out my price."

"What is it?"

"You can't pay off until you've finished chasing this guy," she said. "About how long will it take?"

He looked at her uneasily. "You know, I don't want to be dramatic, but the finish could be that I stop chasing because he kills me."

"I've seen you, and now I've seen him," she said. "I'll take that chance. Give me a call when it's done, and you can pay off."

"Can you tell me what it is?"

"Sure," she said. "There are two things. You'll fly back here to sit for me. I want to paint you."

"What's the second thing?"

"In November I have a one-woman show," she said. "The opening is a big, pretentious party, and they're awful. They're boring, frightening, and embarrassing all at the same time. You will be my escort. The women will be nice to look at, but you won't be able to, or I'll be angry. The men are not all bad, either, but there will be a few . . . you'll want to pinch their heads off. You won't do that, either."

"Why would you want me as an escort?"

She walked toward the steel door, and opened it for him. "I don't have to tell you that, so I won't. It's my price. I'll be waiting to hear from you."

12

Prescott took the film to the photography lab and went to his hotel to sleep. When he awoke in the evening, he picked up the two hundred color prints. The diminished size of the photographs made the painting even sharper and the impression of perfection more striking. He was tempted to call Cara Lee Satterfield and tell her, but she had known long before he did. Instead, he packed his bags, took a cab to the bus station, and bought a ticket to Philadelphia. When he got there, he rented a car and drove west, deeper into Pennsylvania. What he wanted now was easier to obtain in some places than in others. After he had reached the hills, where there were farms and small towns, he made his first stop. He picked up the local newspaper, checked the bulletin boards in the first laundromat he saw, and then looked for flyers left at convenience stores. He was looking for announcements of private sales.

Prescott liked estate sales best, but not if they were big enough to be held as auctions. What he needed was a person he could talk to, and he preferred the closest female survivor. He would look over the dead man's belongings, maybe buy something that was expensive and portable, like a rare book, a watch, or a set of cuff links. That would get

him talking to the woman. He would talk about her wisdom in passing on possessions that someone else could use, listening for her
lament that there were things she didn't know what to do with. He
would let slip that he was sure his wife—or daughter—would have the
same problem: he was a gun collector, and guns were hard to resell. In
some places, this was likely to give the woman the creeps, and the
conversation would be over. But in these rural areas, more often than
not, he would be led into the house to look over a gun cabinet.

Sometimes the cabinet was a metal locker in a den, but sometimes
it was a big, polished piece of furniture like a glass-fronted armoire.
Behind the glass would be a row of long guns: usually at least a pump
shotgun for fowl, a .22 rifle for vermin, and a bolt-action .308 or
.30-06 deer rifle. But plenty of these cabinets had much more exotic
and expensive rifles, custom guns with carved stocks, antiques, military assault weapons. He would look them over, appraise and appreciate them, sometimes buy one or two. But he would make it clear that
what interested him most was handguns. In a few minutes he might
be on his way out with a pistol or two that, if they had ever been registered at all, were still the official property of a dead man.

In the first town, the estate sale included no guns. After he left the
turnpike near Hoyerstown, he passed a large building on the road into
town. It was surrounded by fields, and backed by a long, low barrow
that looked like the back of a sleeping animal. The big sign above the
door said THE GUN CLUB, and the small one said OPEN.

He pulled his car into the lot and got out. Before he had taken two
steps he heard the familiar thud of a gun being discharged behind a
soundproofed wall, then several more shots. He opened the front
door and the noise was louder. Three men wearing yellow earphones
stood beyond a Plexiglas window, firing down adjoining cinder-block
tunnels at small paper targets on wires that ran overhead. A wooden
counter enclosed with the same thick Plexiglas dominated the entrance.

The slight man inside was only about thirty, but he had a shiny bald
head. Prescott smiled at him and rested his elbows on the counter, so
the man came to the window and opened it. "What can I do for you?"

"I'm from out of town," said Prescott. "Is it possible to rent a
weapon and get a little practice while I'm here?"

The man said, "Sure. For twenty bucks an hour, I can give you a .38 Smith & Wesson revolver. Ammo and targets are extra, and the range fee is fifteen bucks a half hour."

Prescott said, "How about ear protectors?"

"Those are five."

Prescott gave him sixty dollars, accepted a weapon with a big red number 12 painted on the grip. He bought a box of twenty-five rounds and went to the range. He could tell from the expression of habitual worry on the man's face that this was a business that had not lived up to his hopes. Probably he had told himself that indoor shooting would catch on as a family sport, and then the world would flock here to hand him money. The world seemed to be otherwise engaged.

Prescott clipped his target to the wire, pressed the button on the pulley, and watched the target skitter down to the end of the range. He loaded the pistol and snapped the cylinder into place. The .38 was lighter than the weapons he was accustomed to, and he expected it would have little muzzle rise with target ammunition, so he took a comfortable one-handed stance, extended his arm, and squeezed off six shots in rapid succession. Then he pressed the button again to bring the target back on the wire. He unclipped it, held it up to look at it, then turned to set it on the shelf beside the ammunition. He found that the owner was out of his booth, standing behind Prescott's tunnel to watch.

The man's eyes were on the target, looking at the six holes all within the inch-wide black circle. Prescott knew he had him. The man was one of those guys who were so hooked on a hobby that they could think of little else.

Prescott knew that he needed to appear careful and methodical. The man owned a business, after all, and since the business involved handing a firearm and ammunition to a total stranger and telling him to fire at will, he was understandably anxious. Prescott sent a new target down the wire, emptied the pistol of its spent casings, set them on the shelf neatly, held the weapon so the muzzle was low and downrange, then reloaded and fired his second six into the bull's-eye. He cleared the pistol again, brought the target back, and took his time getting around to unclipping it, so the owner could satisfy his curiosity. Prescott was getting used to the feel of the gun, so this time the pattern was even tighter. He kept at it, showing the man that he was a consistent, practiced, competent marksman, and that he was never careless. That part was important.

When he had finished, he brought the gun up with the cylinder open, and set it on the counter. The man had warmed up considerably. "You're a hell of a shot."

Prescott said, "Shooting relaxes me. I spend a lot of time on the road, though, so it's hard to keep my hand in. When I'm away from home I try to keep a list of places where I can fire a few rounds."

"You come through here often?"

"Never have before, but I expect to be in the neighborhood for a month or two. I'm a civil engineer, and there's a project going up near Philadelphia that I have to keep an eye on." He paused. "Maybe you can help me. I live in California and I don't travel with my own firearms. You know where I can pick up a gun around here?"

"What are you looking for?"

"What I'd like would be a good used nine-millimeter. I've been looking for a couple of days, but haven't seen anything I liked. Something like a Beretta Model 92. Maybe a Glock or a SIG if one turned up."

The man looked disappointed. "You know, I sold a Model 92 about two months ago." He seemed to feel uncomfortable, and said, "I wasn't the one that sold it, really. It's just that when somebody has something to sell, they usually tell me; and I mention it to the people who come in and ask."

"I hope you get a commission," said Prescott. "It's only fair."

The man looked down slyly. "Well, yeah. Usually I get ten percent."

"I'd like something right away, so if you hear of anything, keep me in mind." He started to go, then said, "In fact, I'll tell you what. I'll be in the neighborhood for a while. If you find something for me today, I'll pay you twenty percent above the sale price, and what you get from the seller is between you and him."

The man looked pleased. He held out his hand. "I'm Dave Durbin. What's your name?"

Prescott said, "I'm Mike. Michael Kennison."

"I'm going to put in a call to the gunsmith who maintains our weapons for us. He refurbishes used guns and resells them. If you'll

hang around for a few minutes, I'll find out what he's got right now."
He retreated behind the counter with the Plexiglas window and went
to his desk.

Prescott could hear him on the telephone between the rounds fired
on the range. Durbin held his hand over his free ear and spoke loudly.
"He's not just the average customer, he's a real shooter . . . and he's a
friend of mine, so I'd like to find something good for him. Nine. He
wants something like a Beretta or a SIG. Got anything?" In a moment
he hung up and beamed as he came to the window. "He's just down
the road, so he'll bring a couple of things in here for you to look at."

Prescott smiled. "Well, that's great. Thank you very much."

Durbin seemed to notice the revolver on the counter. "Hell, this
thing's got to be cleaned anyway. Why don't you go back and shoot
until he gets here? I'll call you."

Prescott bought another box of bullets and went back to the range.
Fifteen minutes later, as he was unclipping a target from the pulley, he
turned and saw Durbin with another man, knocking on the Plexiglas
to get his attention. He lifted his ear protector and shouted, "I'll be
right out."

He carefully unloaded his pistol and took it out into the open space
behind the range. The man with Durbin was a tall fat man in his six-
ties with white hair in a crew cut. He was holding a hard-sided suitcase.

"This is Billy," Durbin said. "And this is Mike. Why don't you come
on into the office?"

The area behind the glass was more like a booth than an office, but
it had a desk. Prescott and Billy went in, and it was slightly quieter
there, with an extra layer of Plexiglas separating them from the range.
Prescott began to understand Billy after a few minutes with him. He
was a retired machinist who worked on guns as a hobby. The reason
he had driven here was that he wasn't interested in making a deal for a
gun with a total stranger unless he was in the presence of third and
fourth parties who were also armed. He opened his suitcase on the
desk, and Prescott could see pistols arranged neatly on a stenciled
cutout foam rubber pad in rows of three.

Prescott looked respectfully at the guns. He spotted a Beretta
Cougar in a space that didn't quite fit it. He said to Billy, "May I?"

Billy nodded, and Prescott lifted it and looked closely at it. The slide was worn, the barrel burned out from too many rounds. He set it back without comment, but Billy said, "Dave told me you wanted a Beretta, and that's the only one I have now. I can work it over for you, get a new barrel, maybe reblue the slide. But that Walther over here is good, and you can have that right away. It's a P99, a year old. Been fired maybe once, and the woman who owned it didn't like it. Little bitty thing—she liked the name because of James Bond, but when she fired it, she found it a little hot for her. I traded her a nice .38 Special and a hundred bucks."

"What are you asking?"

Billy acted as though he had never considered the question before. He thought, calculated, estimated. "Four hundred would probably do it."

Prescott examined the weapon, and saw that Billy was only exaggerating the gun's condition slightly. He transferred it to his left hand and held out his right to shake with Billy. Billy started to take it, then held back. "I'm not actually a licensed dealer, so I don't have no papers for you. I've got to trust you not to get in trouble with it."

"I'll try not to," said Prescott, smiling. He opened his wallet, took out four hundred-dollar bills, and handed them to Billy, who stared at them for a moment, folded them, and put them under the foam rubber in his carrying case. Prescott chatted for a few more minutes, then said, "Well, it's time for me to get back to Philadelphia. Thanks again." As he left, Durbin escorted him to the parking lot. Prescott handed him a hundred-dollar bill. "This is for your trouble, Dave." In another minute he was on the road again. He drove northwest as far as Binghamton, New York, then turned in his rental car and rented another with New York plates.

He continued west, assessing his progress. He had his gun, a high-end nine-millimeter that had been gone over carefully by a gunsmith, cleaned, oiled, and in perfect working order. It was probably still registered to its first owner. Billy might very well have been lying about the woman who had only fired it once, but it didn't matter. No attempt to trace it would lead to Roy Prescott. If an investigator ever traced it far enough to force Billy to admit he had sold it illegally, he could only say he had sold it to a man named Mike Kennison who had told a story about a construction project in Philadelphia.

Prescott had a clean, fast rental car with 250 miles on its odometer. He had his pictures, so good that they were probably better than photographs. He supposed that he should be feeling amazed at how easily this was going. But there was something about the hunt this time that was a bit different, and it disturbed him.

At each of these stops, he had devoted himself to studying the people around him, and found that his old ability to figure out what he needed to know had sharpened and expanded. He knew more about them than he had ever known about the people he had used and left before. He could tell things about them from the way they held their heads or walked or moved their hands. He looked into their faces and read things: stupid misconceptions that they stubbornly clung to in the face of all evidence, bad decisions they had made years ago and still thought about sometimes and regretted. He sensed the things they worried about late at night, and he saw the courage and will it took when they woke up each morning to take up the weight of their lives again.

No, he decided, knowing wasn't the odd thing about this trip. He had always been good at analyzing people instantly because his life sometimes depended on it. He had been like a dog sniffing for danger and always smelling more subtle things in the process, noting them and pushing them aside to think of things that would help him survive. What was different now was that he was interested. The isolated qualities he had noticed had grown into parts of stories. People were poor, lonely creatures who had come into the world unready and helpless, and by adulthood had only partly managed to change that, and by the time they'd made much progress, they had already started to die. That was what was odd, that feeling.

He supposed that the change had come from spending too much time visiting the mind of Cara Lee Satterfield. He had stared so hard at her paintings for so many hours that he had begun to see what she was actually doing when she made a portrait of a person. What she did was an abbreviated version of what old portrait painters had done. In old paintings, a man would be standing in the foreground, staring at the painter, and at his feet and behind him and beside him in artistic arrangement would be the symbols of his trade—orb and scepter, guns and swords, maybe astrolabes and maps, as though those were the contents of his mind. A woman might have children, lapdogs, flowers, fans, pens and paper. Somehow Cara Lee Satterfield had managed to show what her model had in his mind without the objects. It was as though she had painted the whole portrait—the props, the face, the expression in the eyes, the subtle curl of the lip—and then painted over the objects that had inspired and stimulated the face to assume that habitual pose.

What worried Prescott was the eerie feeling that the sudden expansion of his receptivity was beginning to give him. It could be a sign that he was now reaching a new level of perception that was going to make him harder to beat. But it could be what people felt after they'd had a premonition. They took a long, quiet look around them, appearing to an observer as though they were counting the leaves on the trees, memorizing the exact blue of the sky, saying good-bye to the world.

13

Varney had very carefully, cautiously made the trip to Buffalo in stages. His first step had been to buy a set of clothes that didn't smell like seawater and gasoline. He didn't try to get on a big transcontinental airliner like the one he had taken west, because he was intensely aware of what Prescott must be thinking. As soon as Prescott had gotten his message about the people at the hotel in Marina del Rey, he would have gotten into his car again and driven to Los Angeles International Airport. He might think that Varney had gotten out right away, gotten onto a plane and left town, but Prescott had undoubtedly been around long enough to know that things were hardly ever that simple. Chasing a man down often just involved following as well as you could and waiting for something to go wrong for him.

Varney had driven his rental car to John Wayne Airport in Orange County, gotten on a plane belonging to an airline he had never heard of that seated about twenty-five passengers, and flown to Las Vegas. From there, he had flown to Toronto, taken a bus to Niagara Falls, walked across the Rainbow Bridge into the United States, and then taken a cab south to Buffalo.

He had arrived late at night. The house was east of Delaware Avenue, off Hertel Avenue in a neighborhood that was full of big nineteenth-century two-story houses with wooden porches and little squares of front lawn that a person could just about cover with a blanket. Someone had told him once that it had been part of the era when they'd been built: people were just moving off farms and into towns, and the epitome of being modern and prosperous was to be able to walk out the door onto a pavement in as few steps as possible without interference from things that grew in mud.

All of the houses had long ago been broken up into apartments and rented to students and young families. He had spent a couple of days and nights in the neighborhood before he had given it his approval. About half the men he saw on the street were not easy to distinguish at first glance from himself. The bars in the area were mostly old neighborhood taverns that lived off their kitchens. There were two newer establishments that sold draft beer to students, but they didn't have the sort of music or live entertainment that attracted unruly crowds and the police cars that attended them.

He had bought the house and moved into it without changing the provisions the previous owners had made to split it into an upper apartment and a lower. The lower floor had furniture in it from the last tenant, so he kept it and put timers on the lights to make it look occupied, and to avoid walking into a darkened entry and finding someone waiting. He lived on the upper floor. It had a side entrance with its own staircase, but he had bolted it off so that opening it from the inside required a key, and opening it from the outside was difficult enough to be effectively impossible without causing visible damage.

Varney approached his house on foot and in concentric circles. He studied the cars parked in the neighborhood, then the buildings that were close enough to offer a good view of his windows. This took a bit of time and patience, because nearly all of the houses were rentals, and even in a short period away, a tenant might have been replaced. He connected parked cars with apartments, looked for dog bowls or toys left out, or familiar curtains, lampshades, framed pictures that were visible from the street. The last place he studied was his own.

He had no theory on how Prescott might have gone about finding his real address this quickly, but that did not convince him that it would be impossible. Prescott was the enemy, and the enemy always had the resources of authorities at his disposal. It was the nature of authorities to be shadowy, potentially numberless, and possessed of capabilities that were most worrisome because they were unknown. Authorities didn't necessarily advertise everything they could do. In Varney's mind, the authorities did not merely include police agencies but also everyone else who imposed rules: the phone company, the credit card companies, the post office, the airlines.

Varney watched his house patiently as the lights went on and off, the television sets he had tuned to particular stations cast their bluish glow on the upstairs and downstairs ceilings. After he had seen enough, he entered: nothing had been changed, nothing touched since he had left.

Varney waited indoors through the first day, and then another, a gun always within easy reach. He watched from the upper windows of his house, trying to see into each car that passed, to stare at the face of each pedestrian. He slept on a mattress on the floor of the upstairs kitchen beside the door, so he would hear anyone mounting the staircase.

After three days, Varney began to feel assured that Prescott had not used some esoteric method to locate him. Varney had simply been alarmed by the miserable way things had worked out in Los Angeles. He was now convinced that he had let his imagination go too far. he didn't know the way Prescott could find the address, because there was no way.

He concentrated on analyzing his defeat. He had been overconfident about his ability to fly into a distant city, pop the target, and vanish, all within a few hours. He had done it so many times before that it had come to seem routine, then obligatory. He had not taken into account the fact that this target was more dangerous than usual, and that by killing the two cops, Varney had announced to him that he was on the way. Prescott had been ready for him.

He consoled himself with the thought that the whole episode could be considered less than a defeat. Prescott was supposed to be the best, the invincible hunter, after all, and Varney had walked into his office under his nose, taken out the two armed security guards, and walked out again. He wasn't sure how he had failed to erase the videotape that showed his rental car in the parking garage, but it had been a new building with a complicated system. When Prescott had tried to ambush him at the motel, Varney had left him standing around like a moron. The more Varney thought about it, the more certain he was. The mistakes he had made had not been so shameful. The hours he had spent shivering in the water under the dock were his own secret. Prescott didn't know how he had escaped: he had vanished like a ghost. Varney had won: he had made Prescott look sick. It was time to forget about Prescott and go back to his regular life.

The next morning, Varney went to the grocery store to buy fresh food, then walked to breakfast at Sterling's Diner. He bought the *Buffalo News* and carried it under his arm until he got to his booth, taking pride in each act of normalcy as he completed it. Going after Prescott had just been a momentary lapse in judgment, that was all.

He resumed his usual warm-weather routine. He ran in Delaware Park for an hour, and ended the run at the gym. He had spent two days doing very little for his body, so he decided to make this a full workout day. In a few days he would probably be working again, but a few days could easily stretch into months. Discipline was the reason for his success. He kept himself alert, busy, and in training during the slow periods.

He ran the circuit of the park around the small lake, past the marble columns at the back of the History Museum, down near the old pavilion by the shore, along Delaware Avenue, then beside the high, spike-tipped brick wall around the zoo.

Sometimes he could hear the animals on the other side of the wall, but he could always smell them. There was a thick, acrid barnyard smell that made him veer outward a bit. There were always a couple of soccer games on the flats, and he looked without slowing down. The white-and-black ball looked big and bright on the deep green lawns. While Varney was running each day, he often thought of the park as his. That was why he usually didn't run in the early morning or the evening. He didn't like it when other people were jogging too. The people who were doing other things were simply sights, put there to amuse him, but the joggers tended to follow him—even to try, with futile gasping breaths, to run with him for a stretch.

He checked his watch now and then to be sure he was running long enough at this speed to complete at least five miles. Then he left the park, crossed Delaware, and ran south a few blocks to the gym. Today he was pleased when he reached the gym. He was winded and puffing hard, feeling the sweat dripping down his nose and chin to his soaked T-shirt. He would do some stretches, cool down, and then complete a few reps on the machines before he jogged the last few blocks home.

He pulled open the glass door and stepped into the cooler, climate-controlled atmosphere. He could see the row of older men along the back wall on treadmills and stationary bikes, doing what their cardiologists had been begging them to since way before their heart attacks. Off to the right, through the glassed-in aerobic area, there was a class of thin, wiry young women dancing around, kicking and punching the air to music that he couldn't quite hear. There were a couple of gay guys who worked nights as waiters spotting for each other on the weight bench, but the big machines were clear. He took a step toward the desk and glanced at the bulletin board.

There, in the middle of the board, among the flyers advertising rock-climbing trips, hang-gliding lessons, and concerts, was a picture of Varney—an eight-by-ten glossy color photograph. He glanced at the young man on duty at the desk and felt heat grow in his temples and wash down the sides of his neck to his shoulders. The young man wasn't looking up, but Varney didn't recognize him. He must have been hired recently, or transferred from an evening shift.

Varney walked past the board, bent to adjust the weight on the nearest machine, saw the young man turn to gaze at the women in the exercise class, snatched the picture down, and shoved it into the back of his shirt. He went into the men's room, stepped inside a stall, and took the picture out.

It had looked at first like a photograph of him, but his mind rebelled at the proposition. He had never posed to have a professional picture taken. He looked more closely, and formed a different theory. It was a fake of some sort, maybe a computer-enhancement of some tape in a security camera that had caught him during the past few days. His heart was still pounding from his run, and the sweat was still coming, but his body's reaction seemed to intensify. He read the print at the bottom of the picture.

"Do you know this man? Age 25–30, five feet ten to six feet, 175 lbs., and in good physical condition. Substantial cash reward offered for reliable information." Varney studied the telephone number. Area code 716. It was a local number. Prescott was here.

14

It was late at night when Varney approached the darkened one-story commercial building on the corner. He could see that it had been divided into three storefronts facing Cumberland Avenue. He walked along the street behind it at first to see if there was a car parked in the small blacktop lot, but there was no vehicle. Next he walked back on Cumberland to the storefronts along the street side.

The back windows of each section of the building were small and high, with permanent iron bars to prevent burglaries. Only one had a rear door, and Varney could tell by the position that it opened into the tiny grocery store. None of the windows along the back was lighted, and one even had boards nailed up across it from the inside.

He moved farther off and then came around the block to see the front of the building from across Cumberland. The only possibility seemed to be the one with the boards over the rear window. Prescott could not have rented the grocery store, and the window of the thrift store was hung with a rack of used women's dresses, while the back was shelves of shoes and ancient toasters and toys. But the store on the end was in a state of remodeling of some sort. The front window was covered with brown butcher paper. Maybe Varney had made a mistake about the address.

He had used a telephone directory on the Internet. He had typed in the phone number and clicked on SEARCH, and found this address. But maybe the phone number was an old one for the store that had been in this building and had gone out of business, and the number had been reassigned to Prescott. The website claimed all the numbers were automatically updated every day, but how could he know whether that was true?

Varney looked around. There was a pay telephone on the wall in front of the liquor store. He made his way to the store, put in two quarters and dialed the number, then set the receiver on top of the telephone and trotted across the street. He moved around the building, put his ear close to the boarded-up back window, and listened. He heard the faint ringing of the telephone. There was a click, and a recording. "You have reached the offices of Prescott Enterprises. Please leave your telephone number and your name, unless you wish to remain anonymous. Your call will be returned within twenty-four hours."

Varney walked back to the front of the liquor store and hung up the telephone, then kept walking. Prescott had found his suitcase, opened it, and seen the plane ticket to Buffalo. Then he had gotten the pictures made somehow, and come here. He was in the process of setting up a local field office, like he was the F.B.I. or something. Prescott was not a single frustrating experience that he could put behind him and forget. Prescott was a monster. Varney had somehow, unaccountably, attracted his attention, somehow awakened him. He had come, and he kept coming and coming. He couldn't be scared off or ignored. He had to be killed.

Varney circled the place warily, looking this time at all of the sights besides the new office. He looked at nearby windows for signs that somebody was watching, scrutinized the eaves of buildings for surveillance cameras. He walked up and down the streets around the neighborhood searching for closed vans that might be listening posts. Then he simply left. If Prescott was watching, how could he let Varney come into sight and disappear again? He couldn't.

Varney walked, scanned, and listened, his body poised to run, his hand close to the pistol in his jacket, his mind concentrating on the buildings ahead. He evaluated and chose the spaces between buildings ahead where he would duck out of sight, the straight passages where he would sprint, the dark pockets where he could crouch and wait for Prescott to come running after him. He kept walking until he was sure: he had not made a mistake. Prescott had.

He went to his car and drove home. It took Varney an hour to gather his equipment, make a few modifications and adjustments, and drive back to Prescott's new office. A rule of Varney's discipline was keeping a small but well-chosen supply of the implements of his trade. Now he went through his inventory, running in his mind each of the possible problems that could occur. In Los Angeles he had tried to succeed by speed and audacity, because he had not known enough about his opponent. This time he prepared.

When he returned to the neighborhood, he parked his car in an un-occupied space in a lot behind a big three-story apartment building two streets from Cumberland. Then he took his small backpack and walked to the store. He looked in where the butcher paper didn't quite reach the edge of the front window to be sure that nothing had changed in the past hour. There was nothing in the plain white room but a metal desk, a chair, and a few two-by-fours and sheets of ply-wood left by the carpenters.

He stepped to the door. He had two locks to defeat, a dead bolt and a double-plunger door lock. Probably Prescott had assumed that if he found the place, he would not be up to that, but Prescott had been wrong. Varney had done more than break into a few crummy apart-ments. When he had worked with Coleman Simms, he had learned.

During those years, when they weren't traveling, they had stayed on Coleman's ranch in California. He remembered a day when he had awakened in his room upstairs, and known instantly that there were strangers in the house. He had looked out the window and seen no ve-hicles, but that had not dissuaded him. He had taken the pistol from under the unused pillow beside his, crept down the stairs, and lis-tened.

Coleman had been sitting in the kitchen talking to two men when Varney had appeared in the doorway. Coleman had looked up.

"This is him," he had said.

The two men were dressed like workmen, in jeans and identical light blue work shirts with names in embroidered script above the left breast pocket—Dave and Tim. They looked at Varney a bit anxiously, and Varney knew that the two men were all right: Coleman must have told them who he was.

Coleman said to him, "Dave and Tim are locksmiths. They're going to teach you." It had been much harder than community college. For five weeks he had studied books and diagrams of shafts and tumblers and springs and cylinders. Each day he had practiced the use of the pick and tension wrench on door locks that Dave and Tim had mounted on boards. Under their supervision he had taken locks apart and studied their mechanisms, then put them together again.

At the end of the five weeks, he and Coleman had gone out of town to do a minister. It had struck Varney as a joke. The man was the pastor of a huge congregation in Kansas who had a foundation devoted to lobbying for laws to outlaw the teaching of evolution, and it brought in millions of dollars a year. Most of the donation money came from a few rich men who were bent on raising the issue once again in a series of trials that would be made into a feature-length documentary film. But the real prize was still in the future. The minister had just signed a contract to put the church's weekly service on television.

This had been a problem for another preacher who already was on television in that part of Kansas. He didn't want the competition, so he had visited one of his parishioners in his temporary home in Leavenworth, Kansas. The parishioner was a reformed man doing long time, but the word Varney got from Coleman was that his preacher had convinced him that the other preacher was a heretic and false prophet, and probably a precursor for the Antichrist. The prisoner had gotten the word to the right people, and those people had gotten to Coleman.

Varney had gone to the preacher's big brick church at night and seen moving shadows on the ceiling of an upstairs office. He had found the outer doors locked, but he had used his new skills to pick the lock on a maintenance door that led into a small room just off the sanctuary that was full of folding chairs and tables. He had pulled his gun and made his way upstairs to the office, quietly placed his hand on the doorknob, and found it locked. He had picked that lock too, swung the door open quietly to reveal a reception area, and had seen the preacher, a tall, heavy man in a pair of suit pants and white shirt but no coat, forty feet away inside an inner office. The preacher had looked at a sheaf of papers he held in his right hand, and then begun to speak and wave his arms with animation. Varney had crouched in alarm, then realized the man was rehearsing a sermon in front of a mirror. He'd watched the preacher raise both hands, his hair in disarray and his eyes wild, and say, "Am I my brother's keeper?" before he'd fired a shot through both doorways into his right temple.

The day after he and Coleman had returned, Varney had gone back to his locksmith lessons for ten more weeks. He learned about house locks, car locks, commercial locks, and dead bolts. It was only after he had mastered the traditional skills that they had introduced him to electronic pick guns and magnetic bolt-sliders that could do the same things more quickly.

He opened the shiny new locks on Prescott's office door in seconds. He pulled the door open and slipped inside, then let the door swing gently shut without touching the inner doorknob. He walked directly to the back of the dark room, found the desk by the glow of the answering machine, set his backpack down, and looked around him, waiting for his eyes to reach their maximum adjustment to the near darkness.

Everything about this place was right, as though Prescott had been on Varney's side. The front window was covered with brown butcher paper, so very little light came in or escaped, and a passerby would not see Varney unless he put his eye to the uncovered edge. The back window had been boarded even though it had bars on it. Only the single side window was functional, and it was covered with blinds.

He decided there really was no reason he had to work in complete darkness. He reached into the backpack and took out his Mag-lite, adjusted the beam so it was narrow and bright, and let it play along the floorboards and the baseboards and the suspended acoustic ceiling tiles, then over the desk itself. It was perfect: one room, twelve feet by fifteen feet, with only the desk and chair in it. Even better, there was only one entrance. Varney rigged the pipe bombs very carefully. There was one taped under the center of the desk, with the switch set against the back of the top center drawer, and the drawer a little bit open. If Prescott sat in the chair to listen to his phone messages, he would push in the top drawer of the desk, complete the circuit, and the bomb would cut him in half.

Varney armed the bomb, then went to work on the main charge.

This one was set at the edge of the floor, covered only by a paper wrapper left over from the already installed wallboard. He ran the wire around the room, pushed it into the space below the baseboard, where it was covered by the new industrial carpeting and could not be tripped over. Then he set the end of it to a pair of magnetic sensors made for a burglar-alarm system. One would go on the door and the other on the jamb. When the door opened, the magnetic contact between them would break. That would permit a magnetic switch to trip, giving the electrical current a path down the wire. A less thoughtful man would have wired the blasting cap right into the circuit, but Varney had imagined the entire sequence. He had put the blasting cap into a parallel circuit with a time-delay relay. The door would open, five seconds would pass while Prescott stepped inside, closed it, took a couple of steps toward the desk, and then the cap would initiate the bomb. The narrow room would be filled with flying bits of the metal pipe, mixed with a pound of nails.

As he thought about it, Varney wondered if five seconds were enough. Maybe he should set the relay to ten. That way, Prescott could get all the way to the desk and close the drawer to set off that bomb first. Most likely, the main charge would go off after Prescott was dead, but that would be fine. He decided against the change. Prescott was not a stupid man. In ten seconds, he might have time to see that something had changed, and maybe even to disarm the charge.

Varney took his backpack, ran his light around the room one last time to be sure he had not left anything showing, then walked to the door to pull the two wires under the lower hinge. That way, he could connect the two wires to arm the circuit only after he was outside. He brought them to the spot, then reached up to put his hand on the knob, and knew there was a problem. The knob was a simple brass one, with no inner lock button or keyhole. It turned, but when it did, there was a spongy, unchanging resistance, not a spring pushing it back to its original position. He rotated it a full turn without feeling any effect. He switched on his flashlight again. The knob was a dummy. It was mounted on a steel plate that was welded to the steel door.

He stood and tugged, but it had no effect. The front door had been rigged so that it would not open from the inside. Varney felt a growing sense of alarm, but he knew what to do. He would take the pins out of the hinges and get out of here. He shone his light on the center one. The head of the pin was welded into the top bracket. He moved the flashlight. They were all dummies, welded in place. The real hinges were invisible and beyond his reach, built into the jamb.

Varney examined the parts of the front window that were not covered with butcher paper. He looked at it from an angle, then shone his flashlight along the edge. The glass wasn't the regular kind. It looked about three quarters of an inch thick, and the edge was set deep into the steel frame. The outside had the same steel grating across it that the windows of the other storefronts had. He moved quickly to the smaller window at the side of the building. It was the same.

Prescott's little office was not an office at all. It was a trap. Once a man was inside it, there was no way out. He would have to sit in here until Prescott came for him and opened the front door. Varney's eyes went narrow with anger and hatred. His breaths came in short, rough rasps that dried his mouth. He felt as though the veins in his arms were swelling with the blood surging into them. He wanted to tear his way out of here, punch and kick his way through the wall, but he had to think. Prescott might already be on the way. Whatever Varney did, it had to be now, and it had to work.

The outer walls of the building were brick. But maybe the wall that separated this small room from the grocery store was just the usual frame of two-by-fours covered with wallboard. He took out his knife, selected a spot a yard from the corner of the room, and carved away a bit of wallboard. He worked in a circular motion, making a little pile of gypsum and plaster at his feet. Finally, the blade went through. He worked the knife around to make a bigger hole, his heart beginning to beat with anticipation. All he had to do was cut away a foot and a half between a pair of studs and the same size hole in the wallboard nailed on from the other side, and he would fit through. He could arm the circuit of the main bomb without the bother of connecting the last wires from outside. He would slither into the grocery store, go out the rear door to the parking lot, and he would be gone. Then Varney's blade hit something that made a *skritch* sound.

He turned on the flashlight, shone it into the hole in the wall, and saw the rough, reddish surface. It was brick. The little office was not just a walled-off section of the grocery store; it was an addition. The brick had once been the outer wall of the building, and it was still there.

Varney stood still. He was surrounded by brick on four sides. He looked up at the suspended layer of acoustic tiles. Whatever was up there, it couldn't be brick. He glanced at his watch. He had been in here for twenty-five minutes already. Prescott could be here at any moment—might already be out there waiting in the dark for him—and he was wasting time. He reached gingerly under the desk behind the center drawer and disconnected the wires, then pulled the pipe bomb out.

He felt as though Prescott had his arm clenched around his throat, choking off the air, making him flail around desperately, tiring himself with futile struggling. He could picture Prescott, not as just the tall, thin, middle-aged man he had seen slouching in the car in the California parking lot, but as he really was: the cold eyes watching him with sadistic amusement, the thin lips curled just a little at the corners in a mocking smile.

Varney pushed the desk toward the corner of the room. He bent at the knees, tipped it up on its end, and prepared to climb up on it to reach the ceiling, then stopped. Prescott had selected this place. He had chosen everything in it, and modified whatever wasn't suited to his purpose. Prescott was cunning, calculating in a way that nobody Varney had ever met had been. He was perfectly capable of seeing that the desk could be tipped up on its end and used to climb to the ceiling.

Varney looked around him. Prescott had made sure the room had four brick walls. Varney could tell by the feel of the floor under his feet that the addition had been built on a concrete slab. Could Prescott have neglected the roof? He had probably had a layer of corrugated steel laid in, covered with tar paper and asphalt. He had thought of everything else. What had Prescott not known?

Varney looked down at the floor. The only thing that Prescott had not known was what Varney would do, what Varney would bring with him. Varney tipped the desk again and brought it back down.

He stood on it to reach the back window, then used his knife to loosen the screws in the plywood that covered the glass. He removed the square, opened the window, and examined the steel bars. He could tell by feel that the bars were in a frame anchored in the brick by four bolts at the corners.

He lifted his two pipe bombs from the floor and set one in the frame at each of the two lower corners outside under the windowsill. He opened his backpack and took out the third pipe charge he had brought but not installed, and used duct tape to secure it to the frame at the third bolt. Then he set himself to rewiring the three bombs in three parallel circuits, so the electrical current would reach all three at the same instant. He spliced the three entry wires and the three exit wires into two little twists. He took the insulated cord from the answering machine, cut it, stripped an inch of it, separated the two wires, and spliced one to each of his two twists.

Varney brought the window down, leaving only enough space for his cord. He used the rest of his duct tape to cover the glass, then screwed the plywood back over the window. He pushed the desk into the rear corner of the room near the electrical outlet, and crawled under it with his backpack. He used his knife to cut two small squares of cloth from the bottom of his shirt, rolled them into balls, and stuck them into his ears, took off his jacket and wound it around his head so it covered his face, ears, and neck. He curled into a ball under the desk and felt for the plastic plate of the electrical outlet. He opened his mouth to keep his eardrums from blowing out, took three deep breaths to calm himself, then inserted the plug.

The noise was so loud the air seemed to turn solid. The concrete foundation under him jumped to slap against his body as though he had fallen. He was aware that the big, heavy metal desk hopped above him and came down askew. The hand that he had extended to insert the plug had been punched aside so hard it tingled.

Varney lay still. He felt as though he had been injured in some way, jolted like a person in a high-speed crash, shaken by an impact so that his joints were strained and everything inside him had been shaken. It was silent. He tested his muscles and found he was able to stir, and when he did, his presence of mind gathered itself out of fragments and returned. He remembered he was in a hurry. Time was passing. He slowly crawled out from inside the desk and pulled the jacket off his face.

The room was dark, the air so thick he could barely breathe. He held the jacket over his nose and mouth and found his flashlight with his knee. He turned it on. The air was a cloud of plaster dust, but he could see that up and to the side, the plywood had been blown inward off the window. About half of the acoustic tiles in the ceiling had been knocked out of their metal frame, and the others were tilted, the frame still swinging on its wires.

He moved to the window, and his heart stopped. The bars were still there. He moved closer. They weren't at the right angle. He reached out and gave the nearest bar a push, but it burned his hand. "Shit!" he hissed, drawing his hand back and sticking it in his mouth. But he had seen the bars move. He pushed the desk the couple of feet to the side so that it was under the window. He lay on its surface and kicked at the bars with his feet. They moved, then jerked out farther. He kicked again and again, until the lower bolts were out of the brick. He rolled, stood on the desk, used his backpack to brush the broken glass off the sill, then used it to hold the bars away from the wall. He eased himself onto the small window.

He stopped for a moment to shine his flashlight around the inside of the office to be sure he had left nothing. Then he lowered himself to the ground, trotted up the dark street for a half block, cut into the backyard of a house to reach the next street. He heard the faint, far-away sound of sirens. Lights were going on in houses, the glows of lamps falling in squares on the spaces of darkness where he had wanted to walk, so he dodged them, ducking low and stepping quickly along the walls. He broke into a run. He was out of the box. He could breathe the soft, cool air of night.

15

Buffalo was not a huge town. Whenever Prescott had asked somebody how to get to his next stop, the person would say, "It's about fifteen minutes away." In Los Angeles they would usually say, "It's about an hour from here," and they would mean on the freeway, if traffic was moving. Earlier today, he had sometimes found himself in sluggish spots, but not like the ones at home. By evening the lines of cars had thinned out, and the fifteen-minute drives could be done in ten.

He had made twenty-two stops before it got to be too late in the evening to go on. He had made a list of the places where this particular killer probably spent time. There were only seven gyms in the area that would have appealed to this man. Those were the ones that were fairly new and spacious, had huge numbers of people coming in each day, and catered to the twenty-to-thirty crowd. The small, hard-core places that were in tiny, dark buildings and smelled of ancient sweat would not have seemed safe to this man: his best defense was protective coloration. The old iron works where men turned themselves into something like small steers would have been too intimate for him. But Prescott was sure that this killer was in the habit of going somewhere to work out, so he had put pictures in every gym where nobody stopped him.

Prescott believed that this man also spent some time shooting. He was too accurate not to be getting regular practice. Prescott had found only four ranges in the area where people were allowed to shoot handguns, and all were private clubs. None of them seemed to Prescott to fit his image of the man. Two of the clubs were meeting places for men cradling Purdy shotguns over their forearms and wearing sport coats with suede padding patches at the right shoulders. The other two were a bit more plebeian, but both seemed to consist of older men biding their time until hunting season—not practicing, exactly, but rehearsing.

Prescott was not hopeful about the gun clubs. They didn't feel like places that would attract this killer. But men engaged in a pastime sometimes saw others engaged in the same pastime without socializing, so he knew the clubs were not a waste of time. He had left his pictures and moved on. He had tried a few gun shops, but he had not felt hopeful about those, either. Nobody who engaged in shooting sports wanted to be reminded that guns were used to kill people. The topic was depressing, and the shopkeepers were not enthusiastic, because it might put a damper on sales. But Prescott had kept at it until he had hit all the larger stores.

All that had to happen was that the killer come along and see his own picture, so any place might work. He put a few pictures up near big shopping malls. Then he drove back toward his new office. It would be one more day before the place was exactly as he wanted it, but he had begun posting the pictures as soon as the trap was strong enough to hold a man.

It was late when he returned to the spot where he had planned to park while he watched his office, but when he reached Cumberland Avenue, he could tell that he had arrived too late. There was a crowd of people in sweatshirts and T-shirts, and even pajamas and bathrobes, all gathered in the street and staring toward his building.

He could see four police cars, two of them with flashing light bars above their roofs, alternately turning his building red and blue; two that were dark; a fire truck; and an ambulance. He pulled his car to the curb and stared through the windshield. He forced himself to breathe normally. He hoped there wasn't another body, some innocent by-stander who happened to be in this man's way at the wrong time. He hoped it was . . . He didn't finish the thought. The ambulance doors weren't open, and it wasn't in a hurry to get moving, so either there was nobody in it, or the occupant was dead.

He got out of his car and walked up the street toward the low build-ing. As he came closer he could see the police officers milling around in front, on the sidewalk and the street, but there seemed to be more of them in the back. He came to the corner, and started down toward the rear of the building. He could see the yellow POLICE LINE tape blocking the entrance to the little parking lot, and now he could see a big panel truck. He slowly, patiently made his way through the crowd to the police tape, saying over and over, "Excuse me, that's my build-ing. Excuse me, that's my office." People parted, not so much to make room as to spin their bodies to the side so their heads could turn enough to see him. When he reached the tape, he took out his wallet, opened it, and waved it at the nearest cop.

The cop was a tall black detective who had been giving orders to a couple of uniformed officers at the edge of the parking lot. The de-tective's eyebrows went up as he looked at Prescott, and Prescott watched him decide that whatever this man meant by waving his wal-let around, it had better be pertinent.

"Did you want something, sir?" The controlled tone was a warning to Prescott.

"Yes, officer. My name is Prescott. I'm the one who is renting that space on the end, there."

The detective's eyes followed Prescott's gesture to the building. He reached down and pulled up the yellow tape so Prescott could step under it. "We've been looking for you." He led Prescott into the lot, and Prescott saw the rear window. The bars had been torn out of the wall, but not as though they had been pulled. Bricks around the win-dow were chipped and cracked apart. Above and below the window, there were big, fan-shaped marks that were part black carbon, and part gouges and nicks.

"What kind of bomb was it?" he asked.

The detective glared at him sharply. "What kind were you expect-ing?" He led Prescott around the building to the front. "This is Mr.

Prescott," he said to the two uniformed cops loitering beside a patrol car. "Let them know we've got him."

The two cops quickly and expertly whirled Prescott around and began to frisk him.

He said evenly, "I'm not carrying anything dangerous."

The cops finished patting him down, then one of them conferred in a whisper with the detective, and returned. He didn't handcuff Prescott, just opened the door to the back and said, "Have a seat."

Prescott ducked down to sit, and the side window just ahead of him shattered, showering the inside of the car with bits of flying glass. The report of the rifle reached Prescott a half breath later. He was already curled into a crouch. He ducked to the pavement and rolled as the next three shots punched through the door of the police car. The two cops scattered, one to the rear of the car and the other to the front, where they knelt, drew sidearms, and aimed uselessly into the darkness, their heads swiveling to find the target.

Prescott's mind carried several thoughts at once: The bullets had not exited through the opposite window, so the angle meant the killer was high. Prescott's roll was a practiced move, and he knew that it had taken him much farther from the car than the killer would anticipate. The old sniper's motto burned in his brain: "If you run, you'll just die tired." He had to get out of sight.

He came up from his shoulder roll already leaping forward, because the shooter would already have adjusted the elevation of his rifle for the next shot. Prescott dived at an angle to the left, and the shot he'd known was coming pounded into the sidewalk to his right, throwing chips and powdered concrete into the air. Prescott saw the open door of his office and scrambled into it as the next shot pierced the carpet at his feet. He moved to the left, and three more shots smacked the thick bullet-proof glass of the front window and ricocheted into the sidewalk.

He could see by the light of the empty-framed rear window that the office was a ruin. The desk was moved, the ceiling tiles were covering everything. He could see that the answering machine was on the ground, its cord severed. He heard an insistent beep. Could the telephone have survived? He looked at the phone jack and followed the cord a couple of feet before it disappeared under acoustic tile. He could not ignore the sound. He leapt across the open doorway to the most likely area, kicked a few tiles aside, and found it. He pushed down the button under the cradle, heard a dial tone, and punched 911. He spoke calmly and crisply as soon as he heard the click, cutting into the voice. "We have police officers under rifle fire at Cumberland Avenue and Maplestone Street. The sniper is up high about one block to the west, possibly on a roof. He is a white male, twenty-five to thirty years old, one hundred seventy-five pounds, dark brown hair." He heard a female voice begin to say, "Who—" but he interrupted, trying to be sure all of it was said, if only to be preserved on the tape recording that kicked in on emergency lines. "It is essential that the units responding approach from the west, behind the sniper."

"Yes, sir. What is your—"

He left the phone off the hook and stepped away quickly. He knew that the shooter was out there trying to change his angle enough to fire into the doorway. Prescott couldn't close the steel door, because the first cops to arrive had battered it so much it had bent inward. He wasn't sure whether the police officers outside were calling in contradictory messages on their radios. He couldn't tell from their actions whether they knew that he was the only target.

He waited, looking at the ruined room, piecing together what had happened. The front wall and part of the floor had been peppered with holes. He looked more closely and saw a couple that were perfect outlines of short roofing nails, and a few that looked like jagged strips of scrap metal: a pipe bomb.

The killer had not come here, pounded in the back window, and tossed in a bomb. He had come in here to set up a booby trap, and gotten stuck. He had used his bomb to free himself. Prescott slowly overcame his shock. He had been surprised that the man could have found the place and coolly destroyed it so quickly. But he had not. The desk had not been blown into the safest corner of the room: it had been pushed there by the killer. He had used it for protection from the blast.

He thought about the man, and the hairs on the back of his neck began to rise. The man had fallen for the trap, just as Prescott had predicted. But he had not uselessly pounded on brick walls, or waited for Prescott with the gun he'd brought, or even sat in the corner and used that gun to blow his own brains out. He had placed the antipersonnel bomb he'd prepared at the only possible exit, the weakest part of the trap, maybe eight feet from his own head, and set it off. He was like a wolf caught in a trap that was willing to gnaw through its own leg to get away.

Prescott heard a sudden volley of shots, all in rapid succession, the popping sounds of handguns. He listened for the louder, sharper report of the rifle, but it did not come. One of the cops must have gotten optimistic and mistaken a shadow for the real thing. The wolf had already slipped off into the night.

16

After the first salvo, the shooting stopped, and the silence returned. Prescott sat with his back against the brick wall and waited. There would be a SWAT team searching the streets to the west, and then some kind of sweep of the neighborhood before the police would be willing to relinquish their state of readiness. Everything about these situations worked that way. It was oddly comfortable for a man used to fighting to be crouched behind a car with a gun in his hand, even when he knew that the car was not much protection from a high-velocity rifle round, and that a suspect with a good scope could pick out the place on his chin that he had nicked with his razor that morning. Readiness was something that cops found hard to give up. As long as they remained in a standoff, the opportunity was prolonged: there was still a chance to see the shooter and get him. The moment the bosses gave the all-clear signal, the chance was over. The man who had shattered the public tranquility and done his best to kill somebody had gotten away with it.

The end of the emergency was also the end of clarity. A man cornered while firing a gun at police officers was finished. But if he stopped and got rid of the gun before they saw him, he entered the realm of lengthy, unpromising investigations, painstaking accumulations of evidence, formal accusations, and snide counterattacks by defense lawyers. Prescott was sorry for the cops. They felt the way he did.

He had done his best to take advantage of his chances, but each time, the same thing had gone wrong: this killer had gotten to the trap before it was fully cocked and baited, and gotten out again. This time he had done it especially convincingly, and Prescott had found himself doing shoulder rolls on a concrete sidewalk to get himself out of the crosshairs. Now he seemed doomed to sit here in his own brick-and-mortar box waiting for first light to show at the window so the cops would feel safe enough to finish arresting him.

He had gone into this with a strange, almost unnatural feeling that he understood this man. He had looked at the sights that the killer had seen, put his feet on the spaces where the killer had stepped, and discovered that he could imagine the killer's thoughts, maybe even think them. But tonight this killer had done the unexpected, and the unexpected was something unnerving. He had done what—given the predicament he was in and what he had to work with—Prescott would have done.

For the past twenty years or more, Prescott had hunted men. He had devised a great many deceptions and snares. Always, the purpose of them was to put Prescott and some killer in a place by themselves, where no external force could intervene.

It had been a mind-enlarging experience for some of them, a moment when they had suddenly realized that their most deeply held belief about themselves was completely wrong. Even mired in the self-hatred and guilt that had given them a certain attraction to risk, their desperation was not dependable. It had only worked in their favor while they were courting risk, playing with it, doing things that might put them into real danger but probably wouldn't. When positive, verifiable danger arrived in the form of Roy Prescott, they found that their immunity to fear had involved a certain amount of self-deception.

Prescott was a man who would not give up, could not call for reinforcements, and would not stop coming. For him, defeat while he was still alive was not unthinkable merely because he had made a rule for himself that he wouldn't allow it; it was unthinkable because it had not, literally, been thought. Each time he met one of these men, he had already determined that only one of them was going to be able to walk away. Tonight, Prescott was having his own moment of revelation. This killer was not as different from Prescott as the others had been. He was doing what Prescott would have done.

Suddenly Prescott stood up. The killer wasn't gone. Prescott moved through the doorway quickly, striding along at his full height. He stepped around the building. He found the detective he had spoken to before, crouching beside a black-and-white patrol car, the microphone in his hand and his eyes on the tall trees on the far side of the next row of houses. When he saw Prescott, he looked as though he were watching a man in the process of stepping off a cliff. "Get down!"

"No need," said Prescott. "He's not up there anymore. He's moved a couple of blocks down."

"What are you talking about?"

Prescott allowed one of the other cops to lurch closer and pull him down behind the police car. He said patiently, "He's not interested in bagging a cop tonight. He's completely focused: the only person out here he can even see is me. He broke into my office carrying a bomb he was going to use to make a booby trap. He saw that he was locked into the office, so he used the bomb to blow off the bars on the window. Then he went out there to wait, because he knew that sooner or later, I would show up."

"Interesting story," said the detective. "So what?"

"So I know where he is. He saw me arrive, he took his shots, and he knows he missed. For a lot of people, that would be enough. There are a few dozen cops around, and he can't fight all of us. But for him that won't be enough."

"Won't be enough?"

"He knows I must have driven here. He saw the direction I came from when I walked up to the building. He knows that right now you'll think he's gone home, because it's the only sensible thing for him to do. But he hasn't, he's just moved down the street a couple hundred yards."

"What for?"

"To get a clear, unimpeded shot at my car."

The detective's eyes passed across the faces of two uniformed cops moving toward Prescott. "What is it that you're trying to get us to do?"

"Make it look like the emergency is over. Send everybody out of here except a few cops who look like they're collecting evidence and a couple to secure the scene. Then you hide two cars out of sight up on that end of the street, and two at the other end, and let me walk down to my car alone. He'll make another try."

The detective's eyebrows knitted and his face acquired a fluid expression: genuine surprise that shaded off into a smirk. For a moment, he made his features assume a parody of contemplation. Finally he said, "This is a case that's beyond my previous personal experience. I do have a certain memory for things I've seen and heard. One of them is that most of the time, when you get a small, nondescript building that gets its windows blown out by explosives, it turns out that it isn't because somebody blew it up. What you find out is that it was an accident. Somebody was using the place to build bombs, and made a mistake or didn't know how to store them." He turned a steady gaze on Prescott. "Now, you may be telling me the truth, and your theory may even be correct. But I did notice that we had a certain amount of quiet around here until the officers started to put you into their patrol car to take you downtown. Then somebody started shooting, and what got hit was the car, which has POLICE in foot-high letters down the side of it. Now, what I'm going to do is similar to what you want. You could even call it a compromise."

"Compromise?" said Prescott.

"Right. I'm going to move out most of these people, just as you requested. I'm going to leave a few officers to secure the scene so the forensics team can do their work. If there is some kind of maniac who is down there waiting to shoot you in your car, he's got to stay where he can see it. I'll have units stationed all around it, where they can move in if he shows himself. What I won't do is let you walk down there by yourself and get into your car."

"Then he won't show himself."

"You seem to be an intelligent man, too intelligent to imagine you can get in and drive off. But you also seem too intelligent to think it's a good idea to walk in front of a rifle. It's a contradiction."

Prescott shook his head. "He's down there, and this is the chance to get him. All he wants is me. The other officer already took my wallet and keys. You can hold on to them, and I can't drive away."

"Thank you." He turned to the two uniformed cops. "Take him downtown."

The two policemen began to help him to his feet. "He's only here because it's my place."

The detective's expression turned stony. "It was your place until a bomb went off in it. Now it's a crime scene, and that makes it my place." He said to the cops, "Take him around the back, and up the side street to the east, so you can't be seen from the front of the building."

Prescott sighed and shook his head wearily. He let the two cops handcuff him, then push him into the back seat of a car. As they drove off, he didn't look back at the building again.

About five hours later, when the detective came into the interrogation room, he looked at Prescott with frank irritation. He sat down at the table across from Prescott and set a file in front of him that was already half an inch thick. "I've been reading about you. I also read the statement you gave Lieutenant Mussanto. Does your statement contain any inaccuracies that you know of?"

"No."

"How about your record?"

Prescott asked, "Where did you get it?"

"It was faxed to us by the Los Angeles police."

"Then it's probably close enough. It was last time I looked at it."

"You think this is the same man who killed the two police officers and the security guard in the office building in L.A.?"

"I know it is."

"I can see why you don't work at home."

Prescott nodded, but said nothing.

"What is either one of you doing in Buffalo?"

"I think he's been living here. I don't know how long. I came to find him."

"Looks like he saw you first."

Prescott sat in silence, neither conceding the point nor contesting it, merely waiting.

After a time, the detective nodded, then took a deep breath and let it out. "There's a local ordinance against remodeling your own office so a person who goes in can't get out: a fire regulation. The fine will be a thousand bucks, and they'll send you a summons you can pay by mail. I'll try to get you out of that, but when firefighters get called out on something like this, they're pissed off. It doesn't seem fair to them to have to get shot at."

"Why?"

"Why what?"

"Why would you try to get me out of it?"

The detective stared down at the closed file folder for a moment. "What would you have done if I had let you go down to your car by yourself?"

"Tried to draw his fire," said Prescott. "If I could survive one miss, I figured I could probably get to him. He was up high somewhere—I think closer to the car than he'd been to the office. It's hard to hold a moving man in the field of a powerful scope. Lowering your aim when a man is running toward you fast is hard to do. The scope is mounted above the barrel, so if you try to look past it, the gun itself is in your line of vision."

Prescott saw that the detective was listening politely, so he continued. "I picked out his problem when he shot the first time. He had a lot of rounds: at least ten in the magazine. He's young and angry, and he let the fact that he had a semiautomatic rifle make him squander that first shot. The first recoil kicked the barrel up, and so he had to horse it down for the next one, and that gave me time to duck and roll. He's better than that, but I think he let his anger overcome his judgment."

"So you could get him. If you survived one miss," the detective repeated.

"Yeah. That would let me see the muzzle flash."

"I see," said the detective. "If I'd known more last night, I still wouldn't have let you do it. But I would have been sorry—curious to see what would have happened. It's why I want to get you out of the fine. You don't need a fine, you need to be put in a home somewhere so you don't do this anymore." He paused. "You can pick up your be-longings at the desk."

Prescott took a cab to his hotel and requested that his locked cash box be removed from the main safe. He brought it upstairs, opened it, and took out the gun he had bought in Pennsylvania. From now on, he would probably be needing it.

17

Varney drove the route he had run just twenty-four hours ago. Now it was a different landscape. He had chosen Buffalo a few years ago because it was a town that had everything he wanted. It was big enough to hide in, but not big enough to require a lot of work to stay alive in it. Houses were cheap and sturdy, traffic was sane. The stories about the winter weather had not been exaggerated, but it had been that way forever, so the people could hardly be taken by surprise when it happened. They had plows out beginning their routes while the snow was still three inches deep on the ground, and all the people knew how to handle their own problems. He liked being at the edge of the state, where he could slip over a border to Canada, or be in Pennsylvania in an hour and a half, even Ohio in two.

Now his refuge had been spoiled. Prescott had transformed it in a day, made it into a rotting, deteriorating place that seemed to him to be dirtier and uglier each moment he stayed in it. He wanted to leave, to never have to look at it again. It took an act of discipline for him to travel this landscape of squat, old brick buildings that housed little shops that had spent decades looking as though they were going out of business. It was a hot, humid night, and he drove slowly, studying the people out walking on the sidewalks.

They all looked grotesque to him: a fat old couple, the husband's big belly jutting out over his belt buckle, almost pendulous, the bottom of his T-shirt stretched not quite long enough to cover it; the wife in a tent dress that hung down loose in front but still made a kind of detour in back to settle on the shelf of her ponderous buttocks. The young men seemed to stare at Varney, drunk and menacing and stupid, some in the baggy shorts that appeared here the second the snow stopped falling and seemed to be worn continuously until the snow returned. Twice Varney went around a block because he saw a tall, rangy man alone on the street. When he got a closer look, the man was not Prescott.

Varney parked across the street from his gym where he could see into the lighted windows. The heart patients were in the back row on the treadmills and stationary bikes as always, plodding along with the same preoccupied look, listening to their pulses in dull fear. He could see the interior window too, where the late class of women were all bobbing up and down on stair-steps in a soundless dance in front of the mirrored wall. The poster he had taken from the bulletin board had not been replaced. Maybe that meant that Prescott would be here soon to put up a new one, but maybe it meant Prescott no longer needed the posters, because someone from the gym had called him. Maybe Prescott was somewhere nearby, waiting for him to come in for a workout. Varney turned his eyes to the streets again, looking for any sign that would indicate which it was. He started the car again and circled the block, searching, and then moved on.

The next place was the small grocery store where he sometimes shopped. It was about a mile from his house. He always walked there because walking was exercise, but also because it took up time in the evening. He could be out and fight the feelings that plagued him when he wasn't working: that claustrophobic sensation of being young and healthy and free, but locked up on the second floor of an old house while everyone else was out, the sense of loss and sadness he felt when he looked at a young woman walking past, and knew that he couldn't just begin to walk with her. Women demanded so much— the right circumstances of meeting, a veiled but still distressingly thorough interrogation that was designed to catch him in a lie—that sometimes he began by being attracted, then felt the attraction turning to hatred.

He studied the interior of the market. He could see the man in his fifties that he thought of as Mr. Smolinski because it was called Smolinski's Market and he seemed to be the boss. He wore a butcher's apron that was always filthy from the boxes he carried pressed against his stomach. Varney could see him taking cans out of a carton and stacking them on a shelf. The only customer was a young woman with a baby propped in a shopping cart. It was nine o'clock at night, and Varney disapproved. She should have a baby in bed by now, not be pushing him around in that store under the sickly yellow lights. She was too stupid to deserve to have him.

Varney drove past the little parking area in the back. He could see the woman's stroller parked beside the door, and wondered how she proposed to get the groceries home. Probably she would pile some of them in the rack underneath, and put the overflow on the poor kid's lap.

He could see Mr. Smolinski's car, and another that was nearly always there that he guessed belonged to the semiretarded guy who worked in the back, but there was no car nearby that could be Prescott's. He drove up and down the two streets on either side of the building, but there was nothing that tempted him to look more closely. He turned his car in the direction of the little office where Prescott had tried to trap him.

As Varney drove, he let nothing escape his notice. Every car that passed was a new opportunity, and Varney looked quickly at the head behind each steering wheel, taking a mental snapshot and comparing it with his memory of Prescott.

He drove by Prescott's building without letting his foot touch the brake pedal. He aimed the car ahead and stared at the place hard once, but did not come around the block for a second look. There seemed to be no police cars around this evening, and there were no lights on in the building, but he knew that stopping would be a bad idea. He had read somewhere that firemen always took a videotape of the crowd around an arson fire because they knew that arsonists often showed up to watch. He wasn't sure what the police did for bombs, but it was reasonable to suppose they would not do less. He wasn't interested in having to kill some cop tonight. All he wanted was Prescott.

He passed a pair of young women walking up the street in sandals and short skirts and tank tops, and was almost tempted to stop. He had found that if there were two of them, sometimes things actually went better. They weren't as frightened of one man that they hadn't met in the right way. If they were bored tonight, he might be able to talk them into going into a nearby place for a drink with him.

A couple of times, he had even seen something happen with two girls that had at first seemed to him to be a miracle. He had walked down a street in New York one night a year ago and gotten stopped for a moment by a traffic light. Beside him had been two girls. They were each carrying shopping bags from several stores, and they had obviously been out all day. One of them had said something about needing a drink, and Varney had been inspired. He had smiled as well as he could and said, "You know, that sounds wonderful. I'd love to buy you one."

The light had changed, and they had started walking. The girls kidded each other all the way across the street, and joked themselves into it. The party of two was three now, and there was a big hotel with a bar right in front of them. One of them said her name was Sherry, and the other Lynn. He was fairly sure they were false names, but he didn't care.

The miracle had come inside the hotel bar. It wasn't his hotel, but it had been the nearest doorway and it was expensive looking, so he had chosen it. The miracle was that after one drink, Sherry and Lynn developed a more complicated relationship. Neither one wanted to be shown up by the other as being the less attractive one, the less interesting one. After a time, they stopped teasing Varney and turned to teasing each other.

Neither of them had any interest in him. Each wanted to demonstrate to her friend that she was more desirable to him than the friend was. He sensed that the object was to force him to choose one—ask her for a date or something—while ignoring the other. Then the winner would grandly refuse, as though the man who had rejected her friend was, nonetheless, beneath her. This was very tricky—not a novice's game, and with painful stakes—because it involved getting Varney very interested without having done or said anything that anyone could define as trying.

Varney simply waited, being sure to pay attention to one, then the other, in equal turns. He made sure that each time, it took a bit more for the one who wanted to regain his attention to get it. What he had been waiting for happened after the third drink. Lynn said she was surprised at the way Sherry was throwing herself at him.

The remark made the competition overt. Sherry said that it had been all in fun, and there was no reason to feel rejected and jealous. In five minutes her icy remarks had driven Lynn from the table and into a cab. Victory had a curious effect on Sherry. She seemed shocked to find she was alone with Varney. She had to convince herself that this was what she had always intended, and that Varney was valu- a pble enough to be worth the trouble. In another ten minutes, she and Varney were in a hotel room. She had her clothes coming off, and no reasonable way of calling a halt to the proceedings without proving to herself that she had been an idiot.

Varney looked back on that experience with a warm, pleasurable feeling. He had tried to repeat it a few times, but only twice with sim- ilar success. Sex was one of the things that this life of adventure made difficult for him.

Coleman had warned him that it would be that way. Part of staying alive in this business was staying out of situations where some woman felt she had the right to ask as many questions as she could think of until her jaw got tired. Most of them thought that having sex gave them the right. Coleman's solution had been to employ prostitutes.

Varney had never known exactly how Coleman had managed it, but in every city, he'd seemed to know an address or a telephone number, even the cities he claimed never to have visited before. One night near the end of his time with Coleman Simms, Varney had been in a room in Indianapolis with a girl named Terry. She had looked young, maybe nineteen, and she had said she had not been in the trade very long. He hadn't believed her at the time, but in retrospect, he decided that maybe she had been telling the truth. She had begun to ask him ques- tions about where a young guy like him got his money, what company he worked for, what city, and so on. Varney was drunk. He stood as much as he could, and in a moment of annoyance, decided to end the questions.

"You know that guy over in Fort Wayne who got his throat cut last night?"

"Yes," she said. It had been on the television news all day.

"Well, that's what I do," Varney said. "I make a lot of money because I'm really good at it."

The next morning when Varney woke up, Terry was gone. He wasn't entirely sorry, because he had a headache and wasn't interested in hearing her voice again. He showered and dressed, then found that Coleman wasn't in his room. Varney waited for a couple of hours, and when Coleman showed up, he was in a jumpy mood. As they walked to the car in the hotel lot, Coleman's jaw was set, and he threw his suitcase into the trunk and slammed the lid so hard that the car rocked on its springs. When he took the wheel and Varney was sitting beside him, he said, "Don't ever do that again."

"Do what?"

Coleman said, "Don't tell hookers your life story. They're not in it to meet interesting people. If you want them to respect you, stay away from them. If you want them to like you, give them some money."

Varney felt a growing sense of dread. "What happened?"

"About four o'clock I saw her sneaking off down the hall like something was chasing her. I decided to see if something was. When I caught up with her, she told me you hadn't said anything about Fort Wayne, and if you had, she would never tell anyone."

"I didn't tell her anything to prove I really did it," he said uneasily. "I just couldn't stand the stupid questions. I decided to shut her up."

Coleman glared at him. "It's a business. Get that into your head. If they ask you questions, it's just like when a waiter asks you questions. None of them gives a shit what the answer is. They're just trying to make you feel important so you'll give them a decent tip and they can go on to the next customer."

"Did you have to give her more money to keep her quiet?"

Coleman took his eyes off the road to turn an irate stare on Varney. "It was a little late for that, kid. I had to break her neck."

After that, Varney had to sit in silence staring at cornfields and now and then a ramshackle house with dusty old cars in the front yard. The midmorning sun heated the endless, straight road until distant pools of imaginary water appeared on the pavement, then dissolved as the car drew nearer. He thought about the girl Terry, the thin white neck, the little wisps of blond hair that grew at the nape, and felt a confusing retroactive arousal that lasted for a few seconds, until memory moved forward and reminded him that it had all turned ugly, and the girl's body was cold and already dumped someplace. Each time he forgot that he didn't want to think about her, the girl's image returned, and he would find himself falling into the cycle again. She should have kept her mouth shut.

After about an hour, Coleman spoke again. "That's the only free one you'll ever get out of me. If I ever have to do it again, I'll deduct my fee from your pay."

At that moment, Varney forgot the girl and began to concentrate on Coleman. He was treating Varney as though he were some weak, inferior creature that he had the right to criticize or punish any time Varney displeased him. Varney began to see the events of the night differently. Coleman had not had to kill the girl just because Varney had made a small mistake. He had done it to exert control and stifle him. Coleman had sensed that Varney had taken pleasure in her, and Coleman had decided for that reason alone to find an excuse to take her away. Coleman was like a father who punished a child by strangling the kid's puppy in front of him.

As the car traversed the hot, flat country, Varney watched the telephone poles go past the window. Coleman was not the wise, generous professional who had taken Varney on as an apprentice. It had seemed that way at first, but from the beginning, the one who had done all the hard, dangerous work had been Varney. Coleman made a phone call or two, acted as Varney's driver and companion, then kept most of the money. Varney sat there quietly for the rest of the morning, staring out the window at the flat country. There was no reason to argue with Coleman about the girl, no reason to say anything at all. It was settled.

Varney came out of his reminiscence and pulled his car up onto the blacktop margin along the side of a gas station in south Buffalo. He got out, stood at the pay telephone, and opened the book to the yellow pages. There were dozens of hotels listed, but he could safely ignore most of them. He wrote down the addresses and phone numbers of the ten biggest and most expensive in town.

It was thinking about Coleman that had given him the idea. Whenever Coleman had come into a town, he had looked in the yellow pages to find the biggest and the best. Prescott was a lot like Coleman—tall and swaggering, with that cowboy accent and that way of insinuating that he knew everything. They were so much alike that sometimes, when Varney was remembering Coleman, he had caught himself letting Prescott's features merge with Coleman's to form a single face.

18

Prescott stepped into the hotel room and saw the little red light on the telephone dial flashing. He turned off the switch by the door to make the room go dark before he went to the telephone. He stood with his back to the wall where he could not be seen through the window, and lifted the receiver. If the man he was searching for had found the right hotel and used some trick to get the right room number, he could leave a message, train his rifle through the window on the phone, and win the easy way.

The computer voice said, "You have . . . one! . . . message." Prescott covered his free ear so he would not miss any vibration of the vocal cords, could judge the tightness of the throat, maybe even hear a background noise. A man who always made calls from pay telephones couldn't always control what went on around him.

The voice said, "Prescott, this is Millikan. I'll be in the bar downstairs at ten o'clock. Come see me." Prescott hung up, looked at his watch, left the room, and took the elevator down to the lobby. It was nearly eleven, but he didn't hurry to step into the bar. He went into the gift shop and bought a copy of the *Buffalo News,* studied the people passing in and out of the bar, studied the street outside the lobby. He scrutinized the faces of the young men who opened car doors for peo-

ple at the curb or carried their luggage. Then he stepped across the
lobby to the bar.

It was an old-fashioned, dark room with polished wood along the
walls, booths with red leather upholstery, and a few potted plants in
unlikely and inconvenient places. He saw Millikan from a distance
and had time to look at him as he walked in his direction. Millikan had
aged in ten years. The disappointed, liquid blue eyes looked as though
they were the same, but the desiccation that happened in middle age
had begun, and the skin looked loose and dry. Millikan's thick, wiry
hair had not receded. It still began too low on the forehead and covered his head like a bristly cap, but now it was mostly gray, and thin on
top. He had a big, thick manila envelope on the table under his forearm.

Prescott walked to the table and sat. Neither man smiled or offered
to shake hands. People at other tables in the dim, windowless room
would have assumed that they had last seen each other ten minutes
ago. Millikan said, "The police knew where you were staying."

Prescott nodded. "This wasn't a good time to come. He's out there
looking for me now."

Millikan rubbed his forehead in a gesture of frustration that Prescott recognized as a habit that had only gotten stronger over the years.
"What are you doing?"

"You know," said Prescott. "You have news?"

Millikan rubbed his forehead again, then left his elbow on the table
and leaned his cheekbone against his fist. "The police in Louisville
have been looking more closely at the victims. The first theory seems
to have been wrong."

Prescott kept his eyes on Millikan without showing much eagerness or interest. "Which one?"

"The intended victim. I mean the first one to be shot—Robert
Cushner Junior. It wasn't what everybody thought. He did have a new
computer-hardware breakthrough, and one of the big companies that
might have felt threatened by it did know about it. The Louisville police started at the top, with the intention of pressing executives to scare
them into cooperating. But all they had to do was ask, and the first one
produced a signed, witnessed, and notarized agreement. They had
bought his company. He was due to get a wire transfer of twenty mil-

lion dollars in cash and fourteen in stock. The transaction went through without a hitch even though he was dead."

Prescott shrugged. "So the company's out. What else are they looking at?"

"Nothing."

"Nothing?"

"They've done investigations on everybody who was there that night. They looked for anything odd at all: old gigs as witnesses or jurors, drug problems, gambling problems, debts, boundary disputes. They worked on the restaurant owner, rival establishments, distributors of liquor, food, and linen. Nothing."

Prescott said, "I still think Cushner's the victim."

"Oh, he's the victim," Millikan agreed. "Got to be."

Prescott stirred in his seat. "I appreciate your coming to tell me that the cops have eliminated a few things. Anything helps."

Millikan said, "You could wait for them. They'll find out who hired this guy. They may not be able to prove it, but they'll figure it out."

"Probably," said Prescott. "Someday."

"I'm doing my best to help them. The minute we get it, I'll tell you." Millikan looked as though he were trying to make himself understood in a foreign language. "You don't have to do it this way."

Prescott said, "If you do find out, I'll have a choice, won't I?"

The waitress stopped at their table, picked up Millikan's glass, and set a napkin in front of Prescott. "Another?" she asked, and Millikan nodded. "And what can I get you, sir?"

"Nothing, thanks," said Prescott. He was staring at Millikan. "I've got to do some driving tonight."

As she disappeared, Prescott leaned forward. "Do me a favor. Go home. This isn't what you do."

Millikan pushed the envelope across the table. "I brought you this."

"What is it?"

"It's why I came. The lieutenant sent me everything: copies of every report you don't already have, copies of all thirteen autopsies, every word the cops wrote down. It's all in there. I didn't want to mail it to some hotel and find out you'd already checked out."

Prescott pulled it across the table onto his lap, but he didn't open it. He looked into Millikan's tired, rheumy eyes.

"Thank you." He opened his folded newspaper and pushed a single stiff sheet of paper to Millikan.

Millikan turned it over and looked at the glossy surface of the photograph. In the dim light of the bar, he couldn't see the picture as clearly as he wanted to; his eyes hungrily traced the outlines. He could see this was a young man with dark hair, small, regular features, a thin nose and lips. The features that were unusual were the eyes. They made him want to hurry to the lobby and hold the picture under the light. They were cold, but they were not the dead, distant eyes of certain killers he had met in his work over the years. They were bright with an inner life that absolutely contradicted the expression of the lips, the unlined, untroubled forehead. It was a frightening picture. Millikan raised his eyes to meet Prescott's.

"That's all I have to give you in return just now," said Prescott. "If you see anybody that looks even a little bit like that, run like hell."

"Have you given this to the police?"

"No, but they've got nothing to worry about. He hasn't seen them on television. He has seen you."

Millikan watched Prescott step away from the table and disappear into the lobby.

It was two A.M. Prescott had read the police reports from the night of the shooting, the notes from the interviews and inquiries they had made about each of the victims. Then he had scanned the autopsy reports to see if there was anything about any of the bodies that would change his impression of what had happened in Louisville. There were surprises. They all concerned the young couple who had been killed together near the front of the restaurant.

The man's corpse had been lying on top of the woman's, the man obviously attempting to shield her from the shooting with his own body. The first story had been that the killer had stood over them and fired two times into the man's back, so that the bullets passed through him into her. But the autopsy on the man said he had one shot through the back, one through the back of the head. The woman had been shot three times—the two rounds that had passed through the man first, and once through her right side, just under the arm.

The police had interviewed members of both victims' families, a few friends, and the people who had worked with them. Nobody had been aware that this man and this woman had ever met each other. They had been in a small, intimate restaurant together for a late dinner, and when trouble had started, the woman had not cowered in a corner somewhere, and the man had neither fought nor run. He had thrown himself over her to keep her from being . . . Prescott stopped. Maybe she had already been hit.

He worked his way back through the police interviews. The man, Gary Finch, was unmarried, age twenty-eight. He worked as an auto mechanic for the Ford dealership down the street from the restaurant. He had showered, dressed in a coat and tie, and gone there for a late supper after work about twice a week.

Prescott looked at the papers on the woman to verify his first impression. She was Donna Halscy, age thirty-four. She was a stockbroker in the Louisville office of Dennison-Armistead. Prescott had a suspicion that began to grow as he scanned the interviews with people who knew her. It wasn't what they said that interested him—none of them seemed to know anything—but who they were. Her boss was a vice president. Her brother was a senior partner in a law firm that the local cops seemed to think was a big deal. Her friends, male and female, were all professional people of some kind—a pediatrician, an officer in a bank. She didn't seem to know anybody who wasn't about as well connected as you could be in a place like Louisville without owning a whole lot of land with horses on it.

Prescott went back to the interviews about the car mechanic. His friends all seemed to be guys who watched games with him, went fishing, went bowling. The cops had even gone to his high school and talked to a teacher and a guidance counselor.

Everybody used the word "nice." They talked about his sense of fun or his good nature. There were a couple of people who used the word "decent," as though to set him apart from somebody who was indecent. Everybody said he worked hard, but nobody said he was especially bright. He had no rap sheet with the local cops. Prescott turned to the autopsy again. He looked at the angles of the two shots, at the pictures of the entry and exit wounds. The coroner had agreed with Millikan and Prescott: he had been lying on the woman, and gotten shot at close range from above.

The exit wound in the face was so bad that a picture that had been taken while he was alive had been added to the file, so that the coroner could tell what he had looked like before. Prescott studied it for a moment, and his suspicion hardened. Prescott had been holding on to the possibility that the upper-class, educated, wealthy professional woman had taken her car in to the dealership to be fixed, seen this nice, manly young guy with a strong jaw, piercing eyes, and whatever else she liked. She would have said to herself, "Aw, what the hell," and gotten together with him, if only for a one-nighter. That would have explained why none of her friends had been aware of him. But Gary Finch was a nice guy, a steady guy, a funny guy, and at least once in his life, a brave guy. He was not a good-looking guy. He had a small, weak jaw that accentuated his double chin, a nose that had been broken a couple of times, and small, close-set eyes.

Prescott looked at Donna Halsey's photograph. She looked better in her autopsy photograph than most of the women he had seen alive on the streets in Louisville. She was slim, very blond, with hair tied back in a tight, shining ponytail. The suit she had been wearing would have looked good in Manhattan. He glanced at the coroner's shots of the corpse: unusually good body.

Prescott quickly set out all the photographs of the crime scene, and his suspicion was confirmed. The table of the first victim, Robert Cushner, had one plate of food on it, almost eaten; one set of silverware; two place mats. He looked closely at the other pictures, trying to determine what was on the tables near the bodies. The pair of men had just about finished eating. Their table was still full of plates and silverware. The table above Donna and Gary's bodies was a small one with two settings: one for a person sitting on the bench along the wall, and one for a person in a chair facing him. The others all seemed to match Prescott's expectations. It had been late. A whole section of the restaurant had already been unofficially closed down, with the tablecloths and settings taken up for the night. That was probably what the waiter killed in the kitchen had been doing. There was only one waiter still on duty serving customers, and the late people had been seated in a small area so he could reach them easily.

Prescott looked at the spot near the entrance where the manager, who had served as maître d', had fallen, and two customers had stepped over him to be shot trying to tug open the padlocked door. There was a table set for one. Prescott went back to the picture of Donna and Gary. There was a napkin on the floor beside Donna's hand. He patiently went back through the pictures, searching. In ten minutes, he knew.

Donna Halsey and Robert Cushner had been together for dinner at a table for two. It was late, and there was only one waiter on duty. He had served everybody, and now he was against the wall chatting with the manager while they waited to close up. In the kitchen, the cook had stopped making food some time ago, and had begun the cleanup. The other waiter had nearly finished clearing the tables.

At Robert Cushner and Donna Halsey's table, things were slower than at some of the others, but the party of two were nearly finished. It was easy to see what had happened. Donna Halsey took great care of her most crucial attribute, her looks. She had ordered something small and low calorie. Robert Cushner had a big slab of meat and a cloud-shaped pile of mashed potatoes. To make the inequity more pronounced, this was a guy who was full of himself. He had struck it rich a few days before. He was out with a very attractive young woman. He did most of the talking, while she gave him admiring glances and nodded her head a lot. Soon she was sitting before an empty plate.

The waiter had cleared her plate and silverware, and probably a wine glass, leaving her sitting with a napkin in her lap and a place mat, talking with Robert Cushner, the former computer guy, while he finished his entrée.

The killer stepped through the swinging door from the kitchen. He saw Cushner with a fork on the way to his mouth: *bang,* through the forehead. The killer had already seen the second half of his contract, and it took no time to move the gun to the left. Now Prescott saw it clearly. The second round was intended for the side of Donna Halsey's head, but the first shot had made her jump, rise from her chair with her napkin still on her lap. Instead of her right temple, it had hit her right side. The killer had not missed: Millikan and the police had not been wrong. But now other things were happening. People were in motion. The killer focused on the doorway, and took the easy shots like a harvest: the maître d', the two customers pulling on the door handle, the waiter. He had done all of that in four or five seconds, from just inside the door without moving his feet. He shot the two parents and the two little girls, then detected more motion in the corner of his eye, and turned his attention toward it.

The woman he had hit in the side had managed to take a couple of steps away from him. As she collapsed, Gary the mechanic tried to reach for her, then dropped to one knee to bend over her. He saw the killer take his first step toward her, and in a horrified, involuntary act, tried to hide and protect her by putting his own body over hers.

The killer took one, two, three steps, and aimed downward. Shot one went through the man's head. Shot two went to his back. Both of them had gone through into the woman. The killer could see she was dead.

He looked to his right, gathered up the two spent casings on the floor, and put them into his pocket. Then he walked back toward the kitchen door. The rounds he had fired before were all in the same area: one for Cushner, the male target at the first table, one for Donna Halsey. One for the maître d', one for the waiter, three for the pair of diners at the door. Four for the family. He picked up the shells, turned off the lights, stepped through the kitchen, carefully staying out of the stream of blood running across the tiles into the drain. He replaced the empty clip in his gun, stepped out, closed the steel door behind him, and walked off, feeling a growing elation as each step took him farther away and deeper into the darkness. He had gotten it done with incredible efficiency and speed, and left nothing to indicate who had done it.

He had fulfilled the contract—gotten both of them. The client would be pleased. Prescott considered who that might be. Maybe it was the wife, whose husband had just made twenty million but hadn't yet gotten around to telling her because he was too busy celebrating with another woman. Prescott would have to look into that. The man had been first, but the one shot three times was the woman. Sometimes it was worth stopping just to count.

Prescott stacked the pictures and reports neatly, reinserted them into the envelope, and put the envelope into his suitcase. He began to fold his clothes and put them on top. He thought about his decision to begin the long drive tonight, and decided he still liked the idea. At night there would not be much traffic, and by sunup he could be half-way to Louisville. He had given the picture to Millikan, so there was no reason to stay in Buffalo. By morning Millikan would have given the picture to the police with a big lecture on how important it was, and sometime tomorrow the killer would be gone.

19

Varney saw the black of night beginning to fade into a dim blue, the big old trees and the shrubs and lawns of Delaware Avenue lightening to green again. In about forty-five minutes the sun would be up, and the people who had vacated the streets of the city for him would be climbing into their cars to infest the world again. He had not found Prescott.

The way Prescott had stayed invisible was not mysterious: all he had needed to do was use a false name to register in a hotel and stay there. But Varney had not expected him to do that. All night long, he had expected Prescott to be around the next corner, or waiting inside one of Varney's haunts, or sitting in his car outside one of the downtown hotels, waiting for Varney to try to find him.

Varney wasn't even sure why he had expected Prescott to appear during the night. He decided it was that he had gotten used to a rhythm, like the rhythm of two men in a fistfight. At first they had danced around a bit, made a few feints and jabs. Then Varney had tried to win the quick way—not an exploratory tap, but committing himself to a sudden, hard attack that would take Prescott before he was ready for anything serious. Prescott had been ready to brush it aside, and the counterpunch had been immediate. Varney had gotten used to a pace that was fast and intense, based on heart rate and the adrenaline that had already infused both of them. But Prescott had unexpectedly dodged, and now he was dancing again, out of reach and gathering his strength.

That bothered Varney. He had been awake for two nights, struggling and maneuvering to move in on Prescott, wasting his anger and determination. He had spent the night exhausting himself, and Prescott had been in some hotel sleeping on crisp, clean sheets and getting stronger and sharper for their next encounter.

Varney stopped at a gas station to fill his tank, drove back to his house, and went upstairs. He showered and lay on his bed. The sounds of cars began to reach him from the street outside, a low, steady hum that was usually soothing. This morning it irritated him, because it reminded him that he was used up, and the rest of the world was in motion. Prescott would be getting up fresh and rested, probably putting some new scheme into operation. Prescott and the police, and all the forces of pursuit and punishment, would be talking and planning and putting themselves into position, while Varney was here alone, unconscious in a room with the shades drawn. He rolled over, couldn't get comfortable, couldn't get his mind to stop foraging for things to worry it.

Varney sat up and looked at the clock. It was six o'clock already. He reached for the remote control and turned on the television set. The head and shoulders that came on belonged to a woman about his age who had perfected that dumb, teasing, "I know something you wish you knew" look. She was saying, "You'll hear if this morning's humid weather might surprise us with a change later in the day. We'll have footage of a melee outside last night's school board meeting, a three-alarm fire in Cheektowaga, and a picture of a man the police would like your help in finding. We'll be right back!"

Varney moved to the foot of his bed and put his feet on the floor. The first commercial was for cars. He had seen it at least a hundred times, and it had annoyed him the first time. There was a commercial for a financial-services company that couldn't quite reveal what it was selling but featured close-up shots of people who looked sick with worry. Then there were a few shorter ones that seemed to have been recorded with a home video camera to advertise a florist, a Lebanese restaurant, and a company that sold appliances but seemed to think that today air conditioners were the only ones people wanted to hear about.

At last, the woman reappeared, sitting behind a desk with a pile of papers in front of her and a pen in her hand. As the camera moved in on her, she said, "Buffalo police have released a picture this morning of a man they want to question in connection with a bombing at a Cumberland Avenue building. He is between twenty-five and thirty years old, six feet tall, and weighs about one hundred and seventy-five pounds."

There was the picture: Varney, staring out of his television set at him. The extreme definition of the color image that Prescott had somehow gotten made Varney's face as clear as the woman's on the television screen.

His stomach tightened in a spasm. He was up, stalking the room as the woman continued. "If you know this man or have seen him, call the special hot-line number at the bottom of your screen. Police have emphasized that he is armed and very dangerous. If you should see him, they ask that you do not approach or attempt to detain him. Instead, dial 911, and let them handle the situation." She took the sheet from the top of her pile and set it aside, giving her special disapproving look. Suddenly she smiled, and turned her head to the side. "And I see Hal Kibbleman has joined us to give a hint of what he has in store for us in the weather department. Are you going to keep us in suspense, Hal?"

Varney punched the power button and the woman vanished. He went to the closet and began to pack. The house deed had a false name on it, and his habits had kept him from being too much in the sight of people in the neighborhood. He had been gone much of the time since he'd bought it, and when he had been here he had stayed out of synchronization with the people who got up in the morning to go to work. It might take Prescott and the police some time to find the house.

When his suitcase was packed, he put it into a plastic trash bag so it would look as though he were simply taking out the garbage when he brought it outside. He considered leaving a booby trap to welcome the

inevitable intruders—maybe using the natural-gas pipe and an electrical switch—but that would be time-consuming, and it would involve
a kind of concentration that didn't fit his mood right now. As he
thought about it, he realized that he wouldn't get much pleasure out
of it, and it might not even be practical. The police had him firmly in
their minds as the mad bomber of Buffalo, so an explosion was precisely what they would be expecting. He was better off getting out of
here, letting them find the place, and leaving nothing around that was
especially incriminating or revealing. He was certain he could accomplish that, because he had always planned to leave that way. He had
stored his guns and ammunition in this single room. As soon as he
had used one on a job, he had gotten rid of it before he came back to
Buffalo.

At the moment, the house contained no more firearms than many
of the houses in this city: a Steyr Scout short-barreled rifle with a ten-
power scope, a Remington Model 70 hunting rifle in .308, and three
nine-millimeter pistols. He had thirty rounds of ammunition for each
firearm. Two nights ago, he had used up his supply of black powder,
blasting caps, and pipes for the bombs. All he had left were two rolls of
copper wire and a couple of homemade switches. He put them into a
second garbage bag with the guns, carried everything out to the car,
and returned.

He spent twenty minutes checking to be sure the timers were set
right, the faucets were closed on the hoses to the washing machine,
the windows locked. He wiped the smooth surfaces with a rag to
make the collection of fingerprints a bit more difficult. He had been
careful since he had moved into the house to keep out of the dummy
apartment downstairs, and had regularly wiped down the items in the
upstairs apartment that he habitually touched. He was fairly certain
that a real expert would find some prints, but it would take time, and
there would be old prints that belonged to other people mixed in.

He went to the desk and collected all the paper. As a habit, he saved
very few receipts or bills, and he kept them all in the same place. He
used a post office box for his mailing address, so nothing came here.
All of his precautions were tempered by the knowledge that a genuine
expert could not be fooled forever if he were ever turned loose in this
house. Varney could not keep him from connecting the house with a

name or two and maybe the post office box, but he could make each step maddeningly complicated and eat up lots of hours making the expert follow trails that didn't lead to an actual man.

He did one last check and closed the door, holding the knob with the rag in his hand. He got into his car and drove onto the street, eager to get out of Buffalo. Varney knew that the police would already have given his picture to the agencies they habitually dealt with: the Canadian officials across the bridges over the Niagara, the New York State Police, and the local cops all over this area. He stayed away from the border and avoided the Thruway, with its entrance and exit booths. He drove the secondary roads. He followed Main Street until it was just Route 5, and then it merged into Route 20. This part of the state was the bed of an ancient, larger great lake, scraped smooth and flat by glaciers. The roads were straight and broad and fast.

As soon as he was outside Buffalo, passing through old towns that had become suburbs, he began to feel slightly better. If he could just stay awake and keep driving for a few hours, the trouble would fall behind. He had spent years studying the habits of pursuers. He knew that the only nationwide manhunts were a creation of television networks. Policemen were municipal employees who answered to city councils selected by local taxpayers. The only time they paid much attention to what was going on in some other city was when they had strong reasons to believe that an identifiable man was about to arrive in their town to kill somebody in particular. The circulars and wanted lists came in by the thousands from distant places, and piled up until they were filed away. Pretty soon, all the faces looked alike.

In a half hour he was nearly thirty miles from the house approaching Silver Creek, and while he thought about that, he had traveled two more and gone past it. He was cruising along at fifty-five miles an hour without a traffic signal to delay him, and the nearest cars a quarter mile ahead or a quarter mile behind. The drivers couldn't actually see him: he was just an assumption they made because a car couldn't be moving along a public highway without a driver.

After an hour, he knew that he was out. The open roads were beginning to be more open, with long stretches of farmland that didn't seem to have anybody in evidence to work it. There were small clusters of buildings at crossroads that did not deserve to be called villages: they seemed to exist only as excuses to have a lower speed limit for a hundred yards so people driving past could read homemade signs that said FRESH STRAWBERRIES or CORN, or have time to notice that there was a gas station on the corner.

Varney kept going. He wanted to give himself enough breathing space, and he knew he wouldn't have it until he had gone far enough to be out of the range of Buffalo's television stations and in the zone of some other city's stations, where somebody else's picture would be on the news.

Varney tried to make himself feel better. He had been the one who had gone after Prescott, and he was still healthy, still free, still anonymous. He had gone right into Prescott's trap and come out of it unharmed. Reminding himself of those things did not help. Prescott had hounded him out of Buffalo: Prescott had made him run away.

He let the car slow down a bit, toying with the idea of going back. Prescott wasn't some petty irritant. When he thought of Prescott, his stomach tightened, his heart began to pound, and after a minute, his jaw began to hurt from clenching his teeth. It wasn't only what Prescott had done, it was what Prescott was, and what he thought. When Varney had listened to him talk he had felt it instantly. Prescott was so sure of himself, so full of confidence that he was better than Varney— the tone of his voice said, "Well, look at us, the two of us. It's pretty obvious, isn't it?"—that Varney had found himself tense, coiled to spring at him, even though he was miles away and the only connection was an electrical impulse over a telephone wire.

Varney sensed something else about Prescott, and he wasn't quite able to grasp it. Prescott was an impostor. He was a fake; the personality was something assumed in order to fool Varney. It was as though he had constructed an identity, a false one, just to use against Varney. Maybe it was only that he wasn't as fearless or as invulnerable as he pretended to be: like a bully who sensed some weakness in a smaller kid and set about systematically probing to find out what it was, tormenting him by building himself up and making the victim feel smaller. But Varney had been getting a strange feeling that maybe Prescott was something else: that the face he had constructed was there to make him look more ordinary than he was—that he was actually worse than he seemed, and that if he showed his real face, Varney would dismiss the idea of fighting and escape him.

Sometimes it felt to Varney that Prescott was a man that he hated not just because he was an enemy, but because he was familiar. It was as though Prescott were the vague, dark presence that he had sensed just out of sight, that he knew was coming for him, or sometimes was just forming, coalescing, when he awoke, sweating, from a bad dream.

Varney drove across the line into Pennsylvania, and a couple of miles beyond, before he realized that he had done it. Being in a new state made him much safer, but he refused to let himself be reassured. He was going to be smart this time. He would keep going into Ohio, and try to get as close to Cincinnati as he could before he slept.

He crossed the border before noon, and made Cleveland an hour later. He stopped there for a hamburger and some coffee, then got on Route 71 and drove south toward Columbus. It was over 140 miles away, but when he arrived, he stopped at a gas station, filled the tank, and bought some more coffee. Cincinnati was now just a bit over a hundred miles away.

It was evening before Varney reached the edge of Cincinnati. He was so tired he had begun to feel dizzy. He knew he needed to stop somewhere and sleep, but he had to take a look at the office building first, just to convince himself that it was still there. He drove through the streets, heading vaguely toward the river until he reached Colerain Avenue and let it take him to the center of the city.

He drove past the building slowly. The old two-story structure had been built in an era when it probably hadn't seemed odd for a commercial building to have a peaked roof like a house, and there had been no compelling reason to build higher, at least in this part of town. But the place was better than it looked: the rooms inside had hardwood floors and big, solid doors, and the red-brick facade was dirty but intact. Varney could see nothing about the place or the streets around it that had changed since he'd last seen it.

He had been here only twice before, with Coleman. The first time, Coleman had warned him. "They're going to be friendly, and easy to get along with, but don't let yourself get too comfortable, and don't mouth off to Mama."

"Mama?"

"Yeah, and don't call her that." Coleman blew out a breath impatiently, in that way he had of signifying that everything he said was something any sensible person should already know but somehow

Varney didn't. "Her name is Tracy. She's the one you have to pay attention to. She has three sons, Roger, Nick, and Marty, and they're the
ones who run the business. All she runs is them."

"You mean they're a bunch of Mama's—"

"No, that ain't what I mean," Coleman interrupted. "Any one of
them would cut you just for the fun of seeing you bleed and dance
around, and that's the problem. They can't trust each other, don't
even seem to like each other much. They're about a year or two apart
in age, so I don't even know which is older. They all had different fa-
thers, and even God doesn't know where they are or what became of
any of them. The boys each know that the others won't listen to them,
but that they will listen to her. She's what keeps them from turning on
each other. Maybe they like her, or think she's smart or something. Or
maybe she's just a convenience, so they can work together. I don't
know, and I don't care."

Varney had followed Coleman up the stairs and into the carpeted
hallway. As he passed each door, he read the sign on it: CHOW IM-
PORTERS, LTD., RECTANGLE TRAVEL, PINEHILL REALTY SERVICES, CREST-
VIEW WHOLESALE. Coleman did not stop until he reached the
Crestview Wholesale door. Coleman knocked, then entered, and Var-
ney went in with him.

The woman sitting behind the desk was peculiar. She had the hair,
the makeup, and the body of a woman about thirty-five years old, but
there was a wrinkling about the pale, almost transparent skin of her
bare neck and hands that struck him. It was not so much a contradiction as a warning, like a slight puckering on a peach that told him the
fruit had been offered for sale much, much longer than it was supposed to be.

"Sugar!" she shrieked. She got up, tottered around the desk on high
heels, smiled, and kissed Coleman on the cheek. "I'm so sorry to make
you come all the way here for your money, but Roger and Marty and
Nicky can't get away just now, with all the salespeople already on the
road, and—"

"It's okay," said Coleman unconvincingly. "I don't mind a bit."

She smiled in a way that would have been—and maybe once had
been—kittenish, but struck Varney as mentally deranged. "I knew
you'd understand." Then her eyes passed across Varney on their way

somewhere else, and she stopped, brought them back, and looked him up and down. "You brought him?"

Coleman nodded, and to Varney it seemed a reluctant nod.

"This is him." To Varney he said, "Say hello to Tracy."

"Pleased to meet you," Varney murmured.

Her eyes seemed to glow for an instant, then to fade again. "Oh, you're just right," she said. "A cop would run right over you without even stepping on the brakes because he didn't notice you were there." Then she half-turned and said in a stage whisper, "Besides, you're cute." She continued the turn and went to a filing cabinet across the room, unlocked it, pulled a thick envelope out of one of the files, and handed it to Coleman.

Tonight Varney could see lights on in the upper windows. He made a quick decision, stopped the car a block past the building, and walked back. He climbed the stairs and knocked on the door that said CREST-VIEW WHOLESALE, then entered. Tracy was sitting at the desk. When she looked up, she took a moment to focus on his face, then stood. "Sugar!" she squealed, and hurried toward him on her spike heels, her arms extended toward him for a hug.

20

Prescott sat in the window of his rented room and watched Wendy Cushner. He knew she was thirty-four, but she had the kind of face that might have been any age from twenty to forty, a small, unlined round face with light skin and a few freckles She was wearing shorts that were neither revealing nor fashionable, a pair of sneakers with no socks, and a T-shirt that was too big for her.

She was filling a small wading pool with water from a hose, her eyes turned down at the blue vinyl bottom of the pool as though she saw something in the water, or maybe just looked for it there because it wasn't anywhere else. She didn't look like a woman who had been left with thirty-four million dollars. She looked like a woman who had just been left.

She and Prescott had a secret that the rest of the people in the world she inhabited did not seem to suspect. She turned off the hose and disappeared into the back door of the low, rambling brick ranch house. A few minutes later, she came out again holding a girl of about four by the hand, and carrying a boy in her left arm who must have been about one. They both had light purple bathing suits—the girl's with a ruffled skirt around the hips, and Prescott could see that the smaller one's rear end was padded with a diaper and plastic pants. Wendy held the little boy over the pool, bending at the hips as women did, so the baby could touch his toes in the cool water. The baby started to laugh and began to run in place, only his toes brushing the surface, until his mother lowered him into the water and he spent a moment feeling the cold creep into his suit. His big sister unceremoniously stepped in and sat down with a splash.

As they played, Prescott noted the appearance of brightly colored plastic objects from a small tub by the pool: boats, ducks, a whale, a bucket. Wendy retreated a bit after a few minutes and sat on the back steps, where Prescott could watch her watching her children.

He had been here for two weeks observing her to determine whether she had paid to have her husband shot through the forehead. At first he had been surprised when he had not detected any sign that the Louisville police were doing the same, but he had welcomed the freedom it gave him in his work. He had already eliminated a few of the signs he had been searching for.

Prescott had seen no indication that she had taken a lover. He had followed her whenever she went out, and found himself not at hotels or restaurants or houses but at a wilting succession of supermarket parking lots, a nursery school where she took the older kid three mornings a week, and a couple of shopping malls where she made relatively brief visits to stores that sold children's clothes and toys.

He had watched her house at night with an infrared scope and listened with an X-phone, an electronic device about the size of a deck of cards that he had plugged into an unused phone jack in her bedroom. Whenever it heard anyone come up the stairs near the room, it silently dialed Prescott's telephone number.

When he lifted his receiver, he could hear everything happening within thirty-five feet of Wendy Cushner's bed. He had learned that she went to sleep at ten and was up at five-thirty with the boy, followed at about six-thirty by the older girl. The only visitors were women about her own age, usually with children in tow, her in-laws, a woman who looked as though she might be a younger sister, and an older woman who had to be her mother, Mrs. Hayes.

Prescott had seen no sign that she had yet taken any notice that she was a rich woman. She had a cleaning woman who came in two days a week to wash floors and windows. When he had understood the schedule, he had searched harder for the lover. A woman with thirty-four million could afford a lot of help, but a woman with any calculation at all would know that she could not hide the existence of a man from another woman who cleaned her house each day. Prescott devoted another week to watching, and found no lover.

Prescott tired of watching Wendy Cushner at about the same time that the children got tired of the water. When she scooped them out, one at a time, wrapped them in towels, and took them in, it was a relief to him.

Prescott had examined Wendy Cushner's credit reports, searched the Louisville and Jefferson County records for any criminal or civil decisions involving Wendy Hayes, and looked for any close relative who might ever have been involved in any court proceeding. He had checked the archives of the Louisville *Courier-Journal* for the high school graduation announcements printed in the spring of her senior year, and found the names of others who had graduated in the same class. He had tracked down a few and called them, pretending to be a reporter. The ones who would talk at all seemed to be primarily interested in making sure no one had said anything negative about her.

On the first Sunday Prescott was in town, he went to the Methodist church where Robert Cushner's funeral had been held, but Wendy Cushner was not there. He went again the next Sunday, and saw her father-in-law, the man who had hired him. Prescott had sat in the back where Cushner would not see him, then made sure that as soon as Dr. Stevenson, the minister, had pronounced the benediction, he was on his way out the door.

Prescott kept up his observation and widened his research for three more days. Then one day he waited until midmorning, when the older child was in nursery school and the younger was in the back bedroom for a nap. He walked around the block to the front of her house, and knocked on her door.

She opened it only a few inches, with a bit of the trepidation that a woman alone often displayed when a strange man came to the door. "Hi, can I help you?"

"I'm Roy Prescott," he said. "I'm the man your father-in-law hired to find the killer."

She looked at him with a mixture of alarm and exasperation, but she let him in. Wendy Cushner was not an especially neat housekeeper, and she was not apologetic about it. The living room had a few of the kids' toys in unlikely places. She simply picked up a doll from the couch, told him to sit where it had been, set it on the coffee table, and sat down across from him. Close up, she looked tired and sad and worn.

He patiently lulled her by asking the questions he knew that she would have already been asked. They were about the enemies her husband might have had, the strangers she might have noticed near the house in the days before the crime, the worries her husband might have mentioned to her. She answered that nothing had come to her attention. He asked about the possibility that a business competitor might have ordered her husband's death. She answered the question truthfully: she didn't believe that could have happened. He had already sold his business before he was killed.

Prescott took that in and kept asking other questions, always sympathetically. After a time he left. The next day, he came again, and asked more questions. He came several times, always speaking gently and patiently, always careful to tell her things that he knew, so she would come to feel that they were sharing information. On the first day, he'd told her what the local police had told Millikan, and what Millikan had seen in the restaurant. On another day, he'd told her about his conversations with the killer, and what they had made him believe about the man. After a few days, he was sure he had convinced her he liked her and felt sorry for her. He left her alone for a couple of days, and kept her under even closer surveillance. Then he was ready for his final visit.

He waited until they were settled in the living room, then said, "I'm afraid that this time I've got a hard question. The police will eventually get to it, so we might as well do it now. It's about Donna Halsey."

He paused, and watched her face grow still and rigid, then begin to waver and get a rubbery look around the mouth. Her eyes were wet, not weeping, but watering as though she had been hit in the face. She said, "You know about Donna Halsey?"

He said, "I figured it out a couple of weeks ago. How long have you known?"

"I never did know. I thought . . . I didn't think he would do that."

Prescott said, "You mean you found out after he was dead?"

She nodded. "He said he was working that night. It was something about trying to get the bugs out of a program to get it ready for production so he could introduce it in some computer show. The show was going to be in—like—January. He lied. He knew that by January the company would already have belonged to somebody else for months. He already hadn't owned it for a week."

"You didn't know he'd sold the company," Prescott said.

"No," she said. "He didn't think I was even listening to what he said about staying late that night. It was just a bunch of words, plausible because they were words he had used a lot. But it's amazing, isn't it? I remembered exactly what he said."

"Did you know the marriage was in trouble?"

"No." Then she shivered, as though she were shaking off something that had clung to her, like dirt. "That's not true. We argued a lot . . . not always out loud. He wasn't happy with the way things were."

Prescott was silent, not even pretending to understand. He just waited, and she spoke again.

"I didn't get it," she said. "I mean, I understood the words he was saying, but I didn't understand that he meant them, exactly as he said them. I thought he was just complaining, whining for attention, like the kids do. What he was doing was something more. Sometimes I think it was his fault for letting it go, saying something and then not saying anything again for a month or two, so that I didn't take it seriously enough. Sometimes I think if he hadn't mentioned anything— just kept his mouth shut—then in time everything would have been okay by itself. I was busy from dawn to dusk with the kids, and cooking and shopping and the stuff that you have to do just to be a family. I was tired, and half the time I was frantic."

She stopped and looked at Prescott with the purest expression of sadness and regret he had seen in years. "He didn't threaten me, or say, 'If you don't start paying attention to me, I'll find somebody who will, beginning next Thursday.' See, in life it would be a lot better if there were big signs that popped up at important times and said, 'Hey! Drop everything and handle this. You're fighting for your life now!' There isn't anything like that. Everything comes at you at once, and you do your best, and then you find out you picked the wrong thing." She was crying now. "I did that. I kept this house as neat as a pin. I took wonderful care of the children. I did everything, volunteered for everything at the school, the church, helped friends and relatives. I cooked nice meals, I . . ." She seemed to hear her own voice and not want to go on.

Prescott prompted her. "Did you ever meet Donna Halsey?"

"I knew Donna Halsey as well as he did. As soon as I learned she was one of the ones who got killed, I said, 'Who was she with?' She would never, in a million years, have gone into that restaurant by herself. The police were positive she was with that man Gary Finch, but I didn't believe it. There was only one person there that she could have been with." She sobbed. "Even my mother knew it."

"Your mother?"

"She had warned me, at least two years ago. She got the feeling one day that things weren't quite the same between me and Bobby. It was something she saw in his face one night when he was talking to me. She sat me down the next day and said, 'It's none of my business, but is everything okay?' I told her she was right: it was none of her business. But she wouldn't give up. She was sitting right where you are. She looked around, not in my eyes, and said, 'You're a good house-keeper. You're a better mother than I was. You're a terrific cook. But I'm going to say one thing because you're also the best daughter in the world and I love you. In the history of the world, no man ever left his wife because some other woman was a better cook, or was more eager about setting the food on the table, or arranging it more attractively on the plate. The way to a man's heart is not through his stomach, it's a bit south of there.' Then she stood up and left. You have to know my mother. She'd never said anything like that in her life. I saw her blush in church one time when the minister read some passage about some-body's loins. But as soon as Bobby was dead, and the paper printed the names of the other people who had been in the restaurant, she knew. She has never said anything about warning me, just come and tried to help me and be sympathetic. But what she said will always be there between us, just lying there. She was right, and I didn't take it to heart."

"I'm sorry you ever had to find out," said Prescott. "It serves no purpose. But I've got to say that you're being too hard on yourself. You have nothing to blame yourself for. You weren't the one who did this. He was."

She sighed, then sobbed a little, so her breath came out shivery and choked. She said, "He paid for being tempted. I'm paying for being stupid." She squinted. "He wasn't bad. Nobody but me can really know that. He loved us. He would have stayed faithful—had been faithful for twelve years, before this. I told myself after it happened what a bastard he was, what a pig, what a rat. The truth is, he wasn't."

Prescott said, "I believe you. People make mistakes, and usually they get the chance to make up for them. If he had been given the chance, I'm sure he would have gotten over Donna Halsey pretty quickly, and your marriage would have been fine."

As he spoke, she began to shake her head irritably. "I'll show you something." She got up and went to a kitchen drawer, and pulled out a piece of paper. She came back and handed it to him.

Prescott took it into his hand, and he could feel that the stiffness was already going out of the paper because she had held it in her hand so many times, folded and unfolded it. The letter was a memorandum of agreement between Vitaltrex Corporation and her husband to transfer his company for $20 million in cash and $14 million in Vitaltrex stock. The entire sum was to be paid to Wendy Cushner. "How did you get this?"

"I found it in his dresser a couple of days after he died. He never showed it to me."

"Do you think he changed his mind?"

"He didn't change his mind. He wouldn't have changed his mind. The marriage was over."

"How do you know?"

"The house. I got the new deed. It had been changed to be only in my name. At first I thought that somehow the county did that kind of thing the minute somebody died, and I just hadn't heard of it before. But then the lawyer called to arrange the bank-account stuff to put the money from the sale of the company into my account, and he told me. After that I found this copy." She took it and folded it up. "The lawyer finally admitted that he had been drawing up divorce papers, too. Bobby was going to give me everything and then get a divorce. That was how he was."

Prescott said quietly, "I'm sorry I had to ask those questions. I had just figured out that with the Vitaltrex Corporation cleared of the murders, the next best suspect was, sooner or later, going to be you. Keep all the papers connected with the sale, and the house transfer, and make sure that the lawyer who arranged them is easy to reach, and you should be fine."

"I'll be . . . fine." The words brought the tears that had been waiting, and she shook her head, but they kept coming. "I'm thirty-four years old, and my husband got killed on a date with another woman. A date. For the rest of my life, I'm going to have in the back of my mind that the only man I loved got killed because he couldn't get laid at home. Not because he wasn't interested in me anymore—because, God knows, he tried enough times—but because I was too tired, from making casseroles for church suppers or taking care of other women's kids so their husbands could take them out, or something. And just to make things more comfortable, pretty soon everybody on the planet is going to know it." She muttered, "Yeah, I'll be just fine."

"You said you knew Donna Halsey. Is there any chance that anybody was angry enough with her to hire a killer?"

Wendy Cushner shrugged her shoulders. "I don't know. You mean maybe another wife, like me?" She sighed. "She's not my favorite person right now, but I didn't think about her at all before. We were friends, sort of, in high school. She was one of those people that other girls don't care much for but find it convenient to pretend they do. She was a cheerleader, and in the clubs most people couldn't get into, and she had nicer clothes than the rest of us, and so on. That was a long time ago."

"What happened after that?"

She shook her head in frustration. "I don't know much. I heard about her once in a while. We went off to college. Both of us married soon after graduation. She sold real estate for her father's company. Then I heard she sold stocks and bonds. Her marriage broke up." She sat in silence for a few seconds, then said, "I hate her. She's dead, and I hate her."

"I don't blame you," Prescott said. "Right now, you probably don't believe your feelings will change, but they will. It won't ever feel good to think about her, but you'll find that it happens less often."

"I don't hate her for wanting him. I hate her because she was smarter than I was. She saw that I was throwing something away that was a hundred times more important than anything I was keeping, so she twitched her butt a couple of times and picked it up, just like that. For a few days after he died, I thought maybe the word had leaked out that he had sold the company and was going to have big money. It hadn't. It was just a lie I wanted to believe. All that really happened was that she was a lot smarter than I was. She had been married to a guy named Carter Rowland when we were twenty-two. He was an older guy. He had money. In those days, Bobby and I didn't, and neither did anybody else our age, so it was just another thing to make everybody jealous of Donna. A few years ago, I heard she was divorced, and had come out of it with a lot of the money. Some people said most of it."

"Where did the money come from?" asked Prescott.

"I don't know anything, really," she said. "People talk, and if they know somebody took a drink, all of a sudden he was drunk. Rowland is in the jewelry business, so I suppose he sold somebody something that wasn't worth what he said. Personally, I can't tell a diamond from a piece of glass, and I know that a lot of people who think they can are fooling themselves. It's not important. She had been married to a man who wasn't nice to her. She saw that I had a perfectly good one, a wonderful, sweet, hard-working man, and I wasn't smart enough to keep him."

"If she had it to do over again, she'd leave him alone," Prescott reminded her. "Being there with him got her killed."

"Don't you see?" Wendy said. "Donna wasn't the cause of this. She wanted what everybody wants. She was just the one who was in that place at the time. The one who would do things differently is me. He didn't want anything different from what I wanted myself. I just thought all those other things I was doing were more important—no, more urgent, that they had to be done first. And second hardly ever came. Now that I look back, I can't even remember what all those things that seemed so important were. I'm positive that nobody remembers I was the one who did them, and if I hadn't, nobody would miss them. Donna wasn't important. If it hadn't been her it would have been somebody else. She was pretty and available, but so are lots of other women. If I hadn't put him off and pushed him away, it wouldn't have mattered what she was, because he wouldn't have noticed."

Prescott glanced at his watch and stood up. "Wendy, I'm sorry I had to bother you again with this, and I appreciate your telling me the truth. I'll try to make sure you never see me again." He went to the door, and let himself out.

21

The sign above the building had tiny white lights arranged in elaborate italic script, so the letters sparkled: *Rowland's Fine Jewelry.* The painted motto underneath said, "Make her happy as a bride . . . all over again. The anniversary diamond collection by Rowland Limited."

Along the front was a row of small, square windows like openings into miniature worlds, one where velvet necks were strung with diamond necklaces and velvet hands wore diamond rings, another where posts wore expensive watches, and one where red, blue, and green stones that had tumbled from a treasure chest served as a background for gold chains. But the fourth and fifth were the ones that caught Prescott's attention. The small engraved signs behind the two glass panes said ESTATE JEWELRY.

Estate jewelry was trade jargon for anything that was secondhand. Most jewelry stores had some of it. But this merchandise was unusual. There was a yellow diamond bracelet with stones that started at chips and went all the way up to two carats. There was a ring in a brand-new setting that had an emerald the size of a dime. People who owned jewelry like that might sell it, but when they did, they probably didn't come to Louisville, Kentucky, to sell it to Rowland's. They would have a better market in New York or San Francisco. And most certainly, they didn't melt down antique settings and put big stones in new ones. It was a fairly common thing to do if the merchandise had been stolen.

Prescott was beginning to feel a sharpening of his interest in Mr. Rowland. The estate jewelry was too good, and there was too much of it for a city this size. Prescott began to entertain the idea that some of it was stolen. If so, these pieces could not have been stolen in the town where he was offering them for sale. It was too risky. That meant Rowland was dealing with some larger group that was capable of buying them in one town and distributing them in places where they wouldn't be recognized.

Part of Prescott's resistance to the idea that Wendy Cushner had hired the killer to get rid of her newly rich husband had been that he couldn't find a reasonable way that she could have found her way to a killer. She had apparently spent all her time taking care of her kids and doing volunteer work. She had no lovers, no male relatives who had been involved in illegal activities, no old boyfriends who might have been able to introduce her to a killer for old times' sake. When a middle-class woman decided to hire a killer, she couldn't just look in the yellow pages. In Prescott's experience, such a woman always needed the help of a go-between. Usually it was a man who had a reason to take a risk for her and knew somebody who claimed to know a man who was in the business of putting holes in people so the blood would run out. Half the time, the go-between managed to offer an envelope full of cash to an undercover cop, and everybody got to see himself on a grainy videotape in a courtroom.

Watching Wendy Cushner had not changed Prescott's opinion. She had done nothing that would indicate guilt. The most important thing she had not done was pay attention to the money. People who were willing to kill for money were sometimes smart enough to convey innocence, but they were seldom good enough to convincingly feign indifference to money. The reason they killed for money was that they respected it. They thought that having money made them important, attractive, clever, worthy. When they had the money, they showed it in small ways, subtle changes in posture or tone. Wendy Cushner did not betray any interest in the money, and she certainly did not imagine that it added anything to her list of accomplishments.

She had declared herself a failure at the part of life that she had made her specialty: being Mrs. Cushner. To her the money was a bitter irony, and maybe even an insult. Before his death, her husband had been planning to toss all of it to her as the price of getting free of her.

Wendy Cushner had not hired the killer. She had not known enough about her husband's activities to be jealous, and the money had not been a reason to kill him. She was not the sort of person who could have found her way to the man who had committed the murders in the restaurant. But Carter Rowland was beginning to look as though he might know some people who could have provided an introduction. Prescott considered how to go about learning more about him.

He began with the legal papers. The papers filed in divorces were in the public records, and Prescott subscribed to Internet services that provided them. He went to a big copying store that offered the use of computers, entered a cubicle, called up one of his services, and got a copy of *Donna Halsey Rowland* v. *Carter Wilson Rowland*. He requested copies of any other civil matters that involved Carter Rowland or Rowland's Fine Jewelry, and finally, any criminal proceedings in which Rowland had been named as defendant or co-defendant.

There had been no criminal proceedings. The civil suits were all ones in which Rowland was the plaintiff. As Prescott studied the filings, he wondered whether Rowland had sued everyone he had ever dealt with. He had sued the man who owned the building next to his for renting the space to a secondhand clothing business that was "inconsistent with oral agreements to maintain a high standard of commerce and clientele." He had sued a woman who lived in his neighborhood for putting a satellite dish on her roof that interfered with his view; another neighbor for "inducing stress and a threat to his health by causing loud music to be played." He had filed a defamation-of-character suit against a customer who had complained about a cracked emerald that had been repaired with a chemical bond.

Prescott went through all of the cases and found that there had never been significant sums of money involved. Rowland was simply a man who must have been pissed off most of the time. He was vengeful, and he was accustomed to paying large amounts of money to law firms so they would carry out his revenge.

Prescott began to pay closer attention to Rowland's lawyer. Maybe he was the go-between. In the course of their work, lawyers sometimes formed cordial relationships with people they wouldn't invite home to dinner and an evening with their wives. But he discovered that Rowland switched lawyers constantly. Two of the lawsuits were against lawyers. They had represented him in cases he had lost, and he had sued them for malpractice.

Prescott had saved the divorce papers for last. He made a copy he could take with him, and went back to the second-floor room he had rented on the street behind Wendy Cushner's. Donna Halsey Rowland had been represented by a partner in her brother's law firm. She had requested spousal support of fifteen thousand a month, a one-third interest in Rowland's Fine Jewelry, half the money Rowland had put into retirement accounts, a new Mercedes convertible that was registered in her husband's name, and the house.

Prescott turned to the papers filed by Rowland's lawyer. First, Rowland had wanted to reconcile, and had asked for more time. Then Rowland had claimed his annual income was $110,000, so that Donna's support request was $70,000 more than he made. He claimed the retirement money had all been deposited before their marriage, and that her spending habits had made further contributions impossible. He said the Mercedes was owned by his corporation, and submitted the pink slip he had signed over to himself as president to prove it. He claimed the house was encumbered with loans that she had co-signed, which had been used to benefit the company. Transferring it would bankrupt them both. Right up until the final decree, Rowland had been requesting more time, supposedly to reconcile.

Prescott studied the disposition of the case. Donna Halsey seemed to have been slapped down a bit, but Prescott could see that it was an illusion. She had done better in court than she had done during the marriage. She had gotten six thousand a month, which was certainly more than she had expected, the Mercedes, a third of the business. She'd also gotten something Prescott had never seen in one of these settlements: half of the growth in the balances of all savings, retirement, and investment accounts that had taken place during the marriage. He went to the table at the back of the settlement and looked at the figures. The accounts had nearly tripled during that period. He looked at the last attachment; she had also filed a petition for restoration of her maiden name.

Prescott went back to the civil suits Rowland had filed. He liked everything he saw in the papers. All of the rhetoric was legal jargon intended to make the complaint appear to conform to some statute or echo a judge's precedent-setting decision, but the substance of the papers was not. Rowland was a man who took offense easily and held a grudge, sometimes for years while his cases made their way to court. His demands were of a special sort, too. He was generally interested not in monetary reparations, but in inflicting maximum damage to an enemy. He wanted his adversary assessed a big fine, or wanted his business license revoked, or wanted him to be forced to tear down an addition and rebuild it.

Prescott went back to the divorce papers and read them once again. The tone of Rowland's strategy was different, a long series of futile attempts to delay an inevitable outcome. The whole agreement at the end must have seemed to Rowland like onerous terms of surrender. Donna Halsey had, almost incidentally, included a permanent restraining order. As part of the settlement, Rowland was supposed to communicate only by having his attorneys speak with her attorneys. He was to refrain from calling or writing to her or speaking to her. The terms didn't sound to Prescott like anything Rowland would agree to, but in the end, he had signed the papers.

There was no question what had happened. Rowland had made claims about his financial status that were false, and produced as evidence papers such as tax returns. Donna and her lawyers had found evidence that he was lying, and had blackmailed him into accepting the terms she really wanted. Rowland's emotions must have been an unsettling combination. He had included in his responses a repeated request for reconciliation, and even in the last filings before the settlement had wanted the judge to delay the final decree for another six months so he could win her back. He had been wooing her through the end of the fight.

Prescott was beginning to feel sure now. He could not have taken a single piece of the information he had found and convinced anyone that Rowland had hired the killer, but Prescott believed he had. Rowland had paid and kept silent, just as he had in his other disputes, waiting for his time to come. All along, he had planned to get even. No, Prescott decided. It might not have been as simple as that. He had not only hated her. He had loved her or, anyway, had wanted to keep her. Maybe the first intermediary he had hired after the lawyers had been a detective, or at least an informant: a person who had not been included in the court's order to stay clear of her. He'd had her watched, probably since the separation.

When he had learned that she was going to bed with Cushner, he had gone about hiring a different kind of intermediary, one who could carry out his secret desires without ever being seen, whose approach would not be noticed. Rowland had needed one whose feelings about Donna Halsey were not an ambiguous stew of hatred and love and desire and anger and remorse and self-interest. He'd needed somebody with no discernible emotions at all, someone who would simply kill her and go away.

22

Varney awoke and lay still for a moment, staring up at the old, irregular plaster ceiling. It had taken him an hour the first night to determine that the texture of it was intentional, and not just the work of some plasterer in the old days who'd had no idea what he was doing. It was supposed to have all those raised places and lower ones, to show it was handmade. It must have been a style sometime in the 1920s, just like the weird tarnished golden light fixture in the center that held one weak bulb behind a whitish half globe, and the lights on the walls that looked like candles with pointed bulbs.

He sat up in bed and picked up his watch: ten o'clock. He rubbed his hands over his eyes, and felt despair. He was letting go of his discipline, losing his will. For fifteen years he had kept himself under control, fighting to make a tiny bit of progress every day. When he had gone to bed each night, he had closed his eyes knowing that he had done his best to make himself stronger, faster, smarter than he had been in the morning. When he had awoken eight hours later he had not needed to prod himself to get started. He had felt eager to build on the small improvements won the day before.

Every second day he had lifted weights, and every day he had done his stretches and crunches and push-ups and pull-ups, practiced the punches, kicks, feints, and combinations he had been working on that month, then gone out to run. By this time of the morning, he would have had his shower and his breakfast, and been ready to go out again. He would go into the day feeling as though he had his edge, and everything he did after that was extra.

Varney had possessed incredible energy, and taken every opportunity to make the rest of the day as good as the beginning. If he had to go to the library to find everything they had on some topic—say, the habits and attitudes of some business guy he had been hired to take out—he would walk miles to the main branch to increase his stamina. He would stare for a long time at the man's photographs and memorize all the details he had read, then test himself on the way home. On the street, he would study everything he saw, trying to notice things that would help him in other places and other times: how new buildings were locked and protected, where the surveillance cameras were placed, and how they were disguised. He watched policemen and security guards, searching for routines that had become sloppy and predictable.

This morning Varney slowly pulled himself out of bed and walked to the window, trying to avoid the mirror on the dresser so he would not have to look into his own eyes. He was ashamed. He had been here over a week, and every day he had let himself slip a little bit further. He supposed that the first day or two he had been tired from his lack of sleep and his long drive. He had been angry and upset and disoriented. Those were the things he had told himself. He had used them to convince himself that what he needed was to give himself a rest.

He had slept in the next morning. The day after that, he had told himself that he was still tired, and the day after that he'd said he needed time to get used to his surroundings and make observations of the area for security's sake. Then, there were more practical matters: groceries to buy, getting rid of the car he had driven here from Buffalo. On the fifth day he had found himself moving furniture around, as though this room were going to be a permanent residence.

He was afraid he was losing himself. He was losing the man he had built from nothing, and the process was frightening to him. The deterioration seemed to happen so quickly. Suddenly, he felt lazy, tired all the time. He seemed to be breathing in shallow drafts, not getting enough oxygen to allow him to move the way he always had.

It had been a hot, humid week, and the sunlight looked strange and dull to him, filtered through a thin gray haze so that the glare came from every direction and nothing stood out in sharp relief, or had a definite shadow.

He turned from the window, determined to save himself. It was too late to salvage the past week, but today was a new start. He dropped to the floor and did push-ups, counting as he went. When he reached forty, a part of his brain said, "Why fifty? Why isn't forty enough? It's the first day. I can do more in my second set, after the sit-ups." The internal, unvoiced sound of his thoughts horrified him. That was the way of weakness, the way losers thought. He pumped out the fifty, then rolled to his back and rushed into the sit-ups. As he worked, he could feel the effect of his lazy week. Two hundred was going to be too many. Why not a hundred now and a hundred later? The words were so distasteful that he felt disgust and shame. When he had finished the two hundred he punished his abdominal muscles by doing fifty slow, agonizing crunches. Next he went to the empty closet, pushed aside the hangers, and did fifty pull-ups on the clothes pole, and did his second set of push-ups with his eyes already searching the room for his running shoes and shorts. He put on a heavy sweatshirt with them so he would sweat harder when he ran.

He had degenerated so badly that in the seven days, he had not even selected a route for his daily run. He found a way that kept him off the crowded business streets, and eventually came to a large high school field where other people too old to be students were jogging and some kids were playing basketball on a blacktop square with a row of baskets on poles. He used the quarter-mile track to make sure he had covered five miles before he jogged out the gate.

Varney jogged back to his apartment building on a street parallel to the one he had used before, short of breath and feeling a tightness in his calves and thighs that he had not felt in years. That made him more angry. He had been living in a stream, swimming against the current. The moment he had rested, he had begun to drift backward, losing what he had accomplished in the past two months.

When he had dressed and eaten, he walked downtown to the office building. As he walked, he began to feel better. The idiotic interlude with Prescott had not killed him, and the disappointment he had felt since could not be allowed to destroy him.

He climbed the stairs, walked along the hallway, and opened the door to Crestview Wholesale to find Tracy at her desk again. As she looked up at him, her eyelids half-closed wearily.

"Hello, sugar. Nice of you to grace us with your presence this afternoon."

He knew that look, that tired, quiet look as though she had tried to help him and failed a hundred times. He had grown up with it. He had spent his early childhood trying to fight it, to remove it from his mother's face by trying to do things that would please her. After that had failed, he had tried to avoid the look, to keep from attracting her attention, or simply to evade her and be somewhere else. "I was working out."

"You mean lifting weights and all that?"

He shook his head. "I didn't bring any weights when I came. But that's the sort of thing."

She raised her eyes and made a cradle for her chin out of the backs of her hands. She blinked once and smiled sweetly. "I always wondered about that. Why would a person do such heavy work for nothing? Why not just get a job running around and lifting heavy things?"

Varney said, "It's part of the life. You have to be stronger and faster, or the other guy will kill you." He was pleased that she had given him the chance to remind her that he was not just some sap who was paid to listen to her. She seemed to feel it too. She wrinkled her forehead further and shook her dyed red hair in a manner that suggested that the ways of men were far too mysterious for a young girl to understand, and returned her eyes to her bookkeeping.

He stood and waited until she looked up again. "Is there something you needed, sugar?"

"Yes," he said. "I want you to help me change some things."

"Like what?"

"I want to look different—change my hair, get some new clothes, that sort of thing. You probably know the best places in Cincinnati."

She compressed her face into a worried, vexed expression. "I could do better than give you a list of stores and stylists," she said. "I have some experience with this kind of thing, but you know, to do it right, it runs into a bit of money."

"I can pay."

"Really?" She pretended to be uneasy. "I didn't like to embarrass you or anything, because I thought you must be broke. I didn't mention it, but that apartment usually rents for a hundred dollars a day."

Varney watched her face. It had changed from a disapproving irony that was cautious, because she was delicately testing how far she could go without being in danger, to a still-cautious hopefulness, the greed she was feeling rapidly beginning to overwhelm her. He said, "Oh," in a toneless voice. "Here." He watched her eyes when she saw the thick sheaf of folded hundreds emerge from his pocket. "Here's for the time I've been in it." He tossed the three bills on the desk and watched her eyes follow the rest of the bills back to his pocket, then linger there.

Pointed red fingernails that grew into little curves like claws scraped on the wood as her fingertips touched the money lightly and drew it back into her lap. It was not until the money was out of sight that she said disingenuously, "I didn't mean to sound inhospitable, sugar. I could have waited. Now, about the changes you're making. We can get started this afternoon, if you like. You come back here around three, will you?"

"Sure." He turned and left the office. As he walked down the hallway two of the brothers were coming in the other way, but they weren't walking together. The older one, Marty, was almost to the door. Varney smiled and said hello to him, but Marty seemed to pass through the greeting, not slowing, just making a barely perceptible nod as he continued on his course. The second brother, Nick, seemed to have noticed the exchange and decided that if his older brother had been cool, it must be the wrong decision.

He was warm. "Hey, buddy," he said with a grin that seemed to be an unfortunate inheritance from some ancestor who had lived in the hills and eaten raccoons. "How you getting by? Everything comfortable over there?"

"Yes, thanks," said Varney. "I appreciate everything you folks have done." He had used the word "folks" with no time lost in calculation. He had always had an ear for other people's diction and a tendency to fall easily into it that was almost a weakness. He kept walking because it was not the time, and certainly not the place, for the conversation he was considering. Tracy and Marty were too close, just beyond the door.

Nick said, "Glad to do it. Is she in there?"

Varney nodded. "I just left her."

Nick disappeared inside the door and Varney went on. He wondered if he should have come to Cincinnati. It had seemed to be the best way to counter Prescott's latest stratagem. Prescott had made Buffalo an impossible place for him, then abruptly disengaged. Varney could wear himself out looking for Prescott and hiding from a horde of cops while Prescott rested up and concocted some grand plan to take him by surprise after he had defeated himself. It had seemed to Varney that he had been brilliant in sidestepping before any of that happened. He had selected Cincinnati because it was far enough away to keep the Buffalo police from being a problem but close enough to reach in a day. There were other people in other cities who had served as front men to bring him jobs from time to time, but there were none he would have come to like this; each of them had some quality he didn't like. They were too unpredictable, or too closely connected with the powerful, or too involved in some business that brought with it worse risks than his did—schemes like bringing drugs into the country or shipping stolen cars out of it.

But now he wondered if the wholesalers might create problems he had not expected. He amended the thought: Tracy was going to be a problem. He had been here a week, and she had already begun looking at him with that bored, detached expression that showed she was wondering when he was going to leave. And now Marty, the oldest son, had begun to look at him with a debased, cruder version of it. He wasn't sure whether Nick had simply not yet had the conversation with his mother that would make him do the same, or if he had, and had decided that a separate relationship with a man like Varney might be a good idea.

For Varney, being in a place that Prescott didn't know about, and where he could not find him, was not a mistake. Every minute that Varney stayed out of sight, Prescott would be forced to consider the possibility that Varney was nearby, preparing to kill him. Maybe Pres-

cott would be curious enough to begin searching, and not doing whatever he had intended to do. But Cincinnati had not been what Varney
had expected. He was going to need to be watchful.

He went to a big discount store off Beechmont Avenue near the
mall, bought some supplies, and brought them back to the apartment.
He spent the next three hours making small improvements. He installed dead bolts on the doors. He fitted sawed-off sections of broom
handles to the windows so they could not easily be opened from outside. He installed shades. Then he wrapped the handles of the set of
steak knives he had bought with electrical tape to improve the grip and
hid them in convenient places: in the bathroom cabinet, in the refrigerator, taped to the wall of the closet. If an intruder got very lucky
sometime and managed to get between Varney and the gun he'd hidden under the bed, the luck would not necessarily bring a lasting advantage.

He walked back to the office building at three, and found the boys
had gone off again. They had to deal with the messengers and mules,
who kept arriving in town at intervals known only to the family. Tracy
liked to have the boys and their helpers handle buys and payoffs and
exchanges away from the building in hotels and apartments, and then
bring her only the proceeds.

Tracy was not visible in the Crestview Wholesale office, so he sat
down in one of the guest chairs in front of her desk and pretended to
wait patiently and politely while he listened for sounds coming from
the other offices.

After about ten minutes, he heard Tracy's distinctive shriek and
cackle, then another, softer female voice. They seemed to be coming
closer. A door opened at the end of the big room, and Tracy came in.
She was wearing a different outfit, this one a business suit with small
white gloves of the sort that women had not worn for a generation.
She tottered forward on her spike heels, the hoops hanging from her
earlobes bouncing as she came. "Here we are, sugar," she said. "Right
on time!" Varney didn't bother to correct her, because he could see she
was aware of what the clock said.

The door opened again. A young woman he thought of as foreign-
looking, with long, thick black hair, and wearing a white lab coat, appeared. She lingered in the open doorway, looking in his direction.

Tracy clutched his arm to make him stand up, and held it tightly to her bosom as she conducted him past the rows of empty desks toward the door. "Honey, this is Mae. She's an expert cosmetologist and hair stylist, and she's going to handle everything you need for your make-over." She released him at the door. "I've got to go out, but I'll be back around seven to see how you look." He felt her hand settle in the space between his shoulder blades and give him a push, then heard the *pock-pock-pock* of her heels taking her out to the hallway.

The woman she had called Mae smiled faintly and held her door open for him to enter. As he moved past her, he got a very close look at her. He judged that she was what Tracy had said. Her skin was extremely smooth, but her makeup was elaborate and, he supposed, artful. She wore silver-blue eye shadow and dark mascara that made her eyelashes long and curved upward. He had noticed before that the women who worked behind the cosmetics counters in department stores seemed to work there just to be near the stuff, and to get the first shot at the latest shipments. His impression that she was foreign had been from her eyes, which from a distance had looked like the almond-shaped eyes of Egyptian women in ancient paintings, but that he could see now had simply been shaped by the use of some dark pencil at the corners, and by her cheekbones, which had been accentuated with some kind of coloring. Now that he was close, he could see that the eyes were blue, and the expression in them was amused and maybe a little contemptuous. He tried to analyze it, and realized it was the attitude girls in school had shown who were a couple of years older.

She had a soft, musical voice, but the pronunciation was in the local accent, and he suspected that if she had wanted to, she could still scream at a football game. "Sit down over here," she said, and pulled a swivel chair away from a desk.

He sat down and looked up at her. "Do you do Tracy's makeup?"

"Shit, no," she said, and her accent seemed to become more pronounced. "I wouldn't do that to anybody. I just get the white out of her hair and glue on the nails."

He decided that he didn't mind the fact that she wasn't impressed with him. It was part of being a couple of years older. "What I'd like—"

She interrupted, but she did it by putting her hand lightly on his shoulder near his neck, so he didn't mind. "I know what you need. I'm going to strip your hair and dye it, and then I'm going to style it differently. Have you ever worn glasses?"

"No."

"Good. We'll pick out some for you later. Then we'll work on some other things."

He looked around the room. There was a counter with a sink like one in a kitchen, a hand-held hair dryer, and a large mirror. There were barber's instruments, and a collection of bottles and jars and packages on the counter. "What is this place? The door says it's a travel agency."

She looked around her as though she were looking at it through eyes that had never seen it before. "I don't know what they use it for when I'm not here. It's where she gets herself done up. The boys get haircuts in here, too. That sort of thing. I've cut hair for a few of their road men in here, too."

"Road men?"

"Those guys who travel around and do . . ." She hesitated, as though searching for terms but finding nothing. "Whatever it is they do." She combed his hair quickly, with darting movements.

"Tracy hates it when they don't look nice—you know, like they're supposed to be traveling salesmen. Meeting the public, and all that. One time I had to fit one with a wig."

"What for?"

"Oh, she was pissed!" said Mae delightedly. "He walked into the office, and his head was shaved. She was expecting him, so she started talking to him before she looked up from her desk. So it was like, 'Put it right over there, sugar.' " Mae perfectly imitated the high, saccharine voice. "And she looked up, and without even taking a breath, she goes, 'You dare come into my office looking like skinhead trash!' " Mae managed to reach a tone an octave higher. " 'You get your sorry ass right in that room and stay there until I figure out what to do!' Then she turned to me. All I could do was measure his head and go buy a hairpiece for him. It was about four thousand bucks, and she deducted it from his pay."

"What made him shave his head?"

"It was really hot earlier this summer, and he said it made him feel better. But then he had to wear the wig, and it was worse than his own hair. Another one got a tattoo this spring. Him she didn't even bother with. She made Nicky pay him off and fire him. Come over to the sink. Bring the chair."

She wrapped towels around Varney's neck, leaned his head back against the sink, and washed his hair. He listened to her words, but only so he could keep responding and prevent her from falling silent. He liked the sound of her voice. He liked even better the feel of her fingers massaging his scalp and the smell of her perfume.

He was aware that a long period of time was passing, but he liked it. He was only half aware of what she was doing to his hair, but was always aware of her person—when a hip brushed against his shoulder as she moved to the counter to get something, or a thigh touched his when she leaned close to snip his hair. Finally, she looked at him sharply, stepping around him to see him from every angle. Then she turned him around in the chair and let him look into the mirror.

He was shocked. His hair was light brown and short, but the brown was not uniform, like a dye job. It had some lighter highlights and some darker parts, like the real hair of a man who spent some time outdoors. "That's something," he said. "I really look different." He had seen men who looked like him. He had seen hundreds of them. It was like looking into the mirror and finding that he was invisible.

"Do you like it?" she asked, trying to seem indifferent.

"It's . . . perfect," he said, looking at her in the mirror.

She was behind him, and their eyes met in reflection, but hers lowered to avoid his. She put both hands on his shoulders and began to turn him around. "Oooh," she breathed.

"What?"

"You're so tense. I guess I kept you in the chair too long. We'd better take a break before we go on with this."

"I'm okay," he said.

She began to knead his shoulders and the cord of muscle on each side of his neck. "You just sit back and relax for a minute, and let me take care of you. Close your eyes." She worked on his shoulders and upper back. It felt soothing, the small hands moving tirelessly on him.

He felt awkward. After a short time, he said, "Thanks," to end it. "That's fine."

She said, "We have to wait for an hour or so while your color sets."
She pointed to a high, narrow table across the room that he had not
noticed. It had a thick mat on it. "Why don't you get up on the massage table? I'll give you the full treatment. Take off your shirt."

He went to the table, took off his shirt, and sat on the edge. She removed her lab coat and laid it across a desk. She was wearing a halter
top and a pair of blue jeans. He began to wish . . . he didn't allow himself to form a specific image. She walked to the table and immediately
began to unbuckle his belt, her eyes on his to gauge his reaction. "I
said I'd give you the full treatment."

Two hours later, when Tracy returned, she knocked on the door to
the outer office. Mae went and turned the knob to unlock it, then
went back to the sink. Tracy stepped inside and said to Mae, "Did you
two make good use of your time?" Mae stopped putting away bottles
and cleaning the sink long enough to nod slightly. She began putting
things back into her traveling bag.

Tracy looked at Varney. "Why, sugar! Look at you! I thought it was
my boy Nicky for a minute. Come out here with me!" She had her
arm around his shoulder, and she pulled him quickly through the
doorway to her office. Varney had only a second to look back at Mae
and try to smile, but she was looking in the other direction, as though
he had already gone.

Tracy closed the door on her and kept him moving toward her desk.
"You look great, like a different man, and a good-looking man, too.
That's the tricky part. Most disguises make you look uglier, not better.
That Mae really is an artist, isn't she?"

He nodded. It seemed that she had said everything that was necessary.

"Did you like her?"

He supposed that he had to say it. "Yes. Like you said, she's really
good at hairstyling."

"No," she said, and pinched the back of his arm. "Did you like
her?"

Varney hesitated, but the look on Tracy's face was almost a leer, the
half-averted eyes bright and knowing, the coy smile making the
cheeks wrinkle like the skins of overripe tomatoes.

"Yes," he said. "I liked her a lot."

"Good," said Tracy. "Good. Then you can keep her for a while. It'll make it easier for her to get the rest of your changes done—take you shopping and so on. Whoever this person is that's after you, he isn't looking for a couple."

"You mean, she'll stay with me?"

"Isn't that what I just said?"

"Is she a hooker?"

Tracy stopped and put her hands on her hips, her head tilted. "How could you say such a thing? Of course not!" She pulled him, leaning close to him. "Don't think that way. It would hurt her feelings. A girl can't get by on cutting a little hair and doing makeup consultations. Once in a while she does little favors for close friends, and maybe they'll give her a few extra dollars, that's all. Nothing that's not perfectly tasteful and refined. I could tell she liked you and would be willing to make you one of those close friends."

"How could you tell that?"

"Women have ways of communicating without cupping our hands around our mouths and shouting like hog callers, you know. You don't have to engage in any embarrassing discussion about this. If you'd like, she'll just go home with you now. You'll pay me, not her."

His curiosity easily overwhelmed his revulsion at Tracy.

"What's her fee?"

"Give me five hundred for each day that you keep her, and I pass it on. And don't worry about extras. No big tip or something later. I have to be careful with Mae. If she had that much all at once, she'd go right out and buy enough cocaine to kill herself. You'd be trying to do her a favor, and in about three days, they'd be pulling a sheet over her head in the emergency room. So as a favor and a mercy, I just dole money out to her. It stretches the money for her, so she always has plenty to get by, even when she's not working at all. And she never has enough to hurt herself."

Varney thought for a moment. "All right."

"Good," said Tracy. She hesitated, to show there was something else on her mind.

"Something else?"

She looked at the closed door across the room in mock concern, then leaned closer to him. He could feel her breath on his cheek.

"She's . . . a little short right now. She didn't say it, but I called her only about an hour before you were supposed to be here, and she wasn't doing anything. Rushed right over, just to get some hairstyling work. And the . . . extras, they weren't my idea, I can assure you. She saw you and asked me if it was okay if she went a little further in being nice to you. So I think we should try to give her a little advance, don't you?" When Varney stared at her without answering, she prompted, "It'll put her in a much better mood, I promise."

Varney was aware that he was being fleeced, but he remembered the sight of Mae after the clothes were gone. In spite of himself, he wondered what a better mood would be like.

"How much?"

Tracy shrugged apologetically. "Let's see. I already paid for the makeover she just did. That was eight hundred, but I'll just make that my present to you. Let's give her a week's worth on account. Thirty-five hundred. I'll give her some in advance, and show her I've got the rest in hand for her."

Varney took the roll of bills he had brought out of his pocket and counted thirty-five of them. He was being robbed, but he decided for the moment not to care. Tracy took the money, disappeared into the other room for a couple of minutes, then came back in and shut the door, and waved good-bye to him.

When Varney stepped out into the hallway, he found Mae standing near the other door, leaning against the wall with the strap of her travel bag over her shoulder. When he came to within a few feet of her, she wordlessly pushed off, turned, and began to walk with him. When they were out of sight in the stairwell, she put her hand lightly on his arm. It was a comfortable gesture, just as though she were his girl-friend, and they were walking home together from a day at the office.

23

Prescott had stayed in Louisville watching Rowland's Fine Jewelry for another week before he saw the delivery. Two couriers drove up to the rear of the store in a rented car and parked. The younger one then pressed a bell to let someone inside know they were there. A tall, thin man in a tailored suit and starched white shirt with French cuffs opened the door. He looked up and down the alley, then at all the roofs and windows of buildings he could see, then looked in each direction again while the two men went to the trunk of their car.

Prescott was in the window of his hotel three blocks away, watching through a spotting scope that he had mounted above the curtains. He did not consider himself an expert in the jewelry business, but he was confident that few customers entered a store through a fire exit, and even fewer needed to open their trunks. This was some kind of delivery. He was not sure whether it was legitimate or not, but he watched for signs. The younger man stopped, looked around, then stood still and erect while the older man leaned into the trunk, reaching for a briefcase. The younger man's left hand hung at his side in a position that had to be practiced. When he turned the other way, his right arm hung straight and his left bent. He was keeping a hand close to the floor of the trunk. Prescott switched to sixty power and focused on the open trunk. There were two identical silvery titanium cases about the size of a suitcase, but below them, just under the rim of the trunk, was a towel laid over something. Prescott refocused. A hand came into his field of vision and adjusted the towel. Prescott caught a dull gleam of Parkerized steel. There was a momentary glimpse of a muzzle with a flash suppressor, and the distinctive high front sight. He thought he saw the end of a rounded triangle over-and-under foregrip, but his mind might have added what it knew was there. The two men had an M-16 in the trunk, set where the second man could pluck it out and start firing: if something ugly happened, they could make it much uglier.

Prescott adjusted the scope to look closely at the older man's face. He had graying hair, a small cut and a layer of scar tissue above the right eye. The eyebrow seemed to have an interruption there, where the hair had stopped growing. He seemed to have done some boxing; he was right-handed; he had managed to keep his head down, but had neglected to duck some notable jabs.

Prescott raised the scope to the younger man. He had a strange look about him. It was the hair. At first, Prescott had been fooled. It wasn't the sort of toupee that some old men had, that jutted out like a thatched roof of a cottage, and it wasn't the kind that was just a shade off the color of real hair. It was actually a pretty good wig. The problem was that when this young man had put it on, or maybe later, in the car, it had rotated a bit, so the lowest point in the back seemed to be a couple of degrees to the right, and the front a couple of degrees to the left. When the trunk slammed and the two older men went inside, the young man reached up with both hands and adjusted it, then stepped in and closed the door.

Prescott had planned simply to watch the car until they came out, but he changed his mind. He already had the license number and description. He had been expecting an unobtrusive visit, what he had come to think of as a minimal visit. Stolen jewelry was an easy commodity to move. A ninety-year-old woman could carry as much as anyone could sell. Sending two grim-looking characters with an assault rifle was hardly necessary, and didn't contribute much to the security of the merchandise.

It occurred to Prescott that he might be seeing something other than a delivery. Maybe whoever had acted as middleman in the Donna Halsey killing had decided that Rowland was not a man to trust with any secrets. The wig might just be incidental, a sign that the young man had lost his hair early, but it might be that he was wearing a disguise because he was about to grease Rowland.

Prescott took his suitcase, hurried down to his car, and got behind the wheel. He had planned to wait, but he could see no purpose in waiting while these two blew Rowland's head off. He drove to the front of the jewelry store, parked, and stared through the glass doors in the center. He could not see Rowland or his visitors, but there were two armed security guards near the door, three jewelers talking to customers at the glass cases, and another who was watching a group of browsers to see which one would try to catch his eye first. Prescott continued on around the block. He let his body relax. The two men weren't here to kill Rowland in front of all those people.

Prescott came around the last corner and waited until he saw the two men driving out of the lot. He followed them up the commercial street and out onto the highway, then settled back into his seat and turned on the radio. They had not been close enough to see his car well, and now he was far behind them. The car he was driving was a dark green compact that was so much like a million others that when he parked it, he had to remind himself of the license number so he could find it again. He let up a bit more on the accelerator to allow a couple of cars to pass and move back into line between him and the two men ahead. Unless the two men were much better at this than he thought they were, he had disappeared. No, he corrected himself; he had never existed.

Prescott followed them very carefully and conservatively. They drove south 175 miles to Nashville and stopped at two more jewelry stores. One was called Patrickson's, and it looked to Prescott as though it catered to people in the country-music business who needed to wear jewelry the people in the back row could see sparkling. The other was called Bangles n' Batik, and it seemed to be for younger women who went in without men and bought earrings and things for themselves. Then the two men made a stop that was closer to what Prescott had been expecting: a pawnshop. It had one window with a row of guitars hanging like dead turkeys in a butcher's shop, and another that looked like an indoor garage sale. He added the address to his list and drove around the corner to fill up his gas tank and use the rest room, then parked on a side street where he could see the men's car.

Prescott had been following people for over twenty years, and he was good at it. Part of the trick was to relax and let the quarry make all the decisions. Prescott never missed a chance to top off his gas tank, use a rest room, or stretch his legs. When he went inside to pay for the gas, he bought snacks, bottled water, and a road map. If there were items of clothing for sale, like baseball caps, he bought one, and wore it for a while to keep his silhouette from becoming too familiar.

When he was in motion, he never had fewer than two vehicles between him and the one he was following. He always picked the lanes on the right or directly behind his prey, because they were the hardest for the driver ahead to watch. He sometimes did tiny things to change the appearance of his car from the front. He would lower the left sun visor and clip a folded map to it, then take it off after a time and lower the right. When the other driver stopped, he went around a block before he stopped, or went on past and pulled over. He never waited where the other driver could see him, and never started up after him until the man's car was nearly out of sight.

The two men left Nashville in rush hour and began the 210-mile drive to Memphis, so by the time they had gone far it was late afternoon. Prescott turned on his headlights for a stretch, then turned them off again until the rest of the cars turned on theirs.

In Memphis that evening, the routine was nearly the same as it had been in Nashville. The two men stopped at three jewelry stores. This time one of them was a huge place that seemed to exist mainly to sell wedding and engagement rings at a deep discount, and the others were midlevel places in blocks that were lined with restaurants and women's clothing stores. The next stop was the one that interested Prescott. The two men pulled into the parking lot of a shopping mall, parked, and walked down the street to a store with a banner that said USED AND RECONDITIONED APPLIANCES. EASY CREDIT.

When they came out, they drove to another part of town and went into an office on the second floor of a small building that seemed to be a poor man's financial-services conglomerate: check cashing, car loans, bail bonds.

By the time they had finished their business it was nine o'clock.

The two men checked in at a big hotel on Airways Boulevard, and went out for dinner. Prescott didn't care where they went for dinner, or what they ate, so he stopped following. He went to a car-rental agency, traded in his green car for a blue one, checked in at the same hotel, bought a simple dinner at the coffee shop, then went to sleep. At four-thirty, his alarm woke him. He showered, dressed, had breakfast in his room, and checked out of the hotel, then waited down the street where he could see the hotel parking lot.

He had guessed correctly. The men were out at six, loading their silvery titanium cases into the trunk of their car. They set off for the north, and Prescott guessed that they must be planning to drive the 283 miles to St. Louis. The younger man drove this time, and Prescott could tell the difference. He was faster, always pushing the speed limit a bit, weaving in and out of lanes as though his impatience was not with the slow pace of the cars he passed so much as with the sameness of driving. He had been confined in a car for at least a couple of days now, and the act of simply keeping a vehicle aimed in the right direction with the wheels between a pair of painted lines was not enough to occupy him. Prescott drove steadily, staying well back and keeping his own speed constant. After all of the young man's maneuvering, he would invariably find himself stuck behind a truck that was slowly inching ahead of the one beside it, and Prescott would make up the difference, still hidden in a pack of other cars that made his invisible.

In St. Louis, there were two stops at jewelry stores, and then a stop at a big bar called Nolan's Paddock Club, which Prescott judged must live off a small stage with a walkway that was pictured on the sign outside that said LIVE NUDE GIRLS. This was the first building where the two men had led him that had no windows through which he could watch them, so Prescott waited until they had gone inside, then followed to see who would meet them. When he entered, they were just passing through a lounge toward the right side of the stage. A big, bespectacled man behind the bar seemed not to acknowledge or even notice them, but he lifted a hinged section of the bar and stepped off, and didn't seem to be surprised when the two followed him. The three disappeared through a door near the stage.

Prescott heard a sudden deep, repetitive sound like the thumping of a big engine, and realized after a moment that it was recorded music

with the bass turned up too high. A few men in the poolroom drifted
into the lounge, and then a blond woman who could not recently have
been described as a girl, but who was arguably live, stepped out onto
the stage and began to remove parts of a sequined costume, fulfilling
the promise of the sign outside. She seemed monumentally uninter-
ested in the whole empty ceremony, and had the expression of a
woman alone in her room removing the clothes she'd worn to do
some gardening. Prescott bought a beer and went to the men's room.
When he returned, the woman looked about ready to get into a
shower and pick up the kids from soccer practice. He put a tip on the
bar for the bartender, tossed a bill to the woman, and went outside
again to wait.

A short time later, the two men emerged, and began to drive north
on the interstate highway again. They drove the 246 miles to Indianapolis. Prescott now had a clear sense of the way the two men
worked. There was nothing about any of the stops they had made to
indicate that they had not made them all fifty times before. In each
city, the people they met all had been expecting them and were ready
to transact business. No stop ever took longer than a half hour, and
some took as little as five minutes.

They went to jewelry stores, Prescott guessed, primarily to sell jewelry stolen in another town. Most could be safely resold as estate jewelry. If it was too distinctive, a jeweler could break it up and reset it as
new. But in each city they also drove to some blighted neighborhood
to stop in a different kind of business: a pawnshop, a bail-bond office,
a used-appliance store. In Indianapolis it was a barber shop and an
agency that specialized in placing domestic help. None of those places
sold jewelry, but all of them were places where it was possible that
people who came into possession of valuables of suspicious provenance might turn up. Those were the pickup points, where fresh supplies of stolen jewelry came from.

From Indianapolis, the men drove the 110 miles to Cincinnati and
stopped in the evening at a small office building. Prescott saw them go
inside and up a staircase, carrying their titanium cases. He waited for
the usual half hour, and then saw them come outside again. He had
expected them to find a hotel, but they did not. The older man drove
the younger to an apartment complex, waited until his partner had

gone to an upstairs walkway and opened his door with a key, and then drove on. Prescott followed him another fifteen minutes to a small suburban tract, where he turned into a driveway and put his car in the garage. Cincinnati wasn't a stop on the route. It was home.

Prescott drove back to the center of town and spent the evening watching the small office building where the men had made their final stop. He had coffee down the street at a table near the window in a coffee shop, then browsed at the front window of a bookstore, looked at clothes in two different stores, and went for an evening walk that took him up the streets to the sides and back of the building. By ten o'clock the pedestrian traffic had become too thin to hide him, so he returned to his car and drove off.

By then he had seen everything that interested him. No customers or clients had come to the small office building during that time. The only arrivals had been two more pairs of men, and that told him this had to be a far-flung operation. The two he had followed had traveled to Louisville, Nashville, Memphis, St. Louis, and Indianapolis—five major cities in four states—and returned to their home base in a fifth state in under three days. He checked the odometer of his car and added the figure to the one from his last car: a bit over eleven hundred miles. If the other two-man teams did anything like as much traveling, the network would include cities in twelve states.

There would be no trouble selling merchandise in cities where it wasn't hot. The best part was that there was no need for any of the jewelers who were buying stolen merchandise to know which city it had come from, who had owned it, who had stolen it, how long it had been missing. There was no need for them to know much about the people in Cincinnati who ran this business, or even that they were in Cincinnati. All they needed to know was that they were buying goods at prices that meant they couldn't be anything but stolen, and that two men would show up now and then to sell them some more.

Prescott was careful not to assume he knew more than he did. It was possible that the office in Cincinnati was not the tip of the pyramid. This might be one of three or twenty-three regional syndicates that all paid into some larger, uglier national confederation. It might be a franchise that paid a percentage to the Mafia. It might be a secondary invention for the convenience of a silent partner who was washing cash by converting it into jewelry and back. Prescott could not be sure of the exact structure of the business, but that did not, for the moment, matter.

Prescott was sure he had found a route that Rowland the jeweler might have used to hire a killer. During the time when he had watched and studied Rowland, he had found no other way in which Rowland could have met or spoken with serious criminals. Rowland had probably had a difficult time getting himself to make the request out loud. He was a rich, established businessman. Even if there were people who knew he wasn't quite respectable, they didn't know anything specific enough to harm him. It was a risk. He had probably started to speak on a couple of occasions, and changed his mind, or maybe made a joke out of it. Then he had said something like, "I've got a problem, and I wondered if you knew anybody I could hire who might be able to help me." They would have made him say it more plainly, because it wasn't the sort of request that could be acted on without clear understandings. Then the word had traveled upward from the two jewelry couriers, and eventually made it to the killer.

Prescott decided to spend the night in a good hotel, then turn in his rental car in the morning at the airport and get a midday flight. After some consideration, he altered his plan and headed straight toward the airport. It would be better to get out of here now. He already knew the place where he would have to get his request into the system, and it would take time.

24

Varney awoke and his arm moved quickly but silently, his hand sliding into the space between the mattress and springs where his gun was hidden. As his fingers touched the grip, he already knew it had been another mistake. The soft, rustling sound he had heard was only Mae's small bare feet padding across the floor to the bathroom. He turned his eyes in that direction just as the door closed softly.

In a moment he heard the shower running. He rolled over and stared up at the old light fixture on the ceiling, slowly reversing the perspective of his thought so that he was up with the half globe looking down on the bed at himself. Was Varney happy? This seemed to be what other people referred to as being happy. He tried to feel it, to feel anything, but he caught himself calculating again, enumerating the things he now had, and insisting to himself, "That is good. And that is at least okay. And that is something I sort of like . . ."

He had never lived with a person who was female since he had left his mother's house, eleven years ago. At the moment it was not as bad as he knew it would have been if the woman had been confident enough to let her true nature show. Since she had come here, Mae had been on tiptoe, just like this morning, slipping lightly and quietly from one place to another, always on the periphery, where she wouldn't be too obtrusive and get on his nerves.

She almost lived out of the black overnight bag, taking a few of her belongings out of it, putting them back when she was finished, and pushing the bag under the bed. She kept the apartment neat and clean without ever appearing to touch anything that belonged to Varney, and she had quickly gotten used to his preferences.

Varney didn't mind listening to her talk, because she had a pleasant, musical voice, but he didn't like having to give her long answers. He had spent so much of his life alone that he had never developed the habit of talking just to fill up silences, and he didn't feel any need to deliver a running inventory of every thought that entered his mind. But he understood that women needed to do that, so he let her. The surprise was that she had learned to accept the little he said as sufficient. He knew she was on her best behavior. He could tell that in bed, if no other way, because she even talked there. Everything he did was wonderful, every time was the best ever, and nothing was ever too much or not enough. She was always ready, always watching him closely without seeming to. Varney waited: she couldn't possibly be as perfect as she seemed to be.

Varney had always been good at observing people, so that he would know how to behave the way they expected him to. Mae, it seemed, was good at the same thing. Probably he was not as good at it as Mae. But he had watched other women closely at all stages of relationships, and he knew what was probably coming. He remembered talking to Coleman Simms about women once when their two female companions had gone to the ladies' room.

"You offer them a drink, but they say no," he had said. "So a minute later, they reach over and drink yours. You offer again, and they say no, and look at you as if you must be deaf."

Coleman nodded. "She don't want a drink, kid."

"Then why—"

"Because they're like that. What she wants is not a drink. She wants an easement."

"What's that?"

"The right, like a legal right, to drink yours when she feels like it. It tells her something she wants to know, maybe tells other women she claims you or something." He shrugged. "If you don't like them, stay away from them and get a dog."

Varney knew that if he let things go on very long, Mae would get comfortable and begin to do things like that. She would begin bringing possessions in here, moving things around and cluttering everything up. She would have to revert to her nature at some point. He guessed that the past three weeks must have been what a honeymoon was like. Both people were still being very careful, scared to death they were going to make a mistake and fart.

Mae slipped out of the bathroom, holding her hair dryer in her hand. He could see the alert, questioning look in her eyes. "I hope I didn't wake you," she said. "I wanted to get an early shower so I'd be out of your way when you finish your exercises."

He was almost angry at the falseness of it, but he reminded himself that she was trying to please him. "Relax," he said. "I wanted to get up anyway." He put on his shorts and a sweatshirt and began his routines. Before he had worked up much of a sweat, she had pulled her bag out from under the bed and had the strap over her shoulder. She walked to the door and said, "I'll be back at six." She paused. "You don't mind, do you?"

Between crunches, he said, "I heard you."

"If you don't want me to—"

"No," he said, as he dropped to the ground for his first set of push-ups. "No problem." He heard the door close and went back to counting. When he reached fifty, he went to the closet and moved aside the hangers so he could do his pull-ups.

He couldn't blame her for being so careful. All these clothes he had to push aside, he had bought so she would be in a good mood. That was another thing about women that he had learned from careful observation. They had all these strange things about them that made little sense. They liked clothes so much that they sometimes bought new ones they never even wore, just kept them in a closet to make them feel good, as though it made a difference. They all thought they were fat, and even if they knew they were thin, they harbored some suspicion that they were fat inside, and were just managing to hide the truth by being thin. Even then, they had to hear people tell them they weren't fat, so they'd know they hadn't been caught yet.

They also liked to say that other women who weren't very attractive were beautiful. He was not sure why they did that, since they never let on that they knew they were lying. He had tried out theories. One was that if they established an unappealing woman as the standard, then they would be, by comparison, breathtaking. Another was that they all knew perfectly well what all men looked at and how they felt about it, but were trying to be subversive, insisting that the system wasn't fair, and therefore that they could obliterate it by mere denial. None of his hypotheses had been quite satisfactory when applied to even one woman on all occasions. There were a great many oddities. But Coleman's words came back to him: "If you don't like them, stay away from them." It was still astounding to Varney that a man who seemed to know so much about people had been stupid enough to get himself killed.

Varney looked up at the closet ceiling as he did his pull-ups, and once again focused on the square up there. It was an access hatch to the attic—not an attic, really, just a crawl space with bare two-by-fours and insulation. At the top of a pull, he held himself with one hand and pushed up with the other to see how quickly he could open it. Then he did another pull-up and closed it again. He had hidden his extra guns up there, where no casual visitor would find them. When he had finished his second set of push-ups and his crunches and sit-ups, he went out for his run. He completed his usual course to the high school and around the track, then came back and showered.

He tried to keep himself from feeling annoyed that Mae had gone out alone. He would have liked to walk somewhere with her and buy her lunch and listen to her talk. That thought brought back a dull worry. He had only brought with him the cash hidden in his house in Buffalo when he had left, and that had amounted to twenty thousand. The used car he had picked up had cost him eleven, and paying for Mae for two weeks had cost him most of the rest. He owed Tracy about four thousand for various expenses, and he didn't exactly have it where he could easily reach it.

He should just get into the car right now and drive away. These people were taking advantage of him. Tracy was charging him outrageous rent for living in this ratty apartment that had been vacant so long it had smelled musty, and outrageous fees for getting Mae to dye and cut his hair and get him a pair of clear glasses and help him pick out different clothes. She had implied she wasn't taking any of the money he was giving her for Mae, but he didn't believe her. He had asked Mae about it, and she had just avoided his eyes uneasily and said, "Tracy takes care of me okay." He should walk away from this place.

He tried to decide why he wasn't leaving, and it came down to the fact that he wasn't ready to give up Mae yet. He couldn't detect any particular attachment to her when he tried to detect one. He knew that someday he was going to get into his car and drive away, and when he imagined it, he could not imagine wanting her to go with him. He just wasn't ready to leave yet. He liked having sex with her: the shape of her body, the sound of her voice, the shine of her hair, even the smell of her perfume all seemed pleasant to him. He wasn't ready to quit yet.

Even with his new hair and clothes, he couldn't go back to Buffalo and hope to walk into his bank and come out with enough cash to last more than another month. He was going to have to wait longer before he went back there. He had a lot of cash in a safe-deposit box in Chicago. It was over a hundred thousand. Chicago would not be as dangerous as Buffalo, but he wanted to stay invisible for as long as possible.

He decided that on his way to lunch he would stop by the office and try to come to some agreement with Tracy. He walked, and noticed that he was going by a long, indirect route that he hardly ever took. For a few blocks he told himself he was doing it because the extra exercise was good for him, but after he had gone too far to go back to his usual route, he admitted that he had just been putting off talking to Tracy.

Varney remembered there was a good restaurant three blocks ahead. He had been there with Mae about two weeks ago. What was it called? Antoine, or Auguste, or something like that. He stepped inside and ate lunch by himself. The food was still the same, and he noticed that the prices were lower on the lunch menu. He seldom ate much during the day, but he'd made an exception and ordered a steak. By the time he was outside again it was two o'clock, but he felt better, more ready for Tracy.

When he reached the office he climbed the steps and went into the Crestview Wholesale office without knocking. Tracy was sitting behind the desk with her head down, staring from six inches away at a necklace made of silver and turquoise. She raised her eyes at him, sighed, and looked down again. "Damned things," she muttered. "We don't get much turquoise. What do you suppose this is worth?"

"I don't know."

"More than we can get for it. The fake stuff they make now is so good you need a chemist to catch it. And Indian silver work is so distinctive any insurance company can tell you who made it, where, and when, so you have to ship it practically to the moon to sell it." She looked at Varney as though she had just noticed him. "But that's not your problem, is it?"

He shook his head.

"What is? Mae?"

He stared at her. He wasn't sure what she meant.

"I'm afraid I'm going to need her again tomorrow, too. I've got a couple more men coming back from the road, and I promised them a party if they'd behave themselves while they were out there." She chattered on, as he stood there, not quite believing what he was hearing. "I've got two girls out sick. They're roommates, so it's probably some damned thing they ate. But there's nothing else I can do."

"You're using her for parties? I've been paying you, and you're—"

"That's an ugly thing to say," Tracy snapped. "I never said that for five hundred bucks you could own her. She's a free person, and this is America, not some sandbox country where women wear veils and stay home. I just asked her if she wanted to pick up some extra money, and she did." She let her irate glare soften a bit, and she looked at him with bleary, mock-sympathetic eyes. "Maybe the poor thing is worried. After all, you did fall a little behind on your payments . . ." Her voice trailed off so he could finish the thought himself.

"What do I owe?"

Tracy's eyes glowed, opening wide to let a flash of greed show through for an instant. "Let's see. A hundred a day for two weeks for the apartment suite is fourteen hundred. Five hundred a day for Mae for a week is thirty-five. I'll only add a hundred for the lost interest, and keep it at an even five thousand, if you've got it today."

"You want me to pay interest when you're charging me in advance?"

"Sugar," she said in a wheedling voice, "I'm just going by the due date. If money is due on a certain date, and you're late, you always pay interest, don't you?"

"I thought you were doing this as a favor."

"I am, honey, I am. I'm fronting for you, putting up my own money in advance, keeping you safe. If you have the money today, I can knock off the interest, and make it forty-nine."

"I don't have it on me."

"I know you walked here, but I can drive you home to get it."

"It's not there." He could see the skeptical look coming into her eyes, so he said, "I'll have to drive someplace out of town to pick it up. It's going to take a couple of days." He frowned. "I want to take Mae with me."

Tracy sighed deeply and rolled her eyes. "You don't even have the money you already owe me—let alone poor Mae—but you want everyone else to change our plans at the last minute?" She raised a penciled-in eyebrow. "Maybe you ought to get a job."

No sign of emotion appeared on his face. He might have been a photograph of a man looking off into the distance. When Tracy saw that, she felt relieved. She had been surprised by an instant of hot panic after she had said the part about the job, thinking maybe she had gone a tiny bit too far. Her own word "job" had reminded her of what he did for a living. As he walked out of the office, she began to feel the cool relief begin to turn into pride, then anticipation. The next time she saw him, he would be bringing more money.

25

Prescott began to work on his identity the day after he arrived in St. Louis. He rented an apartment in a building that was a new imitation of an old-style residence, designed by an architect who had not been able to resist adding ugly embellishments. He threw away his generic suitcase and began shopping. He bought an eight-year-old Corvette that had been badly rebuilt after an accident. He bought clothes from thrift stores, everything originally on the expensive side, but just a bit out-of-date. Then he went to a store that sold surplus military gear.

He wandered up and down the aisles looking for precisely the right items. He bought a navy watch cap and a black turtleneck sweater, then found a navy blue hooded sweatshirt. He found an olive-drab tool bag, and a pair of thin black leather gloves that were labeled "police-style." He went next to a big hardware store and picked out a selection of tools that looked convincing: a battery-operated drill, a few punches and picks, a long, thin screwdriver, a pry bar. He bought a glass cutter and a suction cup with a handle on it made for carrying sheets of glass. By then the tool bag was full, so he stopped.

The second day, he drove the three hundred miles to Chicago, checked into a hotel, and slept. When he woke, he began to shop in earnest. He went to camera shops, computer stores, electronics stores, buying any item that appealed to his eye. Always, he searched for good deals on high-end merchandise that was used, but sometimes he had to settle for new. He spent most of his time looking at estate jewelry. He bought several watches—a couple of Rolexes, a Cartier tank watch, some women's watches with diamonds, and a variety of others that had some resale value. He bought a wide assortment of women's jewelry, being sure to include some spectacular finds and some junk. He picked up some men's items too—a couple of sets of cuff links and studs that contained a lot of gold and semiprecious stones but weren't in style, a stopwatch, fancy lighters, money clips, rings.

He went to a numismatics show and assembled a collection of gold coins. He went to antique shops and bought a set of ivory carvings and a silver tea set. He spent a day on the South Side searching secondhand stores, buying similar items that might be as old and didn't look any worse but cost practically nothing. For three days, Prescott shopped. He walked through the stores pretending they were houses. If he could imagine an item as the one that would catch the eye of a thief, he bought it. He packed all of his purchases in boxes, shipped them to his apartment in St. Louis, and drove back to meet them.

He spent the next few days refining his identity by rehearsing his anecdotes, inventing and memorizing names, places, and dates, and compiling documents using the computer scanners and printers he had picked up in Chicago.

He spent a few evenings establishing himself as a regular at the Paddock Club. He would arrive there at around eight, go in, and sit at the bar. The man with glasses who had met with the two traveling couriers from Cincinnati returned from his dinner break between eight-thirty and nine, and presided at the bar.

Prescott watched him for an evening and confirmed his theory about him. There were two younger bartenders who did the heavy lifting and all the routine fetching of the endless bottles of beer. This man seldom waited on a customer except during the frantically busy period from nine to one, when all three were pouring drinks with both hands, shoving them onto the wet surface of the bar, snatching up money, and dispensing change on the way to the next customer. The rest of the time, he leaned on the wooden surface behind the bar, usually with his arms folded across his chest. Prescott could see that his eyes flitted to the cash register whenever one of the bartenders approached it, then surveyed the customers ranged around the room at small, round tables and along the bar, then focused for a moment on the front door, where he seemed to be counting the ones leaving and the ones coming in, and finally, went to the woman on the stage.

The women were the constant—hypothetically, the center of attention. But they existed on the edge of the huge room, in the world of the bar but not part of it. The place was like a water hole on a veldt, where two different species were side by side but had very little to do with each other.

The men drank and talked, sometimes laughing and then suddenly tense with anger, the sinews in their necks standing out and their faces acquiring the blank stare that wasn't really seeing. About once a night, two of them would go outside, each accompanied by a companion or two, and then one set of men would return and the other vanish into the night. But the rest of the time, the men slouched in their chairs, now and then staring wistfully at the woman on the stage for a time, but then returning their attention to their friends, or going to join the crowd waiting at the bar for another drink.

Each of the women was alone. A number of the women seemed to have been doing this for a long time. The music would begin, and from behind a small black curtain at the side, a woman in her late thirties or early forties would appear, and she would dance. She would be preoccupied, her thoughts not on the men. When Prescott studied the faces of these women for thoughts, he imagined a compendium of the mundane. This one seemed to be thinking about the things she was going to buy on the way home: milk and bread, of course, and she was almost out of shampoo—had forgotten it the last two trips—plus some Ziploc bags, laundry detergent. Was she out of dishwashing detergent, too? Might as well get some just in case.

The woman Prescott was watching danced, completing the turns and gyrations far below the level of conscious thought, and when the music reached the point where she had taken off her top the last hundred times, her hands performed the practiced gesture, and that was done. She stripped without interest in the process, having thoroughly explored it for implications and possibilities so long ago that it could no longer hold her attention.

She already knew that it wasn't a personal communication, or a step in a career, or a way to start a relationship with a man. The men didn't know who she was, or have any curiosity about her. They looked at her breasts, her buttocks, the space between her legs, in that order, as she bared her body, but what they saw was not she. It was all female bodies, of which this happened to be the one example that was here at the moment, a symbol. What had been advertised as seduction had descended to the level of art.

The weekends were amateur nights. For the young women who competed, this had not yet worn down into a job that was a whole lot duller than checking out groceries at a cashier's stand. They were still up there actually stripping in front of men—not a man, but a whole bunch of them at once—and they couldn't get over it. This was wild, risky behavior, and they did it as though on a dare, took the money slipped into the waistbands of their G-strings like love notes from billionaires.

The customers on the weekend nights were perfectly suited to them. They were boys in their twenties who'd had too much liquor before the shows started, and subscribed to the same illusion that this was a form of communication between this woman and themselves about sex, and that the edge of the stage just might not be an impossible boundary—not for them.

Prescott spent his evenings here, becoming familiar. He always sat at the bar or at a table near it, and gave the bartender a five-dollar tip for each five-dollar drink. He always kept away from the customers who he could see were probably going to cause trouble. He spoke little, and when he'd had two drinks, he left. He kept this up for nine nights, then left town to search for the perfect piece of real estate.

He had a fairly clear idea of where such a place could be found, so he took a flight there. Once he had arrived in the right region, finding the exact spot and obtaining a lease took him only a few days. He spent three weeks getting the place ready, and then returned to St. Louis prepared to change his hours at the Paddock Club. He found that the effect he had anticipated had taken place. His presence, beginning

over a month ago, had been noticed, and his absence for the past three
weeks had been noticed too.

Prescott walked into the bar at eleven-thirty in the morning, as the
proprietor was busy supervising the unloading of supplies. There
were two men from a liquor distributor bringing cases into the building with two-wheeled carts, and two bartenders opening them to re-
stock shelves behind the bar while the proprietor counted boxes and
checked them off an invoice on a clipboard. Now and then the swinging door to the left of the bar would open, and Prescott would see
waitresses hurrying back and forth to prepare the small round tables
for the businessmen's lunch.

The proprietor saw Prescott come in, smiled at him, and nodded.
"How you been?"

"Fine," said Prescott. He stepped closer as the proprietor signed the
sheet and handed it to one of the deliverymen. "How about you?" He
glanced at the pyramid of liquor cases. "Looks like you haven't done
too badly."

"Nope," said the proprietor. "Been pretty fair." He went around the
bar. "What are you drinking?"

"How about a beer and a shot?" said Prescott. He got out his wallet.

The proprietor put the draft beer and shot glass on the bar, and held
his free hand up as he poured the whiskey from the silver spout on the
bottle. "It's on me," he said.

"Well, thanks," said Prescott. He held out his hand. "I'm Bob
Greene, with an *e*. Three of them, come to think of it. You're Mr.
Nolan?"

The proprietor took his hand and shook it. "They call me that." He
smiled. "It's because of the sign outside. Real name is Dick Hobart.
When I bought this place twelve years ago, the sign said 'Nolan's Paddock Club.' I wasn't sure how it was going to work out, so I left the
sign for whatever good will it was worth. Wasn't much, I can tell you.
Otherwise they wouldn't have gone under. But by the time I knew
things were going to work out for me, I was stuck with the name."

Prescott nodded. "I've seen it happen that way before."

"What about you? What business are you in?"

Prescott said, in an affable, confident tone, "I'm kind of between
things right now. I've been out in California for a few years. Had a

couple of car washes, and did pretty well. I sold out a few months
back, and I'm looking around here for the right opportunity."

He could tell that Hobart had instantly evaluated the story and
taken it as Prescott had hoped. He knew Bob Greene was a liar.
Greene had some money to spend, but he probably had not come into
it a few dollars at a time operating car washes in California. Hobart
said, "Well, I'm sure you'll find something you like. This is a good
place to do business." His own words seemed to remind him that he
had to keep an eye on his men. He turned toward them.

"It sure seems to be," said Prescott. "Thanks for the drink."

At one o'clock, when Prescott heard the distinctive change in the
music, as though someone had turned the bass all the way up to vi-
brate so he could feel it, he left the bar and sat at a table. The noon
crowd consisted of men who looked older and more settled than the
evening crowd. About half of them were wearing coats and ties, having come from offices. Two of them had been reading newspapers in
the dim light while they ate lunch, but when the music changed, they
folded them and set them aside.

The woman who came from behind the curtain was announced
only as "Jean." She had her dark brown hair pinned up, and she was
dressed in a business suit and wearing glasses to begin with. She
looked very convincing. She took off the glasses and undid her hairpin
so her dark hair came down in a cascade, shook it out, and went into
her routine. The theatrical lacy garter belt and push-up bra she had
beneath the suit were not what the female business executives Prescott had known well usually wore to work, but he judged it didn't destroy the effect.

It was not until she was wearing only her tiny G-string that she did
one of her turns, looked over her shoulder, and seemed to notice that
Prescott had returned from his trip. She looked directly at him, let her
fixed, professional smile relax for a second, then resumed the mask
again. He stepped to the stage and slipped a fifty into her G-string,
then returned to his table. He drank through the next two women's
performances to see whether Hobart had told them all to notice him.
They were women he had not seen before, and they went through
their tasks without enthusiasm, largely ignored by most of the customers and ignoring them in return.

When Prescott went out to the parking lot to get into his car, he realized that his experiment had made him drink more than he had intended. The sun was impossibly bright, bouncing off the chrome of the cars into his eyes in little semaphores. The red surface of his Corvette seemed to have an aura around it, and the gravel on the ground was like a photograph of the surface of Mars, each tiny pebble bright on top with its own black shadow behind it. But as he carefully steered the car across the lot toward the street, he looked into the rearview mirror and saw Jean and Hobart beside the delivery door outside the building, watching his departure.

Over the next few days, he confirmed his impression that noon was the time to go to Nolan's. The nights in a strip club were businesslike and concentrated. The customers crowded in, and the men behind the bar were frantic, pushing glasses onto the bar and snatching money as quickly as they could move, working like fishermen in a tuna run, making the most of their catch in a three-hour period.

During daylight, the atmosphere was calm and sleepy. The volume of the recorded music was so low that people could speak in normal voices except when a dancer was on the stage. The bartenders had time to talk with customers. Prescott exchanged greetings with Dick Hobart when he came in for lunch each day, and sometimes when he left. He was always good-natured and friendly, always careful to give the impression that he had no desire for a longer conversation but had no reason to avoid one, either. There was an odd easiness to the atmosphere, and Prescott insinuated himself into it subtly and patiently, until he suspected that several of the employees were not sure just how long he had been around—maybe for years, coming in during some other shift. Hobart met with the couriers from Cincinnati once every three weeks, and met with other men more frequently, always during the day.

Prescott waited two more weeks before he decided he was ready to ease himself in further. He was in the bar before the businessmen's lunch when Hobart came past him, checking the tables to see whether they had been positioned and set properly. When he came to Prescott's, he said, "Hey, Bob. Didn't anybody come to take your order yet?"

"Thanks for thinking about it, Dick, but I just sat down," said Prescott. "While you're here, though, there was something I wanted to talk to you about. Got a second?"

Hobart studied his face, as though deciding whether he really wanted to hear this, then said, "Sure. Let's go over to the bar so I can take care of some chores while we talk." Prescott went to the bar and watched Hobart taking inventory of bar supplies: olives, cherries, swizzle sticks, bitters. He emptied old bottles, moved new ones in. "What's on your mind?"

Prescott said, "I was just wondering what your policy was on employees going out with customers."

Hobart put his elbows on the bar and blew out a breath wearily. "Who did you have in mind?"

"Jean," said Prescott. "I was considering trying to talk to her, but I won't if it'll get her fired or something."

Hobart clamped his lips together and nodded sagely, as though it had been obvious. "You were right to ask me first. That's sensible, and I appreciate it. We do have a rule against fraternizing. You start having that kind of thing going on, and the authorities get on you. As it is, every time there's a city council election, everybody in the entertainment business has got to fear for his livelihood. But the truth is, I wouldn't have that rule if the girls didn't want it. This way they can say no, and it isn't their fault. The guy who's been a big tipper doesn't get hurt feelings and go away."

Prescott shrugged. "Okay. I can understand that. No hurt feelings. I'll forget the idea."

Hobart said, "I didn't say that. This is a little different. You're a good customer, and you're not a kid. You seem like a serious man, and the fact that you asked me means you're sensitive to other people's problems." He let a mysterious little smile play about his mouth and disappear. "Jean happened to ask me about you a week or two ago. She's not married at the moment, so it could mean she's interested. Of course, it could mean nothing, too."

"So you think it might be okay if I had a talk with her?"

"I'll tell you what. I have a couple of conditions. You talk to her in private, where the other customers don't get the idea this is a regular thing here. And if she wants to go out, pick her up at her place, not mine, and stay the hell away from here."

"That's not much to ask," said Prescott.

Hobart leaned closer. "There's only one more unpleasant thing to say, and I apologize in advance for having to say it. Jean is a grown woman, and she's free to decide. But if you should happen to be one of those guys who's carrying around some weird fantasy in his head that he's planning on working out on Jeanie, then it had better be one that she likes."

"It's nothing like that," Prescott began, looking surprised.

But Hobart continued. "Because if you were to harm her, you would find that this place works kind of like a family. There are some relatives—distant cousins, you might say—that you haven't met, and that you don't ever want to meet."

"I understand," said Prescott. "I know you've got to be able to protect your workers."

Hobart stared at him in silence for a second, his eyes never blinking. "I've got to say this clearly so we both know exactly what I'm talking about. It's not just getting a couple of ribs kicked in, and losing some teeth. The cops wouldn't find anything as big as the sole of your boot."

"I'm not some kind of pervert, Dick," said Prescott comfortably. "So neither of us has got anything to worry about."

"I was pretty sure that was true," said Hobart. "And I don't mean to insult you. She came in a while ago because she goes on at one. I'll take you back, and you can ask her yourself."

Prescott followed Hobart through the door where he had seen him go with the two couriers a few times. The door led into a hallway of bare cinder blocks and a concrete floor with drains in it, lit by hanging bulbs with green metal shades. The only decorations were fire extinguishers at ten-foot intervals, and a four-foot-high, too expert drawing of a penis with Hobart's face at the top and the words "Dick Hobart, Capitalist Tool" written across the testicles.

Along the outer wall were several doors. One was an office, two were staff rest rooms with posters on them giving dire warnings about washing hands before returning to work. There was one on the right that Prescott could tell led to the kitchen area, and then a short stretch of hallway that ended in a door with a star on it. Hobart didn't knock. He said, "Wait here," then opened the door and entered.

After a few seconds, he came out again, repeated, "Wait here," and went back the way he had come. Prescott called, "Thanks, Dick," before he had gone too far, and heard Hobart say, "Happy to help."

A moment later, the door opened and Jean came out wearing an old, soft chenille bathrobe. She looked at him shyly. "Hi."

"Hello, Jeanie," said Prescott. "My name is Bob Greene, with an *e* at the end."

She nodded, and her shy look tentatively grew into a small smile. "Nolan told me." Then she said, "I noticed you watching me sometimes, and wondered who you were."

Prescott said, "Now you know. I wanted to ask you if you might be willing to go out to dinner with me sometime."

She put her head down, but her eyes were on him from beneath the glittering eye shadow. "You might be disappointed. When I'm not on stage, I'm really a pretty ordinary person."

He grinned. "That's what I was hoping. Ordinary people like to eat regular dinners in nice places, and don't expect the rest of us to be too scintillating."

She let his grin shift to her face. "I think I'd like to. When would it be?"

"I'm afraid I'll have to limit it to tonight, tomorrow night, or any other night in the future," he said. "Last night is out."

"How about tonight, then?" she asked. "I'm only working until three, and I could be ready around seven-thirty."

"Wonderful," said Prescott. "Terrific. I'll get a reservation for Cavender's."

"Cavender's?" she repeated, her expression apologetic and maybe a bit regretful. "I'm flattered. I really am. But you'll never get a reservation for Cavender's at noon the same day."

He looked down at his feet, then back at her and shrugged. "I already have the reservation," he admitted. "I made it just in case you said yes."

Her sad look disappeared, and a look came over her that was partly gratification that he would make a reservation at a famous restaurant just in case, partly pleasure that she was going to get to go, and partly an amused sympathy that he'd had to admit to being so eager. The sympathy made her response excessive, as though to protect him. "I'm so glad. I'd love to go there. What time is your reservation?"

"Eight-thirty, but I could try to change—"

"Perfect."

"Where can I pick you up?"

She frowned. "My apartment, I guess. I'll write down the address." She disappeared behind the door, then came back with an address written on a Nolan's Paddock Club napkin. She held it in her hand, but she didn't hold it out to him.

He detected a tension in her eyes. "What's wrong?"

"This is embarrassing," she said. "But I hope you'll understand. Can I see your driver's license?"

He reached for his wallet and retrieved the Robert E. Greene license he had brought from home. "It's a California license, but it's got my picture on it."

She glanced at it, pushed her napkin into his hand, and closed his fingers over it. "I'm sorry. It's just something you have to do if you're—"

"No problem," he said, making his smile return. "If I were you, I'd do the same." He glanced at the address, and saw that there was a telephone number too. "I'll pick you up at seven-thirty, then."

But he could see there was still something on her mind. He waited. "Would you do me one more favor?" she asked.

"Sure."

"Would you mind . . . I go on at one. Would you mind not watching me work today? You can watch the other girls, I don't mind. And it's just for today. It would be kind of . . . distracting for me, and—"

"Say no more," he said. "I'm on my way." He gave her a warm smile and started down the hallway.

She called, "I heard the lunch is better down the street anyway."

"I'll let you know," he said. On his way out, he passed the bar, smiled at Hobart, and gave a quick thumbs-up sign. Hobart nodded gravely, then looked down to spray soda into a customer's scotch and slide the glass across the bar on a cocktail napkin.

As Prescott walked out into the sunlight, he assessed his progress and felt pleased. He was halfway in now, and the resistance was beginning to soften. The next part had to be done carefully.

26

The apartment complex looked like an island fortress surrounded by a lake of asphalt. There were low ramparts along the sides that held captive plants, but there were no trees. Prescott pulled up to the west end, parked the Corvette, and got out to look for the right staircase. Almost instantly he heard the click of high heels, turned, and saw Jeanie hurrying toward him.

She was wearing a simple black dress and small diamond studs in her ears, and carrying a tiny handbag. Her shining dark brown hair was pulled back in a tight coil that Prescott noticed was more than merely reminiscent of the style she had worn when she was taking off the business suit in Nolan's. He felt a pang of sympathy for her: maybe it was her uniform to signal she was on her best behavior.

He stepped toward her, his expression anxious. "You didn't have to wait outside for me."

She paused about five feet from him, as though she were wondering how to get by him without touching him. "I didn't want to make us late."

He said, "You look terrific." It wasn't a lie. She had a pretty little face with large brown eyes that looked much better without the sparkling blue smears of eye shadow on the lids and the heavily rouged cheeks. Her figure was what she used to make a living, her one reliable asset, and the cut of the dress showed that she was confident about it, relying on it to make everything all right.

She disguised her need to stay five feet from him by using the distance to appraise him critically, looking at his suit, shoes, and tie. "So do you." Then she made a sudden, evasive step to the passenger door of the Corvette. Prescott held it open for her, then went around the back of the car and got in. She seemed to have a list of questions she had decided to ask him, and she started as he drove. "I see you hanging out at Nolan's during the day. What do you do for a living?"

He turned to her and saw that she was nervous, her head quivering slightly as she waited. He looked at the road. "I guess you'd have to say I'm a bum at the moment," he said happily. "I owned a couple of car-wash places in Los Angeles, but I sold them a few months ago, and came east. I haven't decided what I'm going to do when I grow up."

"If you didn't have a plan, why did you sell them?" she asked.

"It seemed like the right time."

"The right time?"

"Yeah," said Prescott. "I was doing okay—not getting real rich, but okay. People in California care about cars. I picked the places up when the price of land was way down, and anything that happened to be on it was down lower. So I bought the corner and got the first car wash almost for free. I hadn't planned to be in that business, but there I was, so I kept it going. A little later the second one was available, so I bought it. Then, about three or four years ago, land prices shot up again."

"And you couldn't resist."

"I did resist," he protested. "I waited for a long time. But I kept asking myself, 'Am I in this because I like the smell of carnauba wax, or am I in it for the money? If I'm in it for the money, I have to sell at the time when there are a lot of people who want to buy, not wait through a boom.' So I sold. One of the car washes is probably a shopping mall by now. The other is going to be a parking lot for the Bank of America." He looked at her again. "How about you? Do you always have a plan?"

She shook her head. "Nope." Then she changed her mind. "Yes, I guess I do, but none of them works so hot."

"Do you have a plan now?"

She looked at him in anticipation of an approaching disappointment. "I'm going to college at night, picking up a degree. That's why I work the lunch hour now."

"That's a lot better than my plans usually are," he said. "What are you studying?"

She said, "Let's talk about you."

He looked at her, puzzled. "What's wrong?"

She sighed, and glared at him with a mixture of frustration and sadness. "I don't like talking about me. You're curious about how I arrived at making a living in a dark saloon taking my clothes off so a bunch of sad, lonely men can stare at my tits. You're too polite to ask straight out, so you work up to it gradually. Only there's no way you can broach the topic without my sitting here cringing and waiting for that part of it to arrive. I can see it coming from a long way off. It's a conversation I've had too many times."

Prescott drove in silence for a few seconds. "I'm sorry. I didn't mean to make you uncomfortable. How about if I promise not to ask you about that, and you just tell me what your major is in college?"

She stared at him with hard hostility, then seemed to see herself. A laugh escaped from her lips. "Accounting. I'm in a CPA program."

"That sounds great," said Prescott. "I admire and approve of it. And I hope you'll notice that it hardly hurt at all."

"I'm sorry," she said, and put her hand on his arm, then seemed to think better of it and pulled it back into her lap. "I just get so tired of it." She sat quietly for a few blocks, but no other topic seemed to fill the void. It weighed on her. "How about if I just tell you quickly, and then we forget about it?"

"No," said Prescott. "I don't think so."

She was very surprised. "Why not?"

"You think I have some eagerness to hear all the intimate details, so I was weaseling my way up to that. Actually, I wasn't. You don't find out much about people by looking into all that. It's mostly decisions they don't feel like defending, and luck. I learn more about people by hearing what they want than by hearing what they have. So if it's a sad story, I don't want to hear it."

"It's a pretty good story," she teased. "And it's not sad."

"You sure?" he said skeptically.

"Yes. I was from a small town west of here, eighteen, and couldn't afford college. I—"

"You said this wasn't going to be sad," he reminded her.

"I know," she said. "That part's over. I came to the big city and waited tables in a restaurant. I was very good at math, so I did a little of the bookkeeping, too: cashing out at the end of the day, and helping with the records. A girl in my apartment building was working at a strip place, and one day while we were doing our laundry, we compared notes."

"Did she work at Nolan's?"

"No, she worked at a different place, called the Harem," she said. "But here's the comparison. I worked at my restaurant five to eleven every night, doing setup, waiting for dinner from five-thirty until ten on my feet, then cleanup after. I made five dollars an hour plus tips, which all added up to about a hundred a night, because it was a nice restaurant and I was really sweet and eager and looked young and pretty. My friend spent two hours at work, which amounted to forty-five minutes of getting made up and in costume, two fifteen-minute dance shows on stage a half hour apart, and fifteen minutes getting the makeup off and changing to street clothes. She got two hundred for the two dance numbers, and her tips came to about three hundred a night. She was making five times what I was making, and working a third of the hours—meaning that she was getting fifteen times what I got on an hourly basis, and was actually doing what I call work for only a quarter of that time."

"That's quite a difference."

"I was off on Sunday night because I worked the Sunday brunch, so I went to see her work. There were four girls on that night. None of them was especially good-looking. They all had lots of long, bleached hair and reasonably good shapes, but that was all you could say. They weren't even very good dancers, except one. It turned out that my friend wasn't exaggerating. They were all making more than she was. They had an amateur night just like Nolan's does on Saturday night, so I signed up for it and called in sick at my job. It isn't nuclear physics. If you can dance and you've seen four or five other people do it, you know about as much as you'll ever know, and if you're used to

waiting tables in six-hour shifts, dancing for fifteen minutes isn't exactly a triathlon, either."

"So you got into it on the arithmetic."

She laughed. "Numbers were always my weakness. I was a little
nervous about it the first time. I didn't know what to expect. Even
though I'd spent a night watching it from offstage, I wasn't used to the
men. I also didn't know what to wear that first time, but then I realized I had the perfect thing hanging on the hook on the back of my
closet door: my waitress uniform. I looked good in it. It was all
starched and ready for Saturday dinner, and I had comfortable shoes
that went with it. A lot of the girls try to dance in spike heels, and you
can do it after a while, but at first it makes you clumsy and stiff. May
Company was having a lingerie sale, so I went and bought some nice
underthings—a slip and everything, because I figured I might need a
lot to take off, just to kill time on stage. So what I took off was the
waitress outfit I was supposed to wear to work that night. I won the
contest, made fifteen hundred for fifteen minutes' work, and got offered a job. I thought about it for a week, and realized it didn't make
any sense to do anything else."

"How long have you been doing it?" asked Prescott.

"About twelve or thirteen years, on and off."

"On and off?"

"Yeah. I got married once, and quit. I met him at the Harem. He
was one of those young guys you see a lot, who go out on a tear on Fri-
day night, drink too much, and celebrate something or other. He was
with about five other guys from a car lot. He was a salesman, and
they'd beaten their quota that month and set some record. I didn't expect to see any of them again, but the next time I came on, there he
was. A little while later, we were dating."

"What made you decide to go out with him?"

"Did I say he wasn't cute?" she retorted. "And he seemed to me to
be the one I wanted. A few months later, he changed jobs so nobody at
work would know me, and we got married in Las Vegas. It didn't last."

"Why not?"

"First he wanted me to quit stripping. I could understand that, so I
quit. Things went on okay for about a year. We didn't have a whole lot
coming in, but I had saved a lot at the Harem. I went back to waiting
tables. But then things started to fall apart. He bought a new car and

put a down payment on a house with most of the money I had saved. Then one day, he came home and said he'd been laid off. He wanted me to go back to stripping, just for a little while, to make the mortgage payments and get ahead for good. I felt really sorry for him because I thought it must be killing him, knowing how he felt. But since he asked me, and I didn't have any better ideas, I did it. By then, Hobart had bought Nolan's and opened it as a strip club, so I got a job there. I figured I'd better make the most of it, so the time I was back at it would be as short as possible. I worked five nights, four shows a night, and five on weekends. Weekends are a rougher crowd, but the money is great. I was taking home at least a thousand a night, sometimes more, most of it in cash. After about two months, I noticed my husband wasn't looking too hard for a job. I kept track of him for a week, and realized he wasn't looking at all. I asked him about it, and he said he already was working. He was acting as my business manager. Investing my pay, making hair appointments for me, and all that was a full-time job. He said it was stupid for him to kill himself trying to sell cars when I could make much more just taking off my clothes. I put up with that for a while, not wanting to do anything too hasty while I was thinking things over. Then I took a look at the bank statements and the bills, and saw that there were no investments, no savings. He had been spending it all, a lot of it on other women. I filed for divorce. My lawyer did a search to see if I still had any money left, and he found no money, but a lot of things I didn't know: that my husband hadn't been laid off from the car lot at all. He had quit, and told them he'd inherited some money."

"After the divorce, you had to go back to work, right?"

"Already was working, remember?" she said. "I paid off the debts, sold the house, sold the new car and bought a used one. I was a little better than broke. I worked nights for another year, saved every penny, and went back to school. I go to class at night, and work the business lunch now. As you know. The crowd then is a nice, quiet bunch, mostly older men, and no rowdy drunks. They tip at least as well, though, because they have more. I'm not going to be able to make a living forever going on a stage and shaking my bare ass, but I'm hoping I'll get away with it long enough to be a licensed CPA." She paused and looked at him with a calm smile. "See? It wasn't very sad."

"Borderline," he said.

"Come on."

"All right. You're only twenty-eight or twenty-nine, right?"

"I wish. I'm thirty-six."

"You look younger. You could do this for a long time yet."

"Maybe," she admitted. "But I'm not the only one getting older. The business is getting older too."

"It is?"

"Sure. It's an old-fashioned thing. Like magic shows, or circuses. It made a lot more sense when you hardly ever saw a woman's legs, or something. But the world is different, and what we do at Nolan's is pretty tame. When I'm done with my act, you've seen maybe ten square inches that I couldn't show you on the beach. Hobart can tell you. He knows. If you turn on your TV, you can see attractive people having sex." She amended it. "Some are attractive, anyway. On the Internet there are sites with girls living in a house where there are cameras on in every room, even the bathroom. You can e-mail them and ask them to do things."

"So you think the clubs will go out of business?"

"I think they'll last a little longer than I do, but not the way they are."

"I'm not sure I follow that," said Prescott.

"A place like Nolan's will either be girls doing the same acts that made your grandma upset—just kind of quaint, making fun of what used to shock people—or it will be stuff that would make you barf."

"Which way is Nolan's going?"

"I don't know," she said. "Hobart thinks like you. He's a businessman. He got the place cheap and thought of a way to make it pay. While it pays, he'll keep it. But he has no emotional investment in owning a club. He's into money. If it brought in more money to replace us with men demonstrating power tools, he'd do it." She considered. "I think he won't go the next step to keep up with the times. He hates legal troubles, so he keeps things pretty conservative. I think he'll just sell out at a profit someday."

"Do you like him?"

She shrugged. "He's okay, I guess. He works hard at keeping the place up and running it. He's good about protecting the dancers: nobody ever gets pawed twice. I guess what I'd have to say is that I understand him, and that makes me comfortable."

"You understand him?"

"Yeah. He's the greediest man I ever met—no, the second greediest. I just told you about the first. But you only have to know one thing about Hobart: he's there to make money. He uses the bar as an office for all kinds of side deals, people coming and going all the time. He looks at the acts, but only to see if they're good enough to keep customers there buying drinks. If we all offered him a choice—our bodies or our purses—he'd take the purses."

"And that makes you comfortable?"

"Yeah," she said. "It does."

He could see her watching him out of the corner of her eye the rest of the way to Cavender's. When they pulled up in front of the restaurant Prescott had to stop and inch forward behind two big black cars, as the parking attendants opened doors to let passengers out. Only then did she look away from Prescott to study the fashionably dressed people stepping from their cars to the big wooden doors. In a moment, the attendant was opening her door, and she stood, catching a glimpse of the big crystal chandelier, giant old-fashioned rugs, and heavy antique furniture.

When the valet had taken the Corvette and Prescott and Jeanie were inside, she was like a cat studying her surroundings intensely, but through half-lidded eyes, without appearing to notice them at all. Cavender's was one of the best restaurants in St. Louis, but it had been since the 1920s: the antiques had aged in place. Prescott ordered them both a glass of wine, which they sipped while they looked at the menu under the watchful eyes of the waiter. She closed hers, set it on the table and said, "I'll just have a small salad, no dressing."

The waiter looked expectantly at Prescott, but Prescott said, "Can you come back in a few minutes, please?"

As soon as he was away from the table, Prescott said, "You're making me feel bad."

"I have to watch what I eat. It's not my fault," she said, not meeting his eyes. "I have to make a living."

"Do you like fish?"

"I love fish."

He beckoned and the waiter returned. "The lady and I will have a salad with no dressing, and we'll both have broiled swordfish and another glass of wine."

The waiter went off, and she looked at Prescott, puzzled.

"It's only a few more calories. We'll have martinis sometime, and you can skip the olive."

She met his eyes this time. "It's much more expensive than I thought," she whispered.

"At a bad restaurant, the food is worth less than they charge—sometimes it's worth nothing. At this place, the food is going to be worth more than they charge, so it's a bargain." He smiled again. "I can't make you eat it, and I can't make you have a good time. All I can do is put them both in front of you."

She said, "You're not like Hobart at all, are you?"

He shook his head. "I like money because it buys things like nice dinners. When I run out of money I get more."

"You're so sure?"

"Yes," he said. "I am. And given the choice of the purse or the body, I don't hesitate, either. If a man even looks at the purse, he loses her, because she knows he doesn't deserve her." He smiled again. "A man looks ridiculous with a purse anyway."

In the middle of the entrée, she said, "You were absolutely right. I would have been stupid not to have this."

"I knew the chef would convince you," said Prescott.

She ate a few more bites, then stopped. "I can't eat any more. I'm just not used to it. I don't want to make you think I'm not doing what you asked, not having a good time. I love this restaurant. I love being here."

"I'm very glad," Prescott said. "It was the right place to take you, then. Being with the most attractive woman in the place is a special treat for me, and the food is the only reward for you."

She looked around the room—a little nervously, he thought—as she compared herself to the other women. Then she looked down at her plate. "You say things that I should think are insulting, because no woman would believe you. But I don't. It's nice."

They lingered for a long time over coffee. He had a small pastry for dessert, but she could not be induced to touch it. When they were outside and the valet brought the Corvette, she turned back toward the restaurant and stared into it. He said, "What's wrong? Did we forget something?"

"No."

"Is there somebody I forgot to tip?"

She got into the car, shook her head, and giggled. "No, I think you tipped everybody—even a couple of customers. I was just taking a last look."

"If you like it, let's come back. When are you going to have a night without classes again?"

"Not right away," she said. "We can talk about it sometime, if you still want to."

He drove along the Mississippi, looking at the lights on the water, glancing now and then at the huge concrete arch that dominated this side of the river. She said, "What do you think of it?"

"I'm not sure," he said. "It's pretty remarkable. I'm not sure yet what it's for."

"I've lived around here all my life, and neither am I."

They drove on for a time, not speaking. Finally, she said, "I'd invite you to my place for a drink, but I'm afraid I don't usually drink, so there's nothing there. Besides, the place is sort of a mess, and—"

"Then let's go to mine."

She hesitated for a few seconds, then said, "All right."

When they entered his apartment and he turned on the light, he could see her looking around with extreme care, like a small animal sniffing for danger. He directed her attention where he wanted it. "The apartment is still kind of tentative. I'm not really unpacked, so try to ignore that stuff." He pointed, and watched her eyes settle on the boxes and open bags of cameras, binoculars, expensive small furnishings, and the smaller, open boxes of wristwatches, women's jewelry, and gold coins.

While he went to the kitchen to make the drinks, he could tell by the sound of her high heels on the bare hardwood floor that she was looking more closely. He returned carrying two martinis, and handed her one. "I remember you said you don't drink very often, so you might want to take that in little sips over time."

She looked at him guardedly. "Are you married?"

He jerked his head back in surprise. "Me? Don't you remember? I'm one of the sad, lonely men you were talking about on the way to dinner. I think I might be their president."

"I said they were sad and lonely. That doesn't mean they're not married."

"Not me," he said. "Never been married. I guess the ones I liked well enough all liked somebody else better. I'm hoping it was the car washes—that they weren't glamorous enough—because that's solved."

She didn't appear amused. "Then why do you have all this jewelry?"

"What jewelry?"

She pointed at the top tray, which was full of rings and bracelets and necklaces in little compartments. "Duh?"

"Oh, that stuff. It's a small speculation. The company that bought one of my car washes is owned by a Malaysian family that has been buying up stuff in Hawaii and California. First they wanted to negotiate the sale in their currency instead of dollars. I said, 'Forget it.' A week later, the son comes back with another deal: half in dollars, and the rest in stock from a pawnshop they just bought in Phoenix. They wanted to close it and turn it into an office building. They had the permits and everything ready to demolish and build, so they were willing to give me an incredible discount. Look at this stuff: cameras, watches, all kinds of things. I figured I could write down the value a bit for tax purposes. Okay, write it down a lot. Come to think of it, I forgot to mention this stuff on my tax return at all. That's why I took a loss on my car wash." He grinned. "This is only part of it, too."

Jeanie took a deep breath and let it out in a sigh, shaking her head in amusement. "You're worse than Hobart. If I were your accountant, I'd have told you to stick with cash. Besides violating tax laws, you probably got screwed."

"Oh?" he said. "Come take a look." He pulled her to the side of the room, knelt, reached into an open box, rummaged around carelessly. He stood up behind her and pulled something around her neck.

"What are you doing?" she said. "That's cold."

He clasped the chain of the necklace and said, "That's probably true. Do you suppose that's why they call it ice? No, I guess it looks sort of like ice." He picked up an antique oval wall mirror with an ornate gold frame and a convex surface. "Here. Take a look."

She stared at herself in the mirror and saw the sparkle of diamonds against the black of her dress. The gold chain held a pear-shaped stone set as a pendant with a pea-sized round stone on either side of it. Prescott could see her chest rise and fall as she looked at herself. "It's beautiful," she said. "These can't be real."

"Of course they're real," he said. "I'm not the one who just got off the boat ready to buy everything in sight. I had all the stones appraised before I went into this thing. It's not the most up-to-date setting, but they can be reset. Maybe the two side stones as earrings or something. That's not important. I got them for a tenth of what you could get them for at Tiffany's." He laid the mirror on the floor beside the wall, picked up his drink again, and walked into the living room toward the couch.

Jeanie stopped beside the row of boxes, her hands behind her neck fiddling with the clasp. "Wait. Help me get this off."

He stopped and looked back at her for a moment, studying her critically. "No, I don't think so. It doesn't look anywhere near as good as that in a box. You'd better keep it."

Her eyes widened, and she froze, her hands still behind her neck. "You can't be serious. You hardly know me."

He smirked and waved a hand at her. "I don't know anybody else any better, and what I know about them isn't all good."

She shook her head. "I can't take something like this." She undid the clasp, carefully lifted the necklace off her neck, and fastened the clasp again.

"I'm not trying to insult you or pay you for going out with me or something," he said. "It's an impulse present. If you'll look in the other boxes, you can see I got more women's jewelry on that deal than I know what to do with. I picked out that one because it looked like something you could use. If you can, good for you. If you can't, pawn it and take a vacation sometime. That's probably what the last owner did."

She came to the couch, watching him as she let it dangle from the end of a finger. She sat down, unclasped it again, and turned away from him, holding the ends over the back of her neck. "Can you fasten it again?"

He clasped it. She stood and walked across the room with her drink, and sipped it. She turned on his radio and fiddled with the dials. Finally, she found a song with a beat. She turned it up and began to nod her head with the rhythm. She set her drink on the shelf beside the radio and began to dance, swaying her hips to the music. Her eyes were closed and her features assumed an expression that was transported. She turned away from him, tugged the zipper at the back of her dress down a few inches, then in a writhing motion reached up her back from below to pull it down farther. Her left hand rested on her thigh and began to slide up beside her haunch, bringing the dress with it.

"Wait," said Prescott. "Hold it."

She half-turned to look over her shoulder expectantly as she let the dress slide down to bare it, still moving with the music. "Something wrong?"

"Yes," said Prescott. He stood, stepped beside her, and turned off the music. "Don't do this," he said.

She turned the rest of the way to face him, holding the front of her dress up at the neck. "Don't?" she repeated, looking alarmed. "You don't want me to?"

"No," he said. "Please."

Her eyes were worried, almost frightened. "Why not?"

"I asked you to go out to dinner with me, and try to have a good time. Not to work another shift."

She shook her head like a person shivering, her eyes now earnest, pleading. "No," she said. "I want to. This isn't working, it's just for you." She seemed to search for an explanation. "It's an impulse present too, not something I agreed to do or planned ahead." She looked into his eyes again. "You have money, jewels. All I have . . ." She shrugged, and the dress slipped a little lower, the diamonds now sliding off the fabric to rest on the smooth skin between her breasts. She felt them and looked down, then quickly back up into his eyes, expecting that she had made the only argument she needed to. She saw something unexpected, his eyes delivering his accusation that her accidental gesture had been premeditated. She recognized it too, and he could tell she was fighting the sensation that nothing she did was, or could be, uncalculated. "Don't you like me?"

He said, "Thank you. I like you very much. I want you to be my friend. But this . . . this isn't the way for me to be yours. It wouldn't be good for you. It's my fault. I wanted to take you out, have a nice time, take you home, have you give me a good-night kiss, and leave. I still want to do that. The diamonds are nothing to me, just a little token like flowers. I didn't even buy the necklace in advance, just picked it, like a flower in my garden, and handed it to you."

Her eyes were beginning to look wet now. "You didn't find me in some art museum or something," she said. "This is what you like. You came to watch me all those times."

He gave her a rueful smile. "You're right. You don't know how hard this is to resist. But tomorrow when you get up, what I want you to remember is that you had a nice date with a man who isn't so bad, and went home without having to do anything but be pleasant. I don't want you to remember that a man gave you a necklace in return for a private strip show."

She shook her head hard, and put her hands on the sides of his head to force him to look into her eyes. "This is not hard for me, not humiliating or anything. I have a beautiful body. I like having you see it." Finally she said, her eyes telling him it was extremely hard for her, "This isn't like work. Don't you get it? I want to have sex with you."

He reached around her and zipped up the dress as he said, "Not like this." He stepped back and walked toward the couch. "Not the first time we were ever alone together."

She looked devastated. She stepped toward the door. "You'd better take me home now, okay?"

He put down his drink and walked toward the door. She seemed to take his acquiescence as a confirmation that he didn't like her. He said, "You said you weren't free again right away. Can I call you and see if we can arrange another dinner the first night you're not busy?"

She looked at him, confused. She said skeptically, "You won't call me again."

"If you think that, then let's arrange something now. Have you ever been to the Veranizzi restaurant at the Prince Andrew Hotel?"

"No."

"Good. Neither have I, so it's worth exploring."

She was silent for a moment, her eyes averted, looking down at her feet.

At last he said, "Well? What's wrong?"

She looked up at him, the tears now coming, but her mouth turned up, trying to keep from laughing at the same time. "I lied to you before," she said. "About my schedule—in case I didn't like you. I'm not really busy every night. I'm on break before summer session starts." She struggled. "I don't know how to tell you this, so I'll just say it. I'm working one to two tomorrow, and I'd like you to pick me up tomorrow at three-thirty, take me to the Prince Andrew so we can check in at four."

"I'll pick you up at six-thirty," he said. "For dinner."

He drove her back to the apartment complex, but when he pulled up to her building, she said, "Not here." She looked at him apologetically. "My building is way down there. I lied to you about that too, so if you were crazy or something, you wouldn't know where I lived."

He drove her to the distant building, let her out of the Corvette, and walked her to the door. She stopped, whirled, stood on her toes, and kissed him deeply, lingering for a long time.

"This is where you pick me up tomorrow. Three-thirty, sharp. Not six-thirty." She released him, then took a step toward the door, came back, and whispered in his ear, "Come and watch me work tomorrow. I would like it."

Prescott watched her disappear through the security door, heard the click as the automatic lock slid in. As he got into his car, he reviewed the evening. If there was any relationship between crimes and punishments, in a minute or two he was going to have to expect a big truck to come through the intersection at seventy, go right over his stupid little car, and drive the steering column straight through his chest.

27

Prescott walked into Nolan's at twelve-thirty, and the usual range of customers were there: men in sport coats, younger ones in khaki pants too well-pressed to be anything but clothes they wore to work. The bartenders and waitresses were busy getting tables set up and bottles and taps in order. But Dick Hobart was waiting for Prescott. It was easy for Prescott to see, because Hobart seldom watched the door until the dancers went on, when he could take his census of customers.

As Prescott stepped in the door, Hobart dropped his polishing rag, poured two draft beers from the tap, and carried them around to a table. He sat down and beckoned to Prescott.

"I've never seen you drink during working hours, Dick," said Prescott as he sat down.

"As a rule, I don't meet many customers I'd drink with," said Hobart. "I just thought I'd have a quick one with you before the crowds come in."

"Well, thanks," said Prescott. He took a sip and smiled. "I appreciate that."

Hobart looked around him as though checking to see that he would not be overheard. "She showed me the necklace you gave her. I was right about you. That was a thing not many sensible men have the class to do right."

Prescott shrugged and took another drink. "It wasn't a big deal. I'm glad she liked it."

Hobart's eyes made their regular rounds of the bar, the door, the stage, the few tables that were already occupied. "She told me about your problem."

Prescott's eyebrows went up. "Problem?"

"Yeah. She said you had a whole bunch of stuff like that. She said you'd taken them in trade or something."

Prescott's eyes settled on the wall across the room. He seemed to find it suddenly interesting.

Hobart said hastily, "Don't get upset. She didn't mean any harm, and I don't either. I like her, and I like you, and I wouldn't mind a bit if you two made each other happy. I actually respect you more for telling her that story." He grinned. "It's about as unbelievable as anything I ever heard, but I wouldn't have any part of a man who hasn't got the sense to feed a woman a bunch of nonsense instead of dumping the burden on her of knowing all about his business. They think they want to know, but after they do, it starts to eat at them."

Prescott sipped his drink again and slowly nodded. He looked at Hobart evenly. "Are you working up to telling me to leave her alone?"

Hobart looked surprised. "Not at all. I just told you, I'm happy for you both. But you know, she's not a stupid person. You give her a present, she's kind of dazzled by the sparkle for a while. Maybe a little later, her business sense is going to kick in: that's what she studies in night school. The story you told her may not sound as good then, and she's going to start worrying, asking harder questions. I think I have a solution." He leaned closer. "I can convert all that stuff to cash for you. When she can't see it, she'll forget it."

"You can do that?" Prescott allowed himself to show some interest.

Hobart nodded. "I told you I have connections. All you have to do is bring in what you want moved. You wait a week or so, and I'll have a buyer." He added, "You do have to give me an idea where it came from—just the name of the city where they're looking for it." He leaned back, drank half his beer, and smiled contentedly. "I'll get you top dollar, and that's the truth."

Prescott studied Hobart, but he didn't answer.

After a few seconds, Hobart began to look uncomfortable, then anxious. He leaned forward. "Look, I know you're not a kid, and I wouldn't try to rip you off. I could tell by looking at you that you've been away."

"How?"

"You drive up in a Corvette that's been up on blocks in some garage for a while, and come in wearing clothes that are expensive, but haven't been in a store in four or five years. And I can see from your face that you've been in a fight or two, so you probably weren't off painting pictures at your château in France." He lifted both hands a few inches above the table in a gesture of conciliation. "I'm not interested in knowing anything. I just figure I can do you some good. I know people who can spread your goods thin all over the place, and give you cash in full. No consignment or anything."

"What's your cut?"

"You and I agree on the price you want for each thing. They come to me and look at it. If they like it, they pay me, they take it away, and I give you your price in cash. I try to jack up the price they pay me just enough to make it worth my trouble. That's no more than anybody would do."

"What happens when they don't make the price?"

"I give you your goods back, and you're out exactly nothing. You don't see these guys. They've seen your stuff, but not you. They don't know who you are or where you live, so you don't have to watch your back."

Across the room, the warm-up music suddenly blared over the amplifiers. The small spotlights came on and threw overlapping circles on the stage. The curtain was pushed aside from the doorway and Jeanie stepped onstage. She was wearing a cocktail dress, as though she were out for the evening. As she stepped under the spots, Prescott saw the rainbow sparkle from the end of the gold chain around her neck. Her eyes surveyed the room, focused on Prescott, and looked glad.

Beside his ear, Hobart's voice came to him. "She's a real beauty, isn't she?" There was a pause. "And smart, too. There aren't many girls in this business who are as quick on the uptake as Jeanie."

Prescott kept his eyes on her. "All right," he said. "I'll bring you a few pieces tomorrow, and we'll try this thing out."

Prescott felt Hobart's hammy hand clap down on his shoulder. "You won't regret it."

"I already don't. Thanks," said Prescott as Hobart stepped off to the bar. Prescott returned his attention to the stage. Jeanie had been marking time, dancing provocatively and building up the suspense by fiddling with her hair and lifting the hem of her skirt to adjust a stocking. As soon as Prescott's eyes met hers, she returned to her act.

She looked into his eyes, her face now set in that watchful, knowing expression, the faint, pleased smile on her lips that he had seen last night. Then he understood it. She was re-enacting what had happened in his apartment last night, in a pantomime like the story in a ballet. She received the necklace, she was overwhelmed, and the gift transformed her. She lowered the top of the dress a little to show him how the diamonds looked on her bare skin, then hesitated. But this time, the story changed. The resistance, whatever its source, was easily, quickly overcome. She was free. The dress was tossed to the floor at the back of the stage. As she removed each garment, she held her eyes on Prescott.

Prescott hid his feelings behind his glass of beer, a good-natured, receptive smile fixed on his face. He could see she wasn't doing this for spite—showing him what he had foolishly turned down last night to tease him. She was making him an offer for tonight. For the next few minutes he sat in affable agony, knowing he must not take his eyes off her, but wishing that he at least wanted to. He felt a growing, gnawing guilt and regret that he had ever seen her, let alone decided that she would be his way to acceptance. But the guilt, the laboriously learned reluctance to do anything to harm an unoffending human being, was so fragile and frail that he could not even get his mind to hold it in place. It was just a bad feeling in his chest. The sight of this woman was bright, clear, and indelible, not a vague principle he had been told forty years ago was something to consider.

She was tantalizing, and the sight of her made his regrets seem empty, distant, and unreal. He tried to tell himself that he ought to find a way to get through this episode by derailing the relationship somehow, cutting it off before she got hurt. But being able to formulate and describe what should happen was not the same as wanting. What he wanted was only to touch her. Then the set was over, and she faded into the dimness at the back of the stage, snatched up the clothes, and dissolved into the curtain. He noticed that a second beer was beside him, waiting. He placed a twenty-dollar bill under it on the table, stood, and went out into the sunshine.

The fresh air and the bright light on the metal of the cars should have made him think clearly again, but he put the thinking off. He had coldly manipulated this young woman to get Dick Hobart's confidence, and to have her be the one who told Hobart that Bob Greene had a hoard of stolen valuables. He knew he was supposed to feel extremely happy that he had succeeded, but he was not.

He drove to his apartment, showered and dressed, then spent some time selecting the items he would bring to Dick Hobart. He put them into the zippered pockets of a leather jacket: two men's Rolex watches and one women's, several women's rings and a gold bracelet that had some good Burmese rubies set in it. He put the jacket into the trunk of his car with his overnight bag, and drove to Jeanie's apartment complex.

She wasn't waiting outside this time, so he was able to go to her door. She was ready, but she let him come in and pick up her overnight bag. She insisted on leading him from room to room to show him the apartment. There was a bedroom, and a spare room with exercise equipment, a desk, bookcases, and a computer. When the tour was finished, she said, "There. That's done. Let's go."

"Why did you want to show me your apartment? It's nice, but . . ."

"Because I made the mistake of telling you it was a mess. I didn't want you to think I was a pig."

He let her into the car, and they drove to the hotel. He had chosen the large, opulent, anonymous Prince Andrew because it was a place that was unlikely to cater to anyone who had also been to the Paddock Club. Jeanie saw that this was really where they were going and looked pleased, but did not mention it. She waited patiently while Prescott registered, then seemed to enjoy walking across the enormous marble floor to the elevator behind the bellman. She took Prescott's hand in the hallway and looked at the vases of flowers they passed at intervals as the bellman conducted them to their room. As soon as he left, Prescott said, "Would you like a drink?"

She put her arms around Prescott and kissed him. "What time is the dinner reservation?"

"Eight."

"Good." She turned around. "Unzip me."

He pulled the zipper down, and she stepped away. "You were right. We're both going to take our clothes off—no music—and meet in bed." She stepped to the closet to get a coat hanger, went into the bathroom, and closed the door.

Prescott undressed and got into the bed. When Jeanie emerged from the bathroom, she was wearing only the diamond necklace and a pair of diamond studs in her ears. She stopped and stood under the small spotlight by the closet, reached up and pulled the pin from her hair to let it fall to her shoulders, then shook her head to make it spill down her back. Then she walked comfortably to the bed, pulled the covers off Prescott to the floor, and lay down beside him.

Prescott had not exactly planned what he would do, or guessed how she would be with him when this time came, but he had not kept himself from imagining it. Now he found that his imagination had been pessimistic and impoverished. Prescott's mind was divided, reveling in the touch, sight, sound, taste, and smell of her, and concentrating on making her happy, then happier, trying to keep himself from giving in, to make it last. Finally, she put her hand on his cheek. "Now, Bobby, now would be a good time." He ended it, letting the glad, delicious feeling of release take him. They lay together in a long, quiet embrace.

Slowly, he became aware of the sounds of cars outside the hotel, then the quiet padding of feet moving along the hallway. She pulled away and lay a foot from him, stretching like a cat. "Now, that was really something," she said softly, as though to herself. Then she turned to him. "You were right to make me spend all day thinking about it first."

"I'm glad you think so," he said. "I was kind of thinking I was stupid to take the chance of missing it. You could have changed your mind. I could have gotten run over by a truck."

She sat up. "Good. That means you won't turn me down next time I ask." She stepped off toward the bathroom. "Let's take a shower. It's a respectable hour to go down and have a drink before dinner."

"Respectable?"

"Well, sure. Respectable people don't rush down to the bar at four o'clock in the afternoon. They stay upstairs in bed until seven, and then go down."

"I guess that's true."

"Of course it is." She began to run the shower.

Later, when they were in the bar, she sipped her drink thoughtfully. "This is perfect."

He tried his, and nodded. "I suspected the reason that lady was standing behind the bar was that she knew how to make a drink."

"Not that," she said. "The whole thing. The package."

"Thank you," he answered. "I'm happy with it myself."

"I want to be your girl," she said.

"What?"

"You heard me," she insisted. "I know that you think of me as a victim. Some men get a charge out of that, and if you do, go ahead. It doesn't hurt anybody. Some women like it too, I guess. It helps them be less inhibited, because they didn't do what they did: somebody did it to them. And it kind of makes the man seem extra forceful and aggressive—she couldn't say no—and I can understand that, too. They want a man who's male. You're male enough."

"I'm not sure I understand."

"I'm not a victim. I saw you, thought you looked nice, and tried to attract you—which isn't that tough to do if somebody's there to watch you take your clothes off anyway. You turned out to be a lot nicer than I thought. I'm smart enough to know you're not going to be in St. Louis long. And I'm not interested in falling in love and getting married. I know exactly what I'm doing for the next five years, and could make a guess about the next twenty. I'm not in a position for a long commitment."

"I thought you wanted to be my girlfriend."

"I do, for now. You and I both are here on our way somewhere else. A couple of days ago, we each, for our own reasons, decided to take a step off the path because it looked appealing. It's been better than

either of us thought it would be or was ready for. And now I'm heading off trouble."

"Trouble?"

"You're starting to feel upset because you think you took this dumb
little stripper and led her on and gave her false hopes, just to get into
her pants." She laughed. "You feel guilty because you've been too nice
to me. Do you realize how stupid that is? Do you think it's possible
that any woman somehow manages not to know what's on your
mind?"

"I guess it's not a good idea to answer rhetorical questions," said
Prescott.

"No, it isn't," she said. She placed his hand in hers.

"This is really nice. In a week or a month or whenever, one of us is
going to have to move on to something else, maybe even someplace
else. I want to be able to enjoy it without watching you feel guilty
about it. Letting you do that would make me feel guilty."

"Are you telling the truth?" he asked.

"Sure." She patted his arm. "We're each committed to what we're
doing—school for me, and for you, whatever—and a temptation came
up to have some fun. I took the chance, and it worked out great. Now
that it's gone this far, I've gotten some worries behind me that only
women feel. Trust is one. You're not rough or weird or scary. You
don't act nice until you come, and then throw me out of bed or something. But now I have a new worry, which is that you'll decide it's
mean to lead me on, and turn cold. So I'm making you a proposition.
Your part of it is that while you're around St. Louis, you're mine. You
take me to places like this, be sweet to me every day, whether we're together or not. I won't see you walking out of Nolan's with one of the
other girls."

"And what's your part?"

"I don't pay attention to other men. Except for when I'm at work or
in class, I'm available to you. . . . Completely," she added with empha-
sis. "Now that I know what I needed to about you, I'll do anything
you want." She smiled. "Maybe even some things you don't know you
want."

His eyebrows went up.

"People who are interested in hurting you show it before this. And they don't feel guilty about using people. I know you're using me, and I'm using you too, in a nice way, to be happy. When it's over, we're both going to regret that it's over, not that it happened. We'll smile when we go. So?"

"That's quite a proposition," he said. "You're my girl." They ate in the restaurant and walked under the stars. The night was hot and the air was lazy, and the sounds of their footsteps seemed to be the only ones to reach their ears. They came back into the air-conditioning of the hotel lobby, had a drink in the bar, and went back up to bed.

For the next week, Prescott divided his time between Jeanie and Dick Hobart. When that week was over, another began and ended in a quiet, calm, and untroubled way. Hobart took each parcel of suspicious goods that Bob Greene brought him, sold it at the price he and Greene had agreed upon, and gave him the money in bills taken from the cash receipts at Nolan's. Bob Greene was well liked, an increasingly familiar face in some of the most exclusive hotels and restaurants in St. Louis, and in one of the most obscure dives. There were times when Prescott almost forgot.

28

Varney felt as though he were underwater, swimming upward toward the light, holding his breath, trying to break the surface. The pressure in his lungs was unbearable, but the water level kept going up as he rose. When he awoke each morning, he would be relieved that it had not been real. Then he would remember what was real, and begin to feel hot panic. Each morning when he sat up, he knew that he owed Tracy and her sons one hundred for the apartment, three hundred for general services that amounted to no more than keeping his presence in Cincinnati a secret. He would look down at Mae's head, her hair spread out on the pillow and her body an inert lump under the covers, and remember that she was part of it. Having her here was costing him not just the original five hundred a day, but now sometimes a fee to hire another girl to do whatever Tracy wanted done. Sometimes that was another five.

Varney had stopped adding up the money he had spent this way. He knew it was already so much that the number would have made him sick. He didn't even count the money he had left from the visit to the safe-deposit box, because counting would have told him when he was going to run out again. He would not have been able to see the date on the morning newspaper without thinking about the final day, worrying about it, feeling its approach. None of this was his fault. Being here wasn't self-indulgence, because that was a kind of weakness. This had been a calculated strategy made necessary by the intrusion of Roy Prescott.

It was Prescott who had done this to Varney. There was not a day when Varney didn't go over the chances that he'd had to kill Prescott, wincing at the mistakes he had made, the opportunities he had not recognized until just after they had passed. He had not known Prescott was waiting outside the office building that night in L.A. until it was too late to kill him. At the storefront in Buffalo that Prescott had rented, he had not noticed that there was something wrong with the doorknob before the door had closed. He could have seen that it was a trap without opening the door at all and could have waited for Prescott outside the building with the rifle. He had not seen any of those things in time, and now it was too late. Prescott had become more than a person he hated. Prescott had begun to enter his dreams.

Varney got up and slapped the part of the covers that he judged was Mae's bottom. "How about some breakfast?"

She lay there for a second, then slowly stretched and rolled over to look at him. "What time is it?"

"Drag your ass out of bed and look at the clock," he said. "I'm going out, and I want to eat first."

She sat up, swung her legs out of the bed, and walked stiffly to the bathroom. She stood in front of the mirror, brushed her hair back, and then went out into the kitchen. Varney stood a few feet away, watching her impatiently. In a minute she had started the coffee and she was standing in front of the stove with a pair of frying pans on the burners with bacon and eggs popping and sizzling. When they seemed to be going the way they should, she set the table hurriedly, tossing the silverware into approximate positions, then pulled the pans off the stove. She came back with Varney's plate. He was carefully moving the knives and forks to their correct spots. He sat down and she set the plate in front of him, poured a cup of coffee, and turned to go back to the bathroom.

"Aren't you going to sit down?"

"I wasn't going to," she said. "You know I can't stand the smell of all that bacon and butter and stuff when I just wake up. It makes me sick."

He glared at her, and she came back and sat down across from him, holding the coffee just below her chin and sipping it now and then as she watched him. Finally, he put down his fork. "Don't you think that for nearly a thousand a day, you could act like you want to be with me?"

"I'm sorry, Jimmy," she murmured warily. "It's just that you're not nice to me sometimes. I had to brush my hair first, or you'd be finding it in your food. And I didn't know you wanted to get up this early. I mean after last night . . ."

He rolled his eyes and shook his head slowly, then muttered, "Forget it."

He had awakened in the middle of the night, thinking about Prescott. He knew that he'd had a dream, something about Coleman, maybe a job they had done together, but then Coleman had somehow stopped being Coleman. Varney had looked at him again, and he had become Prescott. It seemed that Coleman had been Prescott all along, watching Varney do the job, and so he knew everything. Varney had no way to slip away or hide or claim it was self-defense, because Prescott had been there.

Varney had jerked awake in a sweat. It had taken a few minutes to calm himself, but then he was alert. He had lain there for a few more minutes, but then it became an hour. He couldn't get back to sleep. He had reached out and touched Mae. He had done it without any particular intention, but as soon as he had felt the small shoulder, and run his hand down her side to the thin waist and felt the curve of the hip, he had known. She had still been asleep, and the warmth of her skin felt comforting.

As consciousness had threatened her rest she had resisted, stiffening, then tried to shrug him away to preserve her sleep. That had changed everything. It had made him resentful. He had firmly pulled her to him, and in a moment she was no longer asleep, but trying to cut through the fog of sleep to full consciousness. She'd seemed to sense that something had begun before she'd been aware of it and she should have been aware, and she'd had to catch up with it. The look in her eyes had changed. He had seen them widen in the dark as he'd kissed her, hard, his hands already tugging the nightgown up to her neck.

He had probably been rough—had been rough—but it had been impossible not to be. Last night it had all seemed to come together in the simple, annoyed movement of her shoulder as she pulled away from him in her sleep: being stuck here in Cincinnati with Tracy and her sons bleeding him to death instead of hiding him, everyone taking advantage of his sudden vulnerability, most of all Mae. If it weren't for her, he would have burst through his lethargy and gotten out of here. When he had been feeling troubled and worried and sleepless she'd had no business jerking away from him like that. What was he supposed to do?

She seemed to see his resentment growing again. She said hastily, "Not that I didn't like it. I did," she assured him. "I always like to be with you. I just thought you would probably sleep late this morning, that's all."

"Forget it," he repeated. He stood and went into the bedroom to put on his shorts and sneakers to begin his stretches. He was glad when she went into the bathroom for her shower, because he didn't have to listen to her or feel her eyes on him. He cut the stretches short and walked toward the door. The telephone rang, and made him jump. He snatched it up. "Yeah?"

It was a man's voice. "Is Mae there?"

"Yeah, but she can't come to the phone now. Can I say who's calling?"

"It's Duane." Varney knew who that was. He was one of the messengers that went around distributing stolen stuff all over the Midwest. About a month ago, when Varney had gotten into an argument with Tracy over her wanting Mae to work a party, Duane had been one of the ones the party was for. Varney glanced at the calendar. It was not about a month. It was exactly a month.

Varney said, "Wait a minute. I'll tell her."

He went toward the bathroom, his mind gnawing at him. Something was going on. He stopped before he got there, and returned to the phone. "Duane?"

"Yeah?"

"She says to come pick her up at eleven."

"Really?" Duane sounded pleased. "Eleven? Where?"

"Here," said Varney. "You know the address?"

"Yeah, I been there," he said. "Thanks."

Varney hung up the telephone and went back to stretching. When Mae came out of the bathroom, he had begun lifting weights. Her head gave a little jerk, as though she were surprised and a little frightened to see him there. She said, "I thought you were going out for your run."

"I am," said Varney coldly. "You lift, then you run."

"Oh, yeah," she said softly.

"Can you do me a favor this morning?"

"I guess," she said. "What is it?"

"Go out to the Sportmart on the mall. I need a new pair of shorts like these—any color as long as it's dark—and another twenty pounds of weight for this bar. See? Two ten-pound disks like this? They're all standard, so you can't screw it up."

"Okay . . ." she said doubtfully. "They don't have shopping carts at the mall. Will I be able to carry them?"

"Hell, yes," he said. "You can carry twenty pounds. If you can't, get the clerk to do it. The mall opens at ten, and I'd like you back by one."

"Okay," she said. "I'll go as soon as I'm dressed. I'll be there when they open."

He went into his sit-ups. When she left, she said, "See you later."

"Yeah," he muttered. He heard her steps on the stairway, then stood beside the window to watch. She went outside, got into the car, and drove off. He closed the window and lowered the shade. He changed his clothes, went to the closet, and took out the two bags he had bought a week ago from the hardware store. Mae had been begging him to brighten the place up a little, so he had bought what he needed to paint the kitchen.

He laid the plastic tarp on the floor, moved the furniture out of the way, set the two gallon cans on two opposite corners and the roller and pan on another, then sat down on the bed and waited patiently.

At exactly eleven he heard the car. He moved to the kitchen and listened carefully to the sound of the footsteps. They were quick and heavy, but there was only one set. He looked outside and saw the car, and verified that there was nobody waiting in it. He heard the knock and opened the door.

Duane was big, with a puffy pink face and a shock of blond hair that seemed to be duplicated on his thick forearms. He was wearing blue jeans, a short-sleeved shirt, and a pair of wraparound sunglasses that were too small for his face, so they looked like the useless little masks across the eyes in drawings of comic-book superheroes. Duane stepped back and stood uncomfortably outside the doorway. "Hi, I'm Duane. Is Mae ready?"

"Just about," Varney said. "Come in and sit down." He set a chair in the center of the tarp.

"I'll wait out here," Duane said.

"Come in," Varney repeated, his dark expression telling Duane he meant it. Duane looked at the tarp, pan, and roller. Varney said, "I don't want people hanging around the hallway, spooking the neighbors." Duane stepped in.

"I see you're doing some painting," said Duane, as he obediently sat in the kitchen chair.

Varney said, "Yeah," as he went to the refrigerator and reached into the freezer. He could see that the sound of the freezer made Duane feel less awkward and worried. His shoulder muscles relaxed, and he reached up to take off his sunglasses. Before Duane's hand could touch the frame of the glasses, Varney pulled the knife out of the freezer, turned, and shoved it up into the space below Duane's ribs into the vicinity of his heart. Duane looked down, as though to see what the source of his sudden discomfort might be. He saw the darkening spot at the top of his paunch, gripped it with both hands, and lunged forward, his mouth open in a silent circle.

Varney's knee came up quickly and snapped the sunglasses neatly at the bridge of Duane's nose, so that the glasses came apart, dangling from Duane's ears. Varney gripped Duane's hair with his left hand, brought the knife across Duane's throat, and shoved him down so that his face hit the pan on the tarp.

Duane's heart was still pumping, but only half the blood seemed to be spurting into the pan. Varney judged that the rest of it was leaking into Duane's chest cavity or out onto his shirt. Varney raised his knife to the side, spun it in his fist, and exerted his right arm muscles hard to drive the blade through the thin wall of bone into Duane's temple. Duane's body jerked once more and went limp.

Varney stood and looked around him. There were no blood spatters on the floor or walls. He heard no sound of footsteps. It had been unusually quiet. Varney moved the kitchen chair off the tarp, waited a few minutes, then checked Duane's carotid artery. He had no pulse, and his skin was already beginning to feel cooler to Varney than it had at first. He dragged the head back, and saw that the blood that was dripping now was just running down from Duane's chin. The roller pan held only about two quarts, and the overflow had pooled under and around Duane, soaking his clothes.

It took Varney a few minutes to clean the knife, return the paint cans and roller to the closet, pour the pan out into the sink drain without getting much on the porcelain, and wash it too. He used a few week-old newspapers to soak up the pools of blood on the tarp.

He took Duane's wallet, removed $620 from it, and then found his car keys in his pocket. Varney went downstairs, moved Duane's car to the back of the building beside the door, and lined its trunk with plastic trash bags.

When Varney returned, he was pleased to see that most of the blood had soaked into the clothes or the old newspapers or thickened and begun to dry a bit. He rolled Duane up in the tarp, tied it securely with twine, and then ran duct tape around the ends to hold it. It occurred to him that Duane looked like a big blue sausage, and he laughed. He put a trash bag over Duane's top, and another over the bottom, tugged them until they met, and secured them with more duct tape.

Varney moved all of the furniture back into the kitchen, took a last look around to be sure there was nothing he had forgotten to clean, then knelt and used his legs to raise Duane to his shoulder in a fireman's carry.

He staggered getting Duane up, then steadied himself and stepped out the door. He could feel the strain of the extra weight on his back and knees as he went down the stairs, but he breathed deeply, kept his shoulders flexed and his back straight. When he bent his knees to shift Duane into the trunk of the car, then straightened, he felt as though he were rising into the air. He was proud of himself: there weren't many men his size who were strong enough or in good enough shape to do that. He was sweating a bit, but he wasn't strained or winded.

Varney drove to the south for an hour before he saw the right kind of wooded area. He used the knife to loosen the top layer of leaves and dirt, then dug a bit more with a spare hubcap he found in the trunk. He worked hard, dug two feet down before he went back to get Duane. He unrolled the tarp so that only Duane and his glasses went in, then gathered the tarp, knife, and newspapers into one of the trash bags and tied it shut. He filled in the hole, covered it with leaves again, and took the trash bag with him to the car.

Varney drove back to Cincinnati, stuffed the bag into the bottom of a dumpster, then parked the car on the street five miles from his apartment. He searched it for any paper that might tell the police anything, but found none. He wiped the prints off the door handles, steering wheel, and trunk, walked the first two miles, then jogged the rest of the way home. He was back at one, but he could see that Mac had not returned from the mall. He took his clothes off, put them into the washing machine and started the load, then got into the shower.

When he got out, he heard Mae laboring up the stairs. When she was outside the door, he heard a rustle, then a heavy clank as she set the weights on the floor and put her key into the door. It swung open, and he saw her raise her hand to push a strand of black hair out of her eyes. She looked beautiful to him, and he discovered he was not angry at her anymore.

It was five days later that he had to go into the office and pay Tracy for the next two weeks. He walked into the building, climbed the steps to the second floor, and stepped into the big wholesale office.

Tracy was busy staring at a column of figures on a piece of paper. He had to wait until the sharp pencil point had put a dot beside each line and come to the bottom. Then the sharp fingernails released the pencil and let it fall on the desk.

"Oh, it's you," she said. She was not smiling.

"I brought you some money," said Varney.

She raised the pencil again, holding it before her, pinched between the thumb and forefinger of each hand. "You're not going to say anything?"

"Like what?"

" 'I'm sorry, Tracy,' or 'Forgive me, Tracy, I didn't mean it.' "

He stared at her, and he could see she knew. "I'm sorry." Then he said, "Why am I sorry?"

"Because you have risked my life, my sons' lives, the very people who took you in when you needed it. You showed no regard for our safety, or even your own. You killed a man who worked for me. Do you have no feelings?"

"What are you talking about?"

She raised her voice almost to a shriek. "They warned me. Everybody warned me. You can't keep a killer around and expect he's not going to do something. That's why I never did it before. You fooled me, with your baby face and your 'Yes, Tracy, no, Tracy.' I should have cut out my tongue before I said yes to you."

"He called the apartment. You should have kept him away from Mae," said Varney. "I was paying you for that."

"He never asked me, or I would have."

"His mistake."

"No, yours."

"How's that?"

"You think I'm the only one who knows? He had a family. They know you did it. He called you from home!"

"Give me their address, and I'll take care of it."

The suggestion seemed to further enrage her. "He was a hillbilly. You can't kill them all. There are brothers, sisters, cousins all over Ohio, Kentucky, and Indiana. They want money. They wanted a hundred thousand to keep quiet, but I beat them down to seventy. If you don't think that's a good deal, here's the phone book. Kill everybody in it named Perkins. Then you can start on the sisters under married names, and the cousins and aunts and uncles."

"You got them to agree to one payment to shut up and forget he's dead?"

"I told you, they're trash. They know it's either seventy grand, or they get to talk and have the pleasure of seeing you go to jail, which is worth nothing."

"Have you paid them?"

"No, I haven't paid them," she shouted. "I didn't kill him. And where am I going to get seventy thousand dollars? But if I were you, I'd get it, and bring it here today. They're not real good at waiting."

He nodded, numbly.

"And while you're at it, don't forget the thirty-five hundred you owe Mae, and the seventy-five hundred you owe me."

He walked to the door, then stopped and turned to look at Tracy. "Does Mae know?"

Tracy sighed and shook her head. "No, she doesn't. If she did, it would scare the poor girl to death. You pay, and she never has to know." Tracy's voice lowered a bit. "This can be just between you and me." Her heavily made-up eyes were reproving, but he detected a hint of the tentative, conditional forgiveness that his mother had sometimes teased him with. "Just don't ever do that again."

29

The northern end of the San Fernando Valley was only a few miles inland from where Millikan lived, but on nights like tonight, the air seemed to have drifted in from the desert and then remained still all day, heating up on the treeless boulevards and vast, blacktopped parking lots. The sweat had already begun to form droplets on his forehead. "She ran this place all alone—did the cooking and handled the cash register?"

"That's right," said Carrera. "The register's got over two hundred in it, and nothing else seems to be missing either."

Millikan went behind the counter into the little kitchen and stared down at her body. She was Hispanic, not much over five feet tall. She looked about sixty years old, but he knew she could have been much younger. Life in this tiny, sweltering space, standing over a griddle, squinting to protect her eyes from smoke and getting peppered with grease spatters, wasn't much of a beauty treatment. He supposed it wasn't always this hot, but after she had been shot, the killer had not bothered to turn off the oven or the deep fryer.

Lieutenant Carrera stood on the other side of the counter, leaned over it, and pointed. "See, she got just the two shots: one through the chest, and the other in the back of the head after she was down."

Millikan had to step through the narrow door to go outside and then come back in through the front entrance to reach the small porch that had been enclosed and converted into a dining room. There was a big blue B grade from the Los Angeles County Health Department posted on the window. There were only four tables, and from the look of the place, all four had probably been filled at once only during lunch hours. This was not a night spot.

Millikan took a few steps, then stopped and stared down at the third man on the floor. Like the other two, he was Anglo, not Hispanic, and moving into middle age. He estimated that they were all in their late thirties to early forties. The man wore blue jeans that showed some wear, but not the wear that came from physical work. They were slightly faded because somebody had washed them a couple of times to make them soft and maybe to shrink them to give a custom fit.

Millikan would not have needed to look at the jeans to know that these men had not been laborers. Their hands were soft, not callused. Millikan knew that if he wanted to figure out how much a man made, the place to look was where the money showed. Car keys all came from the factories now, because they had computer chips and remote door-lock controls. They had the make of the car stamped all over them. And Millikan had become very good at identifying men's shoes and watches.

The three men were arranged roughly in a line across the room. There was a hole in the forehead of the man on the right, a hole in the back of the man in the center, near the front door. The third man had ducked down behind a table, and gotten shot through it at least four times: Millikan could see several holes in the tabletop, and entry wounds in the man's thigh, stomach, chest, and head.

Millikan had collected a great many tiny bits of mostly useless information over the years. He recognized the one that was in front of him now. When a man with a gun told a group of victims to line up, the place to stand was the center of the line. Right-handed shooters shot the one on the right first, and left-handed shooters began with the one on the left. There was something in the human mind that always kept killers from shooting the man in the middle first.

He pointed at the man on the right. "That one was first, through the head." He moved his arm to indicate the one on the left. "The one over there saw what was happening—or maybe figured out the sort of trouble he was in after the first shot—and ducked down behind the table. The shooter fired through the tabletop a few times, quickly. While he was doing that, this guy was moving too, so the shooter got him in the back and dropped him before he could get to the door. The shooter is right-handed, probably."

"I'll buy that," Carrera said, then paused for a moment. "Okay, so Danny, what do you think? What are the chances it's the same guy?"

Millikan looked at the group of brass casings on the floor, each of them already circled with chalk. There was a small numbered placard beside each one. His eyes moved to the arrangement of bodies. "Absolutely none." He saw the look of disappointment in Carrera's eyes. "I'm sorry, Pete."

Carrera shrugged. "Just so you're sure."

Millikan knelt above one of the brass casings, with a number 8 placard beside it. "See this? In the Louisville restaurant there was no brass. He picked it all up and took it with him." Millikan stared more closely at the shell, then stood. "Forty-one Magnum. Remember those? You don't see many of them anymore, but they were a big deal for a while. They were supposedly going to be the next standard police load in about 1964 or '65. He probably wasn't alive then."

"But he isn't a killer with a signature," Carrera reminded him. "He seems to be able to use whatever comes to hand."

"He's even better than that," said Millikan. "He can make what he wants come to his hand. There's no reason for him to do a paid killing with a gun in a caliber he's not used to, especially one that's a little bit eccentric and out-of-date. When he killed Officer Fulco at the hospital, he took her nine-millimeter Beretta. When he killed the security guard in the building on Wilshire, he got his gun too."

"Any chance he'd do it to disguise himself, just to throw us off?"

Millikan shook his head. "Not him. But maybe whoever did this heard about him on television and gave it a try." He stepped carefully across the room. "This all looks a little bit like the killings in Louisville—three guys shot in a locked restaurant, and the cook taken out because she's a witness—but it's not. The Louisville killer would never make everybody stand in a row so he could shoot them. It's a step that would never enter his mind."

Millikan approached the table that had been turned on its side and punctured by several shots. "In Louisville he had two people down behind a table like this. He didn't fire a bunch of shots through it, hoping he'd hit something. He took the time to walk around it and shoot what he could see. He stays calm and works efficiently. This just isn't his work."

Carrera looked around him at the bodies. "You think we've got a copycat?"

"Not exactly," said Millikan. "Not the kind who got set off by hearing about the other shooting. I think the one who killed these people just figured his chances were better if you wasted some time thinking he might be the Louisville shooter."

Carrera sighed. "You've got me there. As soon as I heard what kind of shooting this was, I thought of him. So did the first officers to respond to the call. I guess we all just hope he'll do something else here, and this time he'll screw up: leave a print, get noticed, or something."

"Me too," said Millikan. He wrenched his mind away from the direction it was taking, refusing to let himself return to the secret hope.

"Heard anything about how Roy Prescott's doing?" It was as though Carrera had read Millikan's mind, detected the vulnerability, and poked at it.

"I don't know," Millikan said. "I haven't talked to him in a long time."

Carrera nodded, pretending to look at the bodies on the floor but holding Millikan in the corner of his eye. "I suppose not. I don't think I'd want to be in too close touch either."

Millikan took a deep breath, and turned to face Carrera. "You and I have known each other for a long time, Pete," he said carefully. "I won't start hiding the truth from you now. The reason Prescott is after this guy is that I gave the father of one of the Louisville victims his phone number. I was the one who brought Prescott in. The father probably would have hired some private detective and thought he'd done everything there was to do. He had never heard of Prescott until I told him."

Carrera returned his gaze to the floor for a few seconds. "Just now I was about to ask you why, but then I realized that I would be the one who was lying. Asking would be pretending that I didn't understand, that I wouldn't have been tempted to do the same thing." He straightened, sighed, and looked Millikan in the eye. "I would like to have a cop be the one who gets this guy, especially after what he did to Fulco and Alkins. It would be better for all of us. But it wouldn't bother me that much if Prescott got to him first."

"I can't say it was the best way," said Millikan. "I don't even know whether it helped or hurt. I talked to Prescott in Buffalo after he'd had a brush with the guy, months ago. Then he dropped out of sight. Both of them did. I don't know what it means. It might just mean that he doesn't want anything more from me, and I'll hear when everybody else does."

"If anything comes in about him—about either of them—I'll let you know right away," said Carrera.

"Thanks, Pete."

"And thanks for coming to look at this mess. I guess the captain didn't need to spoil both our dinners."

Millikan surveyed the room again. "This one, maybe we can do something about. You have three guys here who all look about the same age, thirty-five to forty. They're all dressed in casual clothes, but not cheap. Look at the shoes: Mephisto, Ecco. I didn't look closely at the third guy's, but they seem to be about the same class, and practically new. All three of them have good watches. I figure they're all in the same social or business set, and it's not one that usually hangs out in a place like this at night. I would guess they're all in the same line of work, and it pays okay. They couldn't have all come here at once, dressed the same, by coincidence. They met here for something. Probably it was some kind of business meeting. Obviously, there was a fourth guy. I would guess he wasn't somebody they just ran into here, some stranger who killed everybody. I would guess he was the one who arranged the meeting."

"A drug deal?"

"It doesn't feel that way." Millikan glanced down at the shell casings on the floor again. "I think it's likely he's a bit older than the others. He's at least fifty, probably closer to sixty. He's never done anything like this before. The brass is tarnished, as though he loaded the bullets into the gun with his bare fingers some time ago, and it's been sitting there ever since. I wouldn't even be surprised if he bought the gun twenty or thirty years ago, and never used up the box of ammo he bought at the same time. It will be something like this: these three business guys all conspired to cheat a supplier, and it's putting him out of business. Or the three are partners who were just about to fire an older employee, and he found out about it. It had to be something that would make him angry long enough to plan this and go through with it. Find out what they did for a living, and how they knew each other, and you'll be halfway there."

"I've already got people finding most of that out now," said Carrera. "We'll just see who the older guy might be and try to pick him up quick, before he calms down."

"That's what I'd do," Millikan agreed.

The two men stepped outside, and Millikan could feel the air immediately begin to pull the sweat off his body and cool his skin. A young woman from the forensics team he had never seen before tonight slipped past them through the doorway and returned to her work. Two others joined her, and he realized they must have finished out here a while ago, and waited.

"I guess I'll get out of the way now, Pete," said Millikan. "I appreciate your giving me a call. It wasn't him this time, but it could have been."

"Yeah," Carrera agreed, unconvincingly. "By the way, I told Denise I'd seen you. She said to tell you hello." He chuckled ruefully. "I think she'd probably invite you folks to dinner, but you and I were really the ones who knew each other. She'd be afraid she'd have to invite me, too."

Millikan hesitated, not quite sure what to say. "I was sorry when you told me about the divorce. I hope you know I wish you both well."

"You too. See you, Danny."

Millikan walked uncomfortably to his car, leaving Carrera to turn away toward the tiny white board-and-stucco building. Millikan got in, started the engine, and quickly drove away. Being with Pete Carrera had induced a kind of tension in him that seemed not to disperse as they talked, but to mount and become worse until the awkwardness of each word he said became an overwhelming embarrassment. He intentionally drove down the street in the wrong direction just because his car had been pointed that way when he'd gotten into it.

Then he drove around the block to keep from having to go back past the place.

He had been working homicide cases with Carrera when he had finally conceded to himself that it was time to leave the police force. They had gotten along well enough, but they had been different. Carrera had wanted to clear a case, make an arrest, and go home to dinner. Millikan had wanted something more: he'd wanted to get better at it, to understand what had happened, to be able to look at the evidence a killer left behind and figure out how he had done his killing and what sort of person he was. Each night, after Carrera had gone home, Millikan had devoted extra hours to preparing himself to become the department's resident expert on homicide scenes. He had studied the photographs in old case files, compared investigating officers' reports with the transcripts of confessions, and gone to examine scenes he had not been assigned to, just to see how more experienced detectives interpreted the things they saw. After a conviction, he would sometimes go to speak with the killer to see what he could learn. The hours he had put in astounded him now. He could barely remember the way it had felt to have that kind of stamina. But gradually he had learned and his judgment had improved, and soon, the officers in his division had noticed it.

In time, homicide detectives from other divisions, and then other cities, had begun to ask his advice. Because cops habitually worked on the basis of personal relationships and systems of reciprocal favors, the requests had not been directed to LAPD Van Nuys homicide, but to Sergeant Daniel Millikan. His superiors had not liked that. Eventually there had been a reprimand that had actually made it into his file. The union had managed to have it suppressed, but by the time they had accomplished that, he was already gone. The incident had convinced him that he had already hit the ceiling. No matter what he had already learned to do, or how he might work to improve himself in the future, his life as a police officer would be about the same. There seemed to be no choice for him except to get out.

Seeing Carrera always brought those days back, the sick, bitter feeling of the end of the experience, but also the sweet days when they had both been young and feeling their strength. That was nearly as bad, because it reminded him of loss. Being the youngest had meant

being surrounded by older men—uncles and teachers and enemies—
who had, in the years since then, disappeared. It was a different department, a different world, because those men were not in it. Carrera
had become one of the old-timers now. In another year or two, he
would probably either make captain and become an invisible adminis-
trator or be passed over again, retire, and get started on drinking himself to death alone in the apartment he had rented when Denise had
thrown him out. As Millikan had the thought, he could not avoid the
knowledge that he looked forward to losing touch with Carrera. It was
painless to deal with a department made up of young strangers who
knew him only as the professor, the man who wrote the books, and
not the cop who had quit.

Millikan reached the small, two-story house on the quiet street in
the northern part of Sherman Oaks, and pulled into the driveway. He
got out of the car and closed the door as gently as he could. He looked
around him, as he always did, but this time his mood made the sight
irritating. When he and Marjorie had moved here, the whole neighborhood had been single-family houses much like theirs, but now on
the busy east-west boulevards on two sides, he could see tall apartment buildings. Down the next street they had just bulldozed another
house and begun digging a hole for a foundation that could hardly be
anything but an underground parking garage for another big apartment building. It frustrated him that he had no memory at all of the
house that had been destroyed.

He was also frustrated because it should not have been allowed: this
area had always been zoned R-1. But Millikan had enough connections in the local government so he should have been incapable of surprise at the granting of exemptions. The lives of politicians were a
tormented rush to collect money for the next election, so their fre-
quent meetings with developers were a degrading alternation of
bribery and extortion. He only hoped that it would remain tolerable to
live here for the years he and Marjorie had left.

Millikan took a step toward the front door, then stopped and stood
motionless for a moment breathing the hot, still air and listening to
the distant, whispery sounds of cars speeding along Chandler. He
knew that he had just been distracting himself from his personal dis-
comforts by railing against the anonymous forces he liked to blame

for ruining things. He leaned against the door of his car and considered what was really bothering him. It was that the Louisville restaurant killer had caused him to do things that he had never intended to
do, never would have believed he would do.

There were homicide detectives who had never actually solved a
murder in their careers. What Millikan meant when he used the word
solved was that there was no eyewitness, no confession, no suspect who
was indisputably the only possible killer. What the investigator had
was a crime scene and a mind. Millikan had solved many, perhaps
three hundred. His books and his courses had helped police officers
all over the country solve an unknown, larger number. He had sacri-
ficed security and suffered doubt and long, lonely hours early in his
life in exchange for knowledge, and then worked steadily and tirelessly to improve, but in the end he had made a contribution. If he had
been able to look at himself from a distance, through someone else's
eyes, he would have had to say that he had been a reasonable success.
But the premise was false: the distant observer would not know that
after a lifetime of professing his faith in the slow, logical process of
collecting evidence and helping prosecutors present it in courts of law,
he had finally resorted to sending someone like Roy Prescott out to
get a killer.

It suddenly occurred to him that Marjorie had probably heard the
car drive in, and she would be wondering what he was doing out here.
He stepped to the door, unlocked it, and opened it, ready to turn off
the alarm. There was no alarm sound.

"Dan?" It was Marjorie's voice, the sound of all the good in his life:
warmth, softness, a bit of concern.

"Yeah, honey," he called. "It's only me."

She padded into the kitchen on bare feet, wearing a soft flannel
nightgown, her long dark hair hanging loose, a hairbrush in her hand.
She came close, stood on her toes, and kissed his cheek as he took off
his coat.

"You forgot to turn on the alarm again," he said.

"I was going to go to bed without you, and if I fell asleep and you
came in late, it would go off and scare me."

He kept himself from repeating his lecture on precautions; she
knew. He put his arm around her waist and felt the soft cloth move

against her naked body, the narrow waist curving outward to the rounded hip. In early middle age, she had been concerned and upset by the graying of her hair and subtle changes she detected in her body, but a few years ago, she had simply stopped. One day she had said, "My body isn't young anymore, but it's a body that somebody loved, and that carried our children and nursed them." She still dyed her hair to cover the gray, she still dieted and exercised, but there was not the same frantic and despairing quality to what she did. He suspected that even now, she did not quite accept that she was a beautiful fifty-year-old, any more than he had been able to convince her that she was a beautiful twenty-eight-year-old at the time. She had always been distrustful of compliments, but she seemed to have grown comfortable in her body again. The way she stood still and leaned to his hand was at once a familiar, comforting assertion of her proprietary right to his affection and a gesture that was intensely erotic to him.

She turned to put her arms around his neck and look up into his eyes. "It wasn't him, was it?"

"No," Millikan said. "Not this time."

"Then come to bed, and forget about it for now."

Millikan waited until she had gone up the stairs and turned on the hall light at the top before he went through the first floor, checking the bolts and locks on the doors, resetting the alarm system, and switching off the lights, one by one. He made his way upstairs as she was leaving the bathroom, then took his turn. It was a ritual that had become changeless, efficient, and nearly silent years ago, to keep from waking Katie and Mary Ann when they were still small. Now they were grown, married women, each the mistress of her own house in another city, and mother of her own children.

He turned off the last lights and slipped under the covers beside Marjorie. She snuggled close to him and rested her head on his chest, as she did most nights, and he felt the calm, comfortable sensation that he supposed must be a quality of old marriages, where all the rough edges had been worn smooth and there were no longer any boundaries that mattered. She knew she was entitled to the spot and was welcome there. "You didn't have to wait up for me," he said.

"Well, yes." He felt her shift a bit closer as she shrugged. "Actually, I did. Unless you're too tired . . . ?" He felt her hand move lower on his belly. "You don't seem tired to me." He could hear the amusement in her voice.

"I'm not." He turned toward her only a few degrees and their position became an embrace. "I can't imagine being that tired."

The hour was late, but the Millikans were beyond worrying about it, having made the decision to ignore the clock many times before and suffered no consequences that either of them cared about. Their caresses were gentle and unhurried, but uninhibited and sure, from deep knowledge of each other. He was not inclined to pull his attention away from his senses at any time during the next couple of hours, but because the mind could do many things at once, it recorded impressions and observations that he would think about later.

He was making love to the woman who had been his girlfriend and then his wife for so many years that she had gone from the desired to the epitome to the ideal and, at last, to encompass all and become the only woman, to whom he was the only man. Neither of them made any awkward, tentative overture, because there was no longer any doubt, no uncertainty in what they might do to give each other not pleasure, but the greatest pleasure. That was one of the secrets between them: there were no limits. Both of them wished they could do everything they knew for each other every time. And they knew so much now—that being touched exactly here in exactly this way made her feel so excited that she couldn't quite contain it, couldn't still her voice or her body, and that her reaction was what in turn made him ecstatic—that it would have taken days, weeks, to repeat everything. And to him each time was better, because it included memories of the others that were strong enough to be partly physical, and each act not performed was an option and therefore a promise for another time.

It ended, and he was lying on his back again in the darkness, with Marjorie in her proprietary place, her head resting on his chest with her soft hair loose and her arm across his stomach. He gently stroked her hair and the nape of her delicate neck and her shoulder, silently bringing down upon her whatever blessing an imperfect man might coax out of a benevolent God for this good woman. Her breathing gradually slowed and deepened to a soft, even tempo, and she was asleep.

Millikan remained motionless, staring up at the ceiling. He began to see again the images of the evening, the four murdered people lying on the bloody linoleum floor in the hot, cramped space of the restaurant. This time it wasn't the Louisville killer, but next time, it might be. He reviewed the places in his house where he had put loaded guns after he had returned from Buffalo, and determined to remind Marjorie of them in the morning. He would also have to beg her again to turn on the alarm system whenever he was out: the killer might very well come here looking for the way he could hurt Millikan most. Under certain circumstances, that would be this killer's next likely move, and tonight it seemed to Millikan that these circumstances might be the ones that had come into being. He had not heard from Prescott for a very long time, and that meant that Prescott was probably dead.

30

It was late summer, and the humidity made droplets of sweat form on Prescott's glass of beer and run onto the table while he watched Dick Hobart getting ready for the day's customers. Every afternoon for the past week, the air would grow heavier and thicker, until it took an effort even to sit still, and then a sudden, faint breeze would rustle the leaves on the trees outside, and the droplets would come, big fat globs of water that exploded on the hot tar of the streets and disappeared in a steam that smelled of dust and plants and electricity. The drops came more quickly then, and the rain pounded down, cooling the hot stones and the cracked, dry ground. It lasted fifteen minutes, until the excess had been exhausted, and then stopped. Ten minutes after that, the air would begin to feel close again, but the sun had lost some of its hard, harsh power, and the long, slow decline into evening began. The day-heated air seemed to be old and static, not moving at all.

People were out in the evening this week. Prescott saw them walking up sidewalks or sitting on their front porches after the sun went down, standing in line to get into restaurants that served food that wasn't as good as they'd have cooked at home if they could bear it, or waiting outside air-conditioned theaters to see movies that they had selected on the basis of starting time. It was ten o'clock in the morning, and as Dick Hobart's helpers and bartenders lifted cases of bottles over the bar to stock the refrigerators and liquor shelves, Prescott could see that their shirts were already wet down the spines. The sweat was forming on Dick Hobart's forehead, and each time he bent over, it would drip onto the lenses of his glasses. He came up with four whiskey bottles, set them on the bar, then walked over to Prescott, wiping his lenses on the front of his white shirt, which just smeared them. "I love this weather," he said.

"It's an ill wind and all that," Prescott said.

"That's the truth," Hobart agreed. "Ever since the temperature went up, I can barely keep the bar stocked, and we've had to keep customers waiting in the parking lot from about eight o'clock until closing." He grinned. "I'd fit them in somehow, but the damned fire marshals come to see me more in this weather, too." He leaned forward on the bar close to Prescott's table and looked significantly at the sport coat Prescott had across his lap. "If you brought me something, I can look at it. I'm ready for a break, anyway."

They walked to the unmarked door near the stage, along the concrete hallway, and into Hobart's office, a converted storeroom with no windows. There was room only for a desk and two chairs, because Hobart's filing system seemed to consist of papers thrown into empty liquor cartons and piled in rows along the wall. Hobart locked the door and turned up the air-conditioning while Prescott sat down. Prescott set the summer-weight sport coat on the desk and reached into the inner pocket. Inside was a small package wrapped and addressed to himself, so that in case of trouble he could drop it in a mailbox. He opened the brown paper and sat back.

Hobart looked at the three ladies' watches, one by one.

"They all run good?"

"Yes," said Prescott. "This Rolex retails for two thousand, two fifty. It's about a year old. The Patek Philippe is thirty-five hundred new, but there's a scratch on the crystal. The Omega is about fifteen hundred. The diamonds on the dial would be extra, but I'm pretty sure that was some kind of special order, so I'll let that cancel them out."

"What should we ask for them?"

Prescott squinted, then stared up at the ceiling. "Let's say three thousand for the lot. If they have to get split, I'd like fifteen hundred for the Patek Philippe, and I'll keep the others." He was aware that Hobart was studiously keeping his eyes from resting on the antique brooch in the center of the open butcher paper.

Hobart lifted each of the watches, listened to it tick, and set it aside. "I'll try." He picked up a diamond engagement ring. "Looks like three-quarter carat."

"That's what I make it," said Prescott.

"A thousand?"

"Done."

He lifted a gold chain, tossed it up and down to feel the weight, examined the jeweler's mark. "The workmanship is good, not too distinctive. A hundred an ounce?"

"Sounds okay," Prescott said.

Hobart scrutinized each item, giving estimates and receiving Prescott's approval. He never wrote down a price or notation of any kind, as though by tacit agreement there should be no evidence that the merchandise had passed into this little box of an office. He kept going until there was nothing left but the brooch.

He poked it with his finger, then picked it up and turned it around and around, examined the clasp, then set it on the desk.

"What do you want for it? Four or five thousand?"

"The center stone is an emerald, and it's old, so there's zero chance it's been cracked and repaired with synthetic bond."

"You're sure?"

"The setting is Victorian." He was silent for a moment. "I know it'll have to be broken up, but the diamonds alone are worth about four. I'll take eight for it, as is. If it doesn't sell, I'll split the stones myself and sell them off one at a time."

Hobart shrugged. "Eight it is." He looked at the jewelry he had moved to the side. "Three for the watches if they sell together, a thousand each for the six, seven, eight rings. Eight thousand for the brooch, I make it seven hundred for the chain. What's that?"

"Nineteen thousand, seven hundred."

Hobart stared at the merchandise. "If you'll let me give you your money tomorrow, I'll make it twenty even," he offered.

"Okay," said Prescott. He pulled his coat off the desk, but Hobart didn't move.

"Bobby," he said quietly, "if this is none of my business, I'll drop it, but I don't get the feeling you're a happy man."

Prescott stared at him thoughtfully, then shrugged.

"Is it Jeanie? Look, I'm your friend and I'm her friend, too. I know that if there's something wrong, you'll be able to work it out. She's—"

"She's great," said Prescott. "We get along fine." His reticence seemed to collapse as he met Hobart's eyes. "I know you're a friend, Dick, so I won't bullshit you. It's not a permanent thing. I'm too old for her, too old to have that kind of relationship with a woman who's young enough to think about houses and kids." He smiled sadly. "I'm a hell of a boyfriend, but pretty soon she's going to have to put on her clothes and look for a husband. She knows it, and she knows that I know it."

"Is that what's bothering you?" asked Hobart. "I don't want to sound like I'm not taking it seriously, because I am. I'm sixty next May, and I've been having these thoughts for longer than you have. But I'll tell you, life is short, and there's time enough to be dead after the doctor says you're dead." He frowned. "There's more to this, isn't there?"

Prescott was silent for a few seconds. "There is. I guess maybe Jeanie set it off, made me think about it again." He transfixed Hobart with his eyes. "You already know I've been away."

Hobart nodded, slightly, as though he wasn't sure he wanted to know more.

"I keep thinking about all that time. Not just the time I spent inside, but the years it cost me to get to where I was doing okay before that, and then losing it all and having to start over." He took a deep breath and blew it out. "I made a mistake once. It made me a graduate of Corcoran State. Ever hear of it?"

"No."

"It's an ugly place. The guards used to set up these fights, just let two prisoners go at it until one of them couldn't get up. Like gladiators."

"You?"

Prescott shook his head. "No. Not me." He sighed. "They saved that for guys they thought were troublemakers, and I never got their attention. I was in for four and a half years."

"What for?"

Prescott smiled. "You didn't believe it when I told you about the car washes, did you?"

"Hell no. Would you?"

Prescott said, "It was true. What I did was put most of my profits into things like that, so that no matter what I did, I would have a visible means of support that was dull enough to be real."

"What were the profits from?"

"I had a crew. I would pick the place and case it, then breeze through, taking out the locks and alarms. Five minutes later, I'd send in the crew with a truck. I'd have one guy in a security uniform like a rent-a-cop. He'd drive up, open the gate, and then stand by it. The rest would load the truck and pull out. He'd lock the gate, go to his car, and drive off. We did construction sites, warehouses. Once we did a grocery store that was closed for the night. I paid my guys, made money. I bought the car-wash places." He paused. "The mistake I made was branching out."

"Into what?"

"I met a guy. His name was Mike Kelleher. He was a luggage thief."

"You mean like in airports?"

"Yeah. He was the sneakiest bastard I ever saw. When he first talked to me, I went to watch him work one night. It was like he was invisible. People would be on the pay phones, he'd walk past, and their carry-on bags would practically get up and follow him. He would go to the baggage pickup, and if some idiot would stop on the way there to take a piss, Mike would have claimed his bags and be gone before he got there. He knew every trick. So I talked to him, and found that he was a great thief, but no businessman."

"Why not?"

"He would get the bags, take them to his apartment, pop the locks with a screwdriver, and go through them. He took jewelry, money, stuff like that. Then he went out and dumped everything else. I say, 'Mike! What are you thinking? Some woman has five hundred bucks cash and three thousand in clothes in her twelve-hundred-dollar Louis Vuitton bag, so you take the cash and toss everything else?'"

"Sounds stupid."

"It was. He had first-rate hands and a third-rate brain. But first-rate hands are not a small thing, so I made a deal with him. He steals a suitcase. We open it together, only not with a screwdriver. I pick the lock, or cut the padlock off, or fiddle the combination. He takes the money, just like before, and we split the jewelry. I get the luggage, the clothes, whatever else there is, and pay him twenty-five bucks a bag. That works out for a while. I get enough bags, buy some more wholesale, and open up a shop in San Francisco. I also find lots of stuff Mike missed: electric toothbrushes with hollow handles and the good jewelry inside, secret pockets full of credit cards and traveler's checks, a surprising amount of drugs. It grows into a good little sideline."

"It does sound good."

"I noticed a few inefficiencies, so I worked on those. Mike trains eight people— four women and four men, I insisted on that—to take bags off the conveyors in L.A. These are people who look right. No nineteen-year-olds, no minorities that the cops always jump just on spec. I work it out so every one of them is carrying a ticket for a flight to San Francisco. They go into the baggage claim, see the right chance, grab a bag. Do they go out to the street like thieves? No. That's when cops grab you. If somebody misses his bag, what does he do? He looks first at that door, and runs out looking to see who took it. So what my people did was pick up a couple of bags, hand them off to another person, who walks back in the other door, checks the bags to San Francisco, and goes up the escalator to the departure gates. He flies to San Francisco, claims the bags, and delivers them to my store." He stared into the distance. "It worked. Everything we tried worked. I bought the car washes, and made money on them, too."

"So what happened?"

"Michael Jameson Kelleher."

"What about him?"

"He never told me that he had a problem, and I didn't ask him hard enough questions, I guess. He had a conviction. It made sense to me later. The reason he was so good was that he had been doing it a long time. Only nobody starts out being at the top of his game. They learn by making mistakes, and if you're a thief, a mistake sends you to jail. Mike made a second mistake: not a big one, but big enough. He goes to the airport too often to oversee the way things are being done. The cops spot him, recognize him from his picture, and hustle him off to one of those rooms you see in airports with nothing written on the doors. They bullshit him into thinking they have tapes of him. He figures out that this time his sentence is not going to be a short one. It's his second time, and this time he's clearly the boss, and the thing looks very big and organized. He spills his guts, rats us all out, and agrees to keep running the business like nothing has happened until they have enough evidence on us: special bags that are marked with paint that shows up only on ultraviolet light, videotapes, the whole thing."

"You got convicted. What happened to him?"

Prescott's jaw worked, the muscles on the side of his face knotting and smoothing out, over and over. "Nothing. He's not charged with anything. The cops have it all on me, without him even testifying. There's a tape of them going through my shop in San Francisco and nearly every bag glows in the dark, a tape of me paying a couple of thieves. The state declares my house, my two car washes, my bank accounts, stocks, and bonds to be stolen money, and confiscates them. I have some money hidden, but just about all of that goes to keeping my lawyers paid and working. I get ten years. I serve four and a half, which, with good behavior, counts as nine. Then I serve another six months on probation. So at the end of five years, all I have left is two assets: the Corvette outside, which was registered in the name of a girlfriend—she dumped me, so they never made the connection, but she was honest—and a whole bunch of stuff from suitcases that I'd hidden and never gotten around to selling off before I was arrested."

"This stuff?" Hobart held up the package of watches and jewelry.

"No, that's gone. This I picked up around Chicago over a period of a few months before I came here." He shook his head sadly. "I had to go back to second-story work, just to build up some capital again." He narrowed his eyes. "I never stop thinking about Michael Kelleher. You know where he is now?"

"Where?"

"Retired. He actually lives on a farm up in Minnesota."

"A farm? What for?"

Prescott shrugged. "When the whole thing went south—me, the eight thieves, all my businesses—nothing happened to him. He'd made at least a million or two. They didn't charge him with anything, so how could they take it? I know that the reason he left L.A. was that he thought I'd get out and come looking for him."

"To kill him?"

Prescott stared at him. "What would you do?"

Hobart considered the question for a moment. "I guess the same. Why haven't you?"

Prescott's jaw was working again. "They know it."

"Huh? Who knows it?"

"Kelleher, for one. That part is good. I hope the son of a bitch has nightmares every night, and can't eat a meal without getting a belly-ache and throwing it up. But the part that's bad is the L.A. police. They knew it like they could read my mind. My probation officer used to give me lectures about it, after five years. The last time I checked in with him, he said it again." He frowned. "Anything happens to Kelleher, I'm going away."

"Would you kill him?" asked Hobart. "I mean if you had a foolproof way to do it and get away with it?"

"In a second."

"There may be a way," said Hobart. "If you've got the money, I may be able to get somebody to help you."

31

Varney walked toward the office, wary of the world around him, reading the sights as though he were working. For many paces he kept his eyes ahead and unfocused, so they would not be looking directly at anything, but receiving messages from the matrix of sights. Anything that moved was alive or dangerous, and his eyes would focus and evaluate it, then release it and go unfocused and receptive again. He used tricks to check behind him: reflections in windows, pauses and turns that were studied and small and unthreatening but gave him a chance to sweep the street behind. He did not limit his view to the street level but scanned roofs and upper windows while they were still far enough away to make turning or raising his head unnecessary, then swept them again as he passed. His ears were attuned to the sounds of motion and life—footsteps, sudden changes in the pitch of a car engine, a click or slide of metal on metal—because motion and life were the sources of all possible trouble.

He felt his pride in his senses, his cunning, his strength slowly returning, but he was restless and dissatisfied. He had been in a terrible period of his life ever since he had heard of Roy Prescott. He felt as though he had come upon a mangy, growling dog in the sidewalk, and on an impulse—not even a decision—given it a half-hearted kick to get it out of his way and teach it a lesson. It had not yelped and slunk away with its tail between its legs. It had clamped its jaws on his ankle and held on. After that, everything had turned painful and hard. He felt as though he still could not get loose. Everybody that he had met since then had gotten the better of him, because he had not come to them whole and well. He had been feeling the steady grinding of those teeth on his ankle, already through the flesh and into the bone, and dragging the dead weight of that big, filthy, mangy dog. He had let his control of his life go—not in a decision, but in a fit of preoccupation—and had not been able to clutch it again. He was nearly broke, his money leaking away in Tracy's complicated assessments that made him pay for every second he was in Cincinnati, every moment of invisibility.

He had concentrated all of his mental energy on maintaining a small, private discipline. It was not even a plan, just a way of holding on to who he was. After the first week here, he had been shocked and alarmed at what he was doing to himself. He had been letting himself lose his edge. He had been letting his muscles go slack and his perception dull and his will weaken, and these were the same as dying. That day, he had begun to perform his old workouts. When he had felt the agonizing suspicion that doing them was harder than it had been a month ago, he had increased the number of repetitions, added new exercises, run farther, slowly increasing his workouts until they took half the day. He had walked wherever he went, sharpening his sense of the rhythms of the city, using his ears and practicing his night vision so that his mind would supply what his eyes could not see.

After a time, he had begun to shop for places where he could again practice the skills he used in his work. He had gone to a karate dojo and joined advanced classes that met two evenings a week. He had gone to a second dojo and joined an advanced class in judo that met two more. Advanced classes in martial arts were very small, made up almost entirely of men, all of them wearing black belts. They were much more highly skilled than anyone Varney would be likely to meet in the normal course of his trade. They helped him practice how to detect an opponent's intentions from tiny physical changes, then block, dodge, roll, and retaliate ever more quickly.

He had not felt comfortable about going to a shooting range. There were few of them in the area, and he knew that at least some of the customers were sure to be off-duty policemen or people who worked with policemen. He didn't want to be distracted by wondering whether one of them might have seen a copy of the picture Prescott had given the police in Buffalo. He drove around the area and found four pieces of land that were big enough and empty enough and so overgrown with scrub trees and weeds that they could not be used or even visited by the owners much.

He would go at night with his pistol hidden in his coat and walk the woods and fields. He would tread silently, aware of the way the moonlight fell on him and the shapes of trees and bushes behind him. He listened for the sounds of small animals in the brush, testing his patience and alertness by trying to find birds in their nesting places, and to surprise the skunks, raccoons, opossums, and field mice, which moved only at night.

He followed rituals, sometimes walking in the night landscape with his pistol broken down, the pieces secreted in different pockets. When he detected his prey, he assembled the weapon in the dark without looking at it: slide, barrel, recoil spring, trigger and sear, grip. He loaded one bullet into the magazine and slid the magazine into place. Then he screwed the silencer onto the barrel. He practiced until he could do it quickly, all without making a sound that would alert an animal to his presence. He would study the position and attitude of the animal, match it to the features of the landscape. Finally, he would cycle the single bullet into the chamber. That noise would startle the animal. It would panic, skitter toward a hole or a brush pile, or take flight, while Varney took his single shot.

At other times, he would stop in the brush, assemble the pistol with his eyes closed, slip it into his pocket, then move ahead, waiting to startle any animal out of its hiding place. When it happened, he drew and fired.

Now, three months later, Varney's daily life was still out of control, a bundle he had let slip, that was rolling and bouncing downhill, coming apart and spilling its contents. He still had done nothing about that. Maybe it would all be lost and destroyed, and maybe later he would go back to gather up all the bits and pack them together again.

He would not be able to make that decision until it had bounced to the bottom and stopped. For now, he would tolerate the unpleasant sensation. He had made a different choice. Whatever happened to his money, whatever temporary advantage people took of his vulnerability, Varney had preserved what mattered. He had chosen to save himself.

He knew he had wasted three months, given up planning, lost all of the respect he had earned with one of the syndicates that had often provided him with work. But today he had a feeling. He was beginning to feel that things were about to change. It might have been because he had needed to work on himself this hard, and he had been waiting until the self-improvement process had hit a certain high pitch before he could bring on the next change. But the rest had to do with the consequences of letting go of his life. The disaster was nearly complete. In another week he would be out of money.

There was a strange change in the atmosphere of the office when he stepped inside today. He knew that the reason he noticed was that he had trained himself so assiduously to detect tiny, subtle movements and sounds. Something was different. He looked at Tracy, sitting at a desk across the room, and she was holding herself differently. It took him a moment to realize that it was the angle of her back. Usually she leaned forward on her forearms, looking tired and frustrated. Today she was a little straighter, her shoulders held lower. As he stepped in, she fidgeted before she looked up. She was impatient. Her eyes widened. "Sugar!" she said.

"Hello, Tracy," said Varney.

"I was expecting you earlier. Before lunch." She glowered at him, but this time, the expression was not the usual counterfeit hurt feelings because his payment was late. This time it was mock anger, which he was supposed to recognize as a pleasantry.

"I walked here," he said. "It takes time."

She watched him take out the cash from his coat pocket and set it on the desk in front of her. She gazed at it for a moment, then looked up. "I'll bet you're running a bit low about now."

Varney shrugged, but didn't answer.

"I was right," she announced. "Now," she said in a fake-sympathetic tone, like the one people used to give unwelcome advice to drunks and addicts, "don't you think it's about time you got over what's been bothering you and got a job?"

Varney shrugged again. "I guess I'll have to do that one of these days." He hated her. It was amazing to him that his bad luck should have been so relentless and extreme that it was forcing him to listen to this woman doling out these doses of criticism as though she had invented them and provided them for his benefit.

She stared at him with an air of superiority. "Would you even be ready to work if a job came up?"

"Of course I would. I'm healthy and rested."

She looked at him more sharply. "That's exactly why I ask. You're rested, all right: maybe a little too rested?"

"I'm as sharp right now as I've ever been in my life. Something will come up," he assured her.

"It has," she purred slyly.

"What?"

"I said something has come up," said Tracy, her eyes gleaming with self-satisfaction. Then the malice crept into her voice again. "I hope you were telling me the truth about being ready to work, because this is not like murdering Duane, who wasn't expecting it and didn't see it coming."

"Then what is it like?" he asked.

"It's a big job, almost at the level you worked before your . . . little setback," she said.

"I didn't have a setback," said Varney. "I decided to take a break and cool off for a while. I'm ready to work. What is it?"

There was something in his voice that made Tracy's instinct for self-preservation kick in. "I didn't mean to offend, sugar," she said gently. "I just have no way to know without asking. The job came through a man I know I can trust. He's been doing business with us for at least ten years. A man he knows has an enemy."

"What kind of enemy?"

"Some kind of business thing out in California went wrong, the enemy gave him up to the police, and he went to prison." She stared at him and said reassuringly, "The man I know—my contact—stands between us and the client. The client only knows about my contact, and even my contact doesn't know about you."

"Why isn't the client doing it himself?"

She squinted, as though she did not understand, then seemed to sort it out. "Oh, I get the question. The story is that if this enemy dies, there's only one suspect. My friend was very clear on that point. The cops in California made some kind of deal with this guy. He turned informant, and in exchange, he got off completely free: everything he did got blamed on our client. This guy even got to keep his take from whatever it was they both did. The cops knew it wasn't fair, but as usual, they settled for what they could get for sure—one conviction— and let their informant take his chances. If he got killed later, that was his problem. They probably won't be disappointed. But it won't stop them from going after our client. They know the client wants him dead. As soon as this guy hits the ground, they'll be looking for the client." She paused, and said to Varney with false patience, "Besides, I know it's probably hard for you to see, but some people might want somebody dead, but not want to actually do it."

"How is he protecting himself?" asked Varney.

"He wants to get you all hired and ready to do it. Then he goes back to California and establishes a clear, solid alibi. I'm not sure what that will be. Getting himself tossed in jail would be the best, but I doubt that he'll do that. Anyway, when he's sure he's all set, he places a call from a pay phone to my friend. My friend calls me from a pay phone. I call you from a pay phone. No calls get traced later. You kill the guy in Minnesota, a couple thousand miles from where the client is. Everybody lives happily ever after. Or, practically everybody." She smiled. "Satisfied?"

"Not quite," said Varney.

She looked shocked, then mystified. "Sugar, what more could you want? Are you scared?"

"No," said Varney. "How is the payment going to work?"

"Oh," she said happily. "He'll pay a hundred grand."

"No," Varney said. "I asked how. If the police know he's the one who wanted the guy dead, and the guy dies while he's got an alibi, they don't give up. They'll watch him for a while to see who he pays."

She shook her head in delight. "It won't happen, and if it did, it wouldn't do any good. The police don't know he has this kind of money—or any money. He had some hidden when he went to prison.

Nobody knows about it. And," she added proudly, "I took care of the rest."

"How did you do that?"

"I set it up so he pays in advance. He already gave the hundred thousand to my friend. You get fifty thousand as soon as you agree. My friend holds the rest. When the killing is done, my friend passes along the other fifty. There's no transaction that involves the client— or even takes place in the same state."

Varney let some of his suspicion show. "You set that up, huh?"

"Well, of course I did, sugar," she purred. "I can't count on some strange client to protect me. He's never done this before."

Varney nodded, his tongue exploring the outer surfaces of his teeth. "So I get fifty in advance and fifty at the end, both from you."

"That's what I said," Tracy agreed, her eyes settling on her fingernails, as though she were checking their length.

"I'll do it," said Varney.

"That's smart, honey," she said. "It'll do you good. I just hate to see a young man lolling around, aimless, no use to himself or anybody else. It's time that you pulled yourself together and stopped letting Mae lead you around like a little puppy dog, don't you think?"

He said, "When you've got the fifty thousand, the name and address, call me and I'll come around to pick them up."

She brightened and opened the top drawer of the desk, pulling it into her belly. "Got them." She handed him a thick manila envelope that felt like money, and another with some folded paper inside. "I expect the call to come from the client to my friend sometime around the fifteenth. Think you can be ready by then?"

"I'm ready now. I expect I'll go where he is and have a look ahead of time."

"Don't forget to always leave me a phone number where I can reach you."

"I won't." He opened the big envelope and got a peek at the hundred-dollar bills while he slipped the smaller envelope inside it. He lifted his shirt, pushed the manila envelope into the top of his belt, and tucked his shirt in over it. He glanced at Tracy, and saw she had been watching the process.

She saw him notice, and shrugged naughtily. "See you, sugar."

He said, "While I'm gone, I want Mae in my apartment. Alone."

She looked surprised. "Well, of course, as far as I'm concerned. You'll have to make that clear to her. But I certainly won't put temptation in her way."

He nodded without bothering to look at her to detect the lie. "I'll call you with a number where you can reach me." He stepped out and closed the door. As he walked down the long, deserted hall, he noted all the things that were wrong with the deal. Tracy had said the price was a hundred thousand. That meant that it was more—probably two hundred—and she had taken a hundred out. There was no way in the world she would act as broker without a cut. She probably had to give the middleman something, but there was no question in Varney's mind who would end up with most of it. She had also used her position as purveyor of information to exercise power over Varney, to drag out the process and watch him squirm, using every chance to impose her superior smile and tell him how worthless he was. She had sensed that this news was about to make him stronger, and she hadn't been able to resist trying to weaken him, sucking away his strength like a tick.

He noted each of these things, but he only noted them and set them aside in his mind. The news was better than Tracy had imagined, and he only tallied the problems to remind himself that he knew them. He was no longer about to be penniless. He was walking along with fifty thousand dollars pressed against his belly under his shirt, with another fifty on the way. He was going out on the road again to find an enemy and cut him down.

Even the lies that Tracy had fed him about the job were good. She had made it sound as though this target was some hapless, stupid loser who had once simply gotten caught and squeezed and had the cops go easy on him. Varney didn't believe it. Nobody would pay a hundred thousand, let alone whatever Tracy had really charged, to exterminate a man like that. Anybody who had served time would know fifty guys who would take out somebody like that for a thousand dollars.

The client was clearly a smart man. Tracy had not set this up. The client was the one who had fashioned the deal this way, because he had known that the police would suspect him, and he had known what they would do to prove he had done it. He had also known better than

to hire an assassin directly. He was the one who had placed two inter-
mediaries, two bloodsucking parasites, between him and anybody
who hunted men for a living. He knew that the only likely way for
him to get caught was if Varney screwed it up and traded him for a
lighter sentence. This way, Varney couldn't. But the client couldn't
tell the police who Varney was, either. All either of them could sell to
the police was an intermediary who was next to worthless. Varney felt
a certain respect for this client. It was good to know he was standing
in for a man who was worth something, but who simply was too
hemmed in by circumstances to go kill his own enemy.

Before Varney was aware of it, he had already walked a mile from
Tracy's office. He was alive again, in control. He was in the best shape
of his life, he was thinking, making decisions, preparing to set off on a
hunt. The interruption of his life was over, and he was an adventurer
again.

32

Varney was standing by the bed, folding clothes and putting them into his suitcase, when he heard Mae's light footsteps on the stairs. She had never said anything about Duane, but he suspected she knew about him, because since Varney had killed him, she had never raised the issue of painting the kitchen again. She must have noticed that the tarp that had been in the closet with the paint was missing, and figured out where it had gone. She had also changed the way she entered the apartment. He stood in the doorway and looked across the kitchen at the door. The key in the lock was quiet. The door swung inward an inch or two and stopped, as though she was looking for signs of trouble. She saw Varney, came in the rest of the way, and set the bag of groceries on the kitchen table. "Hi," she said, watching him.

"Hi." He returned to his packing, folding shirts expertly and setting them aside. He always took special care with his shirts. They would be the final layer, so when he opened the suitcase he could pull them out quickly and hang them up. When he traveled, he liked to have his clothes professionally washed, ironed, and packaged, because wrinkles made him nervous. Anything that made him the one in a crowd that somebody remembered was dangerous. But this time he was not going to take the clothes to a laundry: he was too impatient to get on the road.

Mae padded around silently, putting away the food she had bought, waiting for Varney to speak, to tell her what was happening. He watched her for a moment. She was pretty, especially when she was alone with him and preoccupied like this. She was alien, like a different species of animal, with thin, birdlike bones and graceful movements. He kept looking at her while he folded the last shirt he had chosen. She wasn't too pretty, he decided. She had probably gone all the way to the store and back without having a man stare at her.

"I'm going on a trip," he said.

"Oh?" She was being careful to sound casual about it, and knew enough not to ask any questions.

He tried to find words like the ones that other people might use, then pitched his voice to sound the way theirs sounded. "Would you like to go with me?"

She seemed to struggle, as though she had never considered that he might say such a thing, and she had to convince herself that it was true. Then she had to select the safest response.

"I think I would," she said. "If I wouldn't be too much trouble." She stood with her shoulders drawn up to her neck in a frozen shrug. "Where do you want to go?"

He let the part about wanting pass, even though it irritated him: wanting to go meant it was just some self-indulgent whim, when it deserved to be dignified with "have to" because it was a job. "Minnesota," he said. "Up north of Minneapolis." He hurried to spare himself the annoyance she would cause with her next couple of questions. "We'd be gone for a while, probably at least two weeks, and maybe a month. I'm driving up."

She stared at him and tiny worry lines appeared on her forehead and beside her eyes. He realized it had occurred to her that maybe he was planning to take her somewhere and kill her. The replacement tarp she had been fearing to see on the kitchen floor wouldn't be necessary if he took her out in some woods.

He said, "It's a job that I got through Tracy. We drive up, I do it, and we drive home. It's a long trip, pretty dull. If you don't want to come, don't do it for me."

The lines disappeared, and her color seemed to return. "I want to," she said. "I do. I like to go places, and I've never been up there." She was suddenly animated. "I'm so excited." She hurried to the closet and started picking hangers off the rod and putting them back. "I don't know what to bring."

"You don't want a lot of luggage," he said. "A couple of pairs of jeans, a couple of sweatshirts, sneakers . . ." He relented. "Maybe one nice outfit. Minneapolis and St. Paul are kind of big, so we may be able to go out a little to good restaurants."

Mae was a person who could actually be seen in the act of thinking. She got through it like a person feeling a pain passing: a slight knitting of the brows, then it was over. Now it was different. She snatched a couple of hangers, threw them on the bed, went to the dresser, pulled a few items from different drawers as she was talking. "I'll be ready in about fifteen minutes, if we need to leave right away. If we don't, I'd like to trim your hair and touch up the highlights a little first." She paused. "Of course, I can do that when we get there, but if you're working, you probably want to look as good as you can, right? I mean, as different from the way you used to look." She didn't wait for an answer, but jumped to the next thought. "I should tell Tracy that I'm going. We should leave a light on in the apartment, and pull the shades down. Maybe the bathroom light, so it's dim, like a night-light, and you can't see it from outside in the day. I'll just take this dress. If you like this dress?" She held it up on the hanger in front of her body.

Varney decided to defend his concentration from her scattered musings by dispatching all of the questions at once. "The dress will be fine. I'll leave the bathroom light on. Tracy knows. Bring the hair stuff, and you can do me in a hotel on the way. I'd like to get going."

He waited until she was in the bathroom before he closed and latched his suitcase, then lifted a second one to the bed and opened it. This one contained his equipment. There were a few pairs of gloves, some hats and shoes, some locksmith's skeleton keys, a couple of sets of picks, a slim-jim for pulling car-door locks, some Mag-lites in different sizes, three nine-millimeter pistols with spare ammunition magazines, a commando knife with a guttered blade and a nearly flat handle. He added his big envelope to the suitcase, and closed it.

He changed into a comfortable pair of khaki pants, some good, casual shoes, and a blue oxford shirt, pulled down the window shade, and waited. A few minutes later, Mae had filled her small bag and looked at him anxiously.

"Do I look all right?"

"You know you do," he said. "Hair, makeup, clothes, all that. It's what you do for a living." Then he frowned. "That reminds me. Where I'm going now, that's what I do for a living. If you're going, you'll want to listen hard to what I say."

"I will," said Mae. "I promise."

"Start now. Once we leave here, you don't call anybody on the phone, or anything like that. You don't strike up conversations with people in restaurants or hotels. What you want more than anything is not to be noticed or remembered. A man or woman traveling alone might get noticed—for different reasons, maybe—but if they're traveling together, they're just a couple. The man isn't dangerous and the woman isn't available, so people won't look hard to figure those things out. So you stick close to me."

She nodded, maybe a little too energetically. He wasn't sure she really had taken it in and understood. "I know that," she said. "I'm ready." He picked up their suitcases and let her open and close the doors for him.

Varney drove out of town with a feeling that was close to joy. He was on the road, with a pretty woman at his side. She was not flashy enough to make him feel visible, but she was pleasant to look at. He knew she probably would have gotten to chattering again if she had been smart enough to realize that she was important to him, that she was the best part of his disguise. He had told her, in case it occurred to her later, but she didn't seem to have absorbed the full meaning of it.

She was the guarantee that when men looked, they would only let their eyes pass over him on the way to her. If they heard later that somebody had been killed, they would not remember Varney as a solitary young man who looked capable of doing someone harm. They might not remember him clearly at all. He was just another family man on his way somewhere with his wife. She could do some of the driving later, after he got tired. He might even use her to go into motel offices to rent rooms, or into fast-food places to get food, so he could remain completely invisible.

The most important feeling Varney had was elation that he had broken out. He had been like a man in a hospital, his mind like a doctor delivering lectures to him every day that being there was the only thing he could do for the present, while the rest of him was screaming for release. That was over now. He had come away rested and sharp, with an envelope full of money, a clean, honest car, untraceable guns, a companion that he was confident would follow his orders. And somebody had hired him to do what he had always done better than anybody else.

He drove for three hours without stopping, without even having to slow the car for any reason except to keep from speeding. His car sliced between the gatherings of cars ahead, then occasionally edged to the left lane to pass the big box of a tractor-trailer rig and moved back into the right. Much of the time, the road was flat and straight as a surveyor could make it. When there were curves, they were gradual, made without haste, as a boat moves from one compass heading to another.

At the end of the three hours, Mae said, "I'd like to pee, if you can stop someplace," and he realized that she must have set this time for herself in advance, waiting for a while and hoping he would spontaneously think of stopping, then telling herself she could wait, that she wouldn't say anything until it got to be three hours.

"Okay," he said. "Next exit."

He pulled off the interstate and filled the car's tank at a gas station while she went inside and got the key to the ladies' room. He pulled the car away from the pump and parked, went to the men's room, then came back and waited. When she came out, he saw her look at the gas pump, then whirl her head around more quickly toward him, an abrupt, unconsidered movement. He could tell that he had scared her. She had come out and seen that the car was no longer where she'd left it, and she had panicked, afraid he had stranded her. He felt a strong distaste. She was weak and stupid, like a child, somebody with all sorts of needs that he would have to take into account.

When she got to the car, she shocked him again. It was as though it had been normal. She wasn't even embarrassed. "There you are," she said with a smile. "I was afraid you'd gotten impatient and left me here. Want me to drive for a while?" He nodded, got into the passenger seat, and watched her closely while she drove out onto the entrance ramp and moved into the line of cars. He decided she was competent enough for this and began to relax. He leaned back in the seat and closed his eyes.

"Do you like to travel?"

He opened his eyes, astounded that she had not understood that he wasn't interested in talking.

"I do," she continued. "It's one of my favorite things. I just love all of it. Being on the open road, packing, hotels. I never got much chance to do it."

He controlled himself and asked the question. "Why is that?"

"Oh," she said, and looked at him uncomfortably. "Just the way things worked out. My parents never seemed to think of it. I got married young, and my husband always said we'd do it, but there was never any money. He was just saying that, because he was like my parents: like a stone that just stays wherever it's dropped, and doesn't move an inch unless it's kicked or something. As far as he would go was saying he would do it, which was more than my parents would do, I guess. They would just say it was stupid. He would lie to me so I wouldn't try to convince him. If he said yes, but that there's no money, then I couldn't say anything, just wait until there was more money. There never was enough. Then that was over, and he was gone, but that meant I had even less money." She shrugged. "I was doing hair and nails and makeovers, and people had to have regular appointments, so if I went away, then I knew that when I got back, they would have found somebody else. It never worked out." He unhooked his seat belt, and she looked alarmed. "What are you doing?"

"Just watch the road," he muttered. He was fast and flexible from his years of martial arts training, and he easily rolled over his seat into the back of the car. He looked over her shoulder at the windshield. "Keep heading north for a couple of hours while I get some sleep." He lay on the back seat and closed his eyes.

"Okay."

He could hear in her voice a quiet, sad resignation. She sounded as though she was being punished. He supposed that she must know he was back here to escape her meaningless, empty talk. He was aware that there was a range of feelings he could select from and she would accept. He could be sympathetic, curious, apologetic, or even angry.

He knew that people felt those things and expected him to act as though he felt them too, and he knew how to do it: how his voice should be modulated, how his face should look. But he did not feel any of them. Sometimes he imitated emotions, practiced them as he practiced his other skills, because they were useful. Right now he didn't need the practice, and he didn't need to know anything she was saying, and didn't need to manipulate her into doing anything. He closed his eyes and let the steady hum of the tires on the pavement below his head soothe him and put him to sleep.

He awoke a couple of hours later, and she was still driving steadily. She went a little bit slower than he had, but she was careful and methodical and had put them a good hundred and thirty miles on. He said, "How are you holding up?"

"Fine," she answered. "Just fine. But I'm not sorry you woke up just now. I'd like to stop again, if you don't mind."

"No," said Varney. "I'm hungry."

They parked at a truck stop, went inside, and sat in a big booth with red vinyl seats and a Formica table. Varney ordered a hamburger, then took it out of the bun, cut it up, and ate it with the garnish of lettuce, tomato, and pickle. Mae asked, "Why do you do that? If you're worried about gaining weight, the milk and meat both have fat in them."

He said, "I eat what I need. I need protein for my muscles. Milk builds bones. Everybody needs plants."

"Why did you ask me to come?"

He stopped chewing and looked up. Her eyes were in his, searching for something. He swallowed. "I like having you around. I thought you might want to get out."

"Why don't you like to talk to me?"

"I never said that."

"You never said anything much," she said. "We've been together for three months. You never even look at me, except at night, naked. And then you don't talk."

"I look at you other times," he said. He put on a false expression of apologetic concern that he had once seen on a man trying to keep his wife from embarrassing him with a fight in public. "I've had a lot on my mind," he said quietly. It occurred to him that it sounded right because the man had said exactly those words. He tried to remember what else the man had said, but couldn't. "I'm not much of a talker," he said. "I think about you a lot, though." He considered saying he would talk more, but it would be like breaking a dam. She would spend the rest of the trip yapping in his ear like a little terrier, and he would have to dream up things to say in return, as though he wanted to keep her talking.

"You never talk about yourself, or where you came from, or anything."

He was astounded. It was like inviting him to step off the top of a building, and she should be smart enough to know that. "None of that stuff is very pleasant. If it had been any good, I'd probably still be there, having a good time. Instead, I got out as soon as I could."

"You don't have to tell me, if it makes you sad." She reached under the table and gripped his forearm. "I was doing a lot of thinking while I was driving. Kind of catching up, because I didn't have any time to think before we left. I was thinking that maybe we could use this trip the way some married people do, to make a fresh start, maybe make everything new again."

He had no choice now. His hand was still clenched in a fist on his thigh. He opened it and put it over hers, then watched her look of discomfort turn into a smile. He said, "I think that's a good idea."

She gave his hand a quick squeeze and released it, but as she looked at her plate the smile lingered on her lips.

When they had finished eating, Varney pulled the car to the gas pumps at the end of the lot and refilled the tank. Mae didn't begin again until he had gotten into the driver's seat and begun to drive back to the highway. She said, "We didn't really need gas. We'd only gone about a hundred and fifty miles."

He resisted the impulse to shut her up. He said gently, "Remember what we said before we left?"

"I think so."

"This is a business trip. Sometimes in my business some small thing goes wrong, and you've got to get away as fast and as far as you can. You don't know in advance when that's going to happen, or you wouldn't let it happen. If we went a hundred and fifty miles, we used a hundred and fifty miles' worth of gas, right?"

"Well, sure, but the tank holds—"

"It doesn't matter what it holds," he interrupted. "It had a hundred and fifty miles less in it than it could have. If things go wrong, you'll be real glad to be able to get an extra hundred and fifty miles away from it before you have to stop and show your face or run out of gas. It's a problem that never happened, because I solved it ahead of time. It's one more thing we won't have on our minds to distract us."

She looked at him with appreciation. "I'm sorry."

"What?" She had surprised him again.

"I'm sorry," she repeated. "That was what you meant when we were leaving. That you wanted me to do what you told me to, no questions asked. I was just afraid that if you got gas now, then you wouldn't want to stop again for a really, really long time."

"If that was what you meant, you should have said it," he muttered. He was silent for a mile, then remembered that he had determined to keep her happy, or at least pliable, for the duration of the trip. "Anytime you feel like stopping, just let me know." He turned to look at her, to let her see the benevolent expression he had placed on his features. "I'll be happy to stop. We should be enjoying this."

That night they stopped at a motel in Wisconsin. Mae took a hot bubble bath, then asked him to get in, and let him soak for a long time. Then she had him lie on the bed so she could give him a massage that was long, elaborate, and led seamlessly into sex. When it was over and Varney was lying on the bed listening to Mae's breathing settling into the soft, slow cadence that meant she was asleep, he looked back on the day. Talking to her in exchange for peace and all the extra attention had not been a bad bargain. But he would have to be vigilant. Women didn't seem to care much about sex. They tolerated it to get things, and it was simple human nature that when they had traded any kind of service for something, they felt entitled to it. She would probably want more and more talk.

The next morning after his exercises, they took showers and had breakfast, then drove on. She was bursting with chatter about everything they passed, even calling out the license plates for different states. He answered direct questions and grunted now and then to show he had heard, and that seemed to satisfy her. By nightfall, they were in Minneapolis. He had her be the one to check them into a big hotel downtown. Then he left her in the room while he used the exercise machines and went for a swim in the indoor pool.

They ate in the hotel restaurant and then went back upstairs. She didn't seem surprised when he took off the coat and tie he had been wearing, but when he began to put on jeans and sneakers, she said, "Do we have to leave already?"

He shook his head. "You don't have to do anything. I'm driving up north to take a look around."

"At night?"

He turned and leveled his eyes on her, without answering.

"I did it again," she said. "I didn't mean to."

He said, "It's easy, and it's safe. This way I can look at the town where he lives, see where the police station is, what the traffic is like at night, maybe drive past his house. They don't move the roads when the sun goes down, but people won't get as much chance to look at me."

She jumped up from the bed. "Can I go?" She saw his frown, and said quickly, "If I drive, you could get a better look. If there are people, you could even duck down, and they'd never have a chance to see you." She hesitated. "You're not going to kill him tonight, are you?"

"No," he admitted. "Put on jeans and we'll go."

The road up as far as Hinckley was a big, fast interstate. It would be an easy route to choke off if things went badly. But he supposed that the chance to cover a lot of miles quickly on the way out of there was likely to be worth some risk. The roads after Hinckley were smaller, but fast too. There were very few cars at night, and the only traffic signs had pictures of deer on them and warnings. When Varney came to the last intersection before the road where the farm was supposed to be, he pulled over to the shoulder and let Mae drive.

The farm was everything that Varney had hoped. The house and barn were set back at least three hundred yards from the road, at the end of a gravel drive. The best part was the trees. There were at least forty acres of woods on the west side of the farm that stretched from the southbound highway almost to the house. He could see lights in the upper windows, and a sport utility vehicle beside the barn, but no people. He had Mae drive the next ten miles so he could see where the other houses were, all the way to the next town. Then he had her drive back past the farm and beyond it to the junction with the southbound highway.

He took over and drove back toward Minneapolis, feeling contemptuous. People who knew somebody might kill them always seemed to do the wrong things. They went to live in some remote, deserted area like this, and thought that made them safe. What it did was make them slightly easier to find, and much easier to kill.

As Varney drove, he saw that Mae had dozed off. He used the solitude to construct a mental list. He would have to give Tracy a call from a pay phone to give her the number of the hotel. Tomorrow he would pick up a few items that might be useful: a shovel, for one thing. He couldn't count on a rich guy from California even having one, let alone leaving it where Varney could find it. He would drive back up and take a look at the place in daylight. Then all he would have to do was wait for Tracy to call and tell him it was time to drive up here and pull the trigger.

33

In daylight, the farm appeared to be a perfect place. The area had the quiet bleakness of a land that was remote, wild, and sparsely populated, like a thawed tundra. This far north the growing season was short, so the fields Varney saw on the way had already been cut to stubble, the crops harvested with the first chill. Varney couldn't tell if Kelleher's farm had even been planted this year. The vast level plot that ran from the road to the left side of the house and took up two-thirds of the acreage looked patchy and unkempt compared to the land on other farms. The stubble was interspersed with weeds. The rest of the farm was covered with thick deciduous woods, all the trees looking exactly the same age. He wondered about that until his second visit.

On his second trip he passed through Hinckley in the daytime, and picked up a tourist map. There was a paragraph on the back about the various attractions, and one was the Hinckley Fire Museum. He read more closely and learned that all the land for miles around here had been old forests that had been logged in the nineteenth century. The cutters had trimmed the brush from the lumber and left it where it fell. When a fire started in 1894, the land had burned uncontrollably, leaving nothing. All the trees had grown in since then.

When Varney reached the road where the farm was, he did his first daylight reconnaissance. The utility vehicle that had been parked outside the house was gone this morning, and no other vehicle was visible, so he guessed that Kelleher had gone out, and probably lived alone. He paid particular attention to the woods that covered the right side of the farm. Since the left side was low stubble and weeds, it would be a bad place to cross on foot.

He knew he was teasing himself, relishing the planning phase because he had been so anxious to get back to work. He knew that most likely, planning was unnecessary. He could have sat in Minneapolis waiting for the phone call, driven right up here that night, pulled up the farm road to the house, kicked in the door, shot Kelleher, and driven off. There were few cars on this road in the daytime, and almost none at night. Minnesota north of Minneapolis was not as crowded as the places where he had worked before. He had driven up here twice, about ninety miles each way, and had not seen a single police car. He'd had to drive around in Hinckley to see a few parked by the station so he would know what colors they were painted. He had also searched out a state police barracks along the interstate highway to look at state police cars.

Varney studied the road near the farm for the best place to park his car. The landscape presented extremes. Long stretches of road were flanked on both sides by endless, swampy, treeless fields where red-winged blackbirds perched on cattails, their weight making the shafts bend, so that they bobbed in the wind as they called to each other. The rest was either farmers' fields or thick forests of the uniform twenty-foot deciduous trees like the ones on Kelleher's land.

When he had first seen them, he had assumed they were young, but now he supposed they must have been what sprouted after the fire over a hundred years ago, and they'd been stunted by the weather. Every place he saw a grove that looked promising he slowed down to look closer and saw an obstacle. In many places, there was a drainage ditch beside the shoulder of the road, or a fence. In other places, the trees had grown in too dense a pattern for a car to slip in between them.

When he worked in cities, he could always find a safe place to leave a car. Cities were full of commercial buildings with small parking areas behind them. Sometimes he would park his car in a shopping

mall or the lot of a big apartment complex, where it would become invisible, just one of a hundred. Here it was different. He could hardly
leave a car on the shoulder of the road, because it would be the only
one visible for miles. He considered leaving the car in Hinckley.
There was a big hotel and casino run by the Ojibwe Indians there,
with hundreds of cars in its lot. But it was too far from the farm. The
casino was surrounded by long stretches of straight, empty highway
where a solitary walker would be a novelty. People didn't go for pleasant ten-mile hikes beside roads around here. There was a big state
park a few miles away, where people could hike along the St. Croix
River if they wanted to.

As he drove back to Minneapolis, he thought of various ways to
handle the problem of transportation. He was already as far south as
Mounds View before he hit upon the right one. For the rest of the
drive, he worked out the details until he was satisfied.

For the next few days, Varney stayed in Minneapolis and prepared.
He would get up early each morning, go down to the exercise room
on the fourth floor of the hotel, and use the weights and machines before the other guests were up. Then he would step through the locker
room to the pool and swim for an hour. Then he went up to the room,
took Mae to breakfast, and walked the streets with her until lunch-
time. He drove her to the Mall of America and bought her some
clothes, took her to parks with little lakes in them, looked at the Mississippi. In the late afternoon, he drove to a park where people jogged
after work, and joined them. He and Mae went to dinner at a different
restaurant each evening, and when they were back in the room, he
turned his attention to his equipment. The kind of meticulous care he
used was best done in quiet times like this.

Varney put on thin rubber gloves, and thoroughly cleaned his three
pistols. He bathed each part in solvent, wiped it clean, and put a thin
layer of gun oil on it, then reassembled the weapon without putting
any fingerprints on its internal parts. He used the same procedure
with each magazine, then loaded the magazine with ammunition
without touching any of the rounds with bare hands. Then he put the
pistols into plastic bags and returned them to his suitcase.

He treated his clothing with equal care. None of the clothes had
anything memorable or distinctive about them. The brands were all

national, the brand names and even size labels cut out. He did not do this because a police force would not be able to find out these things if they had his clothes. He did it because he wanted to make them work harder. If they had to learn the brand name by cut, material, and pattern, it would take time. And that information would give them nothing, because there was nothing special about the clothes.

He washed the soles of the shoes he planned to wear and put them into a plastic bag so no fibers from a hotel rug or a car's interior would stick to them.

His precautions were meticulous and painstaking, but they dispelled the worries that distracted him. He knew a shell casing left near the body would not carry a fingerprint. If he got blood on his clothes, or was seen wearing them, he could change and throw them away. He could drop his gun in a ditch and not give it another thought, because his guns were all ones he'd stolen in burglaries years ago in California.

Mac watched him making his preparations, never coming near the belongings he spread on the table in their room or speaking to him during his period of meditation on risks and countermeasures. It was only after he had performed all the rituals and put away the tools and clothes that she moved within ten feet of him. She said, "Are you done?"

"Yeah," he said.

"It's interesting, the way you do things. So careful, everything in a certain way. It's kind of like a doctor or something."

He gazed at her in wonder. She didn't get it. She kept pushing forward, and she sometimes came right up close to figuring something out, but she just wasn't paying enough attention after she got there. She was doomed always to think she understood things when she didn't.

The telephone rang, and she gave a small jump. It had not rung in the five days since they had arrived. She flopped on the bed and reached for the telephone on the nightstand. "I'll get it."

"No," he said. "I will." He lifted the receiver on the desk. "Yes?"

"Sugar!" came the high, oily voice. "Is that you?"

"Yeah," he answered, "it's me. Did you get the call?"

"About fifteen minutes ago, sugar. The client just called my friend, and said he's all set in California."

"For how long?"

"What?"

"How long is he going to be accounted for? How long have I got to do this?"

The voice turned honey-sweet and dumb. "Well, I don't really know. My friend didn't tell me, and I didn't know I was supposed to ask." The voice seemed to gel and turn cold. "Aren't you ready by now?" There was a distorted windy sound, and he could imagine her blowing smoke from a cigarette across the receiver. "I'm not about to call him back. I'm standing at a pay phone at a 7-Eleven way across town, and he—"

"Forget it," said Varney. "Don't worry. I'll take care of it. See you in a few days."

"Aren't you forgetting something?"

"What?"

"I just told you. I rushed out to a 7-Eleven after dark alone just to do this. Not to mention setting it all up and waiting a week for a stupid phone call."

His jaw worked, his teeth clenched. After a moment he said, "Thank you."

"That's more like it. Good-bye." She hung up.

He placed the telephone back on its cradle, walked to the closet, and put his special suitcase on the bed. He was concentrating now, getting himself ready, and Mae's voice was an irritant. "Was that the call?"

His concentration was broken. "Uh-huh." He took the plastic bags that contained his clothes, tools, and weapons out and set them on the bed, examining them once more, then returned them to the suitcase.

"Can I go with you?"

He turned to her, his brows knitted. "I'm going up there to kill somebody."

"I know," she said, but her features were pinched together in what looked like confusion. He supposed that she must be surprised that she wanted to go, and wasn't sure whether she was being stupid. "I won't bother you or get in the way. I won't even talk if you don't want me to."

"Why do you want to go?"

She shrugged. "I just thought it might be nicer." Then she tried to carry an idea to him, but she didn't seem to know exactly what it was, so she talked around it. "For you, you know? Somebody to listen if you wanted to talk afterward, maybe to drive if you got tired."

He was intrigued. She had absolutely no comprehension of what this was, or how it felt to be the one who did it. But she had been sitting here in silence, talking herself into doing exactly what he wanted her to do. He had been expecting he would have to fool her or threaten her, but she was practically begging him. It made him curious, so he ventured, "It's not going to be fun. You could stay here in this fancy hotel and get some sleep."

She looked upset, as though she was being forced to drop a comforting pretense and admit something. "Please. I don't want to sit here all alone wondering what's happening: if you're going to come back for me, or if I'll just be sitting here for days."

He let enough time pass so she would believe he was slowly working his way through her reasons and overcoming his surprise at her request. "All right," he said. "Get ready."

She stood and flung her arms around him. "Thanks, Jimmy. You won't regret it." Then she released him. "What do I wear? Something dark?"

He went to the closet, pushed hangers aside, pulled a couple out, and tossed them on the bed. "These will do." The hangers held a pair of black tailored pants with a razor crease, and a dark blue blouse.

"What about— "

He anticipated her question. "These." He tossed a pair of flat black shoes onto the bed. They were ones she had worn once when they had gone for a walk. She looked at the outfit critically for a second, then seemed pleased. She quickly began to dress.

When they were both ready, Varney said, "Okay. Now we clean up. We don't know if we're coming back to Minneapolis or not, but probably we won't. So we pack. We wipe off everything that's smooth and might hold a fingerprint: doorknobs, faucets, the phones, the desk, TV, everything. Use a towel."

Twenty minutes later, Varney stopped and threw his towel on the bathroom floor, and she imitated him. "Check the wastebaskets," he said. "Anything in them, we take."

She stood still. "They're empty. I wiped them off because they were smooth, so I noticed."

"Good. Now we go."

They took the elevator to the ground floor, and Mae paid the bill in cash and checked out while Varney waited in a big armchair across the lobby near a table that held a white telephone.

They got into the car and Varney let Mae drive for the first stretch. It was dark, and after a half hour they were beyond the range of most of the cars being driven north by commuters. It was safe for him to change his clothes in the passenger seat.

"You know, I had an idea," he said.

"What is it?" She kept taking her eyes off the road to look at him, and that made him nervous. He had intended to let her drive all the way up so he could stay fresh, but he was tempted to change the plan.

He said, "The problem with that farm is that there's no good place to park where people can't see the car from the road. What if you drove me near the farm, stopped for just a second while I got out, and took off? You could give me, say, two hours to go the rest of the way on foot through the woods, drop the hammer on this guy, hide the body, and walk back. What do you think?"

"What do I do then?"

His confidence that he had constructed a good plan began to seem optimistic. "You come back, stop the car again, and pick me up. We leave."

"No," she said. "I mean, while you're gone. Do I just keep driving for an hour and then turn around?"

He had to stop himself from saying, "Who gives a shit?" He supposed the question was not as stupid as it had sounded. She was right. It could make a difference. He looked at his watch. "By the time you've dropped me off, it will be around midnight. It's probably better not to be driving around alone. After you drop me, go back to Hinckley, park in the lot at that hotel that says Grand Casino. It's probably the only place you could go around here that's not suspicious. Go inside and play the slot machines for a couple of hours and come get me."

"Is that safe?"

"Yeah," he said. "Places like that are full of security people. It's probably safer than a bank."

"But those places have surveillance cameras, don't they?"

He nodded, mildly surprised that she knew. "Yes, they do. If they

get you on tape, you know what it will show? That you were in a
casino pumping quarters into a slot while this guy was getting killed.
And there's going to be fifty other women doing the same."

"Oh," she said. "Yeah. I'm sorry. I just never thought like this before."

"It's okay," he said. "Now I've got to do some thinking, so I'll have
to be kind of quiet for a while." He stared ahead at the road, going
over each part of his plan, forming an image in his mind of himself
performing each step. Within a few minutes, he felt his heartbeat had
begun to go faster, stronger, his muscles had begun to feel ready. He
put on his thin, tight goatskin gloves, lifted the plastic bag that contained his weapons, and set it on his lap. He took out two of the pistols, both Beretta Model 92's like the police used, a silencer, and two
extra ammunition clips, and slid the bag under the seat. He slipped the
knife into the short sheath, strapped the Velcro strips around his ankle,
and covered it with his pant leg. He put the silencer, magazines, and
one pistol into various jacket pockets, then pushed the second gun
under his belt at the small of his back and covered it with his jacket.
They were nearly to the exit for Route 48 now, and when he saw it, he
said, "Pull off here."

When they passed the brightly lit sign for the casino he said, "That's
the place where you go." He pulled out his wallet and said, "Put this in
your purse. There's about two thousand in it. Use what you need to
keep gambling. Nobody in a casino bothers you if you're gambling."
Then he had a sudden worry. "Don't drink alcohol, or try to buy
drugs. When this is over, you can get as fucked up as you want."

"I won't," she said, sounding hurt.

He was silent again until after she had made the turn onto the
smaller road and was headed toward the farm. She had gotten them
here without his having to point out the last few turns, so he felt reassured: she wouldn't get lost on the way back. She said, "Let me know
where to stop."

He watched the sights going by for a few minutes. When they
passed the farm, he looked and his heartbeat strengthened again. The
SUV was parked there, and one light was on upstairs. He was here.
When Mae had gone a half mile down the road, Varney looked back
and saw no headlights. He said, "Right here. Stop."

He slipped out onto the road and closed the car door, then stepped back onto the shoulder. As he turned to go, her voice cut the silence.

"Wait," she called.

He stopped, his senses searching the area for danger, his mind racing. He glanced at her to see what she had meant. She looked as though she knew she had made a mistake. She said, "I just wanted to say good luck."

His eyes flared, but he said, "Thanks," and stepped into the woods at the edge of the road. He saw the lights fade, heard the engine accelerating, and then submerged himself in the silence and darkness.

34

arney took his bearings by looking up to find the North Star, gauging the angle of the road, and then looking for a landmark to aim at. The sky was incredibly clear and the stars appeared big and close, but the woods were too thick to allow him to pick out a landmark on the ground. He knew the approximate direction he wanted, so he set off.

There was something about the night woods that created its own propriety. He found himself stalking through the forest quietly, as he had practiced in Ohio. As he walked, occasionally he startled small animals that rustled the brush and scuttled off. He was in only about a quarter mile before he heard something different ahead. A thicket shook, making a hissing and crackling, the leaves on the ground crunching as something heavy exploded out of the thicket.

He dropped and crouched, the pistol out of his belt and in his hand before his mind even attempted to interpret the sounds. The thumping of feet rapidly moved off somewhere ahead and to his right, and the silence flowed in to fill the vacuum again.

Varney stayed coiled and motionless for a long time, his ears straining and his eyes slowly moving back and forth, up and down. A deer:

it had to be a deer, he thought. It had been absolutely still, maybe lying down, and he had approached so quietly that he had startled it.

He slowly stood. He switched on the safety of his pistol, but he didn't put it away. He reached into his jacket pocket, found the four-inch tube of the silencer, and carefully screwed it onto the custom-threaded barrel. He stepped forward again, this time feeling the cadence of his heart, almost hearing it as it raced, then slowed again. He was probably being foolish, he chided himself. There was nothing to be uneasy about as long as he didn't get startled in the dark and step in a hole.

He had become accustomed to walking in fields and woods at night in Ohio, but this was not Ohio. It had felt the same at first, but it wasn't. There were deer. What about bears? Up here there could easily be bears. These woods and farms had covered all the land that was high, and the rest was marshes and streams, so this was where they would be.

He plotted his course again by mentally tracing his path back to where he had begun, then extending the line forward through the thicket. He kept going steadily, not letting himself be as quiet now as he had been. If there was something big up ahead, he wanted it to have time to get out of his way.

In a few minutes he was feeling better, concentrating on what he had to do. It was simpler than most of the jobs he'd done since he had moved into the upper level of his profession. People only put out the big money he commanded when the job was risky or complicated. In this case, it was only risky and complicated for the client, and whoever he was, he had taken care of most of that himself. He was going to be the suspect, so he had established an alibi, paid in advance, and gotten out of the way. He had even done the work of finding Kelleher himself, so there could be no mistake.

Varney was not a believer in taking work lightly. If you were good enough to do the job, then usually the way you got destroyed was by chance. The best always assumed that something was going to go wrong, and calmly watched to see what it was going to be this time. Some visitor would show up at the front door just as you were waiting for the target to answer it. You would have your car's muffler go just as you were driving off, trying not to be noticed. Guns jammed, fires either went out or roared into life so fast that you could hear sirens before you made it out the door.

Over the past few days, he had anticipated as many of the possible problems as he could, and fixed them. Nobody would see his car parked here. Mae was in a casino alone, and when she drove off, she would still seem to be alone. If his gun jammed, he had another in his jacket pocket. If that failed, he had a knife. If Mae didn't come, he could walk back to the house and take Kelleher's car, or even sneak into town at that time of night and probably hot-wire one. He reviewed his preparations and contingency plans, and found they were adequate. The real certainty was inside Varney. He had exerted self-discipline over the past couple of months, and stayed strong and ready. He had tirelessly worked on his body, his concentration, his skills, his alertness. Trudging out here to pop some solitary traitor was almost beneath him, but he didn't mind. The job had come at a time when he needed to get back to work. He needed a kill.

He sensed that there was more light between the trunks of the trees ahead, and quickened his pace. In a few minutes, he was sure. A hundred feet to his left, he caught sight of stubble and bare ground. He had made a near-perfect diagonal from the road across the woods, and at some point had passed over an invisible line onto Kelleher's property. He stayed well back, where the brush was thick and the trunks of trees made him invisible from outside the woods, and kept going until his eye caught the glow of an electric light just below the canopy of leaves.

He turned toward it and moved forward from tree to tree, until he could see the house. The light was still on in the upstairs window—undoubtedly Kelleher's bedroom. Downstairs, everything seemed to be dark. Varney moved closer, still gliding ahead only as far as the next tree that he could stand behind, then stopping and watching the house for a time while he planned his next advance.

The SUV he had seen from the road was a dark blue Lincoln Navigator. He could make out the name on the back, the beige leather upholstery of the back seats above the window, and the license-plate holder from a lot in Minneapolis. The vehicle was new, and expensive. He felt a moment of empathy for his client. This weasel had handed the client to the police, and managed to hold on to some serious money. He had bought a big farm and a new vehicle, and if he could live up here, he had no need to work.

For the first time, it occurred to Varney that this job might be worth more than he had been offered. All this money had come from some kind of theft that this Kelleher had pulled with the client, and so there was a fairly strong possibility that some of it was here in cash. Varney checked his watch. It was twenty after twelve already. He needed to set aside twenty minutes to get back to the road, and that left an hour and twenty minutes for him to accomplish everything he was going to do here. The thought made him venture closer, his eyes now scanning the eaves of the house for floodlights that might be connected to motion detectors. The roof of the farmhouse was steep and the eaves were high, so he could see clearly: they were bare. There were no warning signs on the lawn or windows that belonged to an alarm company. He supposed that way out here there might not even be such a thing. But he exerted the self-discipline and made himself do the walk-around he had planned. He unscrewed the silencer and put away the gun.

He stayed far from the house as he walked around it, but moved closer when there was cover. He looked at the eaves and gutters all around, studied windows, doors, the foundation. When he had made a full circuit, he had confirmed that there was no sign of an armed security service that answered alarms, but there seemed to be a system of some kind installed. Visible through a window was a keypad near the front door with glowing red and green lights.

At the rear of the house was an open stone patio that looked as though it had been laid recently enough to be the work of the current owner. There was an irregular pattern of sandstone slabs with sand between them, and just one lawn chair in the center not far from a small portable barbecue. Just as Varney was moving in that direction, the light in the upper window went out. He looked at his watch. It was nearly twelve-thirty.

The barn was a small one, not the kind that had been built to house forty cows, but the kind where machinery was parked on the lower floor and bales of hay were stored in the loft. The door had a padlock on it, but it was unlocked and the hasp open at the moment, so he supposed there was nothing of interest inside.

He found the septic tank, and in the dark it looked to him as though it had probably just been replaced, because it had been covered with turf strips that still had lines between them, and there was a hatch that seemed nearly new. There were a couple of long, four-inch pipes on the ground, and he supposed they had something to do with it.

Then Varney made a lucky find. The upstairs window that had been lit was open about two inches, and so was the one on the other side of the house directly across from it, probably to set up a cross-breeze. If the alarm system was on but the upstairs windows were open, then the alarm was only protecting the ground floor. He could go in the window across the hall from Kelleher's room without setting off any bells and whistles.

It was not going to be without risk. He had to make his way to that window, open it farther, and slip inside without letting Kelleher hear him. Nobody who thought there were people who wanted to kill him went to bed without having a gun where he could reach for it in the dark. Varney moved to the corner of the house and judged the possibilities. There was a low roof over the front porch that he could easily climb onto, but he would still be twenty feet from the open window. No tree was near enough to let him climb and jump for the sill. Even if he could have done such a thing and held on, it would have made a lot of noise.

He looked down and saw the pipes on the ground. He raised his eyes to the window, then judged the length of the nearest pipe. He stepped closer to it. The material was hard and heavy and smooth like iron, but it seemed to be made of some kind of ceramic material. He knelt and looked at the open end. It was rougher inside, and narrower. The rim seemed to be three quarters of an inch thick.

He stepped to the center, squatted, and lifted the heavy pipe, then adjusted his grip to find the balance point, and walked toward the house with it. He set it down. Then, below the open window and about ten feet from the house, he used his knife to dig a hole in the lawn. He set the end of the heavy pipe over the hole. He went to the other end and lifted the pipe, hand-walking up its length until the pipe was vertical and the butt end of it was in the hole. Then he stepped between the pipe and the house and slowly, carefully, stepped backward, letting the pipe tip toward the house until its upper end rested against a clapboard beside the open window.

Varney went to the end in the hole and tested its immobility, then gripped it as high up as he could reach and pulled himself upward until he was straddling it. The pipe was at a steep angle to the house, but it was not difficult for him to shinny up to the top. He was beside the window. He lifted his pant leg, pulled the knife out, punched a small slice through the screen, and used a finger to slip the hook out of the eye. He pulled the screen out a bit, and slowly pushed the window open wider. Then he eased himself carefully off the pipe into the window. When he was inside, he pulled the screen back and slid the hook through the eye so it wouldn't make a flapping noise.

He moved to the side of the window before he stood, so he would present no silhouette. He waited and listened. His heart was beginning to speed up again. He had done this a hundred times, and each time still felt like the first. The moment after he had crossed into the enclosed space where the target was, his eyes always grew sharper, his muscles stronger. His ears heard every sound. Sometimes he was sure that he had other, forgotten senses that most human beings had thrown away with soft living. Everything they did worked to insulate them and pad them and put them to sleep. He often felt that he could detect objects in the dark by the changes their weight made in the elasticity of a man-made floor under his feet. He used differences in the motion of the air on his face to help him find a doorway.

He slowly, carefully screwed the silencer onto the barrel of his pistol and disengaged the safety with his thumb. He became still again and listened. Moving silently was not just a question of care, but of time. He had certainly made sounds when he had come in. If they had reached Kelleher's ears, maybe he had explained them to himself. But his subconscious mind would not be so easily reassured, and it was incapable of forgetting anything. Down there below the level of thinking, Kelleher's mind would be waiting to hear them again, its instincts aware that noises at night were never good news. Varney had to be sure the next sounds he made did not come too soon.

Varney was a being that moved through the night with heightened alertness, as though his skin had been peeled off and his nerves exposed. He could feel the rhythms of the enemy. He knew he did not have to wait for any particular number of minutes. He had to wait until the mind in the other room had listened long enough. When it had, it would stop. Any sounds he made would not be grouped with the first sounds as a pattern that had grown consistent with danger. They would be random sounds, maybe the noises that wooden houses made as they settled or stood up to a breeze.

The time elapsed and Varney advanced, placing each small step gently so his foot set flat and distributed his weight evenly. When he was satisfied the floor would not creak, he cautiously let more of his weight onto that foot as he moved the other foot forward. He kept his knees flexed and his body low, in an attitude that would let him leap ahead, back, or to either side, or drop and roll more quickly than an opponent's mind would be likely to expect. If Kelleher saw him, what he would see was not the shape of a human being—something six feet high with a discernible head and shoulders. He would hesitate while he tried to distinguish it from the shadows and resolve it into something he knew.

As Varney moved into the hallway, he felt an urge to put away the gun. The metal, the weight were jarring to his mood. This felt like a time to slip in like a shadow and use only his hands, the strike chosen by the position in which he found Kelleher's sleeping body. But Varney knew he was being foolish. He was letting his eagerness overwhelm his judgment, just because he was so excited to be working again. He would step into the room, see the head against the whiteness of the pillow, and sensibly fire a shot into it. Then he would spend some time searching for the money.

He stopped at the side of the doorway and listened. He could see the window, a bit of a bathroom floor through an open door, a chair, a dresser with a mirror. He leaned outward until he could see a bit of the reflection of the bed. There was a quilt in a dark shade that he couldn't quite decide in the dark was blue, but no lump. Kelleher must be sleeping on the near side, the part of the bed that he couldn't see in the reflection. Varney raised his right arm in a crook, so the pistol was pointed up, pivoted around the door frame to move inside the room, brought the pistol down to aim at the head of the bed on the near side. The bed was empty.

Varney let his pivot continue so he spun to face the bathroom. Nobody was in there.

A high-pitched electronic ring twittered to his right. It was so loud to Varney's ears that he dropped to a crouch and aimed at it, his muscles rigid. But the only object in that direction was the dresser. The sound came again—a telephone. The small lozenge-shaped shadow on the surface was a cell phone. This time he saw the rows of keys light up as it rang. He had to stop it.

He snatched it up, pressed the button, and clamped it to his ear as he crouched beside the dresser, listening with the other ear for footsteps.

"Hello, Slick," said the voice. Varney's stomach sucked inward. There seemed to be no air in the room, and he had to force himself to take a breath. It was Prescott.

35

Varney's whole being seemed to him to be toppling into the silence: Prescott was waiting for him to answer. His instinct was that anything Prescott wanted was something that would hurt him somehow. But he could not break the connection, lose touch. "I can hear you breathing," said Prescott. "I know it's not Michael J. Kelleher, because I made him up. And it's not as though I don't know where you are. I know where I put the phone."

Varney took a moment to swallow and be sure his voice would sound right when it came out. "I'm listening." He held the phone away from his ear, so he could detect it if there was a sound of Prescott's voice coming to him through the air in addition to through the telephone's earpiece. An echo, a slight time dissonance would tell him where Prescott was. He stepped to the doorway.

"That's better," said Prescott. "I apologize for scaring the shit out of you by ringing the phone."

There was no sound that Varney could hear that had not come from the telephone. He said, "I'm not that easy to scare." He concentrated on keeping the anger and hatred out of his voice. He peered into the hallway, but there was no visual sign of Prescott, either. The hallway was just a hardwood corridor with the two bedrooms he had entered, and four closed doors—one at either end, one on his right on this side of the house, just before the railing of the staircase, and another across the hall from it. Wherever Prescott was, he couldn't see Varney, but he knew which room Varney was in. That had to change.

"That's good," said Prescott. "Fear and anger cloud a man's judgment sometimes, and right now I think you need to be clearheaded."

"Why is that?" Varney quickly slipped across the hall into the other room and paused just to the right of the doorway with his back against the wall. He held the phone away from his ear again and held his breath as he strained his ears.

"Because you've got a problem. I wanted to talk to you now, and let you know there are a couple of options, before they get used up."

Varney's chest felt as though it would burst with frustration. He still could not get his ears to detect a sound of Prescott's voice coming to him from somewhere inside the house. He knew it was happening: Prescott had to be in the house, but Varney's ears were not sensitive enough to pick it up. He blew out the air in his lungs as he stepped silently toward the window. He knew Prescott would hear it as an expression of contempt, but it wasn't loud enough for Prescott to hear except through the phone. He took another step and looked out the window. He sidestepped, still not sure, getting worried.

"I wouldn't bother with that," said Prescott.

"What?"

"Just because I bought you those pipes and let you have the use of one of them doesn't mean I'll let you use it forever."

Varney leaned close enough to the window so his face touched the screen. He had been right. The pipe he had leaned against the wall of the house beside the window had been moved. He could see it on the grass below. He quickly ducked and pivoted, then stopped, protected by the wall. Prescott could be out there with a rifle and night-vision scope—must be, Varney decided. The outer wall was a stupid place for Varney to be. Its solidity was an illusion. Even a common hunting rifle would put a hole through it. He went low again and retreated to the inner wall by the doorway. "What do you want?" he hissed. "Haven't you had enough of trying and losing?"

"It's more a question of what you want," said Prescott. "You've got a problem to solve."

"So what's my problem?"

"Here's the way it looks to me," said Prescott. "You're alone, on foot, in a pretty remote place where there are not a lot of people. There's no crowd to fade into, and not much to distract anybody like me. At the moment, you're in a house that I selected. You know I'm not far away, but you don't know exactly where I am. I could be outside with a rifle, waiting for you to try to get out a window. You'll be out there hanging by your fingertips in your dark clothes against those white boards for a good second or two. Tomorrow morning I can go hose off the siding and go up on a ladder to patch the holes. Of course, maybe I'm in the room right next to you with the door closed. Or one of the others. If you open one to go out a different window, it's entirely possible I might be sitting in a comfortable chair holding a shotgun loaded with double-ought. The cleanup would take longer, but I'm a patient man."

Varney said, "You think I haven't thought of all this?"

"I suppose you have. I don't want you to dwell on the specifics. I want you to think past them. I've got you in a predicament. I want you to know that you don't have to die. There are other ways through this."

"Like what?"

"You leave anything made out of metal in that room. You come out. I run a metal detector over you, to be sure nothing slipped your mind. You would have to tolerate handcuffs on the ride into Hinckley, and probably again when they transport you down to Minneapolis, but after that you'd be in a private cell."

Varney thought he saw a movement at the edge of the woods. If that was where Prescott was, he would have been in position to see Varney arrive, watch the business with the pipe, see him come into this room. Varney stared out the window at the spot. "What difference does it make if I let you shoot me or I let them kill me in some gas chamber?"

Prescott's laugh carried with it everything that Varney hated. It was the laugh of a man who didn't think he would ever have to worry about the things that were tormenting Varney, but more important than this, it was arrogant, superior. Prescott said, "You ought to know better than that. If they did get through a trial and prove anything, it wouldn't be good enough to get you executed. The evidence they have isn't that strong. They can't say, 'This guy has been taking money for putting people in the ground for years.' They have to pick one and prove you did it."

"If you think I'd get off, what are you doing this for? I thought you had given up, gotten off me."

"I'll never do that," said Prescott. The sound of his voice was quiet, almost gentle, and the effect was horrible. "I have two reasons. If you go in, get booked, fingerprinted, photographed, and all that, I'm not the only one who knows you. If you ever kill somebody later, you're a manageable police problem. They'll pick you up. They'll know all about you, your habits, the way you do your work, so they'll recognize it."

"What's the other reason?" Varney still didn't see movement out there.

"That's different," said Prescott. "That's for you. Maybe if you got a little time where you would have to stay put and talk to somebody—"

"Psychiatrists?" The anger tightened his throat so his voice came out choked.

"Your own lawyer would call a few in the minute anything about the case looked ominous. It's your escape hatch if I'm wrong and some real evidence turns up." He paused. "I really think you've had a problem for a long, long time. It must be hard. I'm not interested in killing you, kid. I'll be satisfied just to make you stop."

Outrage gripped Varney's chest, pushing his words out in streams. "You lying bastard. I read about you in the papers. Everybody you ever went after is dead. You're a fucking snake. Did you tell them all you were going to take them to a nice doctor? Did you get them all to put on handcuffs before you shot them?"

"Neither one," said Prescott calmly.

"Bullshit!" Varney snapped. "You're the one who's afraid. You're in the same business I am, and you know I'm better than you. I'm going to cut your fucking head off and stick it on a post."

He heard Prescott sigh. "I guess I've said everything I wanted to. If you change your mind, press 1 on your phone. It's programmed to dial me." The telephone went dead.

Varney watched the bushes at the edge of the woods more intently, and he saw the movement again. He silently mouthed the words, "I've got you." He was moving before the plan had solidified in his mind.

Prescott was out there thinking he had the only advantage that mattered. Varney turned off the cell phone and slipped it into his jacket. As soon as he cleared the doorway he began to run. The upstairs hallway was dark because the doors of bedrooms were closed, but the wooden railing began and he put his gloved hand on it and let the hand slide along it to orient him as he moved forward. The railing made a curve and headed down at an angle into the dark. He took the first stair, lengthened his stride to take three at a time, and his foot stepped onto nothing.

Varney's body dropped downward, but his right hand tightened in a reflex to stop himself, clutching the railing in a desperate grab. His right arm elongated in a sudden, wrenching tug. His left hand held the pistol, but as his body swung and his chest slammed against the side of the staircase, the hand pawed at the wood to cushion the impact, and his legs swung into the void. He dangled there for a moment, swinging back and forth. He stuck the pistol into his left jacket pocket, and hung by both hands. He looked down.

The staircase had been sawed off just below the first-floor ceiling. The drop to the floor looked to him like fourteen or fifteen feet, but below him the floor was not clear. The stairway lay intact on the floor, as though Prescott had run a chain saw across it where it connected to the upper floor and let it fall. If Varney had not been gripping the railing when he had stepped off, he would be lying across those triangular ridges that used to be steps. He probably wouldn't be dead, but it would have been impossible not to have broken some bones.

Varney took a second to move through a series of thoughts. Prescott was out in those bushes, but Varney had seen them shake, so he might have been preparing to move on. If he was heading inside, then it was to catch Varney hanging here by both hands. If he wasn't coming in, then Varney had to get out in time to see where he was going. Varney could pull himself up and go tie bedsheets together to lower himself down, but that would take time. If he dropped from here, the only place he could land was the jagged stairway.

He hung by his left arm, pulled his belt off with his right, slipped it around the base of the corner post of the railing, and threaded it through the buckle. He lowered himself to the end of the belt, where he was clear of the ceiling and the upper steps of the staircase, held it with both hands, and bent his legs to start himself swinging. He swung a couple of times, until he judged that his momentum would carry him out over the part of the foyer he could see was clear of obstacles, then let go. The floor seemed to tilt and rush up at him, but he managed to break his fall by hitting on the balls of his feet with his knees bent and translating his forward motion into a roll. He came to rest near a fireplace at the end of the room, rose to his feet, and realized his pistol must have slipped out of his jacket pocket.

He crawled quickly back toward the ruined stairway, felt the familiar shape of the pistol under his hand, and grasped it, already planning. In order to take down the pipe that Varney had left at the window, Prescott had to have been on that side of the house, hiding in the low bushes that separated the house from the stubble fields. Varney moved to the opposite side, and unlatched a window that faced the woods. He tried to lift it, but it was closed too tightly. He looked more closely and let out a breath through his clenched teeth. Prescott had used sixpenny nails to secure the windows. He would have to use one of the two doors, and Prescott would probably have booby-trapped one and be making his way through the brush toward the other with a rifle.

Varney moved to the front door and looked out through the peephole, then stepped to the front window. The place where Prescott had been was not visible from here, so there was no clear shot. If Varney moved quickly, maybe he could slip out to the edge of the porch, go over the railing, and hit the ground before Prescott could aim.

He tried the doorknob, unlocked the door, then pulled his knife. He stood to the side of the door and ran the blade along each side, then above the top, then lay on his belly and slid it underneath. He was startled by the voice from above and behind him: "Front . . . door." He had rolled to the side and was aiming his pistol at the sound with one hand, the knife still in the other, before he realized the voice had not been human. He was aiming at the alarm keypad on the wall. He stepped closer and saw the slits for a small speaker, then knelt and ran his knife under the door again. "Front . . . door."

The blade had interrupted the contact between the two magnets set into the door and the floor beneath it. He took a deep breath and regained his composure. The door wasn't booby-trapped, and that was what mattered. He stood, took two more deep breaths, opened the door, slipped out, and closed it, ignoring the muffled electronic voice. In a few seconds he was at the end of the porch, vaulting over the railing to the ground. He lay still for a moment, listening: no metal sounds, no footsteps. He spider-crawled quickly along the side of the house to the back corner, then lay flat and paused to listen again and stare out into the darkness. He let time pass.

Prescott was devious. He had picked this remote, sparsely populated place just so he could convert it into a field of traps and snares for Varney. He'd had to be in a place like this, where he could run a power saw through a staircase and let it crash to the floor, where he could fire a gun through a helpless man's head and not have to worry about anybody hearing it, or telling him later he had not done it the way the law said he should. The only way ever to be free was to see Prescott first and kill him.

Varney had to read the trap and use it against Prescott. The brush where Prescott was hiding tempted Varney. He stared across the lawn. The shortest way to the low bushes was across the patio at the back of the house. If he could make it across the open space, he could work his way through the brush and come up behind Prescott. The idea was tantalizing. Prescott would think he was still in the house, probably lying on the ruined stairway with a broken back. He had no way of knowing how good Varney was in a field at night. Varney could move more quietly, more quickly than Prescott could. But moving across an open patio to get to the first cover was a risk.

He crouched, still watching the brush ahead. He slowly moved to the corner of the house to get a view to his left. It seemed that the place where Prescott had been was not quite visible from here, but once he was out a few paces, it would be. He would try the quiet, invisible way. He went to his belly and began to slither across the back lawn, his eyes on the row of bushes, waiting for movement.

There was a loud crack as a bullet broke the sound barrier over his head. He was up and sprinting, gaining speed as he dashed toward cover. There was no reason to stay on the grass now, so he let his feet take him toward the paved patio, where he could make better time.

One foot hit the patio and the ball of his foot pushed off, and he knew it was all wrong. There was a spongy feel to it. The other foot hit and the pavement sank. He saw a section of the stones ahead buckle and fold. The patio wasn't stone slabs laid in the ground; it was just sheets of artificial masonry, made of drywall with a plastic veneer. He had broken through. He had to control the fall. He did not impede his forward motion, because he had to keep from dropping vertically. He flopped forward, both arms extended, slapping the next section of artificial stones, pushing down with arms and legs, scrambling ahead on the fragile surface to keep the drywall falling below him. He felt himself going through, then heard the first end of a section hit with a hollow echo. With the sound, he knew there was concrete, he knew it was about ten feet down. He hit, letting his feet break a sheet of drywall wedged beside another, and directing his body onto the next section of drywall.

His fall was jarring, but he felt no sharp pain, and he was on his feet. He could tell he was in an empty swimming pool, and he knew he had to get out. He ran up the steep concrete slope toward the shallow end, where the fragile sheets of drywall overhead still formed a roof to shield him from Prescott's sights.

Varney reached the end, came up without pausing, his head lifting the end of the drywall enough to free him, and he was out and running again. He found himself heading back the way he had come, but for the moment he had no choice. He had to get out of Prescott's view.

As he approached the side of the house, he was beginning to get past the pure anger at what Prescott had tried to do to him, and had begun to wonder at what Prescott had not done. There had been only one shot, and it had gone high. Prescott had had time to fire again. He could have put ten rounds through the half-inch drywall on top of the empty pool, let them bounce around in the dark concrete basin, and probably clip Varney on a ricochet. He must have known that Varney would come out at the shallow end, and should have leveled his weapon on it. Was he that slow? He couldn't be. He had fired his one shot only to make Varney run and fall into the pool. He had to be at the wrong angle, too low and far away to fire downward into the pool, and too far to the left to have the shallow end in view. He must still be across the lawn from the pipes, where Varney had seen the bushes move.

Varney had one clear, simple idea and it would work only if he used it before Prescott did. When Varney reached the house, he kept running along the side. He had to take the chance that Prescott would still be aiming at the back corner of the house, waiting for him to show himself there. Varney came around the front, running harder now. He ran past the front porch, keeping his feet on the grass, where his steps would make no noise. He could see the start of the row of bushes now. It was not neat and thin like a hedge, but deep and unruly, planted there as a barrier to the wind in the summer, when the dust blew off the fields, and probably in the winter a snow fence to catch the drifts before they piled up on the side and front of the house.

He did not pause but moved immediately among the thick bushes, making his way toward the spot where he judged Prescott must be. His ears were sharp. He could hear insects take flight as he came close, hear a leaf fall from the tree above him, but he could not hear his own movements. He had practiced the skill of motion through foliage at night all summer long, and he knew he had gotten better at it. He began to feel the old excitement return, anticipating the sudden, brief, sweet moment when he would emerge from the bushes. He would take Prescott through the head. Prescott would have just enough time for the meaning of it to reach his brain before the bullet punched through it.

He stepped steadily, placing each foot tentatively, to feel the texture under the sole before he eased his weight onto it. He kept going, watchful and eager at the same time. When he reached the spot where he had expected to find Prescott, he was disappointed. He told himself that Prescott had simply moved onward toward the back of the lot, where he would have a better view of the corner of the house. He had no choice but to keep going. He quickened his pace. Then he was near the end of the bushes. Could Prescott have gotten this far?

He crouched, planted his feet, checked his gun to be sure he had not pushed the safety on while he was handling it. Finally, he took the cell phone out of his pocket.

The telephone was his advantage. Prescott had put it in his hands so he could rattle him, make him feel weak and hesitant and afraid. But Varney had immediately seen the potential. Varney's reflexes had been too quick to let him fall across the sabotaged staircase, his body too agile to be trapped in the empty pool, too fast to be picked off on a run across the open. He had fooled Prescott each time, made the house he had booby-trapped into a joke. Now he was going to finish him. Var-ney held the phone at his side, pressed the power button, pressed 1, set the phone on the ground, and crawled quickly into the brush. Var-ney heard the ring, and began to hurry toward it. He had been right. Probably Prescott had planned to do this very thing to Varney, maybe even provided the phone in the belief that Varney would wait too long, and let Prescott use it to find him in the dark. Prescott might have planned, but Varney had done it.

The telephone rang a second time, and Varney held his head slightly to the side, so the wind blowing across his ears would not distort its sound. He was getting closer. He was sure, and then his mind settled on precisely the spot. He popped up to his feet and fired three times, his silenced weapon making a harsh spitting sound, then dropped down again.

He carried with him into the darkness a sight imprinted on his memory like a snapshot. It was Prescott's cell phone, the tiny lights behind the keys flickering as it rang, then going out again to wait for the next ring, as it lay abandoned on the ground.

36

Prescott gave a disappointed, sad shake of his head. "So much for that."

As he stood up, he began the quiet process of clearing his mind. He had always seen the telephone as the last, surest sign. If this guy had carried it and never pressed the key, Prescott would not have been sure. Only if he used it as a way to surprise Prescott and kill him would Prescott be certain.

Prescott could have ended this an hour ago, when his night scope had detected the bright glow of another human being's heat moving through the woods. He had predicted, in a general way, each move that this man would make. Prescott had placed in his path some signs to suggest that Prescott might be too much for him, and pointed him toward the way to survive.

He supposed it had always been this way. He had wasted his advantages and held back each time since he was a kid. An unexpected memory that was more physical than mental gripped him. There was Anthony Meara in the street with his friends already moving to block Prescott's way on the sidewalk. Meara had been a senior, and Prescott was two years younger. It was not the sort of fighting that had gone on

in earlier years, two boys engaging in the series of elimination matches
that established each grade's male hierarchy. This had been something
else.

Meara had stood in the center of the walk: maybe all he wanted was
to force Prescott to step off the sidewalk to get around him. Prescott
had no desire to fight over a sidewalk he could never own, so he
veered a bit to the right. But Prescott had moved from city to city with
his mother twice by then, and he had been in fights, so he was ready.
He heard the faint whisper of the cloth of Meara's shirt, a scrape of
a shoe moving across concrete, and reacted. He raised the books
clutched in his left hand to the side of his head in time to make
Meara's first strike a glancing blow that knocked them flying, the
pages flapping somewhere out of Prescott's vision as he spun and delivered the jab with his right.

Meara had not been expecting a counterpunch. The jab caught the
bridge of his nose, and made him stagger back as both hands shot up
to cover the hurt. Prescott instantly turned on the other two and
charged three steps, knowing that they would scramble a distance off,
then stop and drift, uncertain. He turned again to make the same
charge toward Meara. He knew that if Meara retreated now, it was
over.

But Meara was already in motion, hurling his body toward Prescott,
trying to take advantage of his momentary inattention to push him
into the brick wall of the building and hammer him there. Prescott
made a quick half dodge, tripped him up, and gave him a push to
speed up his motion. Meara bounced off the wall, fell to the sidewalk,
and lay there. He was clutching his shoulder, moaning a little. It didn't
seem to Prescott that he could be that badly injured. "My shoulder." It
was a half-whispered croak. "It's busted."

Prescott glanced at the two others, who were now at least fifty feet
away, moving sideways like runners taking a lead and keeping their
eyes on the pitcher's mound. When he met their eyes, they began to
back away. Prescott's wrath began to cool. There was no reason to be
afraid, and he couldn't leave Meara here with a broken shoulder.

"Help me," Meara whispered. Prescott stepped closer. The plea was
so unseemly that he felt pity. He had started to kneel when the shoe
kicked up from below his vision. It moved with incredible speed,

missed his groin, brushed the front of Prescott's shirt, and barely nicked his chin, so that his teeth clicked together. Prescott changed. The kick, the surprise of it and the sudden jump to save himself from it, made the adrenaline surge. There was an instant when he saw with clarity the sequence of events, the simple fact of what Meara had done, and quickly passed beyond knowing into judgment.

Meara was up and charging toward him again to take advantage of the ruse. Prescott's body devoted its strength to getting both of his hands on Meara's left shoulder. He gripped the shirt, some of the flesh, and swung him back into the brick wall. Meara caromed off it, and this time Prescott met him. He aimed his blows at the head, delivering them with the heels of his hands, not to punch him but to drive his head into the wall.

In a few seconds Meara was on the pavement again and Prescott went about picking his books up from the ground, stacking them, and then lifting the stack into his left hand. He looked up suddenly.

Forty feet off, one of Meara's friends exclaimed indignantly, "You killed him!"

Prescott put a faint smile on his face. "If you come near me again, I might kill all three of you."

Afterward, the three had tried to use those words to get him into trouble with the police and the school administrators, but the version of the story they provided had not been convincing. There had been some kind of quiet investigation, and it had turned up stories of the three attacking lone students on their way home from school and stealing lunch money, watches, and rings.

Prescott supposed that he had been making the same intentional mistake all his life, maybe because he had required clarity—not for any authority, but for himself—before he could do what he had been aware at the beginning he would probably have to do. This time, he had actually thought a couple of times that the obstacles he had put in the killer's way might have served as more than psychological barriers. The guy had actually taken a step off the stairway into empty air before he had saved himself. He had fallen into the deep end of the empty pool. It would have been nice if Prescott could have found him lying there with a broken leg, unable to go anywhere. But Prescott had watched, and he had been awed by what he had seen. This guy was good: so good that maybe Prescott had been lucky to notice him now, before he got any better.

Prescott sighed. He supposed he had just gotten his kick in the face, so it was time to go out and take this man off the census. Prescott took another look out the cellar window, raised the bolt of his rifle, pushed the detent to release it, pulled it all the way back, and lifted it out. He slipped it into the space beneath the old couch he had been sleeping on for the past few nights, up under the torn cloth into the zigzag springs, then left the useless rifle in plain sight, leaning against the wall. He moved toward the cellar stairs, feeling the weight of his weapons on his body without needing to touch them with his hands. He climbed the steps silently, stopped at the landing, and listened. Then he moved to the back door and slipped outside into the darkness.

Prescott stayed low and moved quickly. He was aware at each moment that the reason he had to be out here was the same as the reason why it was the worst idea in the world. Millikan had seen it instantly, months ago. This was a young, alert, agile man who had, for some reason that Prescott would never really know, begun at a very early age to train himself to kill people, and then somehow gotten himself into the underground market so that he'd had plenty of practice. This man could not be allowed to go on, get stronger, get smarter.

Prescott moved with measured, even paces across the open in the part of the yard that he was sure the killer could not see. Right now his opponent was near the telephone Prescott had left in the brush, wondering why he had been allowed to go there and fire his weapon without drawing Prescott's fire. Probably there was nothing in his collected knowledge of human behavior—surely of combat—that could explain it to his satisfaction. He did not know that Prescott, before he could foreclose all the offers and options, had to see the kick swinging toward his face. After the killer had thought about it for a few minutes, he would conclude that the telephone had been placed there to attract him. He would think Prescott wanted his exact location so he could zero it in his sights, take one calm, leisurely aim with the rifle propped to steady it, and cap him.

Prescott held his pistol muzzle-downward in his hand, and floated smoothly and silently into the woods. He knew exactly where he wanted this man to go next, and he was fairly certain he knew how to get him to go there. It was mostly a question of making all of the other places seem impossible.

He made his way along the edge of the woods. He had walked every yard of the woods alone at night while he prepared. He had wanted a piece of forested land, because it made the place seem easy and appealing. It would seem to be a simple matter for this killer to move nearly to the house without being seen. But it also deprived the killer of a car. He would need to leave it before he entered the woods. Once he was here, he was not getting out easily. Getting out meant running through the woods and coming out tired and scratched and maybe injured on an empty rural road on foot.

Prescott was ready. First he would go about denying the woods to the killer. He set the trip wires of his booby traps along the margin of the woods, then made his way to the tree on the edge of the forest that he had chosen in advance. From here he could see the spot where he had left the telephone. He rested his arm in the crook of the tree, took careful aim, and squeezed the trigger. He fought down the recoil, fired four more times so he was sure the muzzle flash had been visible, then ducked and ran back the way he'd come. He heard the thuds of bullets pounding into the trees behind him, knocking chips of bark into the air. He was impressed by how quickly the killer had returned fire, and how accurately. But the shooting reassured Prescott: if the killer was lying on his belly in the brush on this side of the house, he was not up and running.

Prescott slipped in the back door, locked it, pushed a new magazine into his pistol, then moved to the front door. He reached up and flipped the light switch beside it. Outside, the light was painfully brilliant. The floodlights Prescott had installed in the trees above the line of brush where the killer had hidden poured down in a bright, white halogen light that seared the eyes and made the leaves on the bushes shine. Prescott waited. He knew there were only two ways for the killer to react, and either one was going to put him in front of Prescott's sights one final time. He crouched by the window to see which way it would be. The killer could turn and try to run off across the huge open field of old corn stubble, a five-minute run with nothing that rose higher than his socks to obscure the view of his back. Prescott believed he had already closed that possibility: in order to scare him into falling into the empty pool, he had fired a rifle. This killer would know enough not to run across empty, open land, and he could not stay in the suddenly lighted bushes. He had seen Prescott's muzzle flash coming from the woods, so he wouldn't go in that direction. But he knew there was one place left where the odds would be about even.

Prescott stood back from the window, raised his pistol to shoulder level, and waited for the front door to swing open. After ten seconds, he sensed that something was not right. It was a vague, irritating discomfort at first, then a feeling of distraction. It was a sound. It was an unexpected sound, one he had done his utmost to make impossible. He listened more carefully, hoping it was coming from far away—a freak of the damp night air that had thrown a noise across the empty fields. He stepped to the side window in time to see a bush still shaking, a leaf brushed from it falling to the ground. It was too late for a quick shot from here. The killer was out of the brush now, already too close, moving along the clapboards somewhere near the front of the house.

Prescott tried to listen for footsteps. It might be possible to hear the man's shoulder scrape against the clapboards, then put five or six shots through the outer wall about two feet up from the floor. But listening had become futile, because the engine sound was louder now. He heard the springs of the car give a squeak, and there was a metallic scrape as the nose tipped down over the deep rut in the gravel drive. He spun and ran for the back door, stuck the key in and opened it, then dashed outside toward the corner of the house, squinting against the searing light of the floods across the yard.

His experience told him not to pause at the corner of the house, because that was where the killer would fire instinctively. He determined to step out beyond it, where the light would be out of his eyes and he would have a full view of the side of the house.

He reached the corner, dashed out, and pivoted. The killer's shot slashed along the side of the house, leaving a line of bare wood, and ricocheted off into the distance.

Prescott fired. The killer's left forearm was slapped outward from his body, and Prescott knew he had hit it, but the killer was already moving around the corner to the front of the house. If the wound had slowed him, it was too late for Prescott to see it.

Prescott ran after him, his mind flashing images of the front, trying to predict where the killer would stop to aim. The killer would be ready. Prescott would not. He would have to see, sort out the shapes instantly, and place his one, final shot before the killer put a round through his head. Prescott was almost to the corner before he was sure: practice. This killer was good because he practiced. When shooters practiced, what they became good at was what the ranges offered them: they practiced seeing something pop up, aiming, and shooting it. They practiced leading a target that moved side to side. What they didn't practice was the target that came in low, moving straight at them. Prescott veered away from the house, came in at the corner and dived, trying to use the moment of fast motion to see.

He saw the human shape on the porch and aimed at it, but the muzzle flash came from somewhere to the left, beyond it. The shot caught the muscles along the top of Prescott's left shoulder, beside his neck, and sent pain streaking down his shoulder blade. He hit the ground hard, not able to break his fall with his left arm. He tried to aim at the place where he had seen the muzzle flash, but he could make out nothing.

The human being moved away from the door, and Prescott could see better. It was a young woman, thin and dark-haired, and she was bent backward. The killer had his injured arm draped over her shoulder, and the other hand holding the pistol beside her face. She was terrified, her face set in a wide-mouthed, silent wail as the killer held her in front of him and sidestepped off the porch. Prescott aimed, trying to find a bit of the man—an inch or two—where he could put a fatal shot.

"Fire and she's dead!" The voice was the one Prescott had heard so many times over the telephone, and it had lost none of its bravado. It sounded eager and full of hatred.

Prescott lay still, the gun in his hand useless, the house he had carefully selected and turned into a trap now irrelevant. He watched the killer open the driver's door, get the girl into it, and slip into the back seat behind her without ever presenting him with a shot he could be sure would be fatal. He watched the car back down the gravel driveway for two hundred feet before it swung around. He watched the Lincoln Navigator in the driveway slump suddenly as a shot pierced the right front tire, then jump a few times as shots pounded into radiator, engine compartment, and windshield. As the car drove off, he pulled himself awkwardly to his feet and hurried to find the cell phone he had left in the bushes.

37

Varney lay back in the back seat while Mae drove out of the
gravel driveway onto the road.

"I'm sorry, I'm sorry, I'm sorry," she chanted. "All those
lights were on, so I thought it must be over, and it would be okay to
drive in."

Varney spoke carefully, his face set in the effort to overlook the pain
in his arm. "I'm not mad. Just shut up and let me think for a minute."
He knew that she wanted to say something more. "Just drive to the
casino fast. We need a different car."

She reached the casino in a few minutes. She parked the car in the
middle of a long line of vehicles, then sat and watched while Varney
opened the trunk and reached into the suitcase that contained his
tools. He took a long, thin strip of sheet metal, slipped it into the space
beside the window of the car beside theirs, moved it around a bit, then
tugged it to make the lock button pop up. He opened the door, sat in
the driver's seat, used a big screwdriver to pop the silver ignition
switch with the key slot out of its socket, and connected two wires
from the back of it, starting the car. Then he pulled the trunk-release
latch and the trunk popped open. He came back to the car where Mae

sat and said, "Put everything in this car, and then wipe that one down and lock it up."

While she worked, he sat on the rear bumper of the car he had started. "Drive straight to Interstate 35, down to Minneapolis. It's the fastest way, and we want speed. Now shut me in."

She gaped at him. "You're going to ride in the trunk?"

He said quietly, "There will be cops everywhere in about five more minutes. They're going to be looking for the two of us in a red Ford. But it's going to be just you in a gray Toyota. See?"

She nodded.

"Then do it."

He lay in the trunk, and she slammed the lid, hurried to the open door, got in, and drove. When she was on the highway, there were already police cars driving toward her with their lights flashing. She pulled over and slowed, then stopped. But Jimmy had been right. They saw her, drove past her, and went on. She moved back onto the road. When she made it onto Interstate 35, it seemed to her that she saw more police than she had seen since she had been in this state. They seemed to have come from nowhere. She would drive ten miles of empty road, and then four of them would come along in a line, heading north, covering the miles she had just passed, all in the far left lane with their lights blinking so they could go really fast and the few cars going north ahead of them at this time of night would get out of their way.

The car Jimmy had picked to steal wasn't bad. The odometer said forty-one thousand miles, but the engine was powerful and smooth, and she knew that was all that mattered. She wasn't sure whether he had looked at the gas gauge as soon as he had started the engine, but she supposed he had, because it was nearly full, and she knew he cared about that. It would get them to Minneapolis, and then things would begin to improve. She decided that this was the scariest night of her life.

She fought the fear by reminding herself that she had been almost as scared the time when Gwen died, and she had come through it. Gwen had passed out at the party and her chest had started going up and down, not like breathing, but like shivering. Mae had known it was an overdose. It had to be. But Mae had managed to keep her fear under control so she could do what she had to do. She had closed the door of the bedroom where Gwen was lying, so nobody else would see her and start calling ambulances and cops. Then she had stepped outside on the patio, as though she were going outside for a smoke. Only she had just kept walking into the night. She had avoided all the terrible unpleasantness that would have come if she had let herself get stupid and stay around. Just the single question—where did the drugs come from?—led into so many complexities and difficulties that it simply had to remain unsaid. Nobody at that party had known her name or where she had come from, so it had all worked out all right. She had been proud of her presence of mind. It was bad enough to have lost Gwen, who had been her friend for a couple of years, but the rest of it would have been too much.

Tonight she just had to keep her wits above the fear long enough to get them both down into a real city, and things would begin to improve. Jimmy would realize that once two people had been through something like this together, they were forever bonded. He would be grateful to her: she was saving his life, after all. He would take care of her for as long as she wanted. She liked the thought of that.

She controlled her fear and made the long, fast drive through the night, listening alternately to two radio stations: one that played music about two years out of date so consistently that she wasn't sure if it was intentional, and one that had people calling in on the telephone to complain about politicians she had never heard of. When she reached Minneapolis she drove to a street near the hotel where they had stayed, because it was all that she knew of the city. She stopped, pulled the trunk latch from inside, and went to the back of the car. She watched Jimmy sit up and climb out. "We're at—"

He was already looking around. "I see," he said. "I can't go into the hotel." He had wrapped a piece of cloth from his suitcase around his arm to keep the blood from getting all over everything, but he still looked pale and weak.

He said, "We need to get out of this state."

"But you're bleeding."

"That's right," he said. "But I want to be over the state line into Iowa before we rest." He began to walk. "We need another car. I want you to go back to the hotel. Call a cab for the airport. When you get there, rent a car and come back for me."

All the way to the hotel, she whispered under her breath the instructions he had given her. She sat in careful silence with the cab driver, because she was afraid she would say something that would give away her secret. It was more than an hour before she was back on the block where she had left Jimmy. She stopped the car behind the one he had stolen up north, but he was not in it. She faced the possibility that she might have to walk around, up and down alleys and things to look for him, but he was suddenly right beside her. He reached into the window, snatched the keys, opened the trunk, and put their suitcases in it, then sat beside her in the front seat. "Everything okay?"

"Yeah," she said. "How about you?"

"Drive," he muttered.

She supposed that it was a stupid question. He could hardly be okay. What she had been trying to do was convey some kind of concern, make a connection, like a touch. He must know that. Men seemed intentionally to miss the point sometimes, to pretend they didn't know, or that they had forgotten, so they could look at a person with contempt for having said something that was literally stupid but wasn't really.

She decided that he was simply in a bad mood, and she could not blame him. He was in pain. He was tired, and worried about what was going to happen to the two of them now. That was a special part of his problem. He was a man, and that meant he was used to being the one who made things happen. They expected that of themselves. When he couldn't do it, he must feel like less than a man. She decided that all she could do was behave as though she believed everything would be all right.

Mae concentrated on driving. The distance to the Iowa state line from Minneapolis was about as long as the drive had been to get this far. Now she saw few police cars. Her problem was endurance. In the dim gray light before the sun came up, she saw the sign that said WEL-COME TO IOWA, but he would not let her stop. She had to keep driving toward the east with the sun in her eyes until noon, when she could go into a motel and rent a room.

The hours after that were not as easy as she had promised herself they would be. She had to go out again and buy disinfectants, bandages, tape, then wash and dress his wound. It was a strange, ugly hole right through the forearm, and when she washed it, the hole started bleeding again. She could see that when she touched him, it hurt terribly, but he didn't make a sound. Later, she went out to bring back food, and he slept. She managed to get into bed beside him for a couple of hours before he woke her and made her change the bandages, get into the car, and drive on.

Before he let her stop again they were in Indiana. She changed the bandages again. This time he said, "I'll drive." She was afraid. How could he be strong enough? "Are you sure you want to?" she asked. "I can keep going for a while."

He got in behind the wheel without answering. Mae sat beside him, studying his movements, watching his face and especially his eyes. A person who had lost a lot of blood could easily faint. She watched for twenty minutes, her body tense, waiting to grab the wheel, but he showed no sign of weakness. She slowly let her muscles relax: her tight shoulders, her stiff shoulder blades, her tired arms. Then she was asleep.

Mae awoke when the car seemed to slow and turn at the same time. She sat up hurriedly, taking in a quick breath through nose and mouth that was almost a snort. It was night, and the glare of headlights hurt her eyes.

He said, "You're awake."

She was alarmed. She must look awful. Her mouth was dry and her throat was sore from sleeping with her mouth open. She ran her fingers though her hair quickly, and rubbed her face to be sure she hadn't been drooling. She scrutinized him, searching his face for signs that would tell her what he was thinking of her. He didn't seem to be looking at all. She took her brush out of her purse and began to brush her hair. "How long was I asleep?"

"I don't know. A few hours," he said. "I'm stopping because the sign said there were restaurants up here, and gas stations." She was ready for him to look at her now, but he still had his eyes ahead. She knew that was what he was supposed to do, but it would have made her feel reassured if he had just sneaked a glance at her now.

He stopped the car on a blacktop surface facing the back of the restaurant and far out of the glow of its overhead lights. She said, "Can I change your bandage before I go in?"

He nodded, "Okay."

She took out the bandages and the antibacterial salve and got every-thing ready before she opened his shirt and took off the old dressings. She could see well enough in the dim light to tell that when she changed the gauze this time, there was no new blood. He was incred-ible. Over months she had gotten used to his ability to lift things, his ability to keep on running or exercising without seeming to get winded or tired. Those were things that seemed to her to be impossi-ble to evaluate, because his body was so different from hers. But this—hurt and bleeding and healing—was something that everyone had, and it must be the same for everybody. It didn't seem to be the same for Jimmy.

The way he lived had made him into such a healthy animal it was almost frightening. He was beginning to recover from a gunshot wound in just twenty-four hours.

Mae put the new bandages on. She liked the business of touching him like this, ministering to him. She felt as though she was putting good feelings in his mind for later. When he felt better, he was going to know who had gotten him through this. She said, "I'll bring us something to eat. What do you want?"

"I'll go in with you."

They went inside the restaurant, and she was amazed to hear what he ordered, and more amazed to see him eat it. He was healing, all right. Otherwise, he couldn't have eaten all that steak and the potatoes and vegetables, and then order pie and milk too. She had to cut his steak for him, but after that, if his left arm hadn't been resting in his lap while he ate, she would not have known.

When they were finished, he paid the bill in cash and they went out to the car again. It made Mae feel a tiny bit sad to leave the place where there were lights and cheerful voices and the smells of food cooking, and come out here where it was dark and the air was beginning to take on the late-night chill, and the smell of gasoline was so strong while Jimmy filled the tank. It was easy to be lonely when she was with Jimmy. He had started talking a little more before things had gone all wrong the other night, but that had died out.

Varney said, "You ready to drive some more?"

She drove while he slept, but she found as she drove that the night didn't bother her much, because she forgot about it for long periods. She was thinking about Jimmy while he slept. She could tell during dinner that he had become more settled in his mind. It was as though he had been shocked and confused at first, but had finally made some sense of what had happened. To Mae, that was a very good sign. It meant he was going to be all right. He had not lost his health, and he had not lost his nerve. She drove through the night devising ways to make this work. She considered getting him to marry her, but there were too many reasons why that would be unwise. He would have a responsibility to give her money, but he would also have a right to some of hers, including the money Tracy had been paying her to be with him. And that would stop. He wouldn't pay Tracy for his own wife. Mae would have no income at all. No, marriage was not for her.

In the morning, Jimmy took the wheel and drove into Cleveland while she rested. They turned in the car at the airport, and rented a new one at another lot. Mae was preparing to drive on again, but he stopped at noon and checked into a hotel.

Mae was delighted. It was a nice hotel, with room service and a beautiful lobby with a marble floor. She determined to make this phase of the trip the very best for him. He might have been distracted and inattentive while he was scared and in pain, but he had recovered enough now so she believed he would remember what she did next. She made herself devote every moment to him. Now that they were in good light, she could examine the wound better and see that it had no signs of infection. She bathed him, changed the dressing, brought him food from the restaurant downstairs, massaged him. On the second day, he asked her to dye his hair again. "The guy who shot me saw that it's light brown," he said. "Darken it."

This time, Mae did something more radical, a gesture for him. After she had colored his hair, she waited until he slept again, and colored her own too. She made it the same as his, but with lighter highlights. When he awoke, he looked at her for a long time without speaking. Then he wordlessly took off her clothes and made love to her.

At ten the next morning, they left the hotel and drove toward Cincinnati. At noon, Jimmy stopped at a restaurant and bought a picnic lunch. They drove for a time looking for a place to stop, until he found a secluded grove of trees near a river. It was quiet and empty and beautiful, and she smiled at him as she ate.

Mae was fascinated by the sight of three birds high up in the sky, circling one another. They seemed to be playing. She couldn't tell what kind they were. She was just about to turn toward Jimmy to ask if he could tell, but she didn't, because that was when he brought the blade of the knife across her throat.

A bit later, as Varney dragged her body into the ditch he had dug, he felt himself getting angrier. It was outrageous that Tracy and her stupid sons had done this to him, so that he had needed to kill Mae. He felt this betrayal more strongly than the rest of their offenses. Mae was the part that he held against them most bitterly.

Tracy had let herself get suckered. She was so greedy that all she had needed to hear was a high number, and she was in. He supposed that he should not have been surprised. He had even suspected there was something wrong with the way she was thinking about the job at the moment he had heard of it. Varney had not imagined that Prescott was behind the offer, but that was not the point. A man didn't have to be clairvoyant to survive, if only people would take reasonable precautions. Well, she was going to have to make reparations.

38

When Prescott was still four blocks away from the office building in Cincinnati, he knew that something had already happened.

The sidewalk in front of the building was roped off with yellow POLICE LINE—DO NOT CROSS tape. There were three blue-and-white patrol cars parked on the opposite side of the street, three more at the curb just past the tape. There were a number of plain cars, a couple with small insignia on their doors. There were plainclothes cops walking in and out of the building, some of them with tackle boxes that held forensics kits. Prescott turned his car to the right at the next corner so he didn't have to drive past. He found a gas station where he could see a couple of pay phones, and pulled up to the fence and parked.

He picked up the nearest phone, pumped in some change, and dialed the Los Angeles number. "Millikan," he said. "I'm in Cincinnati. There's a crime scene here, and there's no way the police are going to let me near it. One of us needs to get a look at it."

It was nearly twelve hours later that Millikan came out of the building, ducked under the tape, and walked down the block to the car where Prescott sat watching.

Prescott walked with him back up the sidewalk, under the police tape, and to the front entrance. A uniformed policeman inside the door nodded to Millikan, then turned his eyes toward Prescott, but Millikan foreclosed the question. "He's with me." The two went up the stairs quickly instead of waiting for the elevator, so the cop didn't have time to stare at Prescott and wonder whether being with a visiting professor from some college was enough to make a man welcome in this particular spot.

The two walked along the upstairs hallway shoulder to shoulder, while Millikan spoke in a low voice. "The family owned the building under the name of the family's corporation, and charged themselves rent."

"What about these companies?" He pointed at Crestview Wholesale, and swept his hand toward the row of other doors, all with different names on them.

"All of them—the travel agency, the salon and manicure place, the credit lender—were dba's: the mother or one of the sons 'doing business as.' Half of them connect with the others through doors inside, like hotel suites. You'll see."

He opened the door of the wholesale office, stepped around the desk in front, and pointed down at the floor. "It's a shame you didn't get to see this before they took the bodies out, but there will be pictures. This is where he did the mother. I think she was sitting in this chair when he came in the door. She swiveled around and took a step to get away, and he was on her. It was sort of like a big cat taking down an antelope—kind of flings his weight onto her back so she just runs into the ground. He grabbed her by the hair with the left hand and sliced the throat with the right, then shoved the face back down into the rug. He's not hurt as bad as we'd hoped."

Millikan stepped carefully across the carpet to a door that led off to another room. "Next he goes this way. It's the travel agency, according to the sign on the door. I don't know if he made noise doing Mom, or if he knew this one was going to be armed, or what. But as he's walking, he's getting out his gun."

Prescott nodded and waited. Millikan pushed open the door and stood to the side so Prescott could stand where he had been. In the wall at the other side of the room there were three bullet holes with wooden dowels stuck in them. The holes were all spattered with bright spots of blood where they had passed through a body into the wall. Millikan said nothing, only watched Prescott sidestep, bend his knees slightly, and raise his right arm to line up with the three dowels so they pointed up the arm toward his right eye. Prescott held his position for a few seconds, then looked around him to study the room.

The next step came to Prescott immediately, and Millikan could see it happening. He kept his right arm pointed at the three spots on the wall, took three steps diagonally forward, bent over to look at the outline of the body, came to the space at the left side of the door, and crouched.

He glanced at Millikan, and Millikan nodded in agreement. "I think so. I think that's where he waited for the second son to come to him. He stayed low, and put the shot through the spine just under the jaw."

Prescott stepped around the wall into the next room, then hesitated. "Was that it? Two sons?"

"Nope. There's a third body he got in the hallway. It seems he's a son too."

Prescott went out the door and stared. The blood was on the end of the hall farthest from the stairs. Prescott said, "Did the cops do all the searching in the big office, or was that him?"

"He did it," said Millikan.

Prescott stepped along the hall back into the wholesale office, where the first body had been found. The vault at the end of the room was open. Desk drawers were open, papers were thrown on the floor, left that way, apparently, because something the forensics team planned to do had not yet been accomplished. Prescott could see money, too. A few hundred-dollar bills looked as though they had been spilled from a larger pile. "Any idea how much money was in the safe?"

Millikan shook his head. "I don't even know if that's where it came from. If you think it was him, though, it must have been a lot. He's not the kind who would spill eight hundred on the floor and leave it, unless there was so much that carrying it was a problem."

"It was him," said Prescott.

"Agreed. He doesn't panic, so it had to be the bulk of it. He didn't take anything but cash. There was jewelry and stuff, but he didn't touch it."

"Still here?"

"No," said Millikan. "They took it downtown to lock it up."

Prescott walked closer to the desk and knelt beside the pile of papers on the floor. "Did the cops find any kind of customer list?"

"Like a hooker's trick book?"

"They sent couriers all over, picking up stolen jewelry and stuff, then handing it off to other people. There were sales, consignment deals, trades, It's kind of complicated to carry in your head."

Millikan shrugged. "They haven't found anything like that yet." He let his eyes settle on the bloodstained carpet near the front desk. "Maybe that's what the old lady did—bookkeeping."

"I suppose," said Prescott absently. He was staring closely at the pile of papers on the floor, craning his neck and leaning over them to read without touching them. He got to his feet and walked to a filing cabinet that had been opened, the contents of one drawer dumped on the floor. He looked closely at the pile, then used a handkerchief to open the other three file drawers, glanced inside, and closed them.

Millikan said, "What is it?"

Prescott was frowning. "This guy comes to this file cabinet. He opens a drawer, goes through it. He dumps papers on the floor. The other three drawers are untouched. What does that say?"

"He found what he wanted. Otherwise, he would have done the same to the others. It was probably the money, or part of it. I have a feeling this wasn't the kind of operation where the cash is all neatly stacked in the vault. They'll probably find it squirreled away all over the building."

Prescott shook his head. "He found what he wanted, but I don't think it was money. See? The spilled money all fell near that desk. None of it came from over here." He stared at Millikan thoughtfully. Then he began to search through the papers that had been thrown from the filing cabinet drawer.

"What was in it?"

"Old bills. Power, water, janitorial service, gardening, telephone."

"What do you suppose he thought he'd find in there?"

"Me. He's looking for me."

"And what are you looking for?"

"The most recent telephone bill. There should have been one within the last week or two, and I don't see it."

Millikan stepped closer. "Is there any way he could use that?"

Prescott said, "The number of the guy I used as a middleman to hire him is on the older bills, but so are a whole bunch of others. It's a complicated operation, with a lot of couriers visiting businesses all over the map." He stopped and squinted at the wall for a moment. "I set the whole thing up almost a month ago. My guy—Dick Hobart—called here and talked to somebody—say it was the mother—and she said she would have to talk to the shooter. A few days later she called Hobart back to say he had agreed."

"I'm not following this," said Millikan.

"I set this up so everything would be anonymous. I made Hobart insist that all communication be done on pay telephones. I pretended that was so there would be no record of the calls, and that would protect everybody if something went wrong. It was really to convince the shooter that the job was safe, and to keep him from trying to find out more about the client."

"So what's the problem? Didn't they do it?"

"Yeah, they did it. Otherwise, he would have pulled out."

"Then what is he going to use to figure out which number on a phone bill belongs to your middleman?"

Prescott said, "He can't know when Dick Hobart called, and he wouldn't have any way of getting that number. But he knows what day it was when Mom—or whoever it was—asked him if he wanted to go up to Minnesota and kill somebody. He said yes, and she called Dick Hobart back. Even if he wasn't here listening, the killer knows when that was, probably to the minute."

Millikan picked up one of the old telephone bills. "Oh, boy. Number, city, date, hour, time." He looked up and saw Prescott pick up the telephone receiver on the desk. "Wait, you can't . . ." but he saw the look on Prescott's face. "Never mind."

Prescott finished dialing a number. "Hello?" He was talking loudly, as though the person on the other end was in a noisy place. "Is Dick Hobart in? It's Bob Greene, and I need to talk to him right away." He listened, then said, "Do you know where I can reach him?" He paused, then sighed in frustration. "If he comes in, tell him to take the night off, and not come back until I get there." He pushed down the button with his finger, then dialed a second number quickly. He waited impatiently, then rolled his eyes and shook his head. "Jeanie, this is Bob

Greene. I don't know if you're scheduled to work tonight or not. I hope you're in class. Do not go to Nolan's until you've talked to me. It's really important. Call in sick if you have to." He hung up.

He took a card out of his wallet and dialed a third number. "Hello. My name is Roy Prescott. I need tickets from Cincinnati to St. Louis on the next available flight." He looked at Millikan while the person on the other end spoke. "Two. And my companion is an off-duty police officer who will need to fly with a firearm. My card number is . . ."

39

Prescott stood beside the cluster of pay telephones at the edge of the waiting area for gate A-14 and listened to the electronic voice of his answering machine. "No messages," it said. He had been hoping that the killer would have been angry enough to leave a message that would tell him something. He hung up and looked at the desk to see if the airline people were ready to begin letting passengers onto the plane, then turned to see how Millikan's calls were coming.

Millikan was already hurrying toward him from the next set of telephones down the concourse. Prescott could see there was news. Millikan pulled him to the wall away from the other travelers, and said quietly, "The police in Louisville have been leaving messages on my phone all day, and I just reached Lieutenant Cowan."

"Has somebody there seen him?"

"Worse. It's Carter Rowland—Donna Halsey's ex-husband. They found him in his house. He was shot in the head, but nobody heard."

"He's moving fast."

Millikan turned to look at him. "You're not surprised."

Prescott shook his head. "He's cutting all the strings. He's getting everybody who had anything to do with the job that got him into trouble. I was afraid he might do that."

"But Rowland didn't do anything to him."

"Rowland hired him to do the job in the restaurant. He did it, so Rowland was a satisfied customer. How is he supposed to know that Rowland wasn't the one who told me how to get in touch with the people in Cincinnati? He can't know, but now he doesn't have to wonder."

Millikan shook his head. "Maybe we should exchange our tickets and go to Louisville while we can still get a look at the scene."

"Too late," said Prescott. "No point in going where he was this morning. We've got to go to the place where he'll be tonight."

When the plane arrived in St. Louis, the sun was already low. Prescott and Millikan had barely spoken to each other. Prescott had spent much of the time on the airplane telephone trying to call Hobart, then Jean, then Hobart again. Millikan had, at first, not been able to reach anyone in the St. Louis police department who knew him. He had not convinced anyone else that he was expert enough to be able to predict that a killer could be expected at Nolan's Paddock Club. Finally, he had managed to get a captain on the phone who seemed to have some sympathy for his reasoning, but the captain had not been willing to describe to Millikan what, precisely, he was going to do.

The two men strode along the boarding tunnel. Millikan said, "I told the captain the flight number and arrival time, so there will probably be somebody here to get a copy of the picture for the plainclothes guys."

As they emerged from the tunnel into the waiting area, he pulled Prescott to the side to let the other travelers pass, while he turned his head in every direction, searching for a uniform.

"It doesn't look like they're eagerly waiting for us," said Prescott, and began to walk quickly up the concourse.

Millikan had to trot to catch up. He said, "They could have asked the Buffalo police to fax the picture to them. They might already have it, and be at the bar looking for him."

"We'll find out," said Prescott.

Their pace took them quickly down to the car-rental counter. Prescott had called to reserve a car, so it took only a few minutes before they were on the road. Prescott drove with a quiet determination, always pushing slightly faster than the traffic, weaving in and out when he had to.

When they pulled into sight of the building, all traces of daylight were gone, and the big green sign that said NOLAN'S PADDOCK CLUB was a bright splash of electric color against a black sky. The huge parking lot was already lined with cars, pickup trucks, and utility vehicles. "Is it always this busy?" asked Millikan.

"It's filling up a little early," said Prescott. "Let's hope all the extra cars belong to your undercover cops."

He pulled into the lot and found a space in nearly the last row of cars facing the side of the building in a dimly lighted sector two hundred feet away. Both men got out. Prescott took another look around the lot, then handed Millikan a few copies of the picture and took a few for himself. He leaned into the car as though he'd forgotten something, but Millikan could see he was collecting the parts of a gun from several places in his suitcase, and assembling it.

Millikan scanned the lot as he spoke. "How do you want to do this?"

Prescott said, "Split up. You go in, stay close to the bar and away from the stage, where you can watch the front door. I'll try to get in another way and circulate. If you spot a cop, make sure he gets the picture."

"Right." Millikan turned and set off for the front door. This was a moment when he had unexpected thoughts. He had a vivid memory of leaving the police force so many years ago. His strongest sensation had been relief: he was never again going to have to walk through the door of an unfamiliar building feeling the weight of a loaded pistol on his body, looking for a face. The memory brought with it a judgment he could only identify as a disappointment in himself. He had struggled all that way—through college, graduate school, the job as a professor—only to be jerked right back in a day. He felt that he should have known he would be doing this again. He should never have let himself imagine it was behind him, or that it ever could be.

As he walked, he was almost unconsciously remembering tactics, preparing himself. If undercover cops were here, he would have to rely on them to spot him and find a way to identify themselves to him. If they were any good at all, he would not be able to pick them out. He had to concentrate on seeing the killer, identifying him first from his picture, and getting around behind him. He knew that tonight was a perfect occasion for one of his nightmares from the old days to come to pass: that he would be in a closed space, squeezed in a crowd of a couple of hundred people, and the killer would open fire.

Millikan acknowledged the thought and set it aside—still there, but not something he could devote any of his consciousness to right now. He had to go in there, quickly scan all the faces that he could see, and then move into a dim spot where he could watch for the right one.

The music grew louder as Millikan stepped toward the building. There was a glow in the doorway, a reddish tint to the shapes he could see, as though the place he was about to enter were on fire. Three big men in jeans, T-shirts, and work boots were walking toward the door from his right. He judged that they had been working at some kind of construction site until dark, and that it must be at least thirty miles away if they had just arrived. He made sure he reached the threshold after they did and edged in behind them, using their bulk as a way to shield himself from view for a few seconds while his eyes ranged the faces of the crowd ahead, searching for the one right configuration of features.

Prescott studied the small, unmarked metal door at the side of the building. It was the one where he had seen Jeanie and Hobart watching him depart one afternoon three months ago. It was closed, and he was sure it was supposed to be rigged not to open from the outside. Its purpose was as a fire exit, not an entrance. But Prescott had learned early in life that a great many of the things that were supposed to operate under strict rules did not. When Jean and Hobart had come out that day, no alarm had sounded.

He went to the door, tested the thumb latch, and tugged the handle. He remembered the kitchen door at the rear of the restaurant in Louisville. This one reminded him of it. He was not absolutely certain that the two were identical, but they were at least similar. In Louisville, the killer had gone back there and found the door propped open. He had slipped inside and killed the cook. But the part of that night that mattered to Prescott right now was not what the killer had done. It was what he had been expecting to do. The killer had locked and chained the front door of the restaurant, and only then had gone to the rear of the building. Even if he had come up the alley earlier and seen that the door was propped open, he could not have known that it would stay open. He had been certain—not guessed, but known—that if he had come back and found it locked, he would be able to open it.

Prescott turned his head to survey the parking lot. He could see no shape of a head in any of the cars or trucks on this side of the building, and for the moment, there was no sign of a man on foot. He knelt by the door, extracted the pick and tension wrench he carried in his wallet, and worked on the lock. It took only a moment to line up the pins along the cylinder, but he did not open the door. He stood, leaned casually against the wall as he returned the pick and tension wrench to his wallet, shifted the pistol in his belt at the small of his back to make it easier to reach, and surveyed the parking lot again.

Prescott moved his right hand to his back, opened the door with his left, and stepped inside. The concrete hallway was unoccupied. The music was louder, the thumping bass beat that some of the girls liked to dance to because it kept them on rhythm when the lounge was full and the crowd was noisy. He took his first steps along the hallway. To his right was the door to the dancers' dressing room. His face was familiar at Nolan's. If he stepped in and the killer was not there, he could apologize drunkenly that he had been looking for Jeanie while he backed out. If the killer was there, Prescott's sudden appearance might be enough of an edge. He put his left hand on the knob, held the gun under his coat, and pushed.

The door opened a couple of inches and he heard a woman's voice. "So he moves out, and what does he take with him?"

Another woman's voice said, "You're kidding."

"Nope. The dog. The very same dog that he's been whining and complaining about for three months. Supposedly the reason he was leaving in the first place."

Prescott closed the door quietly and went on. He had no idea who the woman was, but he recognized that the voice had no tension in it. She was talking to one of the other dancers. There was no chance that if the killer had chosen to hide in there, one of them would not have noticed him.

He stopped at the entrance to the stage. He would have liked to try to check the crowd from behind the black curtain, but he knew it was too risky. The dancers sometimes did it, but that was the reason he knew it was difficult to do without being seen. The girls knew that it didn't matter if the customers saw the quick sparkle of a feminine eye appear at the edge of the curtain and vanish. It probably helped build the suspense that was part of the appeal of the show. But Prescott could not afford to be seen.

He moved up the corridor to the door of Dick Hobart's office, stepped to the side, and knocked. He listened, but the music from the main room grew louder, so he heard nothing. He knocked again, this time rapping his knuckles hard on the wood so he could hear it clearly over the music. He waited, but Hobart did not appear.

Prescott moved on, opened the door to the storeroom, and switched on the light. The tall shelves shone white with stacked rolls of paper towels and toilet paper for the rest rooms. On the lower shelves there were bottles of floor wax, cans of metal polish, mop heads, sponges. The empty spaces on the floor held buckets, mop wringers, brooms propped against the wall. There was no way for Prescott to know whether anyone had been here who didn't work here, but he could see there was nobody here now. He turned off the light and went out.

Prescott moved toward the door near the side of the stage that led out into the public part of the building, then stopped. There was still a room back here that he could not be sure about: Hobart's office. He could not leave a room at his back that had not been searched.

Millikan had settled into his spot near the bar, where he could keep his back against the wall and not be jostled too often by the men who made their way past him to buy more drinks. The light in the margins of the cavernous room was red and dim: the stage lights were a bit brighter, a compromise between not paying enough attention to the lady who was working up there, and having a stage awash in white light that would make her skin look pink and raw, like flesh in an operating room.

Millikan was in a dim place that was not too visible, but he was not able to see the other customers well either. He concentrated on looking at every face that presented itself. Prescott had warned him that the crowd at night was young, and now he saw that it was making what he had to do more difficult and dangerous. Everyone he saw seemed to be twenty-five and in good physical shape, with shortish hair and an unlined, undistinctive face. It was their height that was bothering him the most at the moment. He had been aware that each generation grew a bit taller than the last. No forensics specialist could possibly not know that, and anyone who spent time on a college campus could see it. But there were few times when Millikan had found himself in such cramped quarters with an audience made up exclusively of young males. He craned his neck, he stood on his toes, he glanced between passing customers, but he never could see far enough to be sure he was seeing even a significant proportion of the men in the big room.

Prescott had told him that in Minnesota the killer's hair had been dyed light brown—or maybe the first time, it had been dyed dark brown. It didn't matter which was the natural shade, or if either was. Once it had been established that the man had ever changed the color, it was simply not something Millikan could use. He had to look directly into the man's face to see if he matched his portrait, and how could Millikan possibly stare into the eyes without having the eyes stare back?

Prescott managed to push the fifth pin into line with the others on the cylinder of the lock on Dick Hobart's office, then turn the cylinder. He gently pushed the knob to let the door swing inward, and in the first fraction of a second he received the first bit of disturbing news: the light was on. In the next fraction of a second, the door stopped. Prescott pushed the door again, and the sound was the one he had already begun to dread. What had stopped the door's arc was the sole of a shoe. He pushed on the door harder, and the side of the shoe scraped against the concrete floor as he moved the heavy weight far enough to put his head in and look down.

Dick Hobart's foot was against the door because his head had a hole in it. It was a neat hole, on the left side. That was the entry wound. The side that was down against the floor was the exit wound, and it would not be so neat. Since the killer's left forearm was the one that Prescott had clipped in the dark in Minnesota, he had certainly shot Dick Hobart with his right. That meant that Hobart had been facing him.

Prescott pulled back and closed the door, then turned the cylinder to lock it again. He was sorry. Dick Hobart had been eager to get involved in arranging a murder. He supposed that this was not entirely an event that Hobart had a right to expect would never happen, but it was something Prescott had tried to prevent. He moved back up the corridor the way he had come.

The beer bottle Varney carried in his left hand was an empty one he had picked up from a table. He had it so that the way he held his injured left forearm resting across his stomach looked natural. He moved with slow, intermittent progress across the big, crowded room. Nearly everyone but Varney had his eyes focused on the woman up on the stage. Varney turned his face in that direction for a few seconds each time he waited. When he saw another gap in the crowd, he stepped into it, then paused again and pretended to watch.

He did not want to be aggressive in making his way out. It would be easy in a place like this to get into a fight if he pushed one of these big bastards too hard. There was no question he could put any one of them down, even tonight, when his left arm was throbbing, but it would require him to do serious damage.

Throwing a punch in this kind of crowd was foolish. They were all big and stupid. Half of them were already feeling the effect of the alcohol, and that was the half that had been most aggressive about elbowing their way to the head of the line at the bar while they were sober.

As he moved, he looked past each of them, not wanting to make eye contact, his gaze on his destination instead. Each time he was forced by the crush of bodies to pause again, he had to look up at the stage, and he hated it. The woman up there was very blond and very tall, but that did not help. The fact that she was not remotely like Mae forced him to think of Mae and compare. When he did, even the dissimilarity was not exactly real: there was a similarity between the shapes of all attractive women, their movements and expressions. The differences were like the differences between two zebras, probably enormous to a zebra, but practically invisible to any other animal.

He turned away again to watch the fluid movements of the crowd, waiting for a path to appear. His eyes passed across two big men who had just come in a few minutes ago, after he had begun to make his way toward the door. At that moment, one of them turned his body to the side to look over his shoulder—maybe in response to something that was said, but was only audible at that end of the room—and his companion took one step toward the bar. In the half second the space between them widened by a foot, and Varney saw something that made him gasp.

It seemed to be the guy he had seen on television months ago, right after the job in Louisville. Varney instinctively turned and drifted to the side along with the pressure of the crowd, toward the bar, so he would be harder to see while he looked. He never took his eyes from the space near the door, barely blinking, trying to be sure.

Another man stopped and looked at the stage just as the one ahead of him took a step toward the bar, and another space opened. Varney got a clear look beyond them, and this time the name came back to him: Millikan. He wasn't even sure why he had remembered it, but the old guy's name was Millikan.

Varney's eyes moved from side to side, looking for a new path through the crowd. He would have to make his way to the front door on the left side, so that he wouldn't pass on Millikan's side. He was sure Millikan must have seen the picture Prescott had posted in Buffalo. He could not have come here by sheer coincidence. Varney decided that as soon as he could make it to the left side of the door, just before he slipped out of the light into the night, he would have to be sure that Millikan got a good look.

Millikan had been wondering what had become of Prescott. He had agreed with the strategy, and had, in fact, considered it inevitable. One man had to gain control of the doorway while the other moved systematically through the crowd from the far wall toward the door, looking at faces. But Millikan had taken his station near the door at least a half hour ago, and he still had not seen Prescott. He caught himself. It probably had not been a half hour. It had been proven experimentally that it took no more than two minutes before the average person began to overestimate duration, and as time went on, the exaggeration grew. Millikan had not looked at his watch when he came in, so there was no point in looking now. He corrected his time sense by looking at the only objective measure he could see. The woman on the stage was the only one in the building who was making visible progress of any kind. He supposed that merely taking off her clothes to music couldn't take more than fifteen minutes, and she had not finished yet. He returned his eyes to the faces in the crowd.

He quickly scanned the faces from the door inward into the big room. There was still no sign of Prescott, but he had just convinced himself that his wait had not been so long. He moved his eyes from face to face, moving back toward the door. He stopped. His eyes were caught by a face. He saw that the young man was standing absolutely still, staring at him too. He took a breath and it seemed to keep coming, his lungs expanding as though he were preparing to shout. The hair was not light anymore, as Prescott had said it had been, but he could not change his eyes.

Millikan moved toward the door, but the crowd seemed to tighten and solidify in front of him. As he struggled, he shouted above the pounding music, "Excuse me! Pardon! Sorry! Coming through!" He gained a few steps, but then there were four men ahead who had all just come in the door. They were staring stupidly into the big room, trying to get their bearings, just as the music told Millikan the dancer on the stage was reaching some kind of climactic moment in her performance. Millikan tapped the nearest man and shouted, "Excuse me," and that made him a few more feet before he was stopped again. Millikan craned his neck to see past the next group of customers. The doorway was empty. The killer had slipped out.

Millikan felt a wave of panicky heat grip his chest and spine. He yanked out his wallet and opened it, waving it in front of him. All it had in its plastic window was his California driver's license, but he shouted, "Police officer! One side! Police! One side." His voice was stentorian, the authority in it only a remnant left for years in storage, like the old uniforms he would never throw away, but the tone of urgency and need was real. The men in front of him might not have been convinced he was a police officer, but they seemed to know that he was not joking, and they made way. In a few more seconds he was through the doorway, patting his coat to put his hand on the gun as he trotted out into the parking lot.

Varney stared at Millikan with intense interest. Millikan carried himself as though he were armed. That didn't seem to Varney to make much sense. On television they had said he was a professor. But Varney did not waste time questioning what he could see. Millikan was here, and he was moving farther from the bright lights around the building and into the rows of parked cars.

From here, looking through the tinted window in the back of the sport utility vehicle where Varney sat, cut off from the sounds of Millikan's feet and shielded from the breeze that ruffled Millikan's wiry gray hair, Varney felt as though he were watching him on television again. Millikan was turning his whole body round and round now, looking in every direction, then walking a few steps and doing it again. That was a look of despair. Even if Varney had not been able to make out the wrinkled brow and the frantic eyes, he could have told from Millikan's body what he was feeling. When a man stopped and began spinning like that, he was out of ideas.

Varney waited until Millikan had turned away from him and stepped off toward the other side of the parking lot before he got out of the SUV and began to follow him. He would get Millikan now, and then go into cover again somewhere near the body to wait for Prescott to show himself.

Varney had a sudden, unexpected feeling of joy. He had just been through the worst period of his life. All this time, he had been upset about it, but had been quietly determined to wait it out and endure until it was over. He had suffered the humiliation of repeated failure, and the shame of having to be dependent on Tracy and her sons, and the pain of the bullet piercing his forearm. He'd had to maintain his discipline, burn out of himself all weakness and hold to his clarity of purpose while it had all happened. Finally, he'd had to make Mae into a human sacrifice, so there would be no barrier, no human connection to put a limit to his rage.

He had gone from place to place, finding the people who must have had a part in his betrayal, and obliterating them. It had taken him a few days, but now he knew. His rage had made him harder and cleaner, and now the rage was beginning to change into exultation. His period of trial was over: he had won. He wasn't fighting now; he was just collecting the last of the enemies, bagging them like game. His period of misery and agony had been a test. If he had been weak and undisciplined, he would have drifted lower and lower until he died. But he had used every day of those hard, horrible months working to make himself better and stronger. He felt he was approaching a kind of perfection tonight, not a mere adventurer anymore, but a perfect warrior, tempered and purified.

He stepped around the building after Millikan. This side was even darker, but he noticed the steel rungs of a ladder built into the side of the brick wall for maintenance men to reach the roof—probably to fix the air-conditioning and clean the vents. That was where he would wait for Prescott after he got Millikan. Once again, he marveled at the change in the current of the universe. For months, nothing had gone right. Now, he reached out a hand, and the things he needed simply came to him, like gifts.

He studied Millikan's form, walking up the aisle of parked cars, the right arm bent, the hand near the lapel of his open coat so he could reach in and pull out the gun. Varney could not allow that gun to come out and make noise. He screwed the silencer on the barrel of his own pistol, stopped walking, and aimed. The bullet would pass through Millikan's temple, he decided. That would keep some half-conscious nerve impulse from reaching the hand and discharging the gun.

"Last chance, Slick."

Varney held the gun at arm's length, but he knew he could not fire. Prescott had to be first. Where had he come from? The roof, of course. Prescott had simply gotten there first. Varney lowered the pistol a few degrees slowly, listening for the sound of Prescott's feet on the gravel, stepping up behind him to take it. "Last chance?"

"Live or die," said Prescott. "You pick."

Varney knew then that Prescott was not going to step forward to take the gun. He ducked, slapped the ground, dove toward the nearest car, and rolled behind it. As he came up beyond the car, his arm already extended over the hood to fire, Prescott's bullet passed through his forehead.

Hours later, there was a moment when the police had finished with Prescott for a time. He took a breath and looked at the crowd of onlookers beyond the barriers. A familiar shape turned and began walking away, but he had already begun to move, and in twenty steps he had caught her. "Jeanie."

She turned and looked at him, but she kept walking. "I'm glad you got that man, and he didn't get you."

"Thanks," he said. "Will you stop and talk to me?"

She stopped, her arms folded across her chest.

He said, "My name is Roy Prescott."

She shook her head. "Whoever that is, it's not somebody I want to know. My time with Bob Greene is over, and that's okay. I was right that I wouldn't be sorry it happened. Good luck."

She turned away and began to walk, but he stayed close to her. "Where are you going?"

"Home."

"What are you going to do?"

She sighed. "What I had always planned to do. If Hobart is dead, then Nolan's is finished a year or so earlier than I thought. I'm just skipping ahead, that's all."

Prescott said, "I didn't mean to hurt you or mess up your plans. Look, this place is closing because of me. I would like—"

"Don't give me anything else," she said. "I don't need it. Just go away now, so it can be over."

EPILOGUE

Only about half the seats on the late-night flight to Los Angeles had been sold. Prescott was resting, lying across the seats in row 16 with his eyes closed, so Daniel Millikan had moved to sit alone in row 28. He had turned off the overhead lights as the plane climbed, so he was in the dark beside the plane's small window, staring down at the rows of tiny yellow lights that formed the traces of streets of one of the towns just west of St. Louis.

He had known that this time would come. It would be over, and he would be alone at night. There was not silence, but the unchanging drone of the airplane's engines enforced his solitude, keeping him from hearing any sound that was human. It had been months since he had answered the telephone and been surprised by the voice of Robert Cushner. He had been startled, but that could not now, or ever, serve as an excuse. He had decided to give the old man the name and telephone number of Roy Prescott.

How many since then? How many dead? Two police officers and two security guards in L.A., the maid and the clerk at the motel, the ex-husband of Donna Halsey, that woman in Cincinnati and her three sons, the owner of the strip club back there in St. Louis. What was that? Twelve? And possibly more. Prescott had said there was a woman hostage in Minnesota, and this killer would not have let her go. Who else? Of course: the killer himself. He came to Millikan as an afterthought. It was because the decision to call Prescott had included in it the death of the killer. To someone else, Millikan could have protested that it had not been the only possible outcome. But he did not now. He had known it was the best one he could hope for, the ending he had embraced in his imagination at the beginning. That was what you were asking for when you called Roy Prescott. He felt an urge to pray, to seek forgiveness for what he had done. He began silently with "Dear God," but his mind stalled. The contrition was only a reflex, not real this time. It was only a grasp for certainty, just a reaction to his discomfort at not being able to know he had done the right thing. He stopped, closed down the channel of communication: "Amen," he whispered. Nobody gets out of this life without doubt.

ABOUT THE TYPE

This book was set in Bembo, a typeface based on an old-style Roman face that was used for Cardinal Bembo's tract *De Aetna* in 1495. Bembo was cut by Francisco Griffo in the early sixteenth century. The Lanston Monotype Machine Company of Philadelphia brought the well-proportioned letter forms of Bembo to the United States in the 1930s.